JÁCHYM TOPOL is the leading Czech author of his generation. Active in his youth as a samizdat poet and songwriter, since the Velvet Revolution of 1989 he is best known for his reportage as a journalist and his fiction capturing the struggle of Czech society to come to terms with the legacies of communism. His previous novels include *City Sister Silver*, *Gargling with Tar* and *The Devil's Workshop*.

MAREK TOMIN was born in Prague and grew up in England, where his family found refuge after being exiled by the Communist regime in 1980. His translations include *Glorious Nemesis* by Ladislav Klíma and Emil Hakl's *Of Kids and Parents*. He lives in Prague and London.

NIGHTWORK

Jáchym Topol

Translated from the Czech by Marek Tomin

Portobello
BOOKS

Published by Portobello Books 2014
Portobello Books
12 Addison Avenue
London
W11 4QR
United Kingdom

Published in German by Suhrkamp Verlag as *Nachtarbeit*.

The original Czech edition was published in 2001 under the title *Noční práce*
by Torst Publishers Praha.

This book has been selected to receive financial assistance from English PEN's "PEN Translates!"
programme, supported by Arts Council England. English PEN exists to promote literature and
our understanding of it, to uphold writers' freedoms around the world, to campaign against the
persecution and imprisonment of writers for stating their views, and to promote the friendly
co-operation of writers and the free exchange of ideas. www.englishpen.org

A CIP catalogue record for this book is available from the British Library

9 8 7 6 5 4 3 2 1

ISBN 978 1 84627 163 2

www.portobellobooks.com

Typeset by Avon DataSet Limited, Bidford on Avon, Warwickshire

Printed and bound by CPI Group (UK) Ltd, Croydon, CR0 4YY

Hey, Ondra, do you see that
smear on the grass? A head
rolls over it every evening.
Someone picked it up once,
thinking it was a hedgehog.
Three days and nights later he
was lying in his coffin.

From *Woyzeck*
by Georg Büchner

On the devils' wedding day,
It was very hot indeed,
They danced around so much,
Their noses started to bleed

The eldest of them, Lucifer,
Jumped around like a goat,
Until he hurt his big toe,
And cried boo hoo, oh woe

Children's song

1

In winter, the river was the only sign of movement in the white land-scape, floating ice battered the river banks, the water beneath the icy crust in the meanders and blind bends pulsated through the landscape, ice floes rolled over one another, breaking up, bristling with branches and tree trunks. The floes were full of stones and pebbles, soil and sand, they collided with each other with a hissing scraping sound, there were cavities filled with black water in the ice, the ice by the banks was the first to be hollowed out by the current. Tiny branches torn off and twisted by the wind had frozen in the opaque mass, as had a small water rat with a pointy snout full of frozen blood. There was rubbish everywhere, splinters of driftwood, torn fishing lines, car tyres, rusty pots, wellies riddled with holes.

He is lying in the little boat, the sweltering heat is lulling him to sleep, he can hear the wind, the water all around, he can hear insects. He had only drifted for a moment, his progress arrested by a mass of tangled wood, the roots of upturned trees jutting up into the air.

Shreds of bark hung down from the trees, the ice floes had left their trunks scarred, they looked like they'd been hacked with axes, the branches of the trees groped in the depths, bubbles burst in water-filled hollows, green with moss and decomposing grass.

He closed his eyes. He was thinking about Zuza. He thought about her long and hard, pleasure washed over him, he curled his toes. The first time it happened to him in the boat, he got into the water and waded through the current so that his arousal wouldn't be visible. He took off his shorts, let them splash about in the water, his hand hanging down over the side of the little boat. The first time he saw her in a dress was by the church. But they had not spoken to each other there.

He called it his little boat. But this tiny raft was a beggar's barge, it had been nailed together roughly, rusty nails and hooks protruded from it, they had tried making it watertight with tar but it still took on water. If the Líman lads knew where he kept the boat they would wreck her. They'd kick a hole in her, weigh her down with a rock and sink her to the bottom of the river. One time he took Squirt on an outing, they came to a halt in an old blind riverbend, Squirt wanted to get out, to get away, even if it meant negotiating the slippery sludge of a muddy bank, he was afraid of water, he was even terrified of the tiny fish used as bait.

He told him he'd no doubt have dreams about sinking into the mud, about falling into one of the muddy hollows and then sinking in slowly, getting stuck, watching as he got sucked in further and further.

Rubbish, Ondra had said to him. I'd throw you a plank, or a stick, or a rope.

And what if you weren't there? objected Squirt.

But I would be, Ondra said.

He was lying in the boat, letting the current carry him off, knowing that the boat would soon get stuck again, its bottom would hit a mud bank, or it would collide with the driftwood left behind by the summer floods. Sticks and branches, held by thin roots hanging down from the crumbling river banks, stirred in the wind. That was his first day in the little boat. Everything was vanishing in the expanse of time that lay ahead of him.

The subterranean laboratories looked like a machine that kept the city in working order. His father had set up his workshop right by the conveyor belts carrying brand-new, shiny devices. He was working on an invention which, he emphasized, was very near to completion. One time he showed Ondra his room.

It's plain, right, almost spartan. But a man who wants to focus on his work doesn't need any more than that. Believe me.

There were women's shoes by the door, red heels. The kind Mother called little boats. Daddy kicked them under the bed with one deft movement of his foot.

Of course, the work goes quicker if I can have my most able secretary here with me.

Dad laughed. He poked Ondra in his side.

I'm glad we can talk to each other like this, man to man, my boy. You're growing up, slowly, that's true, but even so. Hopefully one day you'll have the same experience. You'll father your own son. By then I'll probably be dead and departed. But that doesn't matter.

Now the long corridors of the Patent Office were packed with Father's colleagues. They were scurrying out of their offices, files under their arms, pushing trolleys loaded with documents. He was standing next to his daddy on one of the uppermost floors of the building.

Remember this. This is a historic moment, what you're watching is the destruction of documents.

A fire was burning in the courtyard of the Patent Office. Civil servants were dousing stacks of papers, the expanding fire was lapping up liquid from the canisters, sending motes of soot and tiny scraps of charred paper flying skywards, they turned to ash in mid-flight.

Suddenly, Father was surrounded by a throng of colleagues. They were shouting over each other and chattering with such urgency that Ondra couldn't understand a word they were saying. They pressed the two of them into Father's office. And then everything happened in quick succession, his father seemed to bow in front of the colossal metal safe in the middle of the office, and then, turning his back to it to conceal the lock mechanism, he opened it with a few smooth movements, the pads of his fingers gliding over the cold metal. He extracted a black folder bound with a pink ribbon, inserted it into his satchel, grabbed Ondra by the hand, nodded in the direction of his colleagues and said: Do your duty.

He took a step forward, hesitated in front of the closed door, clutching the satchel under one arm and holding Ondra's hand with the other, one of the clerks darted over and opened the door. They headed out, hurrying down the corridor to the elevator, and as they were descending past the first floor, Father freed his hand from Ondra's grip, tore the tricolour ribbon from the lapel of his jacket, muttered: That really wouldn't be wise. He discarded the flag onto the floor of the lift as it creaked to a halt.

Already in the reception area, Ondra could hear a thundering noise, out on the street it became a roar, a metallic din, they saw a tank. The tank drove onto the pavement, its treads tearing up the paving stones. A little flame came flying out of the bowels of the tank, then they heard a rattle, bullets were pecking at the facade of the Patent Office, smashing the walls, shattering the windows.

Father was dragging him into one of the side streets through which a crowd was now rolling, they were all walking in the same direction, shouting, Ondra saw two men carrying a stretcher, they were heading towards them, Daddy was pulling him against the crowd, they were trying to weave their way through the people, the people kept pinning them up against the walls of buildings, then they were standing by the stretcher, Ondra glimpsed bare feet under a bloody blanket, the men carrying the stretcher were wearing sashes across their breasts with red crosses on them, one of them asked Ondra's daddy: Are you a doctor? No, but I need a taxi . . . then they were in another street, Daddy jumped right in front of a car that was picking up speed, stopped it, pushed Ondra into the back seat, sat down next to him, slammed the door shut swiftly and, clasping his satchel firmly between his knees, said: I'm sending you on a combat mission.

Squirt was sitting on a bed in the hospital, smiling. He was wearing a tracksuit. His hair was combed differently to how Ondra remembered it. There were lots of other boys milling around him. Squirt was smiling at the glass-panelled door. Father opened the door, they went in. The boys scattered in all directions, giggling and shouting. Father carted Squirt out of the hospital in a wheelchair, Ondra dawdled behind them. His eyes were fixed on the linoleum covered with grooves, covered with the marks left behind by other sets of wheels, he was sniffing the odour of the hospital. It was in Squirt's hair. They got into the car again, they kept glancing at each other and then suddenly they were in front of a bus. Ondra was familiar with the bus station. But he'd never seen so many people there. There were queues around the buses. People were shouting over each other and pushing and shoving, they all wanted to cram into the buses. A pungent stench was coming from the exhaust pipes. The engines of the buses, the cars, the clamouring of the crowd, all of this was deafening Ondra, he squeezed Squirt's shoulder hard, bent down to his ear and said: We're leaving town! Squirt nodded, as if to say it was quite clear to him. Father gave Ondra a strict look, nodded at him, as if he suspected that this gesture would nail Ondra to the ground. He dashed off, but he was back a moment later with a driver in a blue uniform and together they picked up Squirt and carried him onto the bus. Ondra elbowed his way through the crowd after them, then he was sitting next to Squirt, he could feel the crush around them, and then they were driving away, as he was nodding off to sleep he actually felt like he was falling.

In his sleep the roar of the tank engine and the whizz of the bullets, the roar of the bus engine and the sound of the people shouting melded into a single backdrop, he slept, dreamt, the whole time immersed in the din, he woke up into silence with a start, Squirt was tugging on his sleeve.

He was wide awake immediately. The bus stopped, the driver came over to them and said: Up you get, you're here! Ondra stood up, Squirt didn't move, the driver lifted him from the seat with both arms and after a few steps all three of them were on the grass outside the bus.

Oh dear, how come no one's waiting for you, eh? said the bus driver.

Ondra was looking around, even Squirt was eagerly craning his neck, but that was farcical, how far could he possibly see when he was sitting in the grass? He was holding a paper bag in his hand.

Looks like you'll have to wait here for a bit, said the driver. Or, you. Go and ask. The village is still a way to go. Ask in the pub. There's a pub there, apparently. What are you gawping at? Your dad gave me some beer money, so I'm looking out for you. Got to be off, now. Take care. He turned round, gave them a wave, by then he had one foot on the steps of the bus, he extended two fingers from his fist, parted them, and whipped his arm up. Victory! he exclaimed. Then he grabbed the steering wheel with both hands. Ondra was eyeing the faces of the people on the bus, astonished by how few people were left on it.

I was asleep, oh well, he said to himself.

He was standing on the dirt road, still engulfed by the cloud of dust stirred up by the bus. Squirt was sitting in the grass, in places it had gone yellow, because of the heat, probably. Now it was no longer hot. He couldn't even see the field. He didn't want to tell Squirt that he didn't know where they were. He'd never taken this road to the village. But maybe they'd gone this way in the car. He could hear insects. He glanced over at Squirt. He was staring at him. Ondra was a little ashamed because he'd slept the whole way. He kicked a stone with his trainer. He tried whistling, but it didn't come out right. He and Squirt hadn't seen each other for quite some time. He took a few steps towards him and asked: What have you got there?

They gave me this at the hospital, said Squirt. He reached into the paper bag. Socks and a T-shirt, have a sniff, they smell real nice.

Ondra plucked one sock from his hand and pressed it against his nose. He made a throaty noise like he was gagging. It stinks! What a horrible stink. Gross!

Rubbish, shrieked Squirt, yanking the sock from his hand. You're talking rot, the lady doctors gave me that. They put it in the laundry for me. So where are we going to go then?

You'll see, Ondra put his hands in his pockets.

And Squirt said: I'm hungry.

Didn't they give you anything in the hospital?

They did, but that was in the morning. We're at Granddad's, aren't we? Why did we go on our own?

And you know what they cook in hospital?

They cook good food, said Squirt, stuffing his socks back in the bag. I ate everything they gave me there. The lady doctors do the cooking.

Actually, said Ondra. Actually, they cook corpses. When the sick people die.

You're talking rubbish, said Squirt. You didn't stay at the hospital, I did.

Don't you start blubbing here, said Ondra in a deep voice. Otherwise I'll thump you one.

He was angry now. He knew it would soon be dusk, yeah, the sun will set and it'll get dark, he wasn't surprised that Granddad hadn't come to meet them, he never left the house. He was angry because during all those days that he'd spent in a slumber alone in the apartment, without Squirt, he'd forgotten that they were supposed to go to the country. Or had Dad not told him?

He wanted to sit down next to Squirt and tell him he'd seen a tank. He wanted to tell him that Dad had taken him to the Patent Office and what he'd seen there. Squirt was sitting down, he looked like he was going to start blubbing. Ondra snatched the paper bag from his hand, tossed the T-shirt and the socks out on the grass, one by one. He inflated the bag, slapped it. Bang!

Squirt was screaming and swearing, Ondra kicked the T-shirt and the socks back towards him. Squirt tried to put them back into the ruptured bag, he called Ondra a cretin and an imbecile, he kept saying it over and over, by now through tears.

And yet Ondra had been so looking forward to seeing Squirt the whole time he'd been in the hospital. He'd even rummaged through his toys, he'd sniffed his sweaters and his jackets. He kept expecting to wake up one morning and find everything as it had been before. In the morning they'd make breakfast with Mum, he and Squirt would have a row, then they'd grab their satchels and go to school. Sometimes he regretted scaring Squirt so much. He scared him before they fell asleep. Their beds were in a corner, they slept with their heads together. At night Squirt was afraid to fall asleep and wanted Ondra to hold his hand. One time Squirt said to Ondra: I'm really glad you're here. Why? Because I can hold your hand! But that's not my hand! Squirt started screaming and bawling, he was inconsolable. Ondra had to turn the lights on, push the wardrobe and the chairs back from the wall, and show Squirt that there was nothing, and no one, there.

When he was in the flat on his own he always had a knot in his stomach. He'd lock himself up in the toilet for hours at a time, reading magazines, schoolbooks, novels, anything. On the toilet he couldn't see how big the empty flat was. He would lie down on the couch, face down, imagining that the ceiling was the floor with the light fixture jutting upwards, he imagined walking over it, having to climb up the wall to get to the door. He would lie there like that until he heard murmuring in his head. He'd close his eyes, letting red and yellow circles of light explode beneath his eyelids. He'd go to Eluzína's little room, lie about there for a change, his head in a pile of battered, broken toys. He'd stare at the little girl in the picture. She was sketched with a few lines of charcoal. A little girl. Wearing a straw hat. Mother's Eluzína.

Once Mother and Squirt were no longer living in the apartment, the neighbour came round. Dad had arranged it with her. When she found him in the little room, she'd stand him up on his feet with a sharp tug and say: Shame on you! A big boy like you should be studying. And for goodness' sake, you're stinking the place out! Do you even wash properly? Let me see your fingernails, dear me! You've got dirt under your nails and I bet there's muck on your knees to boot. And that neck! Off with you to the bathroom.

In the bathroom, Ondra would get into the tub. He'd read chapter after chapter of *The Mars Monolith*. He'd voyage through the cosmos with Captain Nemura until the water had gone completely cold. One time the neighbour burst in. She grabbed a brush. He resisted, but only to begin with, after that he didn't care any more. She gave him a good scrubbing, threw a towel at him, and shooed him off to bed. When she thought he was asleep, she rifled through all the drawers and cupboards in the apartment. He closed his eyes and feigned sleep until he actually fell asleep.

He and Father went for walks together. They talked about Mum, as well as Squirt. They'd become close like this since the time they'd been on an excursion. Sometimes they got as far as the waterfront, they watched the river and Father told Ondra what he should do, and how to go about it. He also told him to use the time he spent on his own for learning. His school marks were diabolical. Yes, diabolical. And Father's face was so sad that Ondra had to make an effort not to start crying. Then Father asked him: Tell me, this life without your mother or your brother, does it bring you anything positive? Ondra said he was glad he had plenty of room in the flat. Father nodded and they walked along the embankment again. There were lots of little boats under the bridge and a band was playing on the riverboat. One day, my lad, we'll all go somewhere together again, maybe on a steamboat like that. Yes, my boy, all of us together, said Daddy and they watched a while longer. Then it started raining, so they quickened their pace.

Ondra hadn't known where they were going. He thought they were going somewhere just beyond Prague, to some grassy hill where they'd talk about learning and how things were going at school. Then maybe they'd have lunch somewhere. He was biting his nails, scraping out the dirt from under them with his teeth. He didn't want to make Dad feel ashamed of him, that's for sure.

He'd only ever seen Father's native village in the summer. He was only familiar with the church, the houses and the pub when the sun was beating down on their walls. In the scorching heat, the dogs stuck their tongues out, rolled around next to the kennels they were chained to, snapped at flies. He spotted one now, a stray, running along the ditch by the side of the road, its fur caked in mud. In the summer he sometimes watched the river through a veil of insects. There weren't so many now.

They ate in the pub. He kept peeking at the bar. They let them eat in peace and then they came over. They came to greet Father. Everyone knew they'd arrived. Ondra also said hello. He hardly recognised them. They were wrapped up in jackets, in padded coats. He went up to the bar to get a Kofola cola. Zuza's dad handed it to him. He kept expecting to see her. At any moment he expected to see Zuza. Why don't you go out for a walk, said Dad. The fresh air will do you good. Go run around for an hour, chop chop! Dad was sitting at the table with Mr Berka, with Líman. He wasn't listening to them. The first time they'd been down the pub his legs hadn't reached the floor when he was sitting down, now he sat comfortably, he leant back in the chair. It took him a while to realize his dad was talking to him. They were looking at him. Everyone that had come to the table. Okay, he said, sliding off the chair.

He was kicking sods of grass, kicking them down into the water. The wind was swishing over the field, whistling through tree branches. It was rippling the surface of the water. The wind ripped the clouds apart, the sun made shadows rush over the ground. They alternated with bands of light, disappearing in the field. It occurred to him to go and have a look at the little boat. But he didn't go to the church, they'd have spotted him. He walked back and forth along the river bank. They'd only come for a brief visit.

Then he heard Milan. Behind him. He didn't even get a start. Most of the time they knew where he was, even if it was dusk or foggy, for

11

example. Maybe they also knew about the little boat. But the river held no interest for any of the lads.

He turned round immediately, he almost spluttered. Milan was wearing black evening shoes, a suit. His hair was combed. Right behind him stood Pavel. And the others. Pepa was laughing at him. They were wearing shirts. They were wearing dinner jackets, their sleeves hanging down loosely. They looked odd. And that girl was with them. She was simpering.

We're going to the funfair, you coming? said Milan. Come for long? We're going with Květa, said Pepa. He chuckled again. He's not going to be sitting in the field today, thought Ondra.

He knew they were going to the tree. He'd gone there with them once. To the maize field by the riverbend. Only one tree stood there. The place was known as Blighter's Bank. They'd gone there with Squirt, walking with the smallest of the boys, right at the back. Květa had waited by the tree.

Back then they'd taken the back road over the fields to the funfair in Zásmuky. The sun was scorching. He and Squirt were breathing all the dust stirred up by the feet of those in front of them. Milan and Pavel turned off into the field. They went towards the river. They could see Květa already from a distance. She was standing next to the tree, leaning back on it. Into the field, scoot! Milan turned round to the little boys. He stamped his foot at them, even the older ones who hadn't passed the test yet. Everyone knew the routine, no one said anything. Ondra and Squirt walked behind Pepa and Jindra, the smaller boys behind them. Some of them were from Zásmuky. Ondra didn't know them. Now they were sitting in the field, giggling. They couldn't see the river through the thick rows of sweet corn. All they could do was look at each other. They knew that the older boys were already by the tree. We have to sit, is that clear? Pepa instructed them with a grave expression on his face. Yeah? said

Squirt, tearing a cob of corn from the stalk. Jindra slapped his hand. It's not ripe yet, you pillock.

I like the tiny ones, they taste good, retaliated Squirt. They're sweet.

You don't eat the tiny ones, you stupid Praguer, said one of the Zásmuky boys. He looked at the sweet corn stalks all around them and said: She's got her tits out by now. No doubt!

Yeah, you're the expert, said Pepa.

She's taking her clothes off, see, said Zásmuky Boy, jabbing Ondra in the shoulder.

Hmm, said Ondra.

They heard the lads sniggering. Květa was also laughing.

She's got nice tits, apparently, said Zásmuky Boy, poking Ondra again. What do you reckon?

Hmm.

You seen a girl naked yet? Would you like a peek? You're scared!

Leave him alone, said Jindra.

Bugger off, Líman, said Zásmuky Boy. Hear that?

They were squatting among the sweet corn. The ground was parched, crumbly. Pepa was sitting with his legs crossed. Squirt was poking around in the soil with a stick. Ants were crawling out of a crack. They had to crawl over his little stick. The sun was directly above them. They could no longer hear the lads. An altogether different sound reached them from the river through the sweet corn. It sounded like whispering. They heard it on and off. Depending on the wind.

That's it, said Zásmuky Boy. They're doing it with her now. That's the sound she makes. Like a cat in heat.

Crock of shit, said Pepa. How do you know?

The men said so, the boy said. Down our pub. Some of them scream when they're doing it, but not this one.

Yeah, yeah, load of old cobblers, said Pepa.

For sure. They're doing it with her. Everyone knows. Would you like to have a go?

Ondra only realised after a while. That Zásmuky Boy was addressing him. Because he'd thumped him. Ondra kept listening to the moaning, to that sound, the sound of Květa. But now he had to do something. Everyone had seen that the boy had thumped him.

I said, they don't all scream, said Zásmuky Boy.

Ondra drew his arm back and thumped him in the shoulder. The boy didn't budge an inch.

It's scorching, said Ondra. He didn't know what to say.

Just you wait, you twat, said Zásmuky Boy. This isn't scorching. Just you wait, it'll get so hot here, you twat, it'll make your hair crawl off your head. You'll be sweating brain, you twat. You don't get that kind of heat in Prague, you stupid bleeding Praguer . . .

Keep your trap shut, said Pepa.

Shut your piehole, said Jindra almost simultaneously.

This heat's doing my head in, said Zásmuky Boy, standing up.

Sit down! exclaimed Pepa.

Fuck off, Líman brothers, coddle your Praguers, the ugly mugs, yelled Zásmuky Boy, then he was running off, he jumped into the sweet corn, scarpering away from them as fast as he could, stumbling over hard lumps of soil, forcing his way through the corn, then they could no longer see him, only the tops of the corn stalks swaying, tossing about, the boy vanished in the field.

Twat, said Pepa. Sit and be quiet, he commanded the rest of the boys. Some of them were from Zásmuky. They also wanted to do a runner, most likely. But they couldn't. They were too small. They couldn't just get up and disappear.

Ondra lay down on his back, he could see the top of a tree. He watched the leaves quivering in the wind, it reminded him of an anthill. It was better than looking down at the ground. There were slits in the ground, cracks. Little rocks sparkled in the dry clods. Yellowed bits of stalk lay about everywhere. His tongue was sticking to the roof of his mouth, he scraped the soil off a little pebble, stuck it in his mouth, sucked on it. He wanted to be alone in the little boat, to stick his hand into the water. They'd gone with them because of Squirt. Squirt wanted to go to the funfair, he wanted to go on the swings, to stuff his face with sweets, with nougat. Ondra glanced at the others. They were sitting around, lying about. Waiting. Nothing else happened. They didn't hear that sound again.

You going to the fair, yeah? said Ondra. Yeah, said Milan. The lads filed past, Jindra nodded to him. Hiya! said Pepa. Květa was going with them. She was wearing a blue dress. He'd never seen her up so close. The lads seemed altogether different to how they'd been in the summer. Alien. They were swaggering around him. It felt like he'd never set eyes on them before. Milan and Pavel stopped and stood there.

Why have you come? said Milan. You came by car! said Pavel.

Why does your old man want those things back? asked Milan.

What? said Ondra.

Tell your old man he's not getting anything back, said Milan.

Squirt's in hospital. He got run over. He thought they'd find that interesting.

You let him know, said Milan. He turned around and walked off. So did Pavel.

Ondra shuffled off along the river. He was expecting them to call him. Expecting Pepa to catch up with him, panting. Or to hear Květa. He was waiting for that as well. But nothing happened. He kept walking. They let him. They had no interest in him whatsoever. He decided to go back to the pub.

He thought he'd come across her by chance. It wasn't until later that she told him she'd been trying to find him. She'd gone out looking for him. She'd also been thinking about him. All the time. All summer, even after he'd left. She thought about how they'd been together. She didn't tell anyone about it. Not even Renata. Now he was pissing her off. From the moment she first laid eyes on him. A little boy. Kicking clods into the river. Behaving like a silly lout, his hands in his pockets.

You going with them? You going to the fair as well? she said as though they'd seen each other just the day before.

He felt he could hear it. He heard the wind, its murmuring. He thought he could hear the same sound as back then in the summer. That he could hear Květa. That her voice was interwoven with the wind and was being carried by it all the way to where they were standing. But that's not possible, he thought. If only because the wind is everywhere. In the tree tops, over the water. The wind swished over the field.

I don't want you to go there! That's why I went to look for you.

He walked up to her, they embraced. He grabbed her hand immediately. They sat down. Maybe she noticed that he'd gone weak at the knees. All of a sudden he was with Zuza now. He felt this was what he'd wanted all along. He wanted to talk, to keep talking. He didn't want them to hear that sound. They were holding each other, their fingers intertwined. Embracing Zuza was immense. There's no more room for anything else in my thoughts, for any of those things, he was saying to himself. You were in my head all the time, he said to her. I thought about you. She pushed him away. They weren't kissing any more.

I didn't want you to go there, she said. I didn't want that. But why am I sitting with you here? You're going to leave again anyway!

Her lips were cracked. Her hair smelled lovely. Her hair reached down to her shoulders.

I didn't want you to go there with them. Do you know why they call that place the Blighter's Bank? This woman gave birth to a child. But it wasn't really a child! When the people saw it, they were aghast! They went to get the Old Hag. The Old Hag took it and flung it in the water. It wasn't a child at all. It was a little man, he had a beard and everything. The Old Hag threw him in the water, so that's where he stayed. He ate fish and leeches, everything. He never moved from the tree. Stayed there for years on end. People wanted to tear him away from there, but it was impossible. They wanted to give him food, but he didn't want any.

What?

Never mind, said Zuza. It's just an old wives' tale. They tell that story so that kids don't go near the water. But you go near the water all the time. I knew where I'd find you. You're a big baby, too. Are you even normal?

What?

She leaned over him. She was leaning on his shoulder, she was standing up. Her skirt seemed to be hovering now. She narrowed her eyes. She was staring into his eyes. He looked away.

A load of piffle, that's all, she said. But she embraced him again. She pressed him down with her body, down to the earth. The soil felt cool on his neck. She kissed him. She bit his lip a little. She ran her hand over his body. She stroked him through his trousers.

I spent the whole summer fooling around with you, she was saying into his ear. So what, just fooling around, I said to myself. Why not? But then you wouldn't leave my mind. You never got in touch. How come? In all that time. Because you're a little boy! she said and slapped him with the palm of her hand.

He rolled over on top of her. She wasn't looking at him. By the weir, she said. I'm such a cow!

She never went into the water when they were up at the weir. She just watched him swimming. She didn't want to get into the little boat, either. They'd been almost naked together by the weir. Many times. But now he felt closest to her. She embraced him again, drew him to her. Her eyes were narrowed all the time. She was the one moving, helping him. She curled up under him, with one hand she took off her panties. Then she lay back again and pressed up against him. Suddenly he was inside her. They were moving together. He didn't know what to do, whether he should stay as he was. She was whimpering, moving beneath him. Faster and faster. She hitched up his shirt and slid her hand on his skin. He pressed his head on her shoulder, he could hear his breath. He did what she wanted, again, again. Then he felt a spasm, a hot wave rushing over him and he slumped down on top of her. Zuza's whole body tensed beneath him. Jesus Christ! she cried. You cretin! She pushed him away. She sat up. You've done it all over me, you idiot. You idiot. He knew she'd got up. She was tucking her shirt into her skirt, shaking the grass off. She was still livid. He resolved to remain lying down. He didn't even want to look at her. He felt her bending down. She stroked his cheek.

He wanted her gone already. He heard her leaving. He was watching the water. He wanted to stay there, as he was. But he should stand up and do up his trousers. The wind had picked up. It was bending the tops of trees, thrashing about, the weather was whirling around in the branches. His ears were throbbing.

The next thing he heard was a car horn.

Father was standing by the car. There was a huddle of men watching them from in front of the pub. Father opened the door and nervously motioned for Ondra to get in, jump to it. Then Ondra heard a smack.

They were splashed with mud. And again. The next stone hit the car. By then Father was driving off. The stone struck the window, but didn't break it. Father was gritting his teeth, pressing his lips together tightly. The stones were also falling on the road in front of them. But only a few. They were driving away fast.

I'm going to try walking then, Squirt piped up suddenly.

What?

Well, I've not walked yet, come here!

Ondra stood next to him, Squirt grabbed on to his elbow and proceeded to wriggle up onto his feet.

I'm standing, look! he exclaimed, immediately collapsing back down into the grass. That was one hell of a crack, that car almost tore my legs off!

I know, said Ondra. I thought you were dead.

Come here! said Squirt, giggling.

And with Ondra's help he stood up again, yelling: I'm standing! And he keeled over into the grass again. They were both cracking up. When Squirt had toppled over for the third, or the umpteenth, time, Ondra leapt on him and they brayed with laughter in the grass, they kept laughing, they just couldn't stop.

I'm! shrieked Squirt, I'm going to split my sides!

Me too, squealed Ondra and for a moment he actually felt physically sick from laughing.

Then Squirt got up and before he keeled over again, he managed to take a few steps.

So where are we going, then, eh? he asked Ondra.

He's right. They should be on their way. They'll get there somehow. They'll just wait a little while longer. Maybe he could carry Squirt. They'll be passing people's houses. And maybe the pub. She might be there. He'd see her. He blushed. He turned around so that Squirt couldn't see his face.

Look, said Squirt.

Hmm.

Do you see that cloud of dust?

What?

Over there. Squirt pointed. A long way off. I've always had better eyesight than you! Maybe someone's coming. Let's wait, yeah?

The first time he saw her was when he was in the pub with Mum and Dad. Everyone came over to their table to say hello. Frída the Constable and his assistant. He didn't sit down, but he bellowed at the whole pub. We're proud of you! he said and gave Dad a salute. Damn it, Evžen, leave it out! Dad said to him. Everyone was laughing. The Constable's assistant also saluted. He was wearing a peaked cap with its visor missing. Old man Berka sat down with them. The pub was packed. The old women sat in the hallway on sacks of potatoes, nattering. It was almost dark in the hallway. It reeked of the toilets. Rolls of yellow flypaper covered with flies hung from the ceiling. The flies buzzed and crawled over each other, writhing around in the slimy coating, trying to fly away.

I'd like another Kofola cola! he said, pushing his plate away.

You know what, then? said Mum, go fetch it yourself. She pushed a banknote towards him. He shuffled over to the counter.

A girl was standing there. She was wearing a skirt and a T-shirt and sandals. Ondra was made to wear socks and shoes. Even in the heat. He stood there, waiting for the innkeeper to arrive, but the girl said to him: What do you want?

A Kofola cola.

She poured him the fizzy drink from the tap, handed him the glass with one hand, taking the banknote with the other, she tossed it in the bowl and was already handing him the change over the wet metal counter.

He pushed the coins away and like Dad said: That's all right. He turned around quickly, he wanted to get away from the girl.

As he was leaving she said: Ah, the gentleman's from Prague. Oh my, a thousand thanks in that case! She chucked the change in the bowl. He could hear her laughing.

He sat down under the flypaper again with his back to her. He was trying to listen to what Mr Berka was saying to Dad. He was glad the girl couldn't see him. He didn't stir until he could feel he was no longer red in the face.

What's the matter with you? said Mum.

Nothing.

You don't say! You're as pale as the walls in here. You're as white as a sheet! Do you want something to eat?

No. Let me be.

After that he met her by the weir, on one of his wanderings. She was the one who started the conversation: My name's Zuzka. Then he spent the entire summer with her. When he wasn't with her, he thought about her. Squirt was peeved, he had to hang about in the yard the whole time. He was there with Mum. She was friends with the girls, they came to see her all the time. Squirt got under their feet. Sometimes Ondra had to go with him and Mum on an excursion. When they were with Mum, the lads left them alone.

Why do you always come this far? she said.

How do you know I come here?

The girls said so. She kicked off her sandals, ran over the stones onto the weir. She never went swimming. She didn't want to get into the little boat either. Sometimes they got into the deep water beneath the weir. They pressed up against each other. They dived under the water. Sometimes when she held him close on the bank or embraced him, he turned away from her. He thought about beetles in the grass, or something. Or he counted to himself. She smelled so good. He couldn't remain entirely engulfed in her scent. He couldn't keep sinking into it like that. Otherwise something would have happened. The coldest water was in the deep pool under the weir.

And if we get married, are we going to live in Prague?

Sure! He was hard-pressed to stop his teeth from chattering.

She cackled and submerged herself in the water. She could stay under longer than Ondra. He pretended he didn't care.

How come you can touch me like that, but I can't do it to you? he asked her once.

Because I'm a girl.

Aha. And why . . .

Don't keep asking questions, it's girly.

He thought about Zuza even when he was alone in the little boat, insects swarming all around, he thought about how she takes all those beers to the tables, walking under the flypapers, sometimes the buzzing became a solid wall, he had to whistle or clap to make an opening in the droning so that he could slip through the wall. He could feel the sun burning even with his eyes closed, he lay face down in the bottom of the boat, he could hear the water beneath him, that incessant movement, he heard the rumble made by the mass of water rolling through the river channel, he would almost fall asleep, thinking of Zuza.

They were hidden beneath the water streaming down from the weir, lapping at the foamy water falling down from the waterfall above them with their tongues like dogs, they squirted water at each other from their mouths, sitting with their backs pressed against the side of the weir, deafened by the roar of the cascading water. The stones in the wall of the weir were covered with bands of brown and green moss, they made their backs feel cool, Zuza was on top of him, she was pressing herself against his chest, tickling him all over his face with her tongue, he wanted to push her away, he wanted to burst out laughing, he was pulling her towards him, if there hadn't been so much water cascading over them he would have smelled the scent of her mouth, she was giving him little kisses on the corners of his lips, she pushed her hand under his shorts, she stroked him there, then she squeezed him, held him tight. Do you like that? she said. Yeah, he exhaled. He could feel the cold skin of her face on his lips, he also pushed his hand between her legs, she whacked him on the nose, he froze, she kept stroking him, saying something, but she was speaking quietly. Also, the water was roaring all around them.

Suddenly Squirt yelled: Watch out!

Ondra jumped to one side, the man on the bicycle almost ran into him, Ondra slid off the dirt road, immediately shielding his eyes with his hand, the summer sun flashed off the metal of the wheel, the wheel forced the sun's rays into his eyes painfully, the man, dressed all in black, stopped.

What are you doing, laddie, tottering about here like that? Do you know the braking distance of my machine? Never fear, it'll get all of us where we need to go! You sure have grown up! You've turned into a veritable ephebe! As for you, you haven't made much progress height-wise, that's for sure. But I'm sure you too are approaching puberty. What are you two gawking at? Much water has passed under the bridge over our very own silvery-foamed river Lethe since the last time I set eyes on you. Back then you were still oblivious to everything around you. But we'll fix all that! Give me your hand!

The man wearing black baggy trousers kept swinging his arms, he was moving about all the time, his black jacket bulged at the shoulders and the elbows, he was wearing a black hat, sweat was streaming from under it and running down his face. That's because he'd been cycling so fast, thought Ondra . . . the man stretched his right arm towards him but didn't even let him touch it, immediately he raised it again, parted two of his fingers, swung his arm up above his head and exclaimed: Victory! Greetings, boys. My name is Polka. Your quarters await you. And now! But you know. We'll make it by a whisker! But . . . what are you wearing? He walked up to Squirt, who was still sitting in the grass, crouched down, grasped his tracksuit top with two fingers, gave it a tug.

We don't know you! said Squirt.

Well, I'm . . . said the man, finally letting go of Squirt's top . . . your banished uncle! Yes indeedy! I've been called to arms. I'm taking charge of the family estate. Those ruins! And you too. After all, does an egghead like your daddy have the time? Well, you tell me.

Squirt said: I don't know!

See! Polka said. What are you wearing?

Uncle, thought Ondra. He's about the same height as Dad, he said to himself.

You don't look like Dad, not at all, said Squirt.

I don't, eh? Polka laughed. Look! And he stretched his whole body, made a grimace that made Squirt splutter, and then he pranced about, pacing up and down, stretching his long thin stork-like legs, knitting his brows . . . Squirt was giggling, Ondra had to laugh too.

There, now you see, said Polka. And they saw. They couldn't stop laughing.

Polka thrust his hands in his pockets and said: Yep, we're from the same litter all right. But your dad is an educated fellow, I can't compete with him. You see, I'm ... it's hard for me to say that forbidden word, but I'm a bit of a ... poet, don't you know? And a globetrotter! Oh yes.

Yeah? said Squirt. Really? And have you been to Greenland?

But my dear boy, now Polka was laughing in turn and waving his arms about, where did you say? You've got me there, Polka laughed, he laughed so hard he had tears in his eyes, he was slapping his thighs, all three of them were hooting with laughter and Squirt was shouting: Greenland! Greenland! And Polka waved as if to say that's enough, he couldn't take any more.

Huh, you really got me with that one, he said, wiping his eyes, and blurted out: You don't know!

What don't we know? said Squirt.

Luckily, luckily ... mumbled Polka, and then he started rummaging around in the pockets of his jacket. Hold this! he bellowed at Ondra, thrusting the handlebars of the bike into his hands, he pulled out a piece of cloth, pecked at it with his fingers ... Here you go. He pulled Ondra towards him by his T-shirt, hooked a safety pin through the T-shirt, a black ribbon hung down from the pin, Polka snapped the safety pin shut, in a single bound he was next to Squirt, putting a safety pin in his jacket, he straightened up, grabbed the bike and said: Done! On you get. The sun is already bowing down.

And they were off.

Squirt's legs were dangling to and fro, he was sitting in the wire basket at the back, Polka had put Ondra on the frame, his chin was touching his hair, Ondra felt his breath, every wheeze, he had to lean on Polka, they were going uphill and only then did Polka really start peddling, he put his weight into the pedals, forcing the bike up the hill, and then they heard Squirt: Ouch, ouch, ouch ... Polka stopped and said: This won't do, boys.

After that he pushed the bike up the slope. Ondra walked at the back, steadying Squirt in the basket, at times it even seemed to him that he was carrying him, but that wasn't the case, he was just lifting him up a little.

At the top of the hill they mounted the bike again. They got on and went rattling down the hill between the first houses of the village, they crossed the stream. Polka made a sharp turn, heading directly towards the church. Squirt was chuckling on and off, the wind whistled past their ears . . . it was a good ride. They knew where they were now.

He'd never heard a bell toll so near, never stood so close as to be deafened by the chime of a bell, he was below the bell tower, watching the procession, they were all walking towards them, Squirt, Polka and he were standing next to a heap of excavated earth, the procession was going around the church, through grass and nettles, and when Ondra turned his head to the side he saw the river sparkling through the thickets, he remembered the little boat, and he wondered if it was still there, there where he'd hidden it, weighted it down with a rock, he wondered if it hadn't rotted away! Been stolen! By then the procession had reached them, they were all dressed in black, familiar faces emerged, the Líman brothers, they walked one behind the other, spanking clean, wearing black trousers and jackets, they had black ribbons in their lapels, the bell was tolling, he knew he'd slept through the whole journey there, but because of the chiming of the bell he was once again engulfed in noise, the chiming of the bell mingled with the cries of the people on the street, the clattering of the tank, the gunfire, he wanted to get away from those sounds, he took a step forwards, Squirt grabbed his sleeve and that was funny because Squirt had to hold on to him, otherwise he'd keel over.

And then they were coming up to them, the old women came first, they were weeping and lamenting, wearing black shawls and black dresses, some of them were holding each other up as they walked. They were walking from the mortuary, it was hardly visible through the thickets and the nettles, a dark house leaning onto the white wall of the cemetery, now they finally came right up to them and hardly had they lowered the coffin into the grave, than the procession moved on again, walking past the three of them standing by the pile of excavated earth, and Polka was the only one to respond when they said: My condolences ... and Chin up, boys ... and other things and other greetings, Ondra was hardly aware of them, he shook the hands they extended, some of the hands only touched him, other people tapped him with their fingers, someone else squeezed his hand, then Polka nudged him in the ribs with his elbow, and then Ondra and Squirt also started saying: Thank you ... to all those suits and black hats, gazing into the faces of the bleary-eyed old women and the nodding old men, the boys who almost burst out laughing when he said: Thank you ... and then the girls were offering him their hands, one of them was Zuza, he hardly recognised her, he was almost startled, it was the first time he'd seen her in a dress, she squeezed his hand, she wasn't looking at him, she offered her hand to Squirt, then she squeezed Polka's hand and disappeared behind the mound of excavated earth just like everyone else.

The sun was setting. That was good. Everyone was staring at them.

They walked out of the cemetery, took off the black ribbons. Polka stuck them all in his pocket. They headed for Granddad's house. They walked along the stream. Squirt was yawning. The gate creaked as always. Mr Frantla was sitting on the bench beneath the window.

Ondra knew the room by heart. Squirt was already nodding off, Mr Frantla and Polka sat him down on the bed and Mr Frantla took his shoes off. Squirt stretched out, Ondra crawled in next to him. We haven't even washed! it occurred to him, he wanted to close his eyes. Polka crouched over him, said: Off to beddy byes. Tomorrow's another day.

Then he switched off the lights and Squirt said: Your hand. Go on.

Ondra grabbed his hand straight away.

You knew, did you? Squirt said. That he was dead.

No. Go to sleep.

I can't, not right now. How come he's dead?

He was dreadfully old.

Even so.

Hmm.

Hey! What about Mum?

I don't know.

I thought she might be here. She isn't, though. I'm going to sleep, yeah?

Yeah. Me too, said Ondra.

Hey, Squirt piped up again. What are you thinking about? Apparently, whatever you think about on your first day will come true somewhere.

What are you thinking about?

I'm going to think about the walrus. Do you remember? The elephant seal?

Yeah.

He was breathing in time with Squirt to make him fall asleep quicker. He didn't understand why, but the entire time he'd also thought that Mum might be there. Well, I thought wrong, he said to himself, I'd better get off to sleep. He didn't manage right away, instead he thought about the times when they'd all been together.

2

They used to walk behind her, getting rid of the bottles. She'd start drinking in the afternoon and by evening she'd forget her hiding places. She'd take a bottle from the linen cupboard, drink from it, hide the bottle again, burying it under a pile of clothes, she'd walk on, dropping cigarette ash in her wake and leaving burning cigarette butts on top of the table, the linen cupboard, sometimes she opened a window and tossed a fag end out. Then she closed the window carefully. The furniture was studded with burn marks, black grooves, even the carpet was dotted with small rust-coloured spots made by discarded cigarette ends. They walked behind her, she bumped into the furniture with her legs, elbows, ribs, she had bruises all over her body. They followed her from room to room, occasionally she stayed in the kitchen, she had wine bottles stowed behind the cooker and the sink, by then they knew those places well. She had one bottle hidden behind the shoe rack in the hall, another behind the mirror.

In the bathroom there were so many cupboards with so many shelves, so many bundles of dirty laundry, piles of dirty towels and bedsheets, Father's shirts, old rags, and their tracksuits and T-shirts, she could hide miniatures in any number of places.

Ondra used to come across those by chance. Squirt loved them. He especially liked their round metallic tops. When they came home from school, Squirt immediately chucked his bag in the corner and dashed off to search the bathroom. But he rarely found anything on his own. He whined and begged Ondra to help him look. He had a whole collection of metal bottle tops. At school he could swap them for bubble gum wrappers.

As soon as she had taken a few swigs from a bottle and forgotten about it, Ondra would take it away and empty it. He poured the contents down the kitchen sink, the smell of wine wafted from the drain, he turned on the tap and flushed it away.

Anyway, said Squirt when they were in bed.

What? asked Ondra.

Why is Mum holed up in the little room all the time, staring at the photo of Eluzína?

It's not a photo. It's a drawing.

What's better? Being a boy or a girl?

Boy, said Ondra.

So why does she keep staring at Eluza?

Go to sleep.

Still, it was better when they both drank, said Squirt.

Guess so, said Ondra.

On one of those summer afternoons long ago when they were all still together, Dad had carved watermills for them. They spent their days in a pub garden near their new home.

Before then, Dad had gone to work every morning wearing a jacket and white shirt. Now he worked in a factory. They'd moved to a workers' housing estate on the outskirts of Prague.

But they liked spending time in that pub garden. Besides, it was the only one there.

I do think the smell of the horse chestnut trees is delirious. Their scent verges on the incredibly sensual!

And I wonder if you know, young lady, that the Czechoslovak Communist Party was founded under horse chestnut trees just like these? Eh?

Daddy's new colleagues often spent those long afternoons with them. Especially his direct superiors, Foreman Dĕtmar and Brigade Leader Dudek. He never took his eyes off Mum.

That scent . . . it really is almost carnal. I love nature. Don't you?

Foreman Dĕtmar, a huge blubbery man, banged his fist on the table. Dĕtmar looked like he'd been born wearing boots, overalls and a cap. He was giving Dad a hug. Dad was trying to keep the glasses on the table upright. There were lots of beer mugs, glasses and bottles on the table, there were plates with frankfurters, baskets with bread and rolls, meatloaf, thick sausages with onions . . . everyone could take what they wanted . . . and they did, with both hands . . . people who worked at the factory went down the pub every day, entire families, after work . . . that's what people did, that summer the sun was always shining.

Listen everybody, roared Dĕtmar . . . to start off with me and the lads, we said to each other, we've got ourselves another one of them ink-stained intellectual types, never got his hands dirty, what should we do with him . . . let's get him sweeping the yard! We've had a lot of their kind sent to us, they're no use to man or beast, says I . . . and look here! He turns out to be a skilful lad, straight away he's checking out the workshops, looking to make himself useful . . . one of the machines gets jammed and hey presto! This here Lipka splices a couple of wires together, cleans up the coils and it's up and running again . . . he can put an old ventilator back in order, he can! That's what I say, he cried, slapping Dad on the back, he's good and proper, this bloke, a bloke with balls in the right place! Begging your pardon, missus . . .

Oh that's all right. Mum nodded, ordering another glass of white wine. Every now and then she'd remember to have a morsel of fish, a nibble of cheese.

Brigade Leader Dudek kept picking at the small white blisters in the corners of his mouth, fidgeting, ogling Mum. He blurted out: Oh, but the way you eat is so lovely! You're not French by any chance, are you?

Oh leave it out, silly, said Mum, dabbing some mustard on his nose with the tip of her finger. Fetch us another round of spirits, instead, shake a leg . . .

Oi! said Foreman Dĕtmar, winking at Dad. Got yourself a nice little number here, eh? You like it here, don't you? Other people are doing time behind bars, or they've done a runner over the border, but no one will hurt a hair on your head while you're with us at the factory . . . and anyway! he lowered his voice, the Communists won't last, they can't, they're done for . . . the Americans and the West won't leave it like this . . . this is no bloody Asia, we're a western democracy, for fuck's sake, well, aren't we?

Shut your gob, will you? snapped Brigade Leader Dudek, slamming a tray of drinks on the table.

Cheers, said Mum.

Cheers, said everyone.

Ondra was watching Dad's hands. Back then something was going on with Dad's hands, his fingers. He kept restlessly skimming his palms over the table, nervously fiddling with his hands, whatever he got his hands on he bent, crumpled, rolled around in his palms . . . most of all he liked to twist wire, plastic-coated insulated wire, he could get hold of as much as he wanted in the factory yard, the wire seemed to turn round in his hands of its own will, Dad twisted it into little animals, space rockets, Squirt brayed with delight ... whenever he wanted, Dad could leave the factory yard that he swept and go to the machine workshops, they were glad to have him around ... he picked up bits of sheet metal, metal clips, various straps ... he made the boys windmills from the sheet metal ... on that gorgeous summer day in the beer garden his fingers were dancing as usual, he reached out, grabbed a branch, snap, he broke it off ... everyone was watching ... he pulled his knife out of his pocket, opened it and cut, cut, snip, snip, he peeled off the bark ... and raised a watermill above his head ... Follow me! he commanded ... and they all rushed after him, the whole gang, all the lads who lived on the estate, Ondra trotted proudly at the front, dragging Squirt along by his hand ... in general, it wasn't easy to get along with those boys, not at all ... but now they had something ... this man was their dad! ... the man everyone was following ... they ran to the tar-coated wooden shack, the toilets, there was an open drain by the wall, water ran down it all the time, flushing away hectolitres of beer piss ... everyone in the huddle around them was now laughing, even the women jostled each other in the doorway ... and Dad was deftly installing the watermill and it started to turn ... the wooden branches clattered in that uninterrupted flow, clickety-clack, turning like the paddles of a real mill ... and Dětmar got into the shack, his colossal figure almost blocking the view, he leant back ... and that's when the mill really started rattling! Everyone liked that.

You should have that patented, damn it, burbled Dudek, he was already drunk and being all matey with Dad, he was pressing up against Mum, thinking no one noticed ... every now and then the other men got their knives out to carve watermills for their sons, they weren't going to let an ink-stained intellectual put them to shame, but to no avail ... their knives slipped over the bark of the horse chestnut branches, it's not easy to find the right kind of forked branch shaped like a saddlebow ...

their mills were bumpy, they had little cracks, in some cases the efforts resulted in bloodshed, in the end all they achieved was tearing branches off the trees . . . Ondra and Squirt, red-faced with excitement, were the heroes of the day . . . Dad also carved watermills for a few of the other boys who'd pleaded desperately, but only Ondra and Squirt were able to position theirs to make them go clickety-clack, making the sound of a flawless machine . . . that requires practice.

And that was merely the beginning. Then came the windmills. Dad could get his hands on as much sheet metal as he wanted. Artfully he shaped it into giant windmills, ingeniously assembling the vanes into glistening structures. No one had ever seen anything like it in the street before.

Ondra and Squirt stood by the window, proud and happy, and the wind did its work, turning the assemblage of interconnected vanes.

It's simple, Dad said to them, frowning, as if they'd been asking him about something. Matter is converted to movement, and that in turn to sound.

The wind turned the windmills, the metal sails seemed to be endlessly waving to someone. There was much jubilation in that movement. Perhaps it was a greeting sculpture. The wind wailed and whistled in every twist of the sheet metal, it sounded like a pixie praying. That's what Mum came up with.

Dad would stand next to the whirling windmills with gauges and a compass, noting the strength and direction of the wind. He recorded his measurements carefully. He was always experimenting. But people from the vicinity came just to look at the beauty of it.

And one time . . . a big black car full of comrades from the district committee stopped in front of the house. Mum's face was as pale as ash as she opened the door for them. But the comrades were jovial and talked merrily. One of the comrades had had the bright idea that whirling windmills painted bright red would enhance the beauty of the May Day Parade. The comrades opened bottles of Soviet champagne. Got any other ideas, dear comrade? They asked Dad questions long into the night.

That's how it was.

Squirt probably doesn't remember it any more.

Are you asleep? asked Ondra.

Not yet.

With Dad it's like with Captain Nemura, Ondra had told Squirt. In the dark recesses of his brain he's conceived an idea that will transform life on earth. Dad is working on an invention of colossal importance. I've been to the laboratories, I've seen it. When he completes it, we're out of here. Lift off!

With Mum? asked Squirt.

The silvery flank of Captain Nemura's spaceship sparkles with the following inscription in shiny letters: No kids, no pets, no brats and no women on board.

Heh, yelped Squirt.

Yep, said Ondra. That's how it is. Hey, what does it feel like?

What?

Well, doesn't it feel weird, stupid?

What?

When she dresses you up like that!

I don't know. Squirt was fidgeting next to him in the dark.

You couldn't go to school dressed like that, you've got to admit that!

I dunno!

What do you mean you dunno? What don't you know? They'd all be in stitches!

But I only wear that stuff at home!

One time Ondra came home from school, Mum was in the bathroom, the door was closed. He heard the shower and also Squirt, giggling. He was in there with Mum.

Hullo! What's going on? Ondra exclaimed, knocking on the door.

He opened the bathroom door and saw Mum sitting on the edge of the tub, the shower was running as always when Mum shut herself in there. She was sitting on the edge of the tub. She was wearing a black polo-neck, she'd been wearing it a lot recently, she also wore Dad's shirts. There was a little girl standing next to her. She had lipstick smeared all over her mouth. There were hair clips in her hair. And she was wearing a skirt. When the girl spoke, she turned out to be Squirt. Hiya, said Squirt.

Ondra slammed the door and went into the kitchen.

After a while, Mum walked in.

Is that any way to come home? Don't be daft, please!

Ondra ran past her into his room, he lay down on the couch, opened some book or other and pretended to read.

A while later, Squirt shuffled over. He was wearing his own clothes.

Dressed up for a fancy dress party, were you?

It's just a laugh, said Squirt. She sings to me and stuff like that.

You're not a little kid any more.

I know I'm not, said Squirt. But it calms her down, you know.

She's calm when you're wearing a dress? A girl's dress! You wait, I'm going to tell the boys tomorrow!

No you won't! Not that! You can't!

And Squirt cursed him and implored him, he would have promised him anything.

But Ondra wouldn't tell anyone anyway. That he's got a brother who dresses up like a girl at home.

Whenever Mum shut herself in the bathroom, Squirt hung around by the door. Sometimes they heard her talking, but because of the noise of the running water they couldn't make out what she was saying. Squirt tried to peep through the keyhole, but he couldn't see anything because of the steam. He pricked up his ears and when there was no noise coming out for a long time, he whined: Muuummy, open up! I'm hungry! I'm thirsty. He waited for a bit and then he mewled again: Mummy! What's the time? The clock has stopped! Sometimes Squirt mumbled something, putting on a voice like he was a stranger, and then he shouted: There's someone here! He was rarely silent. Ondra tried to immerse himself in what he was reading, but when Squirt was hanging around by the bathroom door making a racket, it was impossible.

The first time Squirt shouted: There's someone here!, Ondra imagined a pale man in a black coat standing in front of Squirt, stretching his arms out towards him, his sleeves slowly sliding upwards to reveal his hairy arms and horrid twisted claws . . . He rushed down the corridor to the bathroom, almost knocking Squirt over.

Now Squirt was yelling again: Someone's here! And Ondra got up wearily, closed the Nemura comic book, picked up a pack of cards, shuffled down the corridor, sat down next to Squirt, they leant back on the bathroom door and Ondra said: Stop it. She can't come out anyway. She's naked.

Naked Mum, said Squirt, chuckling.

Ondra was dealing the cards. They were playing Peanuckle.

When she came out, Ondra fumbled around for the tap in the clouds of steam and turned off the water.

No matter how many bottles he was able to find and empty, she always had another one hidden away somewhere. Sometimes she reached into a hiding place they hadn't yet discovered and Squirt would tug on Ondra's shirt and they'd both have to make a real effort not to burst out laughing. When she was drunk she didn't look at them, she looked through them. Sometimes they planted chairs in her way, that was a lark. She walked around them, bumped into them. The expression on her face was ridiculous.

Squirt was already in bed. Ondra followed her until she lugged herself to her bed. Normally once she'd got into bed, fully dressed, he let her be. This time he got an idea. Chortling, he ran into the bathroom, to the baskets with dirty linen and clothing. What're you up to? asked Squirt. He'd scurried over in his pyjamas. Wait here, you'll see. Ondra was choking with laughter. He grabbed whatever he got his hands on in the basket and darted back to Mum. Wait, he said, pushing Squirt away. Squirt was bursting with curiosity.

He dressed Mum in Dad's shirt, he pulled a sweater over her head. He couldn't get the trousers on her, but he draped Dad's dressing gown over her shoulders. It covered her legs. He put some pillows under her, she looked like she was sitting up. She didn't put up any resistance, just waved her arm about a few times. He remembered that Squirt looked completely different with lipstick on his mouth. He rifled through Mum's make-up and found an eyebrow pencil. He blackened Mum's cheeks. He switched on the table lamp in the corner of the room. In the shadow it looked like Mum had a beard. By now he was almost falling over with laughter. As a final touch, he put a woolly hat on her head.

Then he dashed back to Squirt who was fidgeting about in their room, put his finger over his lips and said in a deep voice: There's someone here! Squirt shrieked: Don't mess about! There's a stranger in the apartment, said Ondra in a deep voice again. Rubbish, rubbish! fumed Squirt . . . Come with me, if you don't believe me! And he was dragging him along, they walked down the hall, Squirt was reluctant, but he went along, overcome with curiosity... Ondra was doing his utmost not to break into a fit of laughter, he shoved Squirt into the room, right in front of Mum in her new guise, sitting there wearing a woolly hat . . . Squirt squinted in the light of the table lamp and then he took a step forward, then a second step, he cried: Dad! Then he jumped on the bed, grabbed the skiing hat, pulled it off and Mum's head fell to one side, she gave out a horrible snore . . . Then Squirt leapt on Ondra, hitting him with his fists wherever he could, and even after Ondra had dragged him away down the hall, kicking and screaming, he managed to punch Ondra in the teeth. Ondra didn't defend himself, he just held Squirt's arms, and only later in bed when Squirt kept jabbering and cursing, Ondra said: Shut your trap or I'll knock you off the bed, and Squirt stopped.

During the night Ondra was woken up by the sound of stamping feet. He knew it wasn't a dream, someone was actually in the apartment. He could tell Squirt wasn't asleep either. Let's check it out, said Ondra decisively, throwing the blanket off. Maybe Dad really had come home. Or maybe there were burglars on the rampage in the flat. Or Nazi assassins with syringes. Who is it? whispered Squirt. Friends, said Ondra. Oh yeah? Honest? said Squirt quietly and he also started crawling out of bed.

Mum was standing in the bathroom, staring into the mirror, then she came out, opened the door of the toilet, stepped up onto the toilet bowl, fumbled around in the water tank, pulled out a bottle. She pulled the stopper out with her teeth.

Blimey! said Ondra.

She keeps one there as well, said Squirt. She's so clever.

She lost her footing, she slipped, falling backwards onto the tiled floor, her head struck the toilet bowl, there was a thud. The bottle smashed into smithereens. She leant on the toilet bowl, stood up, walked out. The bathroom reeked of wine, the floor was strewn with jagged shards, as well as lots of tiny fragments of glass, she walked right over them. She left bloody footprints on the lino, on the carpet, there was blood dripping from her toes.

Ondra pulled a rag from the laundry basket, thrust it in Squirt's hand. He started wiping the floor. Squirt discarded the rag, went to check on Mum.

She was already lying in bed. They pulled a few small shards of glass out of her feet, just like that, with their fingers. Squirt wanted to stick plasters on her feet, Ondra said: Wait! and he went to the bathroom to get some hydrogen peroxide. Squirt didn't want to stay on his own with Mum, so they went together, found the little bottle with the peroxide and poured it on the soles of Mum's feet. The skin on her heels where they'd pulled out the glass started twitching, the peroxide bubbled into white foam, just like it did on their knees when they grazed them, or their fingers when they cut them. Do you think it's painful? asked Squirt. Probably not, said Ondra. They stuck plasters all over the soles of her feet and her toes.

Ondra had hardly opened his eyes when he saw Mum opening the window. And then she was standing next to them, clapping and calling: Ahoy there, boys! Up you get, it's a beautiful day! Hi, Muuum! cried Squirt, leaping out of bed. And what about you, chop chop. Mum shook Ondra by the shoulder. Don't be the slowcoach! Quick, breakfast's ready! I'm going to be first! shrieked Squirt, darting off to the kitchen. He dawdled after them. In the kitchen he leant on the door. The table had been laid, there was a table cloth, tea and cakes. Squirt was already sitting down on his chair, stuffing his face. No school! he yelled at Ondra.

Breakfast, a quick wash and off we go! How about the zoo?!

We've already been there, said Ondra. He was gawping at the little cake in front of him. There was a red cherry on top of it.

You were drunk again yesterday.

Please, Ondra, at least don't spoil this morning!

Squirt plucked the cherry from his cake and gobbled it up. He had cream all over his mouth. He tried to wipe it off with his pyjama sleeve, but only succeeded in smearing it more. Ondra kicked him under the table.

How many times have you promised not to do it any more!

But Ondra. Don't scowl all the time. And why are you whimpering?

He kicked me, Squirt said, telling on him. He was rubbing his eyelids together stubbornly to make himself cry.

No school today! Ondra exclaimed, stamping his feet.

Yippee, cried Squirt and burst out laughing through the few tears he'd managed to wrench from his eyes.

Mum was in the hallway. They heard her slamming the doors of the wardrobes.

Boys! Ondra! Where are your white shirts?

Ondra rolled his eyes. A piece of cake fell on his T-shirt. He scoffed the cherry, flicking the stone at Squirt.

Mum poked her head round into the kitchen. Just you wait, boys! I'll dress you up really nice. Dear me! How can you wear those socks? How come you sleep in your socks? Give them to me, I'll give them a quick wash. She disappeared into the hall again. They crammed cake into their mouths and guzzled tea. They put plenty of sugar in it. There were drifts of sugar on the table in front of Squirt.

Then she dashed back into the kitchen with T-shirts, trousers and various other items of clothing flapping from her arm.

Let's see, try this summer jacket. My goodness, you've made a right mess. Ondra! Off you go to the bathroom, right now, wash your hands and face. Let me see. Well, we'll just roll up the sleeves, that's it. We'll put a safety pin here! Can you turn your head?

Yes, Mummy.

And what am I going to wear? said Mum. That blue mac. It's the colour of clouds. It's summery. But which earrings should I wear?

The red ones, said Ondra, they're the best. Now they were jostling for position in the bathroom. He was looking in the mirror, he saw Mum standing next to him, so tall, so thin, her tummy was hardly visible, she was only wearing the black polo-neck and panties. In one hand she was holding a wig, the one with the long blonde hair, she was brushing it. Once she puts it on her head, her hair will reach all the way down her back. It'll look lovely, thought Ondra. He was pulling one T-shirt out of the basket after another, immediately stuffing them back in again, he wanted to stay in the bathroom for as long as possible. He was watching Mum in the mirror. Sometimes she didn't wear a bra, but right now she had one on.

You'd look really becoming in shirts, said Mum. White ones! I'll buy some soon. Stop getting in the way already, she gave Ondra a light smack on the shoulder and tickled him under his nose with her finger, she had a few drops of perfume on it. In the past all four of them used to mill around in the bathroom, every morning, and when Dad was shaving he always smeared some shaving cream under Squirt's nose with the brush. Squirt squealed with joy and one time he snatched the brush from Dad's hand and smeared his whole face with it. Then they grabbed him and pushed him under the shower.

He pulled on his shorts and T-shirt and went to join Squirt. He was standing in front of the mirror, regarding his new jacket.

Look, Mum fixed that with a plaster. Can you see it when I roll it up?

It's far too big for you, you twat, said Ondra.

You're stupid. All you've got is a T-shirt, you twat.

Don't call me a twat.

Twat, twat, twat!

He launched himself at Squirt, they were rolling around on the floor, Ondra was tickling Squirt and he was wriggling and giggling, squealing... Boys! Stop it! Ondra sat up on the floor, gasping for air, Squirt managed to slip from his grip and now his tickling fingers were on the offensive. Come on now, boys, she laughed, sinking down on the bed, Squirt jumped on her knees and now he was trying to tickle her, she grabbed his arms and Squirt writhed so ridiculously that Ondra couldn't take any more and burst into a fit of laughter, he was lying on his back and now he was squealing, kicking his legs around, crying: Stop it, you're killing me ... and when Squirt attacked him again and Mum joined in, he laughed so hard he almost peed himself, it was just too much ...

Outside the sun was shining, they were walking to the tram stop, Squirt was acting all important in that jacket of his, Ondra didn't know why but he was feeling a little fed up again, probably because Mum kept saying: What a beautiful day ... And it was, the sun was shining and it wasn't yet scorching hot, they could hear music playing in the distance but surprisingly the street was deserted, they were the only ones there, and Ondra was glad, one time when they were walking like this they met his teacher and Mum had immediately started telling her that they were just on their way to the doctor's. I'm sure you are, the teacher had said.

There were red and tricoloured flags flying everywhere, the tram didn't stop, flags were fluttering on the tram and the people inside were sticking tiny little flags out of the windows, someone threw a bundle of flyers out of the tram, they scattered in all directions, Ondra reached for one, bending down, but before he could pick it up Mum tossed a cigarette butt on it, smeared it with the heel of her shoe and said: Trash.

The platform was filling up with people, one of their neighbours was standing next to Mum. She said: Hello, Comrade Lipková. Off to the parade, off to the parade are we? And which election district are you in?

They jumped on the next tram, it had just stopped, it too was full, they forced their way to the window . . . Crikey! exclaimed Squirt. And they stared. There were aeroplanes flying across the sky . . . and then another swarm, and another, metal glistened in the sky.

The tram screeched to a halt. There were children walking down the street. It was the head of the parade. There were processions marching along the winding streets all through the centre of town. Until finally they'd merge into a solid mass on Letná Plain. That's how it always was.

The children surrounded the tram, they were stretching up on tiptoe, waving their parade sticks, cheering. Some of them were already losing their voices. Whenever the jubilation abated up at the front, it resurged in the back rows. There were joymongers and cheerleaders everywhere, experienced comrades.

Many of the floats were bigger than the tram. There were stages for children on some of them. Boys in blue shorts and white shirts danced around girls, performing Russian folk dances. Girls in red leotards waved little flags, skipped around, singing:

> *The First of May is here today*
> *Merrily we'll dance the day away*
> *Jump for joy and leap for life*
> *Spread freedom with your song*
> *Welcome May, sing on and on and on!*

Happy May Daaay! Happy May Daaay! Happy May Daaay! they were all shouting. Ondra pressed his eyes up against the window pane. The float was passing close by the tram. Some of the girls were waving bobble-topped parade sticks, others were holding brightly coloured ribbons in their hands. Happy May Day! shouted Squirt, sniggering. The man on the seat in front of Ondra suddenly bent over, buckling at the waist . . . he was making quick stroking movements with his hand under the bag on his lap, panting . . . Aaaargh, the man groaned. Then he straightened up. He exhaled.

Happy May Daaay! shrieked Squirt again. Don't scream in my ear, snapped Ondra. Sorry, said Squirt, shrugging his shoulders, even though he couldn't care less . . . he couldn't give a toss that Ondra had almost gone deaf.

Now there were soldiers marching towards them. Automatic rifles across their chests, helmets on their heads, they were pounding the pavement.

Squirt squashed his face against the window so that he wouldn't miss anything.

Well, said someone in the tram. It's going to take a while.

And it did. The soldiers were marching at the front, behind them a military band and then a procession of blue uniforms.

There's quite a few of them, eh? said Mum. Someone sniggered and said: That's the People's Militia, the vanguard of humanity, madam.

Ha ha, said someone behind them. The aeroplanes were no longer in sight. The sound with which they'd torn the sky asunder hung in the air. The sky was covered with white lines.

You're not taking part in the parade, are you now, sir? said Mum.

Tee hee, mademoiselle, I couldn't give a flying . . . you know what I mean? said the person next to her.

I know what you mean. I hadn't even realised what day it was today.

A day like any other, madam. I'm in favour of sovereignty, you know? But up to a point! So we don't get steamrolled!

Ha ha, steamrolled. The people in the tram were laughing. Pressing up against each other. It was sweltering in there. The driver was turning round and laughing. Why, that army of ours is a circus act with tin soldiers! he shouted.

Oh, well, said Mum aloud. They've passed. Start her up, then!

Ha, ha, ha! People laughed. Someone clapped. Ondra was also laughing. Squirt was pulling a face like a goblin. His hands in the pockets of his jacket. The citizens became merry. Here and there someone gesticulated at the marching army. Get going already! Turn around and head for Munich! they called.

Tee, hee, hee! laughed the driver.

They were off again.

When they reached the gate, Squirt exclaimed: But it's closed!

Dear, oh dear, what a palaver, said Mum.

Oh bugger! Should have gone to the cinema.

Such a beautiful day, not a cloud in sight, I was so looking forward to it, and the rotten pigs close the place!

Look! Sea lion! exclaimed Ondra. And then he was walking along the railing, looking down, far below he could see a little pond, or something, and there . . . he broke into a run, Squirt started running after him.

They almost squeezed their heads through the iron bars, they could see the little pond, a concrete pool, they spotted a shadow darting through the pool's black water, a head emerged from the water, a huge head with whiskers and black eyes, they looked like holes in that head, they heard the animal's growl, a hoarse bark coming from the black water, even on this hot day there were chunks of ice floating in the pool, the dark water glistened, the aquatic beast was swimming beneath the surface, its body was making the icy soup swell, it glided through the concrete pool with the speed of a bullet like a seamless, smooth, contracting muscle, then it dived.

What have you got there, boys?

They were both hanging on to the railing.

Mum! That's really something! Squirt was shouting excitedly. An awesome beast!

Still under the water, said Ondra. He lowered himself down from the railing.

They walked around the gate of the zoo. They walked along the railing as far as possible. They saw fowl. Several kinds of hen. The hens lived in various coops. Some had colourful feathers. Mum pointed them out to the boys. Ondra raised his face up to the sky, yawned. Squirt wanted to go back to the aquatic beast. But it was too far by then.

Further on, boys, is the enclosure of the kudu antelope. They're really sweet. We might see one.

Kudu antelope! Ondra closed his yawning lips, pursing them into a thin line.

Mum, let's go back, let's go look at the aquatic beast.

And if we keep going even further, we might see the aviaries. That's where the parrots are, they're nice, eh?

Parrots. For Christ's sake!

Ondra, don't use the Lord's name in vain.

Christ, Christ, Christ!

The sun was now directly above them. They were dragging themselves along the fence around the zoological gardens in the scorching heat. They were walking along a sandy track. The rubbish bins stank. Wasps swarmed around empty beer and soft drink paper cups.

Mum, I'm thirsty, announced Squirt.

Hold on for a bit, there should be an Art Noveau pavilion around here somewhere.

Mum, I've got a stone in my shoe, said Squirt after a while.

You know what, boys? Let's play a sort of game, all right? Whoever finds a beer garden or pavilion with refreshments first wins, okay?

Oh hell, said Ondra.

Mum shook his shoulder.

Ondra! We're having a day out. I'm trying awfully hard, so make an effort as well. Look after your younger brother. If you had any idea, my head feels like a nail's being hammered into it.

I win, shrieked Squirt. I'm the winner! I can see it!

I want some more green fizz! shouted Squirt. He had ice cream on his jacket, his face was also smeared with ice cream. Mum got out a hand-kerchief, moistened it with saliva and wiped the corners of his mouth.

Would you like anything else, Ondra?

A Kofola cola.

Waiter, said Mum, two more Kofolas and one Amara soda. Or you know what . . . make that one Kofola, one Amara, and a vodka and small beer for me.

Mum, you're going to get plastered again!

Ondra! Leave the table immediately. If you're not having fun here, go play somewhere else, yes?

He walked around the restaurant. At the back he saw grilling grates and large black cooking pots. He peeked into the kitchen. There were cauldrons in there as well. He heard Mum calling to the waiter. She was ordering more drinks. He dawdled along the sandy track. Squirt set off after him. He sat down on a bench.

Hey! yelped Ondra. Did you see that? Did you see them?

What?

The lizards!

What lizards?

They had tiny human heads, honest! They escaped from the zoo!

You're talking rubbish! Squirt was looking around.

Am not.

Are too!

And they asked about you.

Hmm. Do you know what they said on the radio?

What?

That you're stupid.

He approached Squirt from the back. Treading lightly. He raised his arms.

Why don't you like Mum?

What?

You're being horrible to her.

He let his arms fall. He took a run-up and jumped over the bench.

Bet you can't do that!

No, said Squirt. My stomach's full of fizzy drink. Look, he said. He was holding Mum's lipstick. This one's rose-coloured, but Mum's got different ones.

I'm reporting that! That you nick Mum's stuff!

No I don't, she gave it me, actually!

Let's go and ask her, then.

Feel free! said Squirt. I'd like another frankfurter.

Well, I wouldn't.

They ran.

*

They got to the restaurant just in time. They were already closing. There was no one there anyway, except for Mum. Mum was sitting at the table with the waiter. They were talking quietly. The waiter asked them if they got on well with their sister. Then he explained to them that when they have a lot of customers, the rubbish bins fill up.

And then the animals come to eat the stuff, said Squirt.

Exactly so, added the waiter. The sunshades around their table had already been folded. It wasn't baking hot any more. They heard a screech on the other side of the fence.

Could be a night bird that woke up just now, said Mum.

The waiter said it was quite possible. Mum wanted the waiter to call a taxi and have another vodka. When the cab finally arrived, the waiter insisted on paying for the drinks.

Do come again. Bring the boys.

Oh certainly, laughed Mum. It's pleasant here.

This driver didn't talk to Mum. They ruin everything, Mum was saying to him, when we go on an outing to the zoo with the boys once in a blue moon, they have the stupid May Day Parade.

Hmm, said the taxi driver.

They wouldn't have had to go to school anyway, so what kind of a day out is that, then, eh? Mum was prodding the driver in the shoulder with her finger, but he pushed her hand away.

Even the cinemas are closed, Mum was fretting. And the People's Militia everywhere!

Look missus, said the driver. Have you got money for the fare?

Sure I do, you pleb. You one of them, are you?

I'm only taking you out of consideration for the kids, missus.

You'd better step on it, then, matey, Mum started giggling.

As they were getting out and giggly Mum was pulling Squirt out of the car, Ondra leaned over to the taxi driver and said in a deep voice, I'm for sovereignty. But we don't want to get steamrolled!

Out of my way, boy.

The car drove off, they were standing in front of their block of flats. It was the same as always. Mum was dragging Squirt with one hand, he was putting up a fight, and Ondra was dragging Mum by her other hand. In front of the door to the flat he kept demanding the keys until she finally gave them to him, or he may have simply dug them out of her handbag, or pocket. He was glad they lived on the ground floor. At least they got off the street and into the flat quickly.

Mum kicked off her shoes, went into the kitchen without even turning the lights on. She went straight to the cooker. After that she slammed the door of the little room shut behind her.

They were standing in the hall.

I'll show you something, but it's a secret, okay?

Yeah, said Ondra.

It's a laugh, but it's a secret, okay?

Sure.

They went into Mum's room and Squirt said: Close your eyes.

Yeah. Ondra nodded.

He was looking anyway. There was enough light. The streetlamps were on outside. There was one right in front of the building. Squirt threw off his jacket, T-shirt and shorts. He took off all his clothes. He pulled a dress out of the linen cupboard. He gathered it up in his hands. He pulled it over his head. He put Mum's wig on his head. He had it hidden there somewhere.

What are you doing, said Ondra.

The secret is that I'm a girl.

You're not.

Maybe it's good being a girl!

Squirt stepped out of the room, he was taking tiny steps, befitting of the dress. He looked like a little girl. Like a little girl at school, walking down the hall. Ondra followed him.

Squirt stopped by the bathroom. They heard the shower.

Mummmy. Squirt scratched on the door. Your little girrrl is heeere! Ondra almost spluttered. Squirt was winking at him. Making faces, grimaces. Squeaking like a little girl.

I don't like this game, said Ondra.

Oh all right, then, said Squirt in a normal voice. Let's get the bottle out of the toilet tank. Maybe there's another one there. What do you reckon?

All right then.

They opened the door of the toilet, Ondra bent down, lowered his head, Squirt climbed up onto his neck and grabbed hold of him. Ondra stood up straight, keeping his hand on the wall, and Squirt poked around in there. He shouted: Got it! He was holding the bottle in his hand. He pushed away from the wall so hard it made them both sway from side to side.

Take me to the kitchen, yeah?

He trotted down the hallway, Squirt was holding on to him, chortling, the long hair on Mum's wig was tickling Ondra's neck. In the kitchen he opened the bottle and poured the wine down the sink. Whenever they did this, he and Squirt always talked and nudged each other. The drain was making a gargling sound. They smelled the sour stench of wine.

This white wine has a stronger smell, said Ondra. Sometimes she drinks red.

Squirt was holding on to his shoulders.

But you're getting off after this! Ondra said to reassure himself. He turned on the tap, sending a stream of cold water down the drain.

Get off!

Squirt pulled his hair.

Look, if I was a little girl I'd just scratch and bite you, easy. I'll shriek, said Squirt. And he shrieked.

Ondra turned around in a circle a few times, but Squirt was holding on tight. He could have smashed him against the wall, but he didn't want to do that. Then he had to grab hold of the sink with both arms because Squirt was yanking his hair. He shrieked again.

Why are you behaving like a stupid sod? Why do you keep behaving like an idiot? I'm going to switch the light on. Squirt scratched him. He fell on the floor with a thud. Ondra turned the lights on, he had to squint for a while to get used to the light.

Squirt was sitting on the floor. The wig had fallen off. You twat, he said to Ondra in his normal voice. You ruined everything. You threw me off.

Squirt got up. Without the wig he was a boy in a girl's dress. He could go to a carnival dressed like that, though, said Ondra to himself. Then it wouldn't matter. Squirt shambled towards Mum's room. Dragging the wig behind him. Trailing it over the floor. He was shuffling down the hallway. Then he cried out. Mum also cried out.

Ondra peered into the hall. He switched the lights on.

He saw the two of them rolling around on the floor, it occurred to him they might be messing about, tickling each other. Then Squirt stood up, scampered off down the hallway, Mum staggered after him, barefoot, her feet smacking on the lino. Squirt grabbed the door handle, darted out, then Mum ran out, the door slammed shut.

He ran out of the kitchen, the door slammed shut behind him too, and then he was out on the street, so he saw the whole thing.

The car was no longer moving. Mum was sitting on the pavement. He looked for Squirt, found him, sat down next to Mum. They only sat there like that for a moment. Other cars arrived, he watched the blue flashes of their beacons flickering over the surrounding buildings. There were lots of people there, even people from their building, someone threw a coat over Mum's shoulders. The front door kept banging, someone, their neighbour probably, said: How could it have happened? Oh come on, it's always like that with them, said someone else.

I sat down on the pavement, had a little rest. That's what surprised people most. And what would you do, sir, you with your fake doctorate, from Bucharest most likely, if someone ran your child over before your very eyes? You'd become aware that you had another child and you'd sit down for a moment. Drunk, they said. Your honour! Allow me to laugh. I had my first bout of delirium tremens out in the fields. That was the time when my little girl floated away, I really do have bad luck, that's for sure. Then I went somewhere, I was out in the countryside. Now imagine this, Your Munificence. Suddenly, in a single second, every church spire in this adorable vale, they are but a stone's toss from one another, broke off and headed straight for my heart. And then imagine, Professor of All the Human Sciences, that all the sickles on all the little monuments and posters scattered over our glorious countryside by the wise and firm hand of the Party went flying into my little heart, and all the hammers pounded my head, I had an awful racket in my head as a result, I felt like I was standing next to a cascade of crockery, smashing on the ground.

An enchanting place, these Czech lands of mine, really, and I swear: they combine Catholicism and Communism in the most degenerate way possible. And I'd like you to write an essay about this bipolarity for me, to be handed in before the next lecture, five pages will suffice, Comrade

Political Commissar, and that's an order. But the main thing you should keep in mind: What do these two dogmas that rule the world say to a human being toiling away under a low, murky sky? They say: Guilty! Guilty of existing. Always, and under all circumstances. Choose your own punishment. Do it! Mine is alcohol. I must admit I feel somewhat confined. I'd be quite interested to know how long I've been here. So he managed it then, Mr World Shaker! Got rid of me, now he'll get his hands on that business of his, grab the boys, or what's left of them, I might add, in order to dispel heavy gloom with a bit of light cynicism, and he'll scarper. Half the nation is pushing its way to the borders. And I'm lying here all comfy like this, resting, lucky me! They probably strapped me in so I wouldn't squash my belly, or rather wouldn't hurt whoever's in there, no wonder, I'm not important, but a little soldier or a prostitute might fall out of me, they'd come in handy to them.

Well, all right then, I messed up. Forget the cops, I know I'll have to stand in front of a different court of law, the one that's been in session from the first second, from the moment the first living cell came into being, since the Earth's first morning. Bottle after bottle, you drank your brain away. But it's not too late yet. Five minutes to twelve isn't twelve, esteemed Jury. I'll get out of here. This isn't a Soviet psychiatric asylum, this is a bone fide Central European establishment for gravid, homicidal alcoholic women, damn it. I'll crawl after them on all fours, if need be. After my kiddies. Instinctively, like a she-wolf.

Investigating officer! An alcoholic, an insomniac just wants some peace and quiet after a busy day, they call it the oceanic feeling. Not many people know that. And we all know that every day is very busy indeed, especially in this landlocked country, don't we, Mr Bubble and Mr Squeak, dear Hum and dear Drum, dear neighbours.

I want a different life, Mr Science Maestro used to say to me. We have children together, so what are you going on about? He moved out, Mr World Changing Inventor. I gave birth to his children and just as the big four-zero creeps up on me like an octopus, he ups and leaves to devote himself fully to his work. Well that's fucking hunky dory. Is that what you do to someone? That's exactly what you do to someone. Waiter, one more over here. Make it snappy!

When that son of mine sat down next to me on the pavement, he said: Mummy. He was shaking all over, but he was radiating such strength, it warmed me.

He'll pack them off to the scummy countryside again. He wants to emigrate, most likely, seeing as that racket with the comrades didn't come off. I'll sell it to the army, he says. Where do you think you are? If the army wants something, it takes it.

Oh well. And to top it all there are aeroplanes flying over Prague. Probably not bombers, I should be so lucky. More likely they're full of goggle-eyed boneheads from Siberia, so nervous with fear they keep tripping over their Kalashnikovs. If we had what it takes they'd be stumbling over their own guts soon enough. The Czechs. All those tricoloured flags everywhere. National pride. Jesus Christ! If I was at least a tiny bit sane and not tied to this bed, obviously, I'd crawl under it to hide in shame. Or fear, more likely. How can anyone leave a defenceless woman to face an attack by an army with missiles? Hello! Cretins, anybody there?

Nah, they're not bombers. There'd be the noise of explosions by now. If an atomic bomb exploded over Prague right now my heart would burst with joy. When I was a little girl I saw Dresden on fire. From the window of our flat in Prague. I saw the light of a blaze burning in the sky. I'll never forget that. And now I'm going to pray for a teeny-weeny miracle. That when I wake up these straps will be undone and the door open. Maybe it'll happen.

3

Ondra woke up, it was morning, his first morning in the village, he kicked off the quilt and got quite a surprise. He was alone. The window was open, he could hear people talking, he inhaled the morning air, jumped off the bed onto the floor, stuck his head out of the window and saw Polka's beaming face, staring right at him. Polka was standing there, leaning on his bike.

Lo and behold, the second youth is now also up. Come join us. We were just talking about death. I'm telling the reverend here that I firmly hope that death really is the end. What do you think?

Um, said Ondra.

Squirt took a potato out of a large pot, started peeling it with a knife, lifted his head up, laughed and called to Ondra: Come out!

Mr Frantla was sitting next to Squirt. He was holding a walking stick in his hand. His hair was grey. His face was full of wrinkles. His eyes looked like two wrinkles. They were closed.

Thing is, I would consider it most terrible, boys, Polka was expounding, if my consciousness floated on through the universe like a naked muscle, continuing to perceive, you understand? Now that really would be hell!

Squirt chuckled.

Come out and do some work. Behave like a proper Czech boy. The news from Prague is as follows: We've probably been invaded by the Russians. Kamil, give Ondra a knife. We need to arm ourselves and stock up on supplies, said Polka. What does our man of the cloth have to say? Oi!

Mr Frantla budged up, making room for Ondra on the bench.

He's already old, going doddery, said Polka. Been lingering around here on account of being friends with Granddad. Got kicked out of the vicarage, you know. He's handy with a watering can, keeps the graves tidy, can't deny him that. He's neither a habitual drinker nor a retard. The old women help him out. At least you'll have spiritual guidance, boys, ha ha, said Polka.

Is he not the vicar any more? asked Ondra.

He is, and he isn't, son, said Polka. These are strange times.

It occurred to him that what was happening made no sense. How could he sit here and peel potatoes when Granddad was dead? After everything that had happened? The sun slid out of the clouds. He picked up a potato, stared at it. Light was falling all around the potato. Its brown skin was cracked. He was holding the potato with two fingers, they were sticky with soil. I have to rinse it, he thought, before I peel it.

Rinse it first, said Squirt. Like this, see?

He saw. He's sitting in Granddad's yard with Squirt. Mr Frantla is also here, he used to go and visit Granddad sometimes. There's also that new bloke here. So they'll stay here for now.

I know, he said to Squirt.

I see you're making yourselves at home. Have look in the back if you need sweaters. Sweaters in August. That's funny. Prepare the menu, I'm off.

Polka led the bike by the handlebars to the gate, got on, arched his back, pushed down on the pedals and was soon receding into the distance along the stream.

He's odd, said Squirt in a whisper and pointed his chin in Mr Frantla's direction.

Hm, grumbled Ondra, looking for a smaller potato.

Why didn't he die instead of Granddad? said Squirt, flinging a peeled potato into the pot. He's also old.

You don't die the moment you get old, said Ondra.

And how can you tell that you're going to die?

When you stop breathing.

Aha. Squirt took a single breath, filling his cheeks with air. He held his breath, his face went red, his cheeks burst open, he was gasping for air. Huh, I was dying!

How about dying under water, said Ondra. That must be lousy. Or maybe not breathing is not enough. In *The Count of Monte Cristo*, they burn the feet of the prisoners in the Château d'If with iron rods. Before throwing them in the water.

Yeah? Why? asked Squirt, intrigued.

If they weren't completely dead, they'd scream.

Ah, said Squirt. Hey, Ondra, Squirt whispered in his ear.

What is it?

I'll tell you something, but promise you won't get mad. Promise.

I'll see.

Not telling you anything, squeaked Squirt, hurling a potato into the pot. It splashed Ondra in the eye.

I promise, said Ondra.

Come here, then, said Squirt.

Ondra leant down to him and Squirt said: You had a stiffy this morning.

What?

In the morning, you had a stiff willy. No one saw it, only me.

Stupid potatoes, exclaimed Ondra.

Hey, and when am I going to get one?

You're an idiot.

You promised you wouldn't be mad, and you're mad!

I don't want any potatoes, said Ondra.

It wasn't bad being with the lady doctors, said Squirt. I ate everything they gave me there.

Go be with the lady doctors, then.

What?

Go, just go!

But I'm not supposed to walk!

But you walked.

That was at the funeral, I had to.

Ondra kicked the pot with the potatoes.

I peeled those, shrieked Squirt. He turned completely pale.

Quit whimpering, or . . . said Ondra. The little gate creaked, there were old women walking towards them through the courtyard, the neighbour was with them too, Mr Berka, wearing a peaked cap, Mrs Škvorová was walking next to him. There were other people standing by the gate.

Good morning, boys, they greeted them. Good morning, Reverend.

Mornin', said Squirt like a Praguer, and then he said: Good morning. He nudged Ondra with his elbow. They were watching the people. If Mum and Dad had been there they wouldn't have walked into the yard. They would have waited by the gate.

One of the old women, Ferdinandka, pushed a basket towards the boys. Squirt took off the tea towel. Eggs, bread. A glass jar of something.

What is it? Squirt lifted it up.

That's honey. From woodland bees, said Ferdinandka. She stroked Squirt's head.

Yippee, thank you, said Squirt.

The other old women were helping Mr Frantla get up. They were holding him by the shoulders.

Squirt tugged on Ondra's shirt. We going with them?

Ondra shook his head. The old women smelled of . . . yesterday afternoon. He could smell the dug-up soil and the chill coming from the church. He was cold. He didn't want to go anywhere with them.

He jumped up.

What's got into you? asked Squirt.

But he was already on the other side of the gate, walking along the stream, driving the cold out with every step, he was thinking about the little boat. About whether it would be there. Where he'd hidden it. He'd just take a peek! He was already round the bend in the stream, if he turned round he wouldn't be able to see the people any more. But he could still hear Squirt: Ondra! Don't leave me here! Don't leave me! So he broke into a run.

She was leaning on the broom, they couldn't see her in the corner behind the beer tap, she could be alone there for a while, for a moment, so she was resting . . . the sweetness that she felt deep inside shot upwards, forcing its way up from her belly all the way to her throat, blood was rushing to her head through every capillary, it was now full of sweet and thick blood, she must smell sweetly on the inside, and then came what she hated, the acrid waft of fear, the stinging feeling in her bowels, she was terrified she might throw up, not here, not now . . . she heard stomping, he never came down like a normal person, always flying down the stairs, hurtling down, tearing around the pub, tearing around the village, he probably can't bear walking for long, so he has to zoom around on his bike.

I'm such a stupid cow, she said to herself, leaning on the broom, Dad's going to kill me and Mum's going to watch.

Come on, now, my girl, chin up, it's only morning! He stood in front of her, flicked her chin with his finger and gave her a pretend kiss on the hair, like it was all a laugh, a real lark! After all, it's all right for a kind uncle to do that sort of thing . . . she swept around him with the broom . . . everyone was watching, so she laughed, and flicked the broom around him again, Dad was laughing, they were all laughing with him, even Mum, when he speaks, everyone listens.

Polka pointed upwards, he said: They're getting up! He ran past the constable who'd just finished his beer, he put his beer mug on the counter, Zuza grabbed it and tossed it in the dishwater, Polka opened the door, he was out in one stride and then he was back again, saying: Frída, Cougher, my dear comrade, there's no one there. I told you so!

There's plenty of time yet, said the constable. They'll turn up. I went round to all of them.

Certainly hope so, said Polka, pulling a little paper package out of his breast pocket, he opened it, scoffed the pill inside, leant on the counter and said: So what are they saying on the radio?

Not a lot, said Zuza's dad. The shit's hit the fan in Prague. The roads are jammed. Apparently there're even tanks in Osikov now. Otherwise nothing.

Men, you know I'm a Communist, said the constable. But I've never denounced anyone. I haven't done anything to anyone, either.

You explain that to the Yanks when they come storming in.

Hm, said Zuza's dad. You'd better not walk around here in your uniform, Coughy Boy.

If it had just been the Ruskies invading us, said Polka. But it's also the Hungarians, Poles, East Germans. The whole Warsaw Pact. Bloody hell.

Bulgarians too, apparently, said Zuza's dad. He nodded at Zuza. Finish sweeping, pour some more beers and you can call it a day.

You can come to an agreement with the Ruskies, said Zuza's dad. We suffered together under the Germans. There aren't so many of the white ones like us, though. They are driving all that rabble ahead of them, all those barbarians, those Tartars, Kyrgyzstanis, Mongols, that lot.

That's bad, then, said Polka. But I'm most upset about those Bulgarians. A maritime nation. I'd never have said they'd attack us.

Men, you're taking the piss out of me, said the constable.

We're just talking, that's all, said Polka. We're glad to be alive, aren't we, Karel?

Yep, said Zuza's dad. Every day.

Well, get this, said Polka, they were at it again all night last night.

Leave it out! exclaimed Zuza's mum. At least not in front of the lassie!

Zuza hid her head between the beer mugs, she had to, she was shaking with laughter. Everyone listened in disbelief as Polka told them about it. The constable said: It's the end of the world.

I swear, Polka shouted, I can bear witness. That's liberalisation for you. Dubčekism. Dubček is a Slovak, after all, you can't deny that! he said to Frída. He's introducing the ways of Slovak sheep, that's all! The men laughed. But it niggled away at the back of their minds.

The secret cops were coming down the stairs now, the old one and the young one. Just as Polka was recounting how upstairs they had been at it so hard, the whole house shook and he didn't get a wink of sleep. Zuza said to herself: That's twaddle. That young one keeps eyeing me up.

The secret policemen walked into the establishment, made themselves comfortable at the table, Zuza was all red in the face, choking with laughter, hiding behind the beer tap, right away Mum was carrying eggs from the kitchen, done the way they'd ordered, the constable stood up and greeted them, the old cop answered with a nod, the constable sat back down on his haunches, he was sitting alone at the middle table, a folder in front of him, papers inside, a sharpened pencil in his hand.

How did you sleep, comrades? shouted Polka so loudly that everyone jerked to attention.

Satisfactorily, comrade, said the major, cracking the shell of an egg with his spoon. The young cop twitched, or maybe Zuza was only imagining it.

Yeah, but everyone's gawping at me right now, she said to herself, she was pouring out half-litres of beer, the beer from the tap was foaming. Or maybe I'm just seeing things. And that funeral yesterday. He's so small. I fooled around with him all summer, just a bit of fun, I thought. Then when he left I walked around like I was intoxicated. I can't stay here. He came for the funeral, poor thing. Why couldn't he be older? He could have taken me away from here. I'm a big girl already. My boobs are getting bigger. Dad is going to kill me. I'm running out of time.

She pushed a beer towards Dad, took two more over to the cops. She leant over the young one, just a little, she knew Dad was watching. She could smell the copper sweating in his jacket. So it probably is true, she said to herself. That thing about them. That's barmy. Mum's watching me. She must be able to tell. How come she can't tell? She went back, everyone was looking. I'll wash up the beer mugs now, I won't think about it. A wave of pain ran through her. Through her tummy all the way to her spine. She almost cried out. Almost dropped the mugs.

So it seems we've been invaded, said Polka. By the Ruskies. They announced it on the radio. Comrades! Begging your pardon, but what's going to happen now, like?

Nothing's known for sure, yet, said the older cop. I wouldn't discuss it for now.

May I? said Polka, walking up to the cops' table. He took hold of the younger cop's lapel softly with two fingers, kneaded it, saying: Polyester. Beautiful. From the Soviet Union, is it?

I studied there, said the young cop.

Aha, said Polka without moving from the spot. It's lovely there. I travelled all over the Soviet Union with the circus, I worked as a llama handler, snow white animals they are. We journeyed over the mountain massifs all the way to the enchanting steppes. I know that entire country. In the Soviet Union, magic is only allowed in the circuses. So the comrades issued me with a certificate. Llamas are angelic creatures, don't think they're not, their muzzles are as hard as the hooves on which they climb down the mountains. They kick and they spit, but in the land of the Soviets those animals have become veritably angelic. During my circus act, the working masses could take a breather. My angelic llamas and I were invited to as far away a place as the Red Mountain, fancy that.

The young cop stood up.

Believe it or not . . . Polka was recounting . . . many comrades . . . and now he was sort of circling around the young cop a little. He'd let go of his jacket some time ago. But the light in the pub wasn't very bright. There were only candles and petrol lamps. To some it may have seemed that he wasn't moving at all. The cop was turning his head round at him.

Many comrades, repeated Polka, came to my tent behaving like they were intoxicated. They wanted to ride my llamas. And the caravans were beautiful. The steppe opening up before us. Life is boundless over there. I gave the comrades from the Red Mountain a baby llama. It was no bigger than a beaver. The comrades fed it from the bottle. Hopefully they're still looking after it, even now.

Comrade! shrieked the young cop. Your citizen identification card!

That won't be necessary, said the old one. Comrade Frída! He turned round to the constable. What's the situation? What about the citizens?

They'll be here, don't worry.

The young one sat down. He started tapping his egg with a spoon. He cracked the shell, finally.

We're not worried, the old one sniggered.

I know, I just meant . . . it was just a manner of speech, prattled the constable. Come on in, he said with relief, addressing Juza, who'd ambled into the pub. Juza was shuffling along, turned sideways to everyone, as always. He was holding an axe. Get your arse to the woodshed, Frída whispered to him. Juza nodded. He walked through the kitchen and out into the yard. Soon they heard the blows of an axe. An iron rod. He was in the woodshed, smashing the contraptions. The ones that people had already handed in. Frída could see the yard through the window. Then he glanced at the cops' table. The older comrade gestured with his hand in acknowledgement. Frída thought he'd seen a faint smile. But it was gloomy in there. The door opened again. They'd arrived. The first ones. The constable's heart rose on an arc of relief. So they're here after all! he exulted. He knew them well, he did. He'd gone round to see them all. Some he cajoled, some he threatened. They went straight to him. They were dragging their contraptions behind them.

He straightened the papers on the table. He signed the first receipt. They tossed folders with tables and graphs on the table. Then they moved over to the bar. To join the old men who didn't want to miss all the fun with the contraptions. They were raising their arms and forefingers, calling to Zuza. To her mum. Zuza couldn't pour the beer fast enough.

He was signing the receipts exceptionally neatly. He pushed them across the table. Often he didn't even have to look to know who was there. He recognised them by their coughing, by the way they walked, by the hats they kneaded in their hands.

I'm going to feed that piece of paper of yours to the rabbits, Cougher.

Feed it to your better half, said Frída.

My missus doesn't eat paper. She eats meat, like a woman should, said Prošek.

But my woman eats bricks, like a kiln she fires the building blocks of Communism, said Frída. He stretched his legs. He liked this sort of banter.

You don't have a wife, you twat, said Prošek.

But I have the Party, said Frída.

Fuck your Party, said Prošek. In the throat, he added after a while. Ha ha! He'd run out of things to say.

All right then, said Frída. He tossed the paper at him. They'd gone to school together.

And more people were arriving. The door was constantly open. Now and then he joked around some more. So long as people weren't crowding around the table. Graphs here and tables there, he told everyone. Keep it moving.

The cops were finishing their meal. The old one ordered another beer. He wanted another helping of eggs.

I'm not going to muck around here under the flypaper for much longer, Mum, said Zuza to herself. Not for long. I'll take what the Old Hag gave me. Or maybe I won't. She dipped the beer mugs into the cold water. I can't take it. Renata did and she vanished. It made her unwell.

She was pouring more beers for men who were trickling in with contraptions, or for no particular reason, just to have a look at what was going on today, she poured Kofola cola for the boys, soon she would take off her apron and leave. Dad will let her today. He promised. She'll go and join the girls. This was their day.

Some arrived in little groups, others came alone. The old women had boys carry the cabinets with the contraptions, some of them hauled them on carts. They stacked them in the yard. They peeked into the woodshed where Juza was swinging his rod, intent on playing pranks on him. They peeked in, yelled: Boo! The boldest bunged a stone at him, or a cowpat. Juza paid no attention. He chopped the cabinets up with the axe, laying the mechanisms bare, then he levelled them with the rod. Until they were as flat as the floor of the shed. He kicked the splintered wood and bits of metal into the corners. Springs, wires, cogwheels and glass spilled from the wreckage. The boys were keen to swipe a few of those little things, but Juza didn't let them. So they loitered in the yard.

The pile of graphs and tables on the constable's table was growing all the time. He was looking round at the bosses from Prague. No one sat down with them. They ordered more eggs. This time with bacon fat. And an extra portion of bacon fat. They were stuffing their faces. Swilling beer. As though they'd been unloading wagons all night, thought the constable. Huh, he grimaced. Could it be true? That thing about them? Who knows, nowadays . . . back in the old days they would definitely have been shot. Back in the old days. With relish. And without pardons. It's none of my business. Let the comrades shag corpses, if it's to their liking. I couldn't care less. I set everything up, neatly. The contraptions are here. Except for those possessed by this here Karel, and by Líman and a few others. They say they won't give theirs to the Ruskies. Hell only knows why the high and mighty gentlemen from the interior ministry are collecting this stuff. For the government, apparently. There's always a government. Bugger that.

The pile of contraptions in the yard was mounting. The boys were climbing over it. They wanted to storm the summit. Now and then Juza would come rushing out of the woodshed, swinging his rod. They scattered, shrieking and giggling. They waited for him to withdraw. Once they could hear banging at regular intervals, they ventured out again.

By now there was a little throng by the beer tap. The men were leaning on the counter. Thanks to Polka everyone got a snifter upon arrival. The door closed, opened, the draught let in gusts of wind and bursts of daylight, making the little flames flicker. Everyone noticed that the old women had dressed up in their Sunday best. The boys carried small glasses out to the hallway for them. Peppermint schnapps. Caraway liqueur. Aniseed brandy. I bet they sneak sips, the little shits, thought the Constable. But they won't wear my Juza down, no chance.

He stretched his legs again. Anything's possible. People can come to an agreement. And this guy . . . he fixed his eye on Polka . . . will hopefully stop being a nuisance. At that very moment Polka said in the direction of the cops' table: This is a fine part of the country. And his voice was purposefully very loud. I'm telling you, neighbours, I've seen the whole world! I'll tell you one thing. This place is a veritable paradise!

The men were smirking, the old women simpering, they were all waiting expectantly to see what Polka would come up with this time. What he had up his sleeve. Only the cops were acting as though they weren't listening.

The only thing I can't get out of my head is that Cragg lad, bellowed Polka, downing the rest of his glass. He turned round to her. Give me another one, my little doe. She'd told him ages ago not to call her that. Not in front of people. I'm going to do a runner today, she said to herself, suddenly feeling faint, her head spinning. And how did it happen? Him, my beloved! He'd been hovering around her all the time. And those things he said. No one talks like that. Even now he's doing it for her benefit. Showing her he's not afraid of the secret police. Everyone's afraid of the secret police. She put a full shot glass in front of him on the counter.

I thought the comrades here had come to investigate the case, said Polka, leaning back on the bar. And instead you're interested in that motorway project, that's all! Or what?! Comrades! What's all the technology good for? What about human life? You can't measure a human life. Why, they found that boy in the woods. Not long ago. Who could have done it? No one knows. They said it might have been that queer. Am I right, men?

She was staring at the flypaper. Her ears were full of the buzzing of flies. Must be the flies that got caught today. The ones from yesterday must all be dead by now. That's weird. And it's a cold morning. Why's everyone gone quiet all of a sudden?

Mum, said Zuza. I'm going, she whispered.

Let her go, said Polka. He was reeling at the bar. He was doing it for a laugh, pretending he was sloshed. He was propping himself up on his elbows. He turned round to the cops again. The girl's getting herself ready, you know! We still have certain customs here. It's a virgin part of the country. The girls dance on their own. Yep, the people in this part of the country are still pure. And I've been all over the world. Isn't that right, neighbours?

A few people laughed. They didn't have this sort of thing every day. Secret policemen from Prague. Polka drunk in the morning. All that fun with the contraptions. First they install them and pay people so much money. Then they confiscate them. Without wanting their dosh back. Nothing.

How many times have I said to Karel here, Polka went on, decorate the place with some colourful Chinese lanterns, some flashing lights, photos of popular singers, one of Neckář over there, a pin-up of Pilarová over here, and you'll see. You'll draw crowds of teenagers. You'll pull in people from Zásmuky. Bělá. Even Osikov.

Leave it out, I don't want any commotion in here!

Look, get rid of that Švejk and put up a proper photo of Gott instead. What do you think, comrades?

I like it here, said the older cop. It's a homely sort of place.

Well, comrades, said Polka, tottering. So what about that lad they found in the woods?

That's under investigation, said the older cop.

You know, over in Zásmuky, the men exposed a queer. I don't normally drink in the morning, so no offence meant. So basically, they exposed him, he'd said something that made them wise to his ways, or something, so the men dragged him off into the woods, gave him a good hiding, whipped him with a rope, left him there. Did it for their children. I don't have a kid, so what do I know? They go back in the morning, the ropes are just hanging there, looks like he gnawed his way through them. The bloke was gone. People say that fear drove him mad, that he's running around in the woods somewhere on Blahoš Hill. Apparently, he literally turned white with horror. Bloody faggot. And it occurred to me, it's just an ordinary bloke's hunch, mind. Couldn't the poofter have done it? No offence, comrades, just giving you a lead.

Thank you, said the older cop.

You know, sometimes we get together here, just the men, like. It's a tradition. The wives and daughters stay together in the cellars and the attics, the boys, those little buggers, take the livestock out into the woods. These ancient customs date back to times before the Tatars came, apparently. So we're down the pub, men only. We're waiting. Maybe a soldier will poke his nose in for a bit of fun. We're bored. So we dance. Someone dances like a bear, right? And someone else like a woman. Nothing wrong with that, surely. The fur trappers in Alaska do the selfsame thing. I know, I've been there.

You've been to the United States of America? asked the young cop.

Oh yeah, I've been all over the world, continued Polka. He wasn't taking any notice of the young one. He wasn't talking to anyone in particular, he was telling everyone. He didn't care whether a chair creaked

71

now and then, that someone reached out for their glass. An old woman, all done up, had just hauled her contraption in, she stayed where she was. The women in the hallway were helping her. They didn't cross the threshold.

I've been all over the world, listen, all of you! Take Sweden, for example. You know I've got a nose for Death, you know me well. But over there the Grim Reaper played a trick on me, that's for sure! I was abroad, right. I was walking along the seashore over there in Sweden, drinking seawater, made sense, there wasn't any other kind at hand, you see. I'm walking and walking, and lo and behold, Mrs Death is walking by my side, laughing at me, baring her teeth at me, so I start whinnying too. I get to the beach. It's covered with dead bodies. They're lying there, not moving, nothing. I've got salt-water crabs crawling around in my stomach, from the seawater I'd been drinking, they're rubbing against each other, making a really foul kind of music. So I fart a little. I'm watching a naked girl, and at that moment she does it too, under her bum, into the sand. What's that about? A Swedish greeting? I'm wondering whether the people might be from a sect, maybe they committed mass suicide, like some of those religiously minded black folks do, and that's when the dead girl moves, stands up. And she's really something, drop dead gorgeous! I keep watching: two dead men are playing catch. Kids are running up and down the beach and into the water, shouting. All the dead people are swimming, sunbathing, and that sort of thing. Odd, eh? I packed up my stuff immediately and headed home. Take my word for it! Polka slammed his beer mug down on the counter.

Nothing strange about that! shouted one of the men by the toilets. You just had sunstroke, you twat!

He was ogling that Swedish lassie so hard, he fell over. Ha ha ha!

Frída was waving his arms about. He straightened up behind the table.

He wanted to attract the attention of the silent cops. He wanted to tap his forehead and say something like: You know, this comrade is a bit, watchamacallit . . . he knew Polka wouldn't get pissed off with him. Nor anyone else. But Polka was off again.

I've been to all kinds of places! And it's kind of strange everywhere. Take Germany. They've got some motorways there, the cars go whizzing up and down them, it's magnificent. And when you're in luck, the sun's shining and being reflected off those bonnets, then it really is lovely. When you're standing on the hard shoulder, you never get run over. One time I'd been ploughing all day long, so in the evening I went to a lake for a quick wash. I get into the reeds and there's a dead bloke in there. He'd been there a long time, he's all bloated, white. I didn't even bother looking to see if there were any others in there. Didn't go any further, can't swim. Well, Germany, I don't know what to think. They've got nice lakes over there. But here's where I like it best. You know me. You know who I am. Am I right?

The only person laughing was Polka. He was gesticulating wildly, he almost knocked all the drinks off the bar. Everyone in the pub was now sitting down, watching the cops. What's going to happen next? Someone at the back hooted with laughter. You couldn't see who. The young cop stood up, straightening his jacket. He took a few steps towards Polka. And barked angrily: Your citizen's ID!

It was as if Polka had expected it. He had the little red book in his hand instantly. Where did he pull it out from? When? All eyes were fixed on him.

The cop took the little book with two fingers, squeamishly, like he was holding a dead rat by the tail . . . he turned a few pages and suddenly . . . he's standing to attention in front of Polka. And saluting him! Is he taking the piss as well?

The person in the back, whoever it was, was howling with laughter now. Everyone was smiling. Watching. And now what?

That's all right, young man, Polka patted the cop on the shoulder . . . now you could see how much bigger than the young cop he was . . . you couldn't tell when he'd been pacing around, waving his arms as he talked. Why, that cop's tiny! He's got a little pot belly, he's a chubby little fella, but . . . The guy who'd been laughing at the back started choking. The other men were slapping his back for a moment. To help him clear his air passage.

The copper turned around while still standing to attention. He shuffled back to the table. The old one pretended that nothing had happened. He wasn't paying attention to anything. He cracked the shell on another egg with his spoon. The yolk squirted out onto the plate. There was silence. That was uncomfortable. Maybe that's why Polka started up again: You're a young laddie, Comradey, you can't do anything about that. You're, figuratively speaking, still soaking wet behind the ears. You've still got bits of eggshell on your head from when you hatched from your mum's egg! he yelled at the cop's back. You don't know yet that one day you can be saluting a man and the next day you'll be leading him away to a police van on a chain. Or you'll be smashing his head in somewhere in a dark alley, eh? It's chaos, much of the time. I'm right, aren't I?

Polka took a few steps towards their table. The young one was plopping himself down into his chair. The old one was still calmly savouring his food. I expect your colleague here knows what I'm on about, said Polka. He leant over the old one. He's not alarmed by a piece of paper, eh? Eh, Comradey? Tasty?

Yes, thank you, said the older cop. Right tasty. Local eggs, eh?

And hardly had the young one plonked himself down at the table, than the older one stood up. He was about right for Polka, height-wise. He's a different calibre, the men were saying to themselves, gawping. He's got evil eyes, like a hard man should. He's a copper, all right. High ranking, no doubt. A colonel! Something like that. A real animal.

The old one raised his beer mug. He was smiling. Smiling at everyone. Cheers, neighbours! he cried. They raised their glasses. Of course they did. They toasted him back. That was the right and proper thing to do. Let Polka blather on as much as he likes. This old man doesn't want any strife. And the young cop? He should swallow his pride, sit down in a corner for a bit. He'll learn. A little while later the conversation was once again leaping from table to table like a flame in a smoky fire.

The old one was nodding to his neighbours. He kept smiling. At the men. At the old men puffing on their pipes. That smile of his pleased everyone. Some of the women later said he'd winked at them. He was certainly enjoying his eggs. He ordered more bread. He was chewing on the crust, chasing bits of bacon fat around on his plate, fondling the food. They noticed: he'd put a napkin on his knees. You rarely see that. The women liked it. He really knows how to eat! He doesn't stuff himself like some potato picker. But he can eat a pile of food. Let him get his fill. So there's peace and quiet. But Polka! For a moment he was talking to a huddle of men by the toilets. Then he was off again. As soon as they heard him, they cut their conversations short. Everyone was listening to him again.

Maybe those blokes from Zásmuky went a bit far, probably so, said Polka, taking a few steps towards the cops and then out of the blue . . . he sort of danced a few steps . . . and also made like he was lifting . . . a skirt, that's what he was implying, moving the tips of his forefingers like he was pulling a piece of fabric . . . over his arse! . . . everyone was howling with laughter. The joke sent a jolt through everyone. What's the idea?

It's like those dances, comrades! A very long time ago, the teacher told me this, it's in the chronicles, I didn't make it up, Polka shouted, stamping his foot . . . he was stamping his foot on the floorboards by the counter . . . he ran a few steps, raised his arms and started running his hands all over his body . . . when the girls did their dancing, they smeared lard all over their bodies! But it wasn't animal lard, if you get my drift. What they do is take a nice long run-up and . . . Polka jumped up, they leap over a bonfire! cried Polka, making the floorboards creak as he landed . . . and as they're leaping around like that, Polka went on, red-hot lumps of coal flicker before their eyes, they can smell the forest around them, hear the branches rustling and they can feel many pairs of eyes fixed on them, they're in the woods, they feel them tickling them, something scratches one of the girls on her thigh, caresses another on the calf, pulls on a little hair right there as she's jumping . . . Well, that's folk wisdom, cried Polka and stopped. He grabbed someone's beer mug and drank. We're too narrow-minded for that!

Stop it already! Zuza's mum whipped Polka with a tea towel. But she was cackling. Everyone was laughing. The cops finished eating. The older one got up. Polka was pretending that the tea towel had hurt him, winded him in mid-leap, he was leaning his elbows on the counter.

Thanks, Mum, Zuza said to herself. He's repulsive, she thought. I think I'm going to kill myself. She threw her apron on the counter.

Well, that'll do, I think, said the older cop. He was brushing crumbs off his jacket. He was no longer smiling. The young one jumped up in the corner, his legs got tangled up in the chairs.

I apologise! exclaimed Polka, it's the spirits. He moved again, a moment later he was hovering around the cops, pretending he wanted to help the older one, with the crumbs, or something, he was sort of brushing him down with his arms, but without touching him. Then he was by the bar, saying: You know, yesterday a funeral, today important gentlemen from

Prague, I'm all befuddled. It's too much for one person. You know how it is. Those who made the human lard were sorcerers, and when they caught a sorcerer back then, they did the same thing to him as those blokes from Zásmuky did to that poofter. And that was that. End of story!

Polka turned round to the bar, his back to the cops.

Karel, give me another one.

The cops headed towards the door.

The old one exited. The younger one followed. Someone slammed a full beer mug in front of Polka. Someone said: He gave them hell! And someone else said: One more over here! The old men were clearing their throats. The old cronies started twittering. Outside, a flock of little boys was playing. They messed around with a dog for a bit. Then they stood in a line. They were competing to see who could spit the farthest. There was lots of dust around. Lots of mud. You could see the saliva in it.

She was lying in the hayloft, waiting for the other girls to turn up, tear up the turf, get the wood ready, lots of wood, there'll be girls coming for the bonfire all the way from Bělá, from Zásmuky, from isolated dwellings. Vendula, Jolana, Jarka will come, they'll shout: Get up you lazy cow! But for now she had time, she wriggled deeper into the bedding in the nest, they called the place the nest, they'd put blankets on the hay, the air smelled lovely.

She'd run the whole way from the pub, the air cleansed her, washed off all the pub fumes, all that prattle, all that drivel of his. That's how he got his way with me, with talk, sweet talk. That's how it happened. I have to get away. Away from here, she said. She burrowed deeper into the hay. Deeper still. She's got time now. Dad had said: Come in the evening, tidy up, sweep the floor. Get the middle table ready. In the evening.

She lay on her back, put her hands on her tummy. I just want to have things nice and clean, Vendula could tell, she's the only one that knows, they'd been bathing, standing in the river, standing on the stones, Vendula leaned over to her, almost slipping on a rock, suddenly, out of the blue, she touched her. And she said: Oh Christ.

They were sitting on the river bank, she was crying, Vendula said to her: Quit blubbing! So she stopped, but then Vendula asked: What are you going to do? So she started up again.

I don't know!

What don't you know? You'll end up on the bus to Osikov, a girl on her own, and right away people will say, she's off to be with the soldiers, bloody tramp, or they'll say, she's on her way to hospital for an abortion, fucking whore. That's what people will say. So you've got to go and see the Old Hag. Like Renata. Like others before her.

I've already been to see the Old Hag!

And?

She gave me something.

There you go then.

But I don't know.

What don't you know? Your old man is going to kill you. Mine would tear me in half. My brothers! I'd have to run away. But how? Where?

But Renata . . .

What?

Renata used to go to see her down the pub, she drank Fernet through a straw, paying no attention to the old men ogling them.

Just think, they fantasise about you when they touch themselves. Gross, eh?

What?

They think about you when they're having a wank, that's what!

Don't be daft, Zuza exhaled, blushing.

And why do you think your old man has you around? Why do men come here for a beer all the way from Zásmuky? Over there there's an old woman behind the counter. That's how it is.

My dad doesn't think about that at all, now you're talking rubbish.

Everyone thinks about it. I don't think about it, except when I'm doing it. But that's when I think about the fact that later I won't be doing it.

Don't talk rubbish! Why are you so into it . . .

Give me one more.

Don't drink so much!

Look, Zuza . . .

Hm.

And you did it with that young one, didn't you? The Praguer.

You're stupid!

You did, you did . . . you've gone all red! And you're clever. That would be the best thing for you, moving to Prague. But he's too young for it!

No he's not.

So you did it with him, then.

Well, yeah, Zuza nodded.

I knew it! I saw him gazing at you. Have one on me. Rum?

Don't be daft! Dad's here.

Kofola?

I prefer Ovona.

He stares at you like a lost puppy. Wouldn't be bad to get out of here, go to Prague. In time. Right? By then you'd know if he was a retard.

They laughed. They laughed with each other. Zuza liked that: sometimes one of them knew exactly what the other would say. Or do. That's when they were in the hayloft.

She was glad she'd told Renata. She wasn't going to make fun of her. So he's young, so what. At least he's not like the lads here. The lads here are animals. That's what Renata said. Renata was totally different to the other girls. Renata wrote poetry. *May the skirt around your loins be made of nothing but the river's billowing waters . . .* A guitarist I know is probably going to use that in a song. He's got this kind of Pre-Raphaelite hairstyle.

He's got what? Oh, right. Guitarist, eh? What about that soldier?

She and the girls had met Renata and the soldier when they went to visit Jolana in hospital. He and Renata were holding hands. They met them on the street.

That was the time when Jolana fell into the well. Everyone was shocked when they pulled her out. Nothing happened to her. It was an old well, without any water in it. She didn't have a scratch on her.

I was falling through black darkness and suddenly down at the bottom this light hurtled towards me, like a cloud, there were two arms in the light and they caught me. Honest!

Probably whacked your head on a wooden beam! said one of the girls.

Back then they'd taken the bus, it was like going on a school trip, there were so many of them, they got the day off school.

She could have died! Jolana's mum lamented. She deserves a hiding, more like, her dad said down the pub.

After that Jolana almost froze to death in the forest. She went into the woods with her brother, they went to gather spruce branches, they were playing games. She got lost. She wandered around Blahoš Hill for a long time, she almost fell into an old mine shaft. How could you have got lost in the woods?

Dunno! I took a step forward and then I saw the hole. A cloud came hurtling up from the darkness below again, it was white light, I knew that from before, so I was happy. And I heard the voice again and saw two white hands, and they kept me warm by stroking me, so I didn't even freeze. That's something, eh?

A voice? What did it say to you?

That I shouldn't be scared, and that sort of thing. I've already told it all, it's all been written down.

They went to see her in hospital, the teacher gave them permission for that, sometimes they took the bus, or they set out in the morning and walked through the forest.

After that Jolana was in hospital because she was struck by lightning, on a cliff, somewhere near Blahoš.

She should have been in the papers a long time ago, her father said. I'm going to tie her up, I reckon. Like a goat.

She showed the girls the line of burnt skin slithering down her body.

I'm surprised the hands didn't catch it, Vendula said, wrinkling her nose. They laughed.

You're stupid, said Jolana from out of the pillows. They did, actually.

Hey, and didn't the voice tell you to be careful in future? asked Jarka.

I'm not going to tell you what it said, so there! I already told the nuns from the Black House.

The nuns came to see all the children. Jolana too. They wrote down everything she told them about the light and the voice.

They believe me! They don't laugh!

We believe you too, the girls said.

They heard shouting through the open window. There were children playing outside. There were lots of children. They were wearing regulation tracksuits. Lousy little bastards, Zuza said to herself. But she was instantly ashamed. The children's heads were shaven. Everyone called them lousy. The nuns were outside with the kids. The nuns from the Black House wore black habits.

That time they didn't stay long. They wanted to make it to the pictures.

In the hospital, Jolana played with the other children, or just lay there in the white bed. She didn't have to do anything. Zuza envied her quite a lot. Outside they met Renata with the soldier.

Later Renata told her that she'd been to see the Old Hag. She told her in the pub. She told her about the bird bones at the Old Hag's place. The Mother of the Dead, that's what Renata had called the Old Hag when she was drunk. Then she wanted to tell Zuza what it was like.

You don't feel hollow inside, you don't feel anything at all in there. And you see it everywhere. At one time it would have been this big, and then this big. It would have little hands, like this. You come up with of all kinds of twaddle, that's all. You think it exists somewhere. It occurs to you that it's become another little baby. In someone else's house. Daft bollocks! You cry, get plastered and then you cry again. It's impossible to describe.

And what about the soldier? asked Zuza.

Sod him.

Renata also read poetry in the hayloft. Afterwards they'd lie down next to each other in the nest, they'd fool around, tickling each other and cuddling, the nicest thing was knowing that they both liked it. It's just a bit of fun! Zuza would say to herself. Renata gave her a kiss. Lie down like this, she whispered. She kneeled on Zuza's back. She pulled her hair. With one hand she pulled her hair, with the other she stroked her. She smacked her buttocks with the palm of her hand. Just a little at first, then harder. They could hear each other breathing. Zuza turned around onto her back. They kissed. Not on the lips. On the ear, neck, hair. Then they just lay there.

But I just want everything to be nice and good, said Zuza.

But you like that, right? said Renata. A bit of the rough stuff.

But why? said Zuza.

You're just like that, that's all, doesn't matter.

I don't want you to go away. I don't mean just now. Not ever!

You know what people say around here. Brush her hair till she's six, beat her till she's twelve, guard her till sixteen, and once she's over twenty thank whoever gets her out of your house. I've had my twentieth birthday. I'm old.

Hm, said Zuza. Sometimes I think you like Vendula better anyway. Vendula's got big boobs.

Don't be daft, said Renata. Am I a stupid man, or what? We're friends, yeah?

Yeah, said Zuza.

But then Renata ran away. If she'd been here, maybe it wouldn't have happened to me. Dunno. I don't know, said Zuza to herself. And fell asleep.

4

The boys had not been pestering Juza for some time. They were milling around in a huddle in front of the pub, a few had just turned up in a run, two or three of them dashed inside. And straight up to Frída. Panting, the small, nifty-looking one with the haversack bouncing on his shoulder reported the incident. Frída closed his folder, flung his pencil at the table. He went with them.

The children had found him. They'd been out gathering wood, picking blueberries. Frída cut him down, threw some moss on him, some branches. Stand guard here! he ordered the older ones. Keep the flies off him, or something! He sent the tiddlers to get their dads. Tell them to bring some blankets!

That's why he was now trudging in the heat. From Zásmuky. And Nachty? They'd had quite an argument. The place where the lad had been hanging was on a boundary. A disputed one. I might have known Nachty would try to lumber me with it. Just the paper work alone! But the commander had been in a good mood. All right then, I'll take charge of him, he'd said afterwards. It's my last case anyway.

From Zásmuky he'd gone over the hill, through the forest, now for an hour or two he'd been walking over stony ground. He called the rocky hill the Face. The locals called the place the Head. As though someone was wedged in the ground and only his head was poking out. No one hung around there for long if the evening caught up with them. The old women, tired from collecting wood, would sit down together, their eyes flitting in all directions, saying: I'll just have a quick rest, Head! But they were so frightened they never got a moment's repose, they had shivers running down their spines, they moved on right away. Their skirts rustled over the smooth rocks, as soon as they stood up, they stuck their thumbs up, tapped the stones with crossed fingers. Young girls put garlands of flowers around Stony's neck. The place was strewn with dried flowers.

The stones were giving off heat. Sparse grass grew around the Head. Long ago there had probably been a meadow there. The crags were breaking apart of their own accord, crumbling away. In the end everything would be covered with stones. There'd never been any fields there, not there. How many times he'd slogged through the place on his way to see Nachtigal. And back. He could have taken a shortcut through Buny, but he didn't feel like it. But all this plodding would soon be over. Nachtigal had been more than clear about that.

They had known about the soldier. Every now and then someone caught sight of him. They knew he was loitering in the area. Sleeping in the forest. He'd pulled his ID out of the pocket of his uniform. Of course it was him. The women said he'd been wandering around aimlessly. That he'd lost his marbles. Because of a local girl. So in the end he hung himself from his belt because of unrequited love, what an imbecile. A soldier shouldn't do that.

He and Nachtigal would have had to ferret him out anyway in time. In pursuit of a deserter. And now all he had to do was cut him down, oh well!

My last case, Nachtigal had said. He'd been in a fairly good mood.

Since the previous day. So he topped up his tank to keep the mood going. They'd had quite a few together.

But I've got to get on, damn it! said Frída to himself. He stretched out in the sparse grass that had forced its way up through the stones. He closed his eyes. It's the beers. I've got to get up, got to go. Welcome the comrades from the district. The vodka-induced jolly mood was leaving him. He felt jolts of pain in his temples. It's not far from here, bloody hell, he was saying to himself, get up, you bugger. Oh, but the body.

All right then, I'll stay here with you for a bit, Stony. I've been run ragged. They won't even give me that scooter. Suddenly he felt a chill run through his bones. Even though he was lying on the warmed-up stones. Yeah, I feel strange. Sort of weak. I'm all sweaty from the heat, I feel cold in my bones. The weather's gone barmy. Look, Face, said Frída to Stony, and what will happen if I don't make it in time to bid the comrades welcome?

He lifted his arm, ran his fingers over the stone head. You've got a real nose here, a real mouth, eye sockets right there. Did water hollow those out for you?

But I must get there. There'll be sixteen buses arriving in the village. And straight away they'll be asking for me, that's clear. Comrades! Is Comrade Frída here? He had to go to the station in Zásmuky to deal with an urgent matter. He'll be taking charge of the local unit soon. That's what Juza should report, or something along those lines.

The district office had informed them that sixteen buses were coming. That's something. That's already the power of the armed masses. And they're taking members of the Pioneer youth movement with them. They're well trained nowadays. They're small, quick, almost nothing gets past them. Civil defence training, they said, pah. Probably come to search the woods. It's a dragnet. A manhunt. Around Blahoš Hill. But not for some wretched deserters. This must be something damn important. But what? Not even Nachtigal knows. Maybe Teachy knows. Comrade Bohadlo, the teacher. He's a sort of informer, that Bohadlo.

Feels nice lying here, that's for sure. What would the comrades say?

This comrade has somewhat crumpled under the burden of personal concerns, one comrade would say, kicking me with his boot, as if out of jest.

He had a complete breakdown when he heard about the fate of his girlfriend! another comrade would say.

But that's not acceptable, those strict comrades would say. Attention!

Fuck off, comrades, said Frída to the Head. And I bet you, Stony, that if I opened my eyes I'd see that you're laughing. But I'm going to outwit you as well, Face! I'm going to keep my eyes closed. Good one, eh?

Sixteen buses, mused Frída. Maybe the comrades have been taken in by old wives' tales and they'll be combing the woods for old Poskina, ha ha! He laughed. Old Poskina, he was one hell of a border guard, bloody hell. Poskina in the service of the people. I believe in Poskina about as much as I do in the Loch Ness Monster, a load of old cobblers all that. Thing is, you don't believe in Nessie till she bites off your . . . you know what. And then it's no longer a bone of contention, is it.

If I don't get there in time to meet the comrades, Bohadlo will deal with them. Juza will bid them welcome. He's hacking those contraptions up with his axe, smashing them with his rod. In the pub yard. Karel can't say a word against that. Those are the comrades' wishes. And of all people, Karel doesn't want to hand over his contraption. Karel, and a few others. Well, we'll see, men. I never forget what I don't want to, that's just how it is with me. We'll see who gets the better of whom. A lot is at stake for me. The comrades have promised to make me major. Major! If I sort out the business with the contraptions.

Another promise. And they're not just any old comrades. They were forged in the Soviet Union. They were at Red Mountain, apparently.

The older one didn't even bat an eyelid when I told him that the buses were coming. They're not interested in any exercises, that's paltry stuff to them. I have a feeling I know the older one. One hell of a bloke. He's polite, obliging, all smiles, but he's a killer. Old school. And so what. I've known many like that. And how many of them took the fast lane straight to hell. This one must also have studied at the Training Institute. He must have been finishing when I was a fresher.

There were rumours at the Institute that they were going to select a few of the best to go to Red Mountain in the Soviet Union. To the elite little town in the steppes where comrades can go shopping and buy any luxury goods that take their fancy. Red Mountain is supplied from the West. By comrades living in the West illegally, for the time being. The interests and needs of the comrades from Red Mountain are those of the people of the future, our civic sciences professor used to say. The people of the future will be the most humane in human history. Their humanity will be as invulnerable as the mechanism of a machine.

Fuck it, said Frída to himself. I still know my stuff. I covered a mountain of notebooks with notes. I put my hand up, answers at the ready! I was also a student in a jacket and tie, for fuck's sake.

He slapped Stony. What about you, Face. How are you? Does the smell of burning ever waft over this way? Why, Buny's right over there. I don't feel like going yet. I'm nice and comfy here. No doubt that professor of sciences is dead too, by now.

Comrades, he used to say, death is part of life, we'll float off into it like satellites into the cosmos. And a satellite in the cosmos becomes the cosmos, do you understand, comrades? It could even be magnificent.

Magnificent, it probably wasn't so magnificent for the people of Buny and those other people from the villages in the crags. Oh dear, Stony. I let out a mighty sigh just now. She's on my mind, Květa. That's why I'm idling around here.

To begin with she only slept with me so that I'd get her daddy out of the slammer. But how could I, he was put away by the guys at the top. And then she slept with me because she liked it, of that I'm certain. Well, I'm a man at the height of his powers. And she was an eager lassie. They're all like that, once a man brings it out in them.

They had to pick someone, after all. And Juza was the wealthiest small-hold farmer around. Well, he wasn't actually wealthy, nor a farmer, but he was the only one with anything around here. As for the rest, they were a bunch of ne'er-do-wells, people from the crags, smuggling bandits the lot of them, poachers, potato pickers, raggedy gypos, who could you pick from that lot?

And Juza bore scars. He was the only one here who'd hauled rocks. People here are soft as dough, they just want to muck about in the woods. Juza worked himself to the bone. He didn't have sons like his brother. His old woman's belly swelled up, but not in the normal way, like a cow's. There was a tiny little man inside her. All teeth and hair. They got rid of it. The devil only knows who she had Květa with. With someone from another place, most likely. Might even have been my old man of all people, sniggered Frída.

Poor Juza. But who was I supposed to pick? Who? Those comrades from the district committee came up with those trials. The kulak trials. Juza was the scapegoat here. But someone was locked up in every part of the country, that was normal. Whose fault is it that he lost it in the slammer? He didn't know how to behave in there. So a few of the comrades, the prison wardens, gave him the works, oh well! Often those comrades from the prison service had been in the punitive battalions, and they carry all kinds of scars themselves. You can't expect much ordinary humanity from comrades like them!

She ended up without a daddy. Didn't even have any uncles. We were happy together. She was the one who ruined it. So she'd have kids with me, so what! I'd find a place for them . . . and now I'm going to make major. A major's pension, that's no measly thing. We could have lived together, easily. I'd have bought a motorbike, why not? I'd have gone fishing on the bike. Not in this river! We'd have lived together somewhere else, that's obvious. I'd have come home, the kids would have run up to me, calling, Daddy! Have you got anything for us? Of course I do! I'd always have something.

And then it went awry. She ruined everything. What she got up to! Apparently a man is capable of that. Awakening a complete animal in a girl. It's not devilry, or anything, it's common sense. I should have kept a closer eye on her. But how? After all, I didn't know I was going to be made major, did I? Those comrades weren't even on the horizon back then. Hadn't an inkling it might happen, back then.

He took Juza under his wing as soon as they let him out. They lived in the village, in a house. Abandoned by someone. The rooms were inside a cliff. Often they had to heat the place even in the summer. Juza cooked and washed. They took turns going on patrol. It wasn't an official arrangement, that wasn't possible. Not with a man released from prison. But among the people he was always known as Juza the Junior Constable, the Copper's Assistant, Frída's Juza.

Theirs was a manly coexistence, just like at the Institute. Or in the barracks. They were manning the farthest outpost in a remote part of the country. Often Frída would go to bed as he was, without even taking off his uniform, a single thought running through his head: are there actually roads, cars, cities beyond these stony hills, these woods? Over there, do people dress up on Sundays, swagger around with their offspring? Bollocks! Total bollocks. Beyond lies nothing.

I treat Juza like kin. He lives off my soldier's salary. I protect him, after all. It was me who gave Květa that blue dress and all. How did Nachtigal put it? Like a flower! She was floating in the water like a big blue flower, he recounted. I punted over and what did I see: a girl's bum. A blue skirt all around it on the surface of the water.

And I even told Juza about Květa, on many occasions. About our happy times together. He doesn't know, he was in the slammer! But how am I going to tell him this? That she's dead. People will tell him. He'll find out somehow. And he's not going to like it. That it was Nachtigal who found her and pulled her out. Why, he's like some angel of death to his family.

Talk about Nachty. He never takes a rest. Pokes his nose into everything. Even though his time here is coming to an end, Comrade commander still cocked his ears when I reported how Polky had been winding up the comrades from Prague. The way he spoke about Red Mountain! Mentioned it in front of everyone in the pub. And what would Polka say if he knew that Nachty spies on him? Maybe he does know. Polka's from here, but he's not from here. He's an odd one, but there are so many odd ones around!

With Polka, Comrade . . . with Polka around one feels lighter in the heart. You have a drink with Polka and whatever's been eating you suddenly becomes trivial. Polka's a bundle of laughs.

And who is he? Nachtigal had asked.

Believe me, Comrade, said Frída. Comrade Polka is a good comrade.

I believe you, Comrade. But I'm asking you: Is he registered?

I'm sure of it. I'm sure his papers are in order.

Have you not checked his papers, Comrade?

He's local. Everyone knows him.

Are you trying to piss me off, Comrade? I hate this sort of thing. What is it about you lot? Banging on about me being an outsider all the time! The comrades at headquarters put me in charge of these here parts. So I'm just as good as any comrade born here. Attention!

Seriously, recalled Frída. He actually made me stand to attention. We were drunk good and proper, that's true. He'd only just been transferred. He showed what he was made of soon enough, revealed his true nature. The way he dealt with the Lynx Eyes. I'll never forget that. Nor will anyone else.

Sit! commanded Nachtigal. In the Soviet Union you take a bite of cucumber with your vodka, Comrade. Have some! He pushed the little plate with salted cucumber towards Frída.

Not like that, Comrade. You have to cut the cucumber up with your bayonet. You know, Comrade, when I was in the trenches there was an icy blizzard hurtling towards us, we had to leave those trenches of ours. Bayonets at the ready, attack! The young comrades today don't know what it's like any more. And we had a saying: You start by chopping cucumber, and end up chopping onion. You know, Comrade, I've got a soft spot for this kind of thing. You think I'm a hard man. But often I wake up with tears in my eyes. You wouldn't think it, would you?

Well all right then, Frída had said to himself, if antics is what you want . . . he was slicing the cucumber with the tip of the bayonet, somehow trying to explain . . . about Polka . . . excuse him, somehow . . . look here, Comrade commander, this is a sad part of the country, used to be even sadder, Polka provides entertainment and people are grateful . . . there's no problem from a security point of view, it's a good thing for the men to let some steam off . . . these potato pickers, they're all feeble, sad . . . before Polka reappeared, they only knew sad things, do you know the story about the bear handler? No? The bear dance is a sad one, Comrade commander, it's one a bloke dances on his own, stomping his feet like a bear on a hot plate, a flame burning his feet, they heat the plate under him to make him dance, it burns, so the bloke keeps drinking till he keels over. Bear handlers were roaming through these parts as far back as the times of the raiders, Comrade the teacher, Comrade Bohadlo himself, tells this story! If a bloke was on his own with no one to look after, he got himself a bear and wandered through the land. If he'd had a wife, daughters maybe, as it should be, it would be different. But a man alone can't even look after his own cottage, it bears down on his neck. In the end, the lonely bear handler had it off with his bear. And believe me, they were both still sad.

Nachtigal nodded. He was frowning. He was sombre. I've heard these stories, Comrade. It's against nature. Have a piece of cucumber, Comrade, listen. Up to now people have just been part of an experiment, like lab rats. They had to experience wars, the hell of those massacres. That was all just about testing technology. How far it can go. Now we know how far it can go. To the brotherhood of machines and people. Robotics will serve the future like a saddled horse, Comrade, I'm telling you. Today some comrades are tinkers, fraternising with machines. They wear headphones, they have night vision, fingers on triggers. The enormous development of machines will lead to the brotherhood of machines and people. And the rights of the machine? They will be human rights. I can see it coming.

I . . . I can see it too, Comrade.

This here goes with the cucumber, it's dill.

I know, nodded Frída. Thank you.

Dill is nature, said Nachtigal. Nature is dreadful. She's a mother who gnaws her own children. We have nature. So! Now we need the law. That must be a firm father. He needs to be dignified and human. Whoever thinks the rules don't apply to them, they're gravely mistaken. That Polka.

Is he registered, then? Or not? Who is he? Does he follow any rules?

I think so, Comrade, stuttered Frída.

But my question, dear Comrade, is: Can those rules accommodate the world?

Ah, Comrade, I've already had quite a lot to drink. He's from around here.

Look you, don't piss me off with that. Everyone keeps mentioning that I'm an outsider. You remember Jankovský? Sure you do. You were there.

Jankovský was Juza's brother. But he was different. He had sons. They called them the Lynx Eyes. Their irises were as white as the white of the eye should be, otherwise their eyes were dark. With their inverted eyes they could even see at night. They were poachers! They went around shooting game in the woods even under the Germans, they didn't hand in their guns, Jankovský sure didn't. They went wherever they wanted. They shot a gamekeeper. That was the last gamekeeper we ever had. Nachtigal handled everything on his own. He had a promotion to show for it.

The Lynx Eyes. No one could deal with them. Until Nachtigal came along. He executed them, plain and simple, comrade-style.

Frída hadn't known what he was up to. He'd gone to their cottage in the middle of the clearing with a summons. He'd had no idea that old Jankovský's number was up.

And it should have occurred to me. That time I met him in the woods. He was leaning on his rifle, his shoulder torn open.

Comrade! Frída had yelled, looking at the crippled Nachtigal. He was crawling through the brushwood, his black uniform all ripped, dirty, his shoulder covered in blood, shreds of flesh poking out of it.

It was a horse, Nachtigal had told him. A horse in the woods, standing behind me, nipped me, tore a bite out of me, Nachtigal had said, collapsing.

A horse, yeah right, what a load of old bull. It must have been a slug, a dumdum most likely. He'd been shot by the Lynxes while he was spying on them. He hadn't even recovered properly yet and he went: Comrade Frída, you off to deliver a summons? Over to Jankovský's place? I'm coming with you.

He shot the old man and the two young ones in the living room, he was right behind Frída when he started shooting. He shot the others as they appeared. Just like that: Bang. Christ, the Lynx Eyes, everyone was scared of them and their end was that quick. I was surprised, that I was. I felt sick. I was standing by the door, got splattered by the blood. We dragged them off by their legs. We plopped them in the mud. The Lynxes had a bog right behind the cottage. They threw bones in there, all kinds of stuff. Who knows what's in that mud.

Then everyone knew. That this is not a guy to be fucked with. Some people left Zásmuky. Didn't want to live there any more.

Frída got up. He knew he had to get going, fast. Stop messing about, man. That blue skirt is making you go soft in the head. That was the end of Květa. That's why I felt weak all of a sudden. That was the only reason. I had to swallow it on my own. That she was gone. We had a good time together here, Stony. He patted a stone. He unbuttoned his trousers. Ha ha, I'm going to piss on your head, Stony. Then I'll turn my back on you. You'll have my water in your eye sockets. I'll wave to you from a distance! Yup!

5

The little boat was there, behind the church, lying in a muddy puddle beneath intertwined branches. Geese used the muddy path along the cemetery wall to waddle to the river, as did flocks of ducklings. There was a rusty can for bailing out water in the punt. The barge pole was lying in the thickets. He had barge poles hidden all along the river. One time one of them had floated off while he was asleep.

That time the little boat ran aground on some rocks, got mired in the reeds. Tussocks of the previous year's grass left behind by the floods were rotting everywhere in the reeds. He didn't know where he was.

Perhaps he'd slept for a long time, and the river had carried him for hundreds of kilometres. He'll end up in the docks of some harbour, living among stevedores, vagabonds, and pickpockets. He'll not return home until many years have passed, wearing a pilot's uniform.

It would be dark soon. Mum was no doubt looking for him and Squirt was asking around for him. He was going to set off to explore the faraway horizons of the landscape.

He climbed out of the little barge, waded through the mud, the water was up to his calves. Dusk was descending. What now? The provisions have been left behind in the fortress, and the forests are full of blood-thirsty Assiniboine natives. He'll slip into the thick forest silently like a ghost . . . the mud gave way and he dropped into a hollow, all of a sudden he was up to his waist in mud, yelling, his nose full of stench, the stink of mud, he was choking on water, he stepped on a stone, he was standing on a boulder. He jumped towards the boat, grabbed on to the wood, held on with all his might.

He pushed the boat through the reeds, tied it to a tree trunk, scrambled up onto the river bank. His hands were shaking.

He was wiping the mud off with grass, tearing up tufts of it, saying to himself: Well, I came within a whisker that time, and he saw two of the Líman brothers. The worst of them, Milan and Pavel, and also Standa, who hung out with them, and Pepa, also a Líman.

I always said he was a lunatic, said Milan. He talks to himself.

Is there someone here with you? inquired Standa.

Yeah!

Who? asked Pavel.

People I know.

You talk funny, said Milan. Are you, by any chance, from Prague? He barked the word out tersely and sharply, the others were laughing.

He's been talking to the spirits here, sniggered Pepa.

I wouldn't take the piss out of that, said Pavel. When his mum fell into the weir dead drunk, the spirits were the only thing that saved her.

Tee hee, everyone laughed.

Ondra knew that he if he started crying they'd leave him alone. Squirt always started crying.

Admit you're a weirdo, said Milan. Ondra folded his arms over his chest and stared into his eyes. He had to tilt his head back.

I told you about the test already. If you don't want to do it, you don't want to do it.

You'll get your gob smacked, said Pavel.

The Límans had been forcing the test on him ever since he'd first arrived. The Límans were brothers. Every other boy also had to become a Líman.

Pavel told him: You're either a Líman or you're a piece of shit, or a Pioneer, or a dirty gypo who lives on the other side of the river. So take your pick. There's only one choice.

The first time they gave Ondra a beating, he trudged back home with tears in his eyes and the moment Squirt saw him, he also started crying. Dad went to see Mr Líman and the other lads' fathers, and they all got a hiding.

You wouldn't have survived that, you wuss, Milan told him later. By then they were back on speaking terms. They'd made a fire. Squirt wasn't there.

My old man works on a cattle farm, mate, said Valeš. What does yours do, you gypo twat, said Valeš to Standa.

I'm no gypo, my dad works on the railway, cried Standa. They all laughed. Valeš had said it to wind him up. Then Valeš said to another boy: And what does your old man do, matey?

My old man either works in the woods or with your old man, you know that as well as I do, so why are you asking, you twat? said the boy.

I know that, you twat, I want to know what *his* old man does.

Ondra was sitting by the fire, wearing a tracksuit top like everyone else. Despite the cold evening, he went red. He was saying to himself: My old man is an old yarn spinner, you twat . . . or something like that, but then he said: Daddy is an inventor.

He was expecting everyone to crack up, but they were silent.

And that's why our old men, matey boy, those degenerates, are at home right now, said one of the boys. Oh well, he said, spreading his arms out and lying down in the grass.

Father's research. The Patent Office had begun to take a serious interest in the work of Ondra's daddy, or at least that's how Mum had put it. Maybe that was the reason they'd come the first time. To stay at Granddad's house. He couldn't remember. They came the next summer too. And the one after that.

Experts from the Patent Office installed a measuring device in almost every household. The device looked a bit like a clock. The fathers of the village boys placed painted marker poles along the river, as well as in the forest at the foot of Blahoš Hill. Metal rods from the Patent Office, as well as various poles they had at home. When the rods ran out, they used whatever poles they had in their barns and woodsheds.

Ondra's daddy went with them, noting everything down. He fixed triangulation points. The devices measured humidity. Maybe their complicated mechanism also recorded the movement of celestial bodies. Each device had its own folder with technical documents.

Ondra's daddy evaluated the collected data. Every evening he sat under a lamp. Ondra and Squirt were asleep by then. Ondra knew that sometimes Daddy sat under the lamp until morning. Moths flew towards the lamp. They fluttered in the curtains. He pored over the papers. The fathers of the other boys brought them to him. He leafed through them. Examined them. He squinted in the light of the lamp. He was on his way to inventing something phenomenal.

My old man loafs around at home, the whole day, mate, he doesn't give a shit about the field, just gawps at that clock. He's going bonkers, mate, said one of the lads. 'Cos of those graphs that come out of it.

He gets more dosh for it than he does for taking the cows out to pasture, said Valeš. My old man bought a scooter and he's out fuck knows where for days on end. Mother looks after the machine.

Look, Valeš leaned towards Ondra. What's the story? Something to do with satellites, right?

Ondra imagined Captain Nemura in his spaceship, vanishing in the stratosphere at a mind-boggling speed while taking samples with sensitive catalytic converters. Discovering the original essence of the Big Bang. Vanishing behind frothy clouds, his speed exceeding that of light. Going beyond light. Entering darkness, going beyond darkness. Will he return?

Tell us. Pavel leaned towards him. He grabbed his hand.

Apparently, you can drill a hole in a person's head and screw a little radio in there, said Milan. They fell silent. They were waiting for what he was going to say.

A tiny little radio like that is only visible under a microscope, said Milan. You put it in a person's head while they're asleep, or you knock them out with a drug, doesn't matter. They don't know about it. And then via satellite you know about everything they're thinking. The little radios are monitored by the government. And the government then knows everything you're thinking. My old man said so.

Fuck me! somebody said.

Hm, said someone else.

The government knows that Valeš is thinking about Vendula's titties, mate! Ha ha . . .

You're a pillock, you twat! exclaimed Valeš.

The government knows who takes cattle to Poland to sell on the sly, you twat! Hah!

And our old men are scared shitless, mate!

Ha ha . . . little radios!

Tee hee . . . satellites!

Hey, Ondra, said Milan. Tell us. If you tell, it'll count as half the test. Now they all went quiet again. Ondra knew they were watching him. He was staring into the fire. That's what he liked most about a fire. He knew he'd see little flames when he was falling asleep.

Milan pushed him.

Doesn't matter that your old man pays our old men. You're either with us or you're not. Get it?

Yeah, said Ondra. It's something . . . I dunno! I don't know what they measure.

Pavel twisted his arm. But just for a laugh.

It has something to do with the weather, that's what Mum had said. Ondra knew that Pavel wasn't twisting his arm to really hurt him. It only hurt a little. He acted as though it was just a bit of fun and sort of laughed.

It's got something to do with the weather. So there's a good harvest, he said.

That's a load of shite, someone said.

Grandma hates that contraption, she wants it taken off the wall, said Valeš. But then again, everyone's got one.

We haven't, said Standa. My old man's too busy working for the railways, I'm telling you!

Everyone burst out laughing. He wanted to tell Standa that it's not because of his father's work that they don't have a contraption at home.

Driving a locomotive is different to working in the woods or taking the cows out to pasture. Or running around with barge poles. Anybody can do that.

You're going to get your gob smacked, Pavel repeated. Your old man's not here now.

Beat the shit out of Pavel and you'll have done half the test, said Milan, chuckling. Everyone was laughing. No one could deck Pavel.

Why don't you want to be on our side, Milan wanted to know. You a Pioneer now?

Am not!

You lot are weird, said Pavel. You're not a Pioneer, all right then. You don't come to church. And you talk funny, you can't deny that! Are you lot yids?

Yeah, sure! said Ondra. Leave me alone.

We're not going to leave you alone, said Milan. Half the test is that you win a fight against one of us. Not Pepa. Standa here is the same size as you. Standa, come here.

The person who loses will get three slaps from Pavel. To finish them off. Get to it!

Standa walked straight towards him. Pavel and Milan were sitting in the grass next to Pepa.

He wanted to tell them that he'd managed to crawl out of the mud. And there was something else he wanted to tell them. He was thinking about the leaves rotting in the water. About the sticks in the hollows, stirred by the current. He could hear the buzzing of insects. And then everything happened all at once: Standa was walking through the grass, the high grass was swishing around his elbows, he was swinging his elbows, his fists were clenched.

He looked round. He could see that the rope was lying in the grass, that they didn't know about the little boat, he jerked his head towards the boat, the blow missed his face, numbing his shoulder, he sprang at Standa, knocked him to the ground, Standa's head struck a rock, you couldn't see it in the grass, he was beating Standa, his blows weren't landing. Standa said: Ouch. He wasn't moving. He heard the grass rustling, they were coming towards them, Pepa was yelling: That can't be, it can't be! They were standing next to them and Pavel said: It can, they're the same size.

Standa was sitting up, holding his head in his hands, Pavel said: He hit his head on a rock, that doesn't count . . . Milan and Pavel looked at each other, Milan flung his arms out, said: He's on the ground, so it counts. Pavel crouched over Standa, lightly touched his cheek and exclaimed: One! And then Pavel shouted: Two! and he stroked Standa's face again. I'd be getting a different kind of thrashing, occurred to Ondra. Three! cried Pavel, slapping Standa with all his strength, Standa fell back into the grass and Pavel said: Pansy. And he said to Ondra: Now you can go to the bunker with us! Alrightey?

Ondra turned around, ran off through the grass, he heard Milan shouting: What's the matter with you! You won! He could also hear Pepa sniggering.

The time they'd beaten him up, he'd also made a run for it. Ran the whole way, scrambling down the hillside, running over the little bridge across the stream, Mum and Dad were in the living room and Dad asked: How was your day? and Ondra said: Fine! Then they had dinner.

That night his legs felt like they were made of ice, the ice was rising up to engulf his body, he fought to stop the cold in its tracks. He fought with his whole body, coagulating the cold inside him into little grains of ice and then pushing them out of his bones with all his might, forcing them out through his skin. He fought all night and won. He knew he'd won when he saw the sun rising, he got a glimpse of it, he didn't even need to move his head, he was lying directly opposite the window.

Hatman shivered. But he wasn't cold, that wasn't it. He was quivering on the inside. Again and again. Maybe it was because of the cold water. Nah, that wasn't it. He could still see the girl's face. He recalled the time when he shot his first young doe. Shouldn't do it, I know, oh well.

People didn't see it that way back then. He was still a boy, all eager. He howled with joy, running towards the deer, jumping over the bushes, everyone was envious. The morning in the forest. The grass was wet. He crouched over the deer, reaching for his knife to make the incision, mark it the way it should be done, and that's when he saw her eyes. She's dead, he realised. Truly. I did that. A chill ran through him. He stroked the dead deer's nape. Wide-eyed, she was staring somewhere into the distance behind him. Upwards, where the clouds were darting about. He stroked her side, her legs were sticking up, they were stiff. Her tender head lay in the grass where it had fallen. The leaves all around her were splattered with blood. She was beautiful. The sun was already creeping up into the sky. Nonetheless he had the shivers, he felt a tingling in his bones. He could have stayed there, kneeling, touching the deer. But the others were approaching. So he cut her throat, got up quickly. She was his first.

Then he learnt that others had felt the same. Other gamekeepers.

Oh well. The memory of that first deer had never come back to him. Until today. It had never occurred to him that a dead deer could be as beautiful as a girl. He'd never dare say that aloud.

There was nothing pretty about the drowned girl's face. She looked like she was still gasping for air. She was bloated, when he grabbed her calf it felt like squeezing a sponge. Her skin burst open, water spurted out. She'd been there for some time. Poor Květa. Commander Nachtigal had ordered him to take the boat out. Nachtigal punted towards her himself. They already knew it was her by the dress.

Shush, Nachtigal hissed at him. He was getting the sleeves of his black uniform soaked. His gun was in the boat. He never went anywhere without it. They pulled the drowned girl into the boat, Hatman leaned into the oars. There were already people on the shore. And others were running over there. Women were hurrying to get there, holding little children in their arms. Boys were skimming stones on the water. Dogs were lapping at the water, fighting. Then they started howling.

He tugged at the oars one last time and raised them. Streams of drops trickled off, the boat thudded softly to a halt in the mud. And then the women were there and they threw a bedspread over Květa. And a blanket too. Nachtigal kept looking askance at him.

The first time he met Nachtigal was at Žima's pub. They'd had a chat, they did do that. They had a drink together. But Nachtigal didn't keep company with the gamekeepers. He went everywhere alone, combing every hill, exploring every footpath. At the beginning there'd been many times when he hadn't come back from the woods for several days. Even though he'd gone to take a stroll for an hour, as he said himself.

Has he got something there? Is he looking for something? Or does he get lost every time? the gamekeepers speculated. But they didn't find Nachtigal amusing, that's for sure. He was getting rid of them. He confiscated their gun licences under the slightest pretence.

You men, you're the people's armed forest guard. You're the legendary Dogheads, for fuck's sake! So how come you look like bandits, fucking hell!

They looked each other up and down. Wellies, soft walking boots for going in the woods, warm padded jackets, standard gear. Hats when it rained. Overalls, whatever anyone had. No one bothered with stuff like green hunting jackets, no one put on airs around here . . . hats with jay feathers . . . the kids would laugh at them. What does he want from them? What's he blathering on about? They were the only ones who had gun licences, that's true. But that was ridiculous. All kinds of people went around the woods shooting. They couldn't prevent that entirely. Well, there were the Lynxes . . . they tried to avoid that subject. They had no recipe for dealing with them. They knew that.

Whose shoulders is he putting whatsits, dogs' bloody heads on, damn it? mumbled Žima.

Comrade . . . said Sixth. He was scared. He'd done time in the slammer. Nachtigal could do what he liked with him.

And what's your vision, comrade?

He strutted in front of them in polished jackboots and a black uniform without insignia. Rifle over his shoulder. He liked to shout. He liked to give speeches. I'd rather go back to chopping wood, Hatman always thought. I can't bear this bullshit. But this time Nachtigal caught them by surprise. Suddenly he sat down by a tree. He leant on the tree trunk with his backside, slid down and slumped into the grass. They were goggle-eyed. Žima let out a snigger.

Me, Nachtigal raised his head. I am my own vision! he ejaculated. And in that vision . . . I'm flying over the steppes like a steel bullet. I'm the casing of the bullet, I'm even the air, in fact. He looked directly at them. A bullet slices through the air, he said heatedly. It swallows the air and screeches, goes whizz . . . He was silent for a moment. He rested his head in the palms of his hands. He was pretending not to take any notice of them, but there were thin slits between his intertwined fingers. He was staring at them. They were gawping at him. They were shaking their heads.

Men, if, one day, you snap out of your vision, you'll be dead, he said quietly. Get it?

No, said a gamekeeper known as Napalm. We don't get it.

Napalm turned around and walked away. The others slowly dawdled after him. Without saying anything. Some of them didn't even look at Nachtigal. Only Sixth was hesitating. He went after them, and then he came back again. He returned to Nachtigal in a heap by the tree. Then he ran to catch up with the others. Is he plastered? he almost yelled out. No one took any notice of him. No one believed him. Sixth was a dunce.

Hatman sat down now. He was at home. He was no longer cold.

She was sitting on the couch, packing. She was looking at him. He glanced back at her, she bowed her head. Grey hair was forcing its way through the shawl on her head. It was still thick, falling down her back. He felt glad whenever he got back home. He knew she'd be there. He knew she'd been packing all day. Putting things in order. She'd taken care of Grandma.

Grandma was lying in the last room in the house. She was by the stove where it was warm, as always. They'd been heating the place anyway. Grandma was all twisted, she'd become paralysed when he was still a boy. She used to like it very much when he brushed her hair. Her hair was almost as long as she was tall, he used to comb it out, it would take an entire evening. Now the comb he used would literally get lost in his hand, it was so small. His daughter also liked to brush her hair, when she was smaller. He never forgot to go say hello to Grandma when he came back from the woods. It didn't matter that she could no longer answer him.

She'd washed Grandma, dressed her, Grandma had been getting this dress ready for as long as Hatman could remember.

She'd lit candles by her side. They'd leave two coins next to her. That's all they could do.

We were waiting for this, Hatman said to himself. But calmly, quietly, not a word had been mentioned to Grandma.

Hold on, he said aloud. He was racking his brains. He almost went to ask. Then he finally got it. Terezie! Terezie Hatman, born Hladká, that's my mum's name, he said. He wouldn't forget it again.

She'd been crying since she'd started packing. They weren't going to take a lot with them. They'd sold it all. They no longer had any animals. They'd sold them a long while back. They never sold anything in the village. He'd exchanged everything for little gold coins. He knew where to get them. The kind you can use anywhere. Always. Oh well, but . . . She kept waiting for the door to open and for her to come back. She expected it every day. Maybe she'll come and she'll need them like never before. And this'll be an empty house. That could happen.

But I have to leave, that's clear. Sixth was the first to vanish. But no one cared about him. Then two gamekeepers from Bělá failed to come back home. Hm, that was strange. Then they found them. Some of the gamekeepers left of their own volition. Nachtigal seized the gun licences of two or three others. He came up with some excuse, something silly. Hatman had thrown his gun licence down on the floor by his feet. He'd already made arrangements to go back to working timber.

But Nachtigal hadn't said anything.

Here it is! said Hatman.

Pick it up.

Hearing that voice had been enough. He stooped down right away. He could feel Nachtigal tensing like a spring. He wiped the licence on his thigh. He shook the mud off it. He passed it to him between two fingers.

Out of my sight!

From that moment on it was clear to him. He couldn't stay.

Žima lasted the longest. He was the eldest. He spent all his time caring for that zoo of his. He kept it well outside the village, away from the boys. The boys would have liked that, to harass those creatures. To poke sticks in their cages. Žima made the cages himself. He was friends with the boys. When they brought him a creature, as he called those little animals, he didn't mind forking out a penny or two.

You're quite the daft bugger, just the cost of the fodder! Hee hee

hee, sniggered the old men who liked to get together at Žima's secluded establishment, their voices cracking.

Get yourself a travelling circus, ha ha ha, they tittered . . .

Oh no, that wouldn't do, they'd die on me if I took them anywhere else, those darlings of mine.

He brought them from the woods. Only Žima knew exactly where to find them. There was no way he could abandon the forest.

Hatman found those creatures abhorrent. He'd never say that aloud, he laughed, pretended that, yeah, it was . . . a real lark, Žima's pastime, the hobby of an old gamekeeper, that's all.

But he didn't like those feathered fledglings with two little beaks. One made a peep, peep noise in its throat . . . stretching its beak for an earthworm. There was an adder with a head the size of a football. A hare that dragged a fifth leg at the back of his body. He looked like he had two little tails. But one was a paw. He couldn't run very fast. The boys had caught him.

Every now and then someone came across a little animal like that before it perished. They called Žima immediately, or brought it to him. Dead animals didn't interest him. Now and then someone found a live one around Blahoš.

Žima looked after the animals, he fed them, nursed them to health and tended to their needs. Gave them names.

One time they were sitting there, almost all the gamekeepers and a few of the old codgers. There was a bottle going round. Leaning on the fence of his menagerie, Žima was in stitches, squinting, laughing at every joke. The cages with the creatures were on the other side of the wooden fence. At that time he had about sixty of them. A few of the cages were empty.

They spotted Nachtigal when he was still a long way off, coming from the woods. Before he reached them they'd gone quiet. Nachtigal said a word in greeting, otherwise ignoring everyone. He just leant on the fence. He often came there to do just that. Look at the animals.

Apparently, right after Žima had been shot, a lorry covered with a black tarpaulin arrived at his cottage in the middle of the night. They took all the animals. That's what people said. No one knew anything for certain. Or didn't want to say. Žima's house was isolated, no cars ever went there. That one vehicle might not have left any tracks. Once the grass had perked up after the rain.

He knew she was still waiting. She knows how to leave a message. In case she comes back. She'll manage it somehow. She even knew who was going to take care of the dead woman. Hatman trusted her completely. They'll cross the border. During the night. They had relatives there, though they hadn't kept in touch. They'd find somebody.

He opened the door slightly, looked out over the stream, towards the church. He could recognise anyone from a distance by the way they walked. But this little figure . . . Aha! Not a man, it's a boy. The Devil sent us that lot, a curse in disguise. They're the cause of all this. His old man, the engineer, is hiding out somewhere and we're being rounded up. The boy started running.

He flew into a rage. He slammed the door shut, turned around in the hall. He was staring right at the little cabinet. Everyone's got one. He listened to the ticking. The contraption in the cabinet was ticking away, quietly, persistently. He grabbed the metal mallet they used to secure the door at night, smashed the monster on the wall, the wood cracked, splintered, he struck it again, machine parts poured out of it onto the floor, he stamped on them, smashed that jumbled mass with the mallet, and again, and once more.

She was looking around. All day she'd been looking around like this, at everything. Her eyes skimmed over the walls, peeking into every nook and cranny. She was going to leave the place clean and tidy. All four rooms. In the back the candles flickered. Four rooms, good. The beds have been made. We would have had a telly soon enough, no problem. But this place is not for living. What if they found him in the woods as well, one of these days?

The tears again. They keep flowing. There's a whole lake inside me. Since she ran away. She always did as she pleased, that little girl of mine. Well, she made her choice. I'm going to stick with mine.

She heard banging. She saw him smashing it up. Let him blow off some steam. In the evening he'll be walking ahead of me. He'll walk quietly and softly. He's the only one who knows how to walk through the woods like that. We'll take the back way. No one needs to see us. It's not anyone's business, where we're going. We lived here with these people all our lives. Our entire lives! Why, it was like a dream. What you remember is all there is. We'll never see them again. We'll live elsewhere. And so what, Mum, Renata would say. And so what? You're right. I mustn't let it get to me so much. The Poles are people too.

The pot with the potatoes was on the bench. He opened the door to the living room, the bed where they slept was made. Someone had closed the windows.

Had Squirt been around, playing, there'd have been stuff flying all over the place. He went to the back. That's where the wardrobes and the linen cupboard were. That's where their parents slept. He peeked under the bed. He crept up to the wardrobe, gave it a whack. If Squirt was hiding somewhere, he'd have pounced on Ondra by now. He wouldn't have gone up to the attic on his own.

The light in the attic was dim. Sweltering heat beat down from the roof.

Pigeons flew in through the dormers, leaving behind a jumble of feathers, claw prints in the dust. Sacks hung from the rafters in the corners. The place reeked. There was pigeon shit everywhere. Mice scurried around in the attic. Enormous spiders lived in the nooks and crannies. The spider webs were full of soot, splinters of wood chips, specks of dust. Ondra told stories about bats living high up in the rafters. About how they suck the blood of cattle. How they sometimes attack toddlers.

They'd often sat there together, when it was raining, waiting for the bats. Holding sticks. If he scared Squirt too much, he'd start blubbing. Then they'd leave. Squirt would grab his hand. He'd be glad Squirt was holding on to him.

The attic was above the woodshed. Planks lay on the beams. This part of the attic was sectioned off by wooden chests. The chests were stacked on top of each other.

The planks are out of bounds, for ever! We'd fall through them and crash down on top of the tools in the woodshed. The scythes and the rakes. Ooh! exclaimed Squirt. Not going there. We'd fall on the axes.

The planks on the other side of the rampart of chests would buckle, creak. They led into darkness, to the wall of the attic. There were no dormers there.

It's like the palace of the Great Shogun. There the creaky floorboards betrayed the slightest movement of even the best-trained ninjas. And that was how the life of the Shogun was protected!

Aha, Squirt said back then.

He opened the door slightly and let out a shriek. Someone had crushed the chests underfoot, hacked them with an axe. Their lids had been ripped off, they bristled with splinters. Old boots, clothes, yellowed newspapers were scattered all over the place. The attic was strewn with glass shards from broken lamps. He slammed the door shut. He ran down the stairs.

There was no one in the living room. He heard the gate creak. That must be Squirt. He opened the door and collided with Jindra. Hiya, he said to Líman. What do you want?

Running, they reached the little bridge, left it behind them, ran around the church and up the slope. They were walking through the woods to the bunker. They were walking towards Blahoš Hill. Impaled on the trees, the sun was unleashing light. It was bobbing up and down on the moss in front of them.

We're hanging out in Dziga's bunker. He leaves us alone.

What?

His hair's completely white. He only just managed to throw that grenade out. Even the mines next to the walls of the bunker exploded. We've got planks in there, you'll see. Dziga lives behind a line of planks, inside Blahoš. There are old mine shafts down there. There's gas everywhere! We don't go in there, mate ...

Aha.

Blind animals live where those gasses are. You strike a match in there and you blow up! We give him food. The food always disappears. Dziga decided that's how it should be. He doesn't come to our meetings. We always call to him, for real.

What? Bollocks ...

When we get there we call three times: Dziga! Dziga! said Jindra quietly, and then he said: Stop! Ondra stopped. Jindra quietly spluttered into his ear: Dziga!

Then he was striding off again. Ondra wanted to stay level with him. Each time Jindra moved up a bit, intent on walking in front. We'll call to him, so he knows it's us. He won't do anything to the lads. He found the bunker here when he was a boy. I don't think he minds us, eh?

How do you know he's got white hair?

He's been seen on occasion. The women have seen him down by the river. He catches fish and eels. Frogs.

Dziga! Ondra shouted loudly.

Jindra put his hand over his mouth immediately and, livid with anger, he hissed: You can't do that, call him like that! Never!

Jindra was silent. He continued to walk ahead. He was furious. Then he said: Try calling like that three times, anywhere, and you'll see!

What will I see?

Go into the woods and do it! Call once and nothing will happen. The second time you'll see, something will move somewhere, a branch will snap. You'll hear someone breathing. In the thickets. Dziga could be hiding anywhere. Stand there and think about him. But you have to be alone. And call a third time. You'll see!

Hm.

Hey, see those hills over there?

They were walking along a path at the foot of Blahoš. They could see trees below them. Everywhere. The leaves were moving in the wind, quivering. The quivering didn't stop even for a moment.

That's Poland over there, mate. My old man used to haul wood over there. It's lousy there.

How's that?

It's not like here.

Aha.

And if you went that way, keeping between the crags the whole time, and you walked and walked, that's where Germany is.

I know, said Ondra. They were walking through thick undergrowth. The bramble bushes were tugging on his T-shirt, he was sweating. The buzzing insects made his hair itch. He was mad at the Límans. The way they ordered him around. But, oh well. So they'll be with the Límans, so what. Until Dad arrives. He wanted to see the bunker.

Walk right behind me, said Jindra. Follow in my footsteps, right?

He reached into the bush in front of him, pulled out a strand of rusty barbed wire. He jumped over it.

Let's say you see a nesting box, for example, yeah? You want to hit it with a stone. You're looking at it. It's all nicely done up, somehow. It's pretty, just a little weatherworn. And there's no bird living in it. There's a mine inside.

No way! said Ondra. Jindra was now walking slowly.

Or you're walking along a path. Some footpath on the other side of the wire fences. There's a haversack lying there, mate. A military one. Got a few holes in it, but nice enough. You going to pick it up?

Ha ha! Not likely!

Exactly, Jindra let out a snigger. One time some guys tied a whimpering little kid up in a cottage. A blubbing orphan, right? Doesn't belong to anyone. They put a toy on the chair, a teddy bear, say, a cuddly toy. They left. An enemy soldier comes to the cottage, mate, sees the blubbering little brat. He unties him, the kid grabs the cuddly toy and bam. Everything blows up.

Bloody hell! They stuck a mine in the cuddly toy's belly?

Yep.

Jindra gouged a piece of turf out of the ground with his knife. The corner of a tarpaulin appeared. The camouflaged tarp smelled of wax. Jindra pulled the tarp off, raised a little trapdoor with his knife and nodded to Ondra.

They climbed down a few metal steps, walked along a passage, it was illuminated by rays of light coming through the slits of the embrasures.

*

The bunkers were in the hillsides, blasted into the cliffs. They served as shelter for couples fooling around or simply provided cover in inclement weather ... the untiring wind had covered their round lookout posts with soil, the turf was vibrant with all the colours of summer, nimble goats nibbled on the slim silver birches forcing their way through the embrasures.

Some of the bunkers weren't even on the special maps of the general staff. Entire levels beneath the ground ... that's where the comrades stored thousands of trench coats, thousands of mess tins, thousands of rolls of gauze and bandages, vast numbers of folding bunk beds and field spades, the riches of the Czech lands.

People said ... some of the bunkers bustle with activity day and night. Minecarts go up and down, harsh yellow electric lights shine everywhere. Pumps suck in air. Machines break down groundwater into vitally important nutrients. The flawless mechanical activity of metal ceaselessly carves out a slice of eternity. Everything functions, everything is ready.

Perhaps the only way a thorough check of the underground bunkers could be performed would be via an air survey, combined with the use of special periscopes to probe the core of the ancient mountains. The comrade in charge would also have to fly over the village, however. He himself, flying through the clouds, would create a tableau vivant ... for a brief second he would alter the nature of the landscape, his shadow would darken the dusty tracks.

An old woman is weeping. Weeping dreadfully, tears are gushing from her eyes, streaming over her mouth, she's almost choking, coughing and rasping, her nose is blocked ... her friends, her companions, are holding her up, one on each side, they're consoling her: Now, now ... come now ... it's Mrs Prošková weeping, a horrible harridan, she looks like a shapeless blob of yellow butter squeezed into a black dress, a knob of butter slashed with wrinkles . . . she's weeping and weeping, holding on to her left elbow is Ferdinandka, a little old woman with piercing eyes, she's got bristly stubble sprouting from under her lips, a beak-like nose, she looks like a dwarf, this clever old crone . . . hanging on to the other side of the giant Prošková is Grandma Škvorová, she says: Don't cry so much, you'll lose your mind . . . Any comrade who by some twitch of fate ended up gliding above this part of the country would need to have a silent flying machine, however, not a helicopter! That would make the old women scatter immediately, they wouldn't allow him to gain an insight into their sorrow . . . but there's no comrade crisscrossing the sky above them, though perhaps someone else entirely is lowering his huge refulgent face through the clouds . . . An old harridan is weeping on a dusty road, tears are raining down from her eyes, two others are hobbling around her, from a height they look like black beetles . . . Don't cry, that's how it had to be! . . . He was so strong, so well-built, I'll not have another like him ever again, never . . . my handsome, my precious, he was my prized possession, all his life . . . I was the one who nursed him . . . such a tragedy, oh! What a calamity . . . Škvorová is also starting, boo hoo, snivel, snort . . . Ferdinandka's eyes are sweeping over the road, that granny never misses anything, someone's walking over there . . . in the bend of the road!

What a tragedy . . . he was such a looker, that young brown bull, no one had one like him, he broke loose, in the evening dogs ran into the village, dragging the young bull's head in their teeth, his sad eyes covered in flies, one of his horns broken off . . . By now she can see who's approaching, girls from the village, Jaruna and Naďa, they're giggling . . . they've stopped, observing the tearful old women from a distance, Ferdinandka is watching the girls with narrowed eyes, she's rubbing Prošková's shoulder, the girls have gone up the slope, so they don't have to say hello to us, oh well, they're already crawling through the grass, crouching down . . .

they spotted us and scurried off, their thighs flashing . . . they want to go around us . . . hm, they go around in shorts nowadays, like boys . . . oh well, little princesses, strutting their stuff . . . yesterday they were still just little girls . . . now they flaunt their breasts ever so proudly, young girls' breasts with tender nipples like blueberries, as yet unchewed . . . by screaming little nippers . . . Oh dear, oh well, Ferdinandka said to herself, they find us old women repulsive, we're just sagging old flesh . . . they don't even say hello! . . . hm . . . always makes me think of that ossuary in Osikov built by the monks a long time ago, there's men, women, children lying in the pits there, their bones all jumbled up . . . What you are now, we used to be . . . What we are now, you will be . . . yep, that's what the sign there says, rendered in arm and leg bones . . . Hah! Ferdinandka sneered at the girls clambering up the slope through the grass, she almost let out a shriek . . . Prošková is still blubbering, whimpering, staggering, she's crushing them with her dreadful weight, dragging them down to the ground . . . Škvorová has also started sobbing, they're holding on to each other tight, those three old friends, Ferdinandka is now also snivelling . . . she's tottering, I can't hold that Prošková up any more, I'm as weak as a sparrow, my, oh my, I'm an old bat, no escaping that . . . I used to run up hillsides too, now I can barely move my legs and soon my time will be up . . . same as with that young bull! . . . so that was it, an entire life, what happened? That's not possible . . . I believe, I believe, I believe, by touch she found the cross-shaped pleated string under her skirt . . . we don't live like weeds, we're here for a while and then for all eternity we're not . . . Prošková's legs were buckling under her by now, she was toppling over, accidentally she elbowed Ferdinandka in the throat, bending her head backwards . . . they're in a life-and-death struggle with an old hag who's about to collapse . . . why, it's just not possible, surely, flashed through Ferdinandka's head, to live just like that, someone must be adding it all up, must know everything . . . we live for such an infinitesimal fragment of time, all eternity rolling by like clouds, we know nothing . . . Prošková sank to the ground, sending dust splashing in all directions like water . . . the sound of boisterous cackling reached them from the hillside where the girls had hidden . . . Laugh while you can . . . you'll see what it's like later, on your own without anyone's help, not being able to talk about it . . . to anyone . . . oh the girls these days! . . . they all want to go to college . . . a girl with a book, heh! . . . heh heh heh . . .

The sunlight didn't reach down there. Whenever someone spoke you could see their breath. It was damp and cold in the bunker. They were all sitting around a petrol lamp.

He knew they were all looking at him. From the moment he'd entered. They were acting as though they'd only just noticed him.

Hiya, Prague Boy, someone said.

I brought him! said Jindra. He came voluntarily, no probs.

Sit down then, said Milan.

He sat down on a box. Next to Valeš. There were more boxes than boys. The empty ammunition boxes were scattered all along the walls. One of the walls was covered with planks. The planked wall was giving off cold. He was getting used to the darkness. Craggy was sitting there, wearing a beanie. Ploughman was there. They're always holed up like this. They don't know that he lived on his own. They haven't seen a tank.

Milan leaned over to him. What did you see in Prague? Tell us.

He spoke quickly: There's shooting in Prague, mate! I saw a tank. The day we left, mate! It was firing at the Patent Office. The machine gun smashed the windows, the walls. There were people inside. They were running down the corridors. Dad and I made a run for it. What were we supposed to do? Everyone was scarpering.

They were listening. He stood up. He could no longer remain sitting down. He wanted to tell them about the station. But they wouldn't get that. They didn't know how huge the bus station was. There were cigarette butts, bits of paper, paper sausage plates rolling around on the asphalt there. Paper cups. There were puddles. At one point he could no longer see the pavement, the asphalt. There were people running everywhere.

People were piling onto the buses, said Ondra. The tank fired from the machine gun, not the big gun barrel. He sat down.

Did you see any dead in Prague? asked Milan.

I did, said Ondra. He recalled the bare foot on the stretcher. I saw some. Two or three. Guys with crosses carried them.

Blimey! someone exclaimed. They're shooting people. It's war, then.

The only thing here is there's no electricity! And the telly in the pub's on the blink.

How many times that's happened, someone blurted out.

Let's go get us some Pinkos, yelled Pavel. He was kicking one of the boxes. Yeah! someone else shouted.

Hey . . . Milan spoke up. Why are they after your old man?

What?

And why were they shooting at the Patent Office? Why did they send a tank straight to the Patent Office?

And why are they coming here?

Why are they already in Osikov? The boys were shouting over each other.

I don't know, said Ondra.

We wanted to go to the pictures, mate, but nothing doing, said Ploughman. The road's jammed. Patrols everywhere. Checks! There are Ruskies in town. Why? What do they want?

Apparently you fill a bottle with petrol, right, said Tonda Líman, and then you chuck it down the tank's hatch, and bob's your uncle, no more tank.

Or . . . you bust open the barrel of petrol on top of the tank with a pickaxe, strike a match and whoosh . . .

Sure, matey, and the Ruskie inside just sits around waiting, you twat, till you barbecue his arse.

I'm off to get me some Pinkos, someone exclaimed.

Me too. Let's smash some Pinkos!

There's busloads of them. You saw them! By the pub.

Pinkos . . . said Ondra. He didn't know what to say. He was worried about Squirt. He didn't know where Mum was. They'd run away with Dad. From the tank. He didn't want to sit around in the bunker with the Límans. They were all shouting, banging the boxes. The noise was confined to the bunker. Now he was crying. They could see him.

Hah, someone said.

He wanted to tell them about how the tank treads screeched, he wanted to say he'd seen the tank ripping cobblestones up from the pavement. How the bullets scraped against the walls, smashed into the windows.

The tank is enormous, he said.

Look, said Milan. We can hide you and your old man.

And Squirt too?

Of course.

All right then.

The test is at midnight, you know that.

I know, nodded Ondra. He wasn't crying any more. He'd only cried for a moment. No one cared.

You thought you could be here on your own with your brother, said Pavel. But you can't.

Boo, said Pepa. The test is dreeadfuul!

It's a full moon, mate, and the dead are having a ball, someone said.

He chuckled. He knew that making a person scared was part of the test.

It's a different kind of test than the kind you get at a fucking Pioneer Camp, mate. It can make you . . . make you lose your marbles.

Or get lost, fall in the water.

You see a light, you follow it. But the light's coming from the mud! Watch out!

The funeral bier!

You've reached the bier. That's horrifying. The black door! What if it slammed shut? You'd go nuts!

But then the bell tolls, and it's over. You're going home, pal. And you're not a wuss. You've passed the test.

Yeah, that's it!

Everyone's done it.

Standa fell asleep, mate! Eh, Standa?

I'm not afraid of the dead, said Standa. I don't give a rat's arse about them.

Blimey, said Jindra . . . and what about you? Can you handle it?

Milan swung his arm, releasing the blade, the dagger stuck into one of the boxes.

Me, I was afraid, said Milan. Honest. You're looking for a dagger. This one! You have to find it, it's on the grave. There's an old graveyard beyond the cemetery. You have to go all the way to the wall. To the river. And we're not going to tell you about the main thing, the terrible thing, yet.

The petrol lamp was giving off smoke. In the bunker it didn't matter if it was night or day. Milan yanked the knife out. He brushed the splinters off the box with his finger. Someone exhaled: Yeah!

And what about me! exclaimed Ploughman and everyone turned towards him. I was also terrified . . . that I'd get eaten by an earthworm! Bloody test! It's war now! Are we little runts, or what?

Earthworm, earthworm, the boys called. They were cackling.

Hardly scary, all this, Ondra said to himself. I'm not going to be afraid. But Squirt! He wouldn't pass the test! He wouldn't!

No one from our lot, from the bridge, has been a member of the Pinkos, said Pavel. But your brother was, Ploughman.

What are you bullshitting on about? Our old man was in the slammer. Under the Germans, and the Commies. What would I be doing with the Pinkos? said Ploughman. And Granddad was also locked up. In Russia. That's bollocks, what you just said.

My granddad was also locked up, said someone.

But not in Russia, said Ploughman. So keep your trap shut.

His old man did time with my old man, said Valeš. Everyone knows that. He can't help what his brother did, obviously.

But your old man was behind bars for poaching, you twat! cried Tonda Líman.

Not for poaching, he was a resistance fighter, you cunt!

Valeš punched Tonda, knocking him off the box. He kicked his own box to the side, charged at Tonda. The boys moved out of the way. Tonda's legs were flailing. Valeš was already on top of him, pummelling him.

Ondra stood up. Pavel winked at him. Let them warm up. It's always good, when you're about to go get some Pinkos.

Then Milan shouted out: We can't fight here! Let's go outside.

Yeah, let's go outside! someone shouted. They disappeared down the passage, one by one. He followed. Jindra grabbed his hand. Wait, all right? I'm supposed to tidy up. I was the one who brought you.

Tonda went last. He was tripping over boxes. His nose was bleeding, there was blood all over his shirt. He tried to stop it, but only succeeded in smearing it all over his face with his fingers.

They straightened up the boxes. Lined them up by the wall.

Look, said Jindra, pushing one of the planks to the side. He raised the oil lamp that he was holding in his hand. Bits of broken rock, torn from the cliff, adhered to the planks. Rocks shattered by an explosion were lying around in there. The hole widened further in. There was nothing in there. They saw white fog. It was moving. It was hovering, churning. At the edges the mist was transparent, the fissures and grooves in the dark cliff looked like the bite marks of giant fangs. The fog was moving, it was around their ankles, then in front of their faces as well, it was flowing towards them from the mountain.

Hey, now you wouldn't, you know . . .

What . . .

You wouldn't call for him to come now, eh.

That I wouldn't, exhaled Ondra.

I know, said Jindra. He pushed the plank back in place.

Somehow they managed to get the old woman back to her place. Hardly had Ferdinandka got home herself and sat down, than she nodded off . . . She's looking directly into the interior of the mountain, right down to its bottom, where even the rocks look ancient, and there she sees three old women. They're cooking. Boiling coins. And she stares, what are they throwing into the cauldron? They've got long, thin arms, invisible arms, and they need ones exactly like that because they use them to rifle through graves. Not only around here! All over the place, in all graves, all cemeteries, little graveyards, they even use those long, dry arms to fish around in hollows in the forest, they reach down into rivers, they frisk every dead person, people who died alone somewhere and no one found them, died of heat exhaustion, maybe, some wretched old person, or a soldier who'd been shot dead, the long-armed women don't care, they pull belts off the dead, they take women's earrings, they even pull metal from their teeth, they tear off their buttons, they don't even hesitate to take their glasses. Straight away they toss it all in the cauldron. They melt the metal over a fire inside the mountain and after a few centuries have passed they scoop out little coins with an iron ladle. And they're made of gold! How do they do it? No one knows. Those coins, those tiny gold coins can be sewn up in a fur coat, in a hat, you can swallow them. They're not heavy. You can pay with them anytime and anywhere. You can buy bread with them, a life, a pistol, whatever you fancy, you can cross any border as though you were invisible. And now the old women are waving to her! They can see Ferdinandka. They know she's snooping on them, but they're not one little bit upset. Crikey, why, that's my grandmother, for goodness' sake, marvels Ferdinandka. I haven't seen her in a lifetime, and the other one, that's Škvorka, my neighbour of course . . . and the third one, of course! And they're waving at me, should I go there . . . join them? They probably need help. So should I go now? She woke up.

Ugh! No wonder I'm so awfully tired all the time, Ferdinandka scolded herself. With dreams like that. But it was nice! My mind's not what it used to be, but there's nothing wrong with my dreams . . . no doubting that.

They were standing up, squinting. He was looking at the grass beneath his legs. Had he been looking directly into the sun, he'd be seeing coloured spots before his eyes. The air was quivering with heat.

They had dawdled behind the others. Through the forest, up the slope. There was wire fencing everywhere there too. Some of it wasn't visible in the thickets and bushes. Jindra had clambered first.

They walked out of the wood and saw the lads.

They were lying down on the railway embankment. Below them, below the little bridge, below the railway line, an asphalt road led out of the village.

That's where they'll go. On the defence exercise. We'll hide behind the track and when they come past, we'll bombard them with a shower of missiles.

A shower of missiles?

Yeah, nodded Jindra. He blushed a little.

Captain Fredagard's scouts have aimed their muskets, said Ondra.

Fire when you see the whites of their eyes! cried Jindra. *The Mars Monolith*! You know it?

Sure. Hey, you haven't got the fourth issue, have you?

Yeah! Nemura escapes from the monsters' clutches to another universe. I'll bring it tomorrow.

Brill!

We've got to go. If they saw us from the road, we'd be up shit creek.

They walked through the grass and then they were by the railway track. It was strewn with grit.

One of the boys lying at the back was waving at them. Motioning for them to also lie down.

The boys were lying everywhere on the crushed rock. There were lots of white stones between the sleepers, between the rails. There was heat coming off the grit.

I really don't get how anyone can still be a Pioneer, now that the Ruskies have stormed in, said Pavel, shaking his head.

The Pioneers, said Ondra, have air rifles.

Pah, said Tonda, scowling. He was lying not far from Ondra. This is better. He pulled a catapult out of his pocket. He opened the palm of his hand. He had a steel nut in it. He'd wiped the blood off his face by then.

Now he was chortling. He put the nut on the track. He was weighing the catapult in his hand. I've got plastic wire coiled around the handle, mate, that's the best.

I've got plastic wire on mine too, said Jindra.

Green wire's bad, though. You end up losing your catapult in the woods, said Pepa. In the leaves.

I'll never lose my catapult.

The best thing is just to strip the bark off the wood, easy.

Nah, if you coil plastic wire round it, it doesn't matter if you sweat. Steel nuts are the best ammunition, though.

That's a fact, said Valeš. Steel nuts are good. Rocks are good too, though. There was a pile of stones in front of Valeš on the embankment. He kept sifting through the grit on the track, trying out different stones.

Once you learn how to shoot steel nuts, they always fly the same way, said Tonda. Then you always hit your target.

But if you run out of nuts, you're done for, said Valeš. Rocks are everywhere.

True that, someone said. Rocks are everywhere.

Tonda turned onto his back, grimaced at the sun, and said to Ondra: Show us yours.

What?

Yours. Let's see it!

What?

Show us your catapult.

Don't have one.

What? Oi, he hasn't got a catapult! You don't have them, matey? In Prague? Not even bought ones, ha ha.

Ha ha, someone laughed. Buy my catapult, matey! Wouldn't sell it for a thousand.

Wouldn't sell mine for a million.

Everyone around the track was now laughing and sniggering.

Ha! I would for a million, I'd make myself a new one. And I'd buy a machine gun, ha ha.

So he hasn't got a catapult, so what, said Milan. He's new. He'll get everything sorted. Quit yelling!

Standa here gets steel nuts from his old man, said Jindra quietly. His old man works for the railways. Nuts really are good.

I know, nodded Ondra.

His old man gives them to him. You know why?

No.

'Cos if he didn't, we'd nick them off the tracks.

Aha.

His old man steals anyway. Chucks lumps of coal off the locomotive and later they pick them up.

Hey, they're coming… quiet… the Pinkos are coming… The boys fell silent, Ondra hid his head, then he carefully glanced at the road, everyone was watching, some of the boys had made two piles of stones, one to hide their heads behind, the other, smaller, one for ammunition.

They were silent. The sun was beating down on Ondra's back and neck, if he turned around he'd see it above the forest now, he felt the heat coming off the grit, off the tracks, he was sniffing the wood of the sleepers, watching the red ants swarming between the splinters in the sleepers, he lifted his head, saw the Pioneers marching along the road towards the bridge, they were still far off, he could see their light blue shirts, a bloke wearing a peaked cap was walking in front of Pioneers marching two abreast, he was also wearing shorts and a light blue shirt, a knapsack was bouncing by his side, all Pioneers carry haversacks and canteens, said

Ondra to himself . . . Jindra very quietly rolled down the embankment almost down to Ondra's feet, and he was giggling, choking with laughter, he turned round to Ondra, hissing through his teeth: Bloody hell, that's Teachy! Bohadlo's leading them, mate . . . a diehard Bolshie, he's going to get one right on the forehead from me, mate, you can bet on that, fucking wanker . . . Jindra emptied his pocket, making a little pile of steel nuts, he had about six or seven of them, he put one in the catapult and whispered to Ondra: I polish them up, see, when I get them they're rusty, but I rub the rust off . . . they're still too far away.

Bohadlo comes to see my nan, said Standa next to them. So is he a Bolshie? Or not?

He goes to see your nan, yeah? said Jindra. That's weird. What's he want?

I'm not allowed to say, said Standa.

I hate that guy with a vengeance, whispered Jindra. So I'm enjoying myself right now.

Fuck! someone whispered. The police are with them.

Marching in orderly fashion, the front ranks of the Pioneers had by now almost reached the little bridge where the road began to descend. Green uniforms emerged behind the Pioneers.

Let's call it off, someone said.

They're on joint exercises, dickheads, said Jindra.

Let's get off the tracks, said someone. Come on!

Just one shot, Ondra heard someone say. It was Pavel, whispering.

No, forget it, Ondra heard Milan say, let's get down from here and into the woods.

Just one, mate, said Pavel.

Ondra looked around, some of the lads were crawling off the embankment. Two or three were already making their way quickly towards the woods, crouching down, they weren't visible from the road on the other side of the tracks.

The policemen outnumbered the Pioneers. And they weren't marching in formation.

Ondra wanted to slide down from the railway line, Jindra jumped up onto the tracks, catapult in hand, the rubber band already drawn back, he raised his elbow and sent the steel nut flying, then Pavel was standing on the tracks, taking a shot, then Ondra heard the swish of rubber, Pavel crouched down to his knees, he stood up again immediately, rubber band already drawn back with his left hand, and when Jindra let fly, Pavel was kneeling and putting another stone or steel nut into the pocket of his catapult, and when he jumped up, Jindra was crouching down and pulling back the rubber band of his catapult, and Tonda and some of the other boys were also taking shots and because they dropped down quickly right after letting go of the rubber band and moved to a slightly different position, it must have looked like there were people all over the embankment.

Ondra heard shouts, he heard the Pioneers yelling, he raised his head, saw Pioneers leaping into the ditch by the road, Pioneers huddled together with policemen, he heard a bang and something whizzed over his head, he slid off the embankment, running towards the woods, Standa was running behind him, they were all running to the woods now and hardly had Ondra slipped from view among the first few trees, leaning back on one of them, than Ploughman was standing next to him, and someone else as well, they were both breathing heavily, Ploughman was pointing towards the embankment behind Ondra's back: They're coming after us, he shouted, immediately turning round and careering down the hillside, leaping between the fern bushes . . . the person next to Ondra mumbled: That backfired, that did, and then he too was disappearing in the woods . . . the embankment was swarming with green uniforms . . . he ran, he saw the white of the other lads' T-shirts and shirts flashing ahead of him. I'll hide, he thought.

The forest was gloomy. He felt a sharp stabbing pain in his side. He sat down.

Standa flopped down next to him in the grass.

I could easily keep running, said Ondra. But I don't feel like it any more.

Sure, said Standa. I almost didn't catch up with you.

You reckon they'll come all the way up here?

They won't. They're from the district. Odd that, them shooting at us. That's not done. That was a fuck-up, that was.

Shall we go to the bunker? said Ondra.

It's damp. Standa wrinkled his nose. I guess there's a rainstorm on the way. You want to go to the bunker?

Ondra pictured the crush of boys, the reek of the petrol lamp, he remembered the planks and said: Not one bit. He raised his head and saw a basket. The basket was swinging from a tree.

Look! That's the kind they bring us food in.

Oh yeah. Those ones are for food.

There were several baskets on the tree. There were others on the tree next to it.

The women put them up there.

Yeah? Why?

So that hungry people don't come ferreting around the village. It's better to put something out for them.

Ferreting around?

It's not for gypsies or anything, that's the first thing you think of! It's for all kinds of people. The ones hiding out, maybe, I dunno. It's what they do around here. Let's go down, come on.

They were walking down the hill through the forest. Ondra was taking deep breaths of the damp air after a day when the stifling heat had been pounding in his head.

It was drizzling, there was a tiny stream flowing down the slope, they were walking slowly. Standa didn't care who walked first and fastest. They heard thunder.

Thunder rolled over the sky, suddenly there was lightning everywhere above them, the lightning was splitting the sky, breaking it asunder, fiery lines lacerated the sky, it tilted like an enormous plate, a bolt of lightning came snaking out of it, dazzling them, slicing a pine tree in half, a chunk of the tree ripped out by the lightning strike hurtled through the air above them, sinking into the thickets by the footpath, its end sticking out. The tree scintillated with quivering radiance, little sparkling lights slithered around the trunk like tiny purple snakes.

They ran. There was muddy water everywhere, it was splashing over the path, dragging with it stones, branches. The little streams on the slope became torrents. The water was knocking them off their feet, they jump-ed and climbed over upturned trees. They staggered about in the tor-rential rain, if the water had not been up to their ankles, and then their knees, they'd have been laughing. They waded through the ditch onto the asphalt road.

They ran down the road, soon they were among the first houses on the tree-lined avenue. Ondra stopped, he wanted to catch his breath, he heard the clap of thunder, right in front of them a fiery skewer tore apart a lime tree, he heard the screech of wood splintering. Branches swished past their faces.

Suddenly it stopped raining. They walked slowly. The road was covered in mud and puddles.

Ondra sat down. He slumped down on a branch. They were still some distance from the church. He sat there, his hands clasped around his ears. Standa was saying something, he couldn't hear him, he was shaking his head. It's over, he said.

It's the silence that deafened you. Let's go and dry off at my grandma's.

I should go and see my little brother. He's afraid of storms.

You're supposed to be with me. I'm supposed to be your handler and tell you scary stories. But it's no fun for me. You'll go to the graveyard, find the dagger, take the dagger to the mortuary, and that'll be that. The Límans came up with it when they were little, who's afraid to go to a graveyard nowadays? Or Kunert's place?

Shitty test of courage. Ondra shook his head again and stood up.

Yep. You'll find it unbearable with the Límans if you don't pass the test.

Hm.

They were walking through the village, the houses were dark, only here and there candles flickered in the windows. They were treading through puddles. It was cold for August.

I'll lend you my sweater, said Standa. Hey look, I'm freezing my tits off too. He showed Ondra his arm, he had goose bumps.

Ha ha! he suddenly shrieked with laughter so hard it gave Ondra a jolt.

They toil away, mate, for a bit of cauliflower. And look!

The gardens and vegetable patches on the little plots between the houses looked like piles of mud. The tempest had also levelled the trees lining the road. Grains of sand twinkled in the holes left by the upturned trees.

They were walking past the pub. There was light in there.

He stopped. He was thinking about Zuza. Sometimes thinking about her made him dizzy. Everything that was happening was rolling around in his head. Beneath everything that was going on, he saw her face.

I'm not going in there, that's for sure, said Standa.

Hey! I've got a crown coin. I'll buy a Kofola and bring it out, yeah?

Bollocks. There's plenty of Kofola at my nan's.

Now you're bullshitting.

Light, voices reached them through the window. The smell of water and mud hung in the air. No insects were flying after the rain. Not even flies.

She'll be wearing more than just her sandals on her feet now. She'd be cold. He'll go in, say hello to the men as usual, then he'll say to her: One Kofola. And he'll say: Would you like some? Zuza will take a sip from his glass and he'll whisper to her: Tomorrow. Zuza will just nod because her daddy will be there. They'll meet up tomorrow.

He stretched up on his toes, peeked in through the window, he heard singing, grabbed on to the window frame, pulled himself closer, standing on the tips of his toes he could see shadows flitting about inside the pub, the petrol lamps did that, if he didn't have to hold on, he'd have burst out laughing, what were they up to? At first he thought the men were just reeling about drunk, or that they were brawling, but they weren't, Ondra spluttered . . . he saw the constable dancing with a tall thin bloke, he was wearing a beanie on his head, a scarf around his neck . . . they were swinging their arms and legs, dancing . . . slowly, veeery slooowly, and he also heard music . . . that was old man Berka playing the violin and someone else next to him was tapping the floor with a stick in a regular rhythm, there were tin cans tied to the stick, bouncing around and banging together . . . Ondra also heard an accordion, he tilted his head

back, he could see drawings on the walls, he'd never noticed them before
. . . now they were showing through the plaster, there was a bear and also
a billy goat, drawn with black charcoal . . . and a pig . . . he chuckled, he
heard Standa behind him: What can you see? Hah! said Ondra, his head
started spinning, now he could see clearly through the gloom and smoke
in the pub, sharply . . . suddenly he saw all those things and people and
he could see into them . . . the dancers made the animals on the walls
move with their shadows, they were opening their mouths, stomping to
the rhythm, singing, he heard: On the devils' wedding day, it was very hot
indeed, they danced around so much, their noses started to bleed . . . he
wanted to say to Standa: They're singing, matey, like little brats at nursery
school, but he only thought it, his head was spinning: The oldest of them,
Lucifer, jumped around like a goat, until he hurt his big toe, and cried boo
hoo, oh woe . . . the figures of the dancers faded out in the corners, there
wasn't much light there . . . he couldn't hold on any longer, he fell on his
back into a puddle, Standa said: What's your problem? He was trying to
get up, Standa lifted him.

We're not going in there, said Ondra.

Yeah we are, why not? I'm allowed, said Standa.

I'm not sure we should! said Ondra.

But I am, I'm allowed, said Standa. I'm no gypo! he said and he was
off like a shot up the stairs, through the door, down the hall, Ondra
followed, Standa opened the door to the bar, they heard the din of the
pub, suddenly, all at once.

Petrol lamps stood on the tables, they had a candle at the back by the
wall, there were men sitting all around the tables, beers parked in front
of them, the constable was sitting at the middle table, they were talking
over each other, old man Berka was playing cards with the other old
men, cards were slapping down on the table . . . Ondra was squinting, he

couldn't make out the shadows on the walls and the ceiling, his eyes were full of smoke from the pipes, the cigarettes. Oh yeah, she's not here in the evenings, he said to himself, still squinting. Stop gawping, boy, and shut the door! someone shouted, Ondra reached for the door handle . . . he shuffled over to Standa by the counter, it was only a few steps from the door. Kofola, please, he said.

Zuza's dad wasn't paying any attention to them. He was wearing a white apron. He was pouring out spirits from a bottle into little shot glasses. Putting the glasses on a tray.

Kofola cola, said Ondra. He put his crown piece on the counter.

But there's two of you, said Zuza's dad. Or aren't there? he said to Ondra.

Yeah, said Ondra.

So just the one then, eh? said Zuza's dad. He said it loudly. He put the glass in front of Ondra.

The men had gradually gone quiet, now they were all watching them. Ondra didn't know what to say, so he lifted the glass and took a sip.

So the Kofola's for you, laddie, right? said Zuza's dad. So what's the other one doing here, then? Your black shadow, is he?

He heard sniggering coming from the tables, so he took another sip, then he heard: Come on, now, Karel, steady on! Let's have some harmony at least today. The constable pushed back his chair with his backside, then he was standing next to them, saying: A small shot for each of the lads, it's a momentous day today! Oh, give them a large one, then! Ondra didn't even look round, he could hear talking again, the men were laughing merrily, clinking their glasses together.

My dear lads, the constable had one arm around Ondra and the other around Standa, he was leaning on them, pressing them into the counter, we're all Czechs, aren't we? Oi! the constable shouted. My neck was on the line today. He let go of the boys, slapped one of the men on the shoulder, they were jostling all around them now, taking shots from the tray. My life, he said.

And how many of them were there, then? said one of the men. The constable was speaking loudly, so that the whole pub could hear: No one knows how many there were in the woods. There were only a few lurking on the tracks. I'm telling you, they're good at that sort of thing. That's how they clobbered the Germans. Assault squads. They're dab hands at that, you've got to give them that. The Constable plopped down on a chair. He shouted: Victory! He lifted his fist, stuck two fingers out in a V, waved his arm from side to side. A few of the men also shouted Victory!

Zuza's dad pushed two shot glasses towards Ondra and Standa.

They upended the drinks like the men at the table.

The door banged, Polka entered the pub, he was leading his bike, he propped it up against the wall, the bell gave a ping, in no time he was standing next to Ondra, threatening with his finger, shouting: You've been plying him with alcohol ... the constable stood up again, his backside had swelled up in the chair, the chair fell off his green-uniformed buttocks, the constable hugged Polka, saying: Man, my life was on the line ... then the constable sat down again: What will become of me ... The men were silent, only Polka said: What do you mean, like ... Well, the comrades from the district have gone again and I'm here alone with an old rifle and the woods full of Ruskies ... Take your uniform off, Smoky ... The guys from the district won't give a flying fuck about you, Coughy Boy! ... You'll be the first to hang when they come, you tough old bull! ... I never shopped anyone, you know that, right? ... You and Nachtigal had better dig yourselves an underground shelter, you twats ... Better stay under the turf ... Ha ha ...

And Polka leant towards Ondra, hissing in his ear: This is how you guard your brother? Down the pub? He gave him a thump, slapping his back, but he was laughing . . . Well, don't worry, your little brother, the little gentleman, has a bunch of friends over there now, a whole company of girls, ha ha ha . . . Zuza's over at our place! I came to tell you. Karel! called Polka towards the counter, the lassies were afraid of the storm so they took cover in the Lipka household! Polka shouted . . . that Vendula of yours and your Jolana too, cheers! cried Polka . . . They were squealing like little does and scarpering away from the lightning, but you know, they're safe with us, Polka was saying . . . but by then no one probably heard him because the constable was banging his fist on the table, screaming: We destroyed a Russian assault squad, they were firing shrapnel at us over by the railway track . . . Apparently someone was hurt pretty bad, said Polka quietly, he was standing behind Ondra . . . Yep, Bohadlo, they shot half his skull off, Teachy's been taken to the district hospital, said someone at one of the tables . . . Ondra winked at Standa, Jindra's probably going to be overjoyed, he thought . . . then the constable was standing in front of them, he glanced at Ondra, said: You! Where's your dad?

Ondra inhaled and . . . beyond the windows a bolt of lightning slid out of the sky, and another and another . . . they all froze in the yellow refulgence, sitting at the tables, standing by the counter with their mouths open . . . they could easily have been singing another song, he couldn't hear a thing as the thunder roared . . . and under the plaster he saw the drawings, he saw the charcoal drawings in the clear light of the lightning, they'd slapped rough, white plaster on them, the drawings of the animals shone through like when blood and puss soak through a bandage . . . but it was only for a brief moment . . . there was so much smoke in there, the place was so full of fumes, he couldn't see a thing . . . and torrential rain was rapping on the window panes . . . they were all conversing again, the chairs were creaking, the constable was pushing his belly up against him, shouting, and now Ondra heard him: Another round for everyone! I almost got killed today, men! I'm going to have one last one and I'm off. I swear!

And Polka says: You've got that test today, well holy crap, boy, it just struck next to the church.

How do you know that? said Ondra.

Why, we all heard it, the thunderbolts. Didn't you?

But how do you know about the test? Ondra stretched over to him, standing on tiptoe, Polka stooped down: Lots of people know that you boys have your little gangs. You're going to Kunert's grave, hm. That Kunert is considered a sort of bogeyman around these parts. By old women and little girls, you understand, men like you and me aren't afraid. He's, pardon me, he was a Kraut who'd been in the SS, he hid out here in empty houses. He was the last one here. In the end he lost his mind and abducted people and cut them up into quarters in the empty cottages and ate them, you know? bellowed Polka.

He had to shout. The general conversation was in full flow again.

Oh yes, Kunert. Polka made his eyes pop out comically and stuck out his tongue. Boooo! Ondra recoiled.

Ha ha, chuckled Polka. He put his hand on the back of Ondra's neck and pulled him closer.

Listen! Apparently he was in Siberia for years and in the concentration camp over there he got used to eating human flesh. They didn't give them a lot of food over there. But son, I'd say he was just one of them run-of-the-mill, whatchamacallit, perverts, you know.

Hm, said Ondra. Standa was pulling his elbow.

But what is bad is the thing with the eyelids, boy, said Polka. And he blinked. He was now blinking so much it occurred to Ondra that maybe something had fallen in his eye.

He got out of the gulag. Fled home through the woods. As far as here. But there weren't any Germans left here, none at all. We drove those bastards out in double-time with no remorse, the way it should be done. So he must've been a little shocked, see? Empty buildings everywhere, yeah. He'd been taken prisoner near Stalingrad. He was in the tank regiment. Well, and that's where his eyelids got frostbitten, they had to cut them off. Soviet surgeons, chortled Polka. As for Kunert's victims up in the attic, it was all a bit . . . he had them up there day and night. The victims never knew when he was asleep. Seeing as he's got no eyelids, he was always staring at them. So they couldn't even get any rest. Nasty, don't you think?

Yeah, said Ondra. Hm, he said. Standa was also saying something. But he couldn't hear him.

Polka was sputtering in Ondra's ear. Everyone knew about Kunert around here, about how he considers human meat a delicacy, so what were they supposed to do? Wait until they sent investigators from the district authority? Sure! So back then they murdered him and even dug him a grave behind the church, by then Frantla was a whatsit, a vicar, so they even gave him a funeral. But they say, well, the old women say, that Kunert wasn't happy about it. Apparently he always guards his grave when it's a full moon. Imagine! What a load of bollocks, eh?

Standa kept tugging on Ondra's T-shirt and now he was prodding him as well.

And apparently if he catches anyone there on a full moon, then he does exactly what he used to do when he was young. I mean alive. Locks a fellow up in the attic, flays him and eats him. Thanks, said Polka. Someone had stuck a shot in his hand.

Of course Kunert doesn't dawdle around there every full moon, but a few times a year, maybe once, maybe five times. Seven? No one subjects that to scrutiny, believe me, boy. That's the test. Will he come, won't he?

You never know. I'd lend you my torch, lad, but the batteries are dead. But it's a full moon, so you'll have plenty of light to see by.

Polka turned away from Ondra, the men were standing around them now. Polka stood on tiptoe, pushing the beer mugs that the men were forcing on him aside with one hand, reaching into his pocket with the other, he pulled out a little paper envelope, kneaded it in his hand, exclaimed: Forget drinking, my dearest gentlemen, hypnotics, hypnotics, those are my narcotics . . . he popped the pill in his mouth and made such a horrible grimace . . . they all spluttered with laughter . . . then he grabbed someone's beer mug, downed it in one . . . Ondra also had a shot glass in his hand, he didn't know who'd given to him, he drank.

He started coughing. Standa whacked his back, grabbed his arm and was dragging him out of the throng. Towards the door. Past Polka and the others. He wanted to say: Goodbye! as one should. But he could only see their backs, so he went.

They walked out of the pub. Assault unit! The lads are going to be bug-eyed, Standa laughed.

Ondra wasn't laughing.

Look, I didn't want to tell you all that, it's a load of twaddle. I don't believe in Kunert. Come on, he thumped Ondra on the shoulder. Kicks like a mule, eh?

What, said Ondra.

That's what you say when you drink spirits. Kicks like a mule! And Standa reeled, pretending he was plastered.

Kicks like a mule! said Ondra and also reeled, but he stepped into a puddle.

Let me lend you my sweater. For the test. We don't have time to go to my nan's.

All right.

The dogs aren't barking. They've crawled into their kennels.

Standa had his sweater around his waist. He untied it. He sniffed it.

It didn't get too wet.

Look, Ondra said, his teeth chattering, when he'd taken his T-shirt off. Look, I really like this T-shirt. It was his favourite one. The one with Numa, the lion. He pulled the sweater over his head.

I like it too, said Standa. He put on Numa.

They were walking down the avenue again, the one lined with trees. They heard the rumble of water coming from the bridge. They walked past the few buildings. There was no light in any of the houses now.

Hey, said Ondra. I think it's odd, what you said on the tracks. Bohadlo is going out with your nan? But he's young! He's a teacher!

He's not going out with her! Don't be daft! He goes to see her! For advice and that.

How come?

Look, I'm not living with my dad right now. I'm staying at my grandma's.

Yeah?

But we're not dirty tinkers or anything. The gypsies live on the other side of the river. They eat dogs. They're unclean gypos! I hate them, cried Standa, kicking a stone.

Oh yeah, said Ondra. They steal.

You bet, exclaimed Standa. If you come across one, two. Even three, mate! They do a runner. But if there's more of them . . .

I know, said Ondra.

You don't know anything! cried Standa. I could just tell you to fuck off, you twat. I'm supposed to take you to do the test, so that's what I'm going to do, I have to do that. I wasn't the one who told you all that crap about Kunert!

You're plastered, said Ondra. And I'm sloshed too, aha, so this is what it's like!

He was looking directly ahead. He felt warm in the sweater. His eyes were sources of light. They were hollowing out luminous tunnels in the darkness. He liked it. He wanted to tell Standa something. The night is huge! he wanted to say. We're in it. It's good. This is what he felt.

They were climbing over branches hacked off by the lightning. A thunderbolt had ripped a sizeable chunk out of the lime tree. Ondra staggered, almost fell.

Look, I'm tottering! he cried.

Hm. Even the biggest Bolshies come to see my nan, don't think they don't. Even the women who go to church. They're stupid.

Yeah? said Ondra. He remembered the aeroplanes he'd seen in Prague, he spread his arms, going: Vroom. He almost keeled over again, so he skipped forward, extending his runway.

They think she talks to the dead and that kind of bollocks. Standa stepped into a puddle. Stamped his foot in it on purpose.

With the dead, yeah? But that's not possible. Ondra still had his arms outstretched like wings, he wanted to make the sound of the motor with his mouth like this: Vroom, but his teeth were chattering. He put his hands in his pockets.

Grandma just takes them for a ride, that's all!

Even Bohadlo? The teacher! Blimey.

Standa nodded. His uncle died. And no one knows where he put his money. He started coming to see my nan. Not the dead guy. Bohadlo! And Nan tells him: This is a difficult case, this. Your uncle is being rather obstinate. But I'll give it a go. And Nan does a séance. And then another séance. And Bohadlo's forking out. She had magazines about séances sent from Prague, Nan, and I read them to her! I go to school. I'm normal. But my nan, the old pikey, she can't read. Not a word, honest.

She can't, eh?

I've got money. From Nan. On me like, all the time. Could have bought us Kofolas, anything. Didn't feel like it.

Aha!

Nan tells everyone: You want to talk to a dead person, all right! But I need something of worth. And something that belonged to the deceased. Nan knew all the dead people here personally, she's old. She even knew the people that knew them. It's easy after that. People cough up.

They give her money, yeah? Really, yeah?

People are real careful about their readies. But so is Nan. Dosh might not have any value any more, now that the Ruskies are here. I should have bought those Kofolas. Or more snifters! I should have bought chewing gum.

You'll buy them tomorrow! Ondra thumped his shoulder.

Standa stopped. Even girls come to see her! All kinds of women, you'd be surprised.

What?

I saw one of them naked. Yesterday. If I said something to Nan, maybe I could see them all naked.

Yeah?

But I don't want to! I don't give a fuck about them, get it?

Aha!

Fucking prissy cow like that in her neatly pressed skirt, wouldn't waste her time talking to a normal person, they mean nothing to her, and she cries her eyes out when she comes to see Nan.

And why?

You stupid or what? Nan examines them. But ones like her don't have anything, Standa waved his hand dismissively.

No?

Of course not! Nan wants things from them, necklaces, rings, stuff like that. Various things. Have you got a good carpet? says Nan. Let's see, Standa knitted his eyebrows, hunched his back and made like he was kneading a piece of fabric in his hand. Ondra chuckled. Standa was hunching his back like some old gypsy beldame.

Alrightey, said Standa, we'll see what we can do! And he made like he was throwing the carpet on the floor. She takes different things. Whatever people bring. Things people left behind. Things from the houses abandoned by the Germans. Glass figurines, for example. There's one of a stag, one of its antlers has been chipped off, but Nan doesn't mind. People bring old things and laugh at the old woman. But they're total dimwits. Dad sells lots of things for serious dosh.

Really?

Yeah. Dad is on the locomotive all the time, gets to see the world. Yeah, said Standa, squinting with one eye, pretending to lift a beer mug, take a swig, smacking his lips and wiping his mouth. I get to see the world, kiddies, says Dad. There's shops in Prague where they only buy old things. Pictures, for example. A little painting! With a watermill, a tree of some kind and some countess on it. Six thou, kiddies! Standa whistled.

You're kidding!

Am not. There's shops like that in Prague, don't you know that?

Of course I do. I know them.

There you go, then. I've got six crowns right here. From Nan. And other people pay for old things too, they do!

Blimey! Six crowns!

Well, I read those brochures to Nan, that's all. Now she wants a black tomcat. So that people will believe her even more.

Meow, cried Ondra.

Meow, cried Standa. But not a local one, a tomcat from someplace else. That no one knows.

Man, said Ondra. I saw aeroplanes in Prague, warplanes. They flew in formation.

Prague, oh yeah. My old man said there's shops in Wenceslas Square in Prague where they sell ten kinds of ciggies, twenty even!

Those planes were beautiful. Vrooom! And then they were gone!

But my old man! He was supposed to bring home a tomcat from someplace and never came back. I'm standing there by the locomotive, waiting. He's nowhere to be seen. I ask the blokes, they don't know anything. I ask Nan, where was he supposed to bring the tomcat from? She doesn't now. Not good.

Those planes, right, said Ondra. They've got radar that enables them to fly all the way to outer space. They can go to places ruled by gigantic alien civilisations!

You of all people, mate, said Standa. You believe in that stuff?

I always imagine it like this, said Ondra, when I'm on my way to school, mate. Stupid teacher says: So and so, up to the blackboard! And suddenly the janitor, or no, the headmaster, rushes in! Attention everyone! I have news of enormous significance. We've made contact with an alien civilisation. Go home! Or someone on the radio: Alien life forms have been discovered in space, they have huge technical potential, unforeseen parameters, over! New life, a completely different form of life, get it? Everything would be different.

Well, I don't know.

Ondra said: Wait! He sat on a milestone. He was tying his shoelaces.

It was taking him a while. He looked up at Standa, Standa was pacing to and fro. Between puddles. Mud was squelching under his feet. He was kicking branches. He looked ridiculous. He was prodding his belly with his finger. Ondra sputtered.

At school they said we're made of molecules, said Standa. That's a load of bollocks, right? Or water, mate, said Standa and poked his gut again. That's rubbish, isn't it?

Molecules, man, said Ondra, standing up. He reeled a little again, he had to tilt his head back. He felt a chill on his neck. He was looking up at the sky. There were lots of stars after the storm. He wanted to say something. That happened to him sometimes. Sometimes he had to get something off his chest quickly. Sometimes people laughed at him.

Look, look, he bellowed so suddenly it gave Standa a start.

What if everything up there and the two of us as well, in fact all people, mate, what if we're all inside a tiny molecule in the body of a giant, mate, who's also a boy, mate, but on a different planet? And the giant and his people, right, his old man and his mother, his mates, are inside a molecule inside another giant boy, mate, on another planet, blimey! and it never ends, mate, there's no end to it. What do you reckon?

Hm, said Standa. Sounds like a load of bollocks, I reckon.

Hm, I guess so, said Ondra. He was suddenly dreadfully exhausted.

And even if it was like that, doesn't matter! It would still be the same, said Standa.

Aha, said Ondra.

And like you were saying, the aeroplanes and that. Satellites. Apparently it's a right cock-up, man, radiation and that.

Radiation, yeah?

Nan, right, how she says she talks to the dead. Hey! What if there's radiation, and people don't know about it? They're tending to their gardens, they're down the pub, feeding the rabbits, and all the time they're dead. But they don't know it. They're only alive as if, yeah? That's what I sometimes think, said Standa. I'm walking down the road and I'm looking at the people and at my hands, I'm moving and that, but I'm asking myself whether it hasn't already happened.

Blimey, said Ondra. Maybe it has!

Anyway, Nan. The best thing would be if someone who's actually dead came to a séance and told her: You're talking out of your arse! She probably wouldn't survive that.

Hmmm.

What are you gawping at me like that for?

Ondra was walking next to Standa, he wanted to walk like him, he was moving his legs and arms in the same way. He was watching him. He was blinking. He could see through Standa, he could see bits of branches with drops of water, he could see the water streaming over the road. He could see glistening grains of sand through him. Is he breathing? he was saying to himself. Or not? Their breathing was synchronised. They had already reached the little bridge. They heard the bell. They counted the strikes.

6

This is Buny, said Frída to himself. This is where Buny used to be. The moon was shining down on the place. Only the stone foundations of the buildings remained. There were also a few of the thickest wooden beams that the flames had not destroyed. In the summer the beams were alive with insects. Larvae hatched in the wood that had been splintered by bullets. Bullets had also left their marks on the collapsed walls.

Weeds and grass had taken hold in the charred beams. Rusty machine parts were lying about in the grass on the ground. Somewhere there were partly buried wells. That was all that remained of Buny.

He sat down on a rock. He was already worn out. He'd had to wrest himself from the pub. Hurry over to see Nachtigal. Report the embankment incident. What can you do. Times are changing. Now the Ruskies are going to be here. What's going to happen?

Not a lot, Nachtigal had laughed. What are you afraid of, Cougher? Every government needs policemen, gravediggers, and some women to boot, he cackled.

Yeah, said Constable Frída to himself. I guess so.

What a storm! And the laughs down the pub, yeah. But I shouldn't have done that. Scared the boy. I surprised him with that question about his old man. I was sharp, like some detective. He stood there in that dive, all taken aback, soaking wet. Let the comrades find his old man. Why me?

I serve the people of the republic! he'd yelled at Nachty.

The people will gobble you up like a worm and shit you out, remember that, man. And it doesn't matter how big a man you are. This and nothing else is written in blood in the red heart of the Communist Manifesto, Nachtigal had roared at him.

Yeah, I feel sorry for the boy. He was cowering there, chilled to the bone. He's here without his daddy, without his mummy. Oh well, I guess he reminds me of someone, that's all, said Frída to himself. He laughed. Bitterly. Into the night.

This sometimes happened to him. Now and then. Suddenly he felt remorse for everything.

I should have poked the boy in the ribs, should have said to him: You must be strong! And that's an order, all right?

Frída's eyes misted over. He sniffled a little. I'm sorry! But he felt sorry in a warm kind of way. He wiped his nose, his eyes. He glanced around furtively. The blackest night. Oh well, so what. Nachty was also in a sentimental mood today. He's leaving, after all.

In the end he regrets it, Nachtigal, his departure. Nothing can be done about it, though, people even leave a place like Zásmuky. To go and live in the towns. To go who knows where. And some of them, as we know, have done a runner over the border. And what used to be the gendarmerie in Zásmuky will cease to be, it's no longer going to be a police district. And the powers of authority will remain in the hands of Comrade Frída! the constable said aloud. That's how he'd said it, Commander Nachtigal. They drank vodka, just a few glasses, and said farewell in the right and proper comradely way.

All right, I'll hand it over to you! But don't get any ideas, Nachty had said, hiccupping. There's work to be done, comrade. Malevolence is a devil who sticks his snout into human endeavours. You, my dear comrade, are still an inexperienced laddie with tousled locks, said Nachtigal, slapping Frída on the shoulder. Even though you've got a few grey hairs, I noticed that. I take note of that sort of thing. The commander stood up and took a few steps towards the window. Look, he waved into the darkness.

The comrades from headquarters know full well why they issued this simple black outfit to an ace like myself, whose chest in his normal uniform is studded with medals. Our mission is to ensure that people don't live like rabble. That they respect the rule of law. That's Poland over there, Nachtigal swung his arm towards the window, that's a dreadful place, that's clear. But what about our lot? What do you think about our people?

Ahem, said Frída, waving his arm as if to say he knows.

You're right. But pay attention. I'm going to tell you how it is now. Nachtigal leaned over the table towards him, knocking the glasses and plates off, he couldn't care less. He was almost whispering.

Satellites are already peregrinating above the broad reaches of the steppes. An intrepid comrade sits in each one, camouflaged by moonlight. What do you have to say to that?

They were silent.

My lad! Nachtigal exclaimed suddenly and hugged Frída. Then he loosened his grip. They slumped down in their chairs. You'll live to see it! cried the commander. The comrade ensconced in his satellite is travelling through the sky, continued Nachtigal in a firm voice. He's monitoring the ripples on the river, the shaking of cobs of corn, and maybe even the antics of a tiny little hare romping about in a field of maize. He sees everything. Any movement! Any enemy. So. Now you know!

Thank you, stuttered Frída.

But until such a time! cried Nachtigal, standing up resolutely. Frída also stood up immediately. The commander continued: They get together at night. They talk nonsense. They crawl over the borders, to and fro. They get together by smoky little campfires, as well as in cottages. They light their way with battery-powered torches. They clamber over the hills as they please. They go into caves! And they do things that make no sense, they scheme, they violate the law. At night, in the dark. We've got lots of work to do, believe me.

They sat down. Nachtigal's boots were glistening. His belt buckle, all his buckles and clasps, everything was polished. Frída had always admired that.

You're just a tad too old to be my son, dear comrade, said the commander. But you could be my brother. So keep a watchful eye on them. Put a stop to obscurantism. We must finally put a stop to it, we must break the back of evil, that's our nightwork. Get it, comrade? Cheers!

Cheers, said Frída, knocking back the vodka. There was still enough in the bottle for another couple of snifters. Then he'd have to head out.

This place Buny, he surveyed the ruins. They drove them out of here with guns. The scum. A few more winters and no one will remember that there ever was a place called Buny.

There used to be quite a few isolated villages and settlements in the woods, at the edge of the woods. Charred remains were all that was left of them.

And they weren't all forced to leave, driven out with whips, like that other lot back then. Sometimes they left of their own accord. Even years later.

You turn off a road and walk down a new track, you've received a report, from the gamekeepers, for example. That there's someone there.

You're going there to look the place over. And what have we here, there are two or three houses standing where before there was nothing. They're more like huts, but they've got glass windows and everything. People have arrived.

An old woman is feeding the chickens, a man is toiling away on his little tractor. Or he and his sons are struggling with a tree stump. The wife is spreading something on pieces of bread for the kids. The children see you first, they start yelling. You keep going. Watch out for the dog. You give the people a friendly smile. They'll give you something to eat and drink, you'll ask them some questions, then you'll put everything down in writing. Right! But then later . . . you go there again, and there's not a soul in sight. They've left, or whatever. An old shirt is still hanging on the clothes line, it's tattered, patched, hanging there come rain or shine. They've covered the well with a metal sheet. It's already gone rusty from the water underneath it.

Sometimes it takes years before they leave. You've only just got used to them, you know their names, suddenly they're gone. Hell only knows who sets it all on fire afterwards. Maybe a bolt of lightning. Maybe the local lads do it for fun. And maybe those who are leaving feel it would be a pity to leave a house for someone. Well, can't really call it a house, grimaced Frída.

He stood up and stretched. He didn't like to walk in the forest alone. But the way through Buny was shorter than over the stony field. Also: I want to go to the clearing. I have to go there every now and then.

He got into his stride. He saw a path between the trees. He'll be there soon enough. At the clearing. That's where it happened. The Cougher. You'll see. You call me Coughy Boy, copper, nitwit. This Líman fellow, Karel the innkeeper and others too! We'll see who comes out on top.

He glimpsed something moving between the trees. His hand slid down to his pistol holster. The wind, probably. The wind must have bent a bush towards the trees. It was nothing. There's no one there. His fingers were thrumming lightly on the pistol holster. He didn't like the look of those trees.

Three of the trees stood beyond the edge of the forest on the footpath. I don't think those were here before . . . he walked around the trees, stepping over their roots growing into the path, turned his head around at them, watching them all the time, he walked past the trees with his head twisted as far back as possible, until his view was obscured by his left shoulder . . . that's how far he had to twist his body. He knew that this was how one had to walk around trees like that.

He passed them, he felt relief. Hm, fuck it, he said to himself. He glanced round, the trees had disappeared from the path, they were obscured by the forest. He almost tripped over a fallen boundary stone. Ugh, this Buny place. It's as though it still reeks of fire to this day. He spat. He'll be at the clearing soon. That's where he'll sit down. He reached into his pocket for the bottle, he also had some bread wrapped in paper, Commander Nachtigal himself had poured vodka into his bottle, just a little, to keep him warm. So he took a slug.

Květa. So we would have had little nippers together, so what. I'd have looked after them. And . . . what's this popping into my head? Maybe she was my last. I've also got a few grey hairs. And maybe nothing of any worth is going to come my way any more. Maybe it's all already been and gone, my whole life. And if I were to get out of here, where would I go? I don't know anyone, anywhere. I'd planned it all with her.

With Květa, with the kids, I wouldn't have had to give a shit about anything. With a major's salary. People would crawl to me of their own accord, with a wage like that. To our new house. And I'd be selective. I'll talk to you, but not you. I wouldn't talk to everyone any more. Oh well, it wasn't to be.

He corked the bottle, tucked it away in his pocket. He quickened his pace. He kept his hand on the bottle's neck.

He was in the clearing. He went straight to the cross, his eyes sweeping from one tree to the next. If there's someone here, then they can see me. But I've got a pistol. They can see that too.

He was looking up at the cross. At the few rocks around the cross. How many times I've come here like this. If I make major, this'll be the last time. A major can go and live wherever takes his fancy. Even if the Ruskies come, or whoever. He sat down. He stood the bottle on a rock. It clinked. He put the bread next to it. It was dark and the moon was in the sky. It had only just risen. It was burning a hole into the darkness. This is a good cross, he said to himself, made of silver birch wood. Silver birch wood shines like a beacon even at night. This is where it was. The Coughing Hollow.

They'd walked out of the forest. Early in the morning. The sun was rising. The Bandera faction guerrillas came out of the forest, there were seven, maybe nine of them. Infamous insurgents. They had epaulettes with black thunderbolts. They were walking in an extended line towards the hollow. And Granddad shot at them.

They lived in a hole. They had nothing better. Actually, they had nothing at all. In the winter it was warm, they covered the planks with turf, they always had hot coals down there in the soil, it did the job. They spent the summer in the forest. Now they were all in the hollow, because at night it poured down with rain. Granddad, he and his seven brothers, their dad was away. And the girl. Why did Granddad take a shot at them? He spotted them, picked up his poacher's rifle and fired. But he never hit anything! He was almost blind. Maybe he thought he was shooting at a deer, or something. He shot Ataman Avril right in the neck and the man croaked of his wounds right there in the thickets. They killed Granddad, left us in the hollow. They stopped the cracks up with rags, doused them, set them on fire. Those were the evil Ukrainians. Apparently they'd worked in the concentration camps. Everyone wanted to kill them on sight.

They managed to avoid capture by our soldiers and the Ruskies, and then the Poles killed them off. The moment they saw those epaulettes, they started shooting.

Why on earth did Granddad take that shot at them? Because they'd walked onto the clearing? Maybe they just wanted some water and a bite to eat. Why on earth did he shoot their leader? That incensed them. His brothers paid badly for it, they were all roasted alive.

He was the only one pulled out breathing. And how long was he in there? He doesn't know. The bodies were twisted in a jumble above him, everything was smouldering, the clothes too. But the comrades weren't the ones to pull him out, half-asphyxiated! It was the villagers, they came at night. They took him back to their homes.

Then he became a village boy. He took cows out to pasture and all that. He even got a name. He was given an official name. He didn't know what it was while he was living in the hollow, he was still little, after all.

They kept laughing at me. The Líman brothers and everyone else. Always coughing, the Cougher. So they called me: Coughy Boy. He was always coughing because of the smoke, the singed meat, the hair, the clothes. He could still smell it. And the girl? The small one with the bloated belly found by his brothers who dragged her to the hollow? Then they used to do it with her. Not him, though, he was little. But he ogled her. She wanted to run away from them so they tied her up. She had blisters on her skin from the hot coals.

He was the only one who knew what she did when everyone was asleep. She burnt the rope around her hands. It stank. Did she manage to escape in the end? Was she tied up there even when that lot arrived? She's in the hole beneath him with his brothers and grandfather, most likely.

And his old man? Dad never turned up. Probably heard about what happened. Why bother himself on account of one son? Probably didn't feel like it.

I was always checking out strangers, they'd come to the village sometimes. Could that be him? Or that one over there? And when I saw some puffy old fart, I'd say to myself: Well, that's not my dad. And maybe it was. Anyway, by now he's farting inside a coffin. Shitting blood in some slammer. Why am I being so nasty? Because I'm a nasty person. If Granddad hadn't taken that shot that time I'd have seven brothers.

He reached towards the stone. He stood up. The bottle wasn't there. Nor were the slices of bread. Fuck, he said to himself. He started sweating. His brow was suddenly moist.

He scoured all the rocks, one by one, groping around in the dark. He even felt behind them. Then he glimpsed something moving again. Someone was standing beneath the trees. There was something white over there. He pulled his gun out. Waved the barrel at the trees.

Stop, who's there? In the name of the republic! He stared into the dark. He was watching the trees. So hard it made his eyes hurt. No one anywhere.

He got down on the ground, taking cover, feeling around in the grass with the tips of his fingers. He only found the footprints by accident. He knelt next to them, pistol in hand. The footprints of a large man. He'd been there just a moment ago. He was standing behind me when I was drinking from the bottle. He ran the pads of his fingers over the imprints in the grass, it had been trampled down. Then he let out a shriek. The guy hasn't got shoes on. He's barefoot.

He retreated with his back to the path. He was still aiming the barrel at anything in front of him, at the trees. He reached the footpath. He set off. He was still sweating. Yeah. This is the way home.

He put his gun away in the holster. He quickened his pace. This is how he'll walk. Briskly until he gets to the road. And if something jumps me, I'll blow its brains out. Ha, he laughed. But I don't really care. I couldn't care less about anything. He turned round to the clearing. See you later then, he called.

He saw a light above and between the trees. The moon had only just come out. The darkness was being torn apart. There was a chill in the air, he walked quickly. He heard the sound of a bell coming from the village, it was faint, carried on gusts of wind.

The last time I ended up talking to a stone. I was tormenting myself on account of Květa. Because of Nachtingal. Because of the Jankovský family. What a strong family they'd been, the Lynxes. Only Juza was left. And it could have been my family. The world is like a pair of scissors, snipping at my neck. And what'll happen when they come? The Ruskies. Will things be any different?

I've managed to make it so far. I always make it. Somehow. And I could have had seven brothers. But I'm not badly off. Not at all. I'm taking over Zásmuky, and Bělá comes with it. That's not bad. I hope they give me that scooter.

He'd driven a scooter once before. Little stinging flies had flown into his eyes. He had to stop, wash them out. He blinked a lot, his eyes stung for three days.

7

The church bell had hardly started tolling when Standa hissed: Go . . .
Ondra pushed off the asphalt, trotted off, running through the church
gate, and just as the bell struck again, he said: Twelve. He knew that
Standa had also said it . . . by now he was among the graves, running down
the gravel path, here the graves were topped with gold-edged marble slabs,
there were large and small lamps made from rose-tinted glass, crosses and
statuettes, little statues of angels, quite a few of the marble gravestones
bore carvings of the faces of the deceased, their eyes seeking those of
anyone approaching, eyes met eyes, that's also how the Lord Jesus was
painted in the church . . . there were watering cans and rakes in the aisles
between the graves, he took care not to stumble over a wreath, knock
down a candlestick . . . he ran with his shoulders slightly hunched, here the
graves were low, he was among the old graves, he yelled out, immediately
putting his hand over his mouth.

Trees hacked down by lightning lay over the graves by the wall,
the branches had swept away the desiccated old wreathes, broken the
cylindrical lamp shades, been driven into the graves, fresh wood shone in
places where the lightning had severed the branches.

He was climbing over the branches, knowing that the dagger was in the oldest part of the cemetery where there were unkempt graves with upturned headstones inscribed with foreign letters, he could already hear the river, in places the low graves overgrown by nettles merged with the ground, he jumped over a toppled rusty gate, smoke-stained glass was scattered everywhere, the glass shards of broken lamps, he stopped. He extended his arms. There was no wall.

He heard water. He reached into the gap. Damp emanated from the darkness where the water was rolling.

He sat down. He leant on a gravestone. There were clouds around the moon. The damp stayed close to the ground.

The church bell struck quarter past the hour, ding! The metallic strike made him cower, he moved his shoulder, the dagger slid down from the grave, the blade hit the gravel with a clink.

He reached out with his hand and grabbed it, the Líman dagger. The dagger with two thunderbolts and a skull, the one from the bunker.

What luck! he almost cried out.

He heard footsteps. They were coming towards him.

He was crouching by the grave. He realised whose grave it was. He closed his eyes.

He heard feet treading carefully. He heard breathing. Close by.

But I'm not going to yell, he said to himself. I'm not going to scream at all.

Now he heard furtive steps behind him, between the graves. They were moving away from him. He opened his eyes. Slightly. He looked.

They were wearing long white shirts. The tail of Pavel's shirt got caught on the head of a little angel on one of the low graves. Pillock, hissed Milan. Pavel tugged on his shirt. They were walking towards the church.

He ran after them, now they were going to lie in wait at the mortuary, he ran, gripping the dagger tightly in his hand, he was jumping over branches, weaving between the graves. He was happy that the Límans were there, that he wasn't alone.

He could see white shadows on the wall adjacent to the mortuary, they were whiter than the wall, two white shirts were standing there . . . on top of the wall . . . and they jumped off, ran towards Ondra, screaming boo and boo, mouths open wide. He ran past them, forced the mortuary door open with his shoulder, it swung on its hinges with a creak, he drove the knife into the earth, like he was meant to, walked out and called: Test! And Milan said: It's only just starting, you pillock, and slapped him.

He picked him up off the ground, said: Sure, matey boy, people in white sheets don't scare you, you take the piss out of pranks like that, but how about this, and he slapped Ondra again. Pavel laughed and said: Nice one.

Then Milan knocked him down to the ground, knelt over him, said: Look, where's your old man? Where has he got it? And make it quick, or else.

His cheeks stung. He tried sitting up. They let him. He was staring at the door of the mortuary. There were flowers there made from sheet metal. Painted silver.

They came to our house, two of them, went to other houses too, said Milan. They had Patent Office ID cards. Said they were looking for your old man.

But they're secret police agents, said Pavel. Everyone can recognise secret cops.

For years, you twat, Milan was shaking Ondra, every summer your old man has been dragging our old men over the hills. Over Blahoš, you twat. Is he looking for treasure, or what?

Get your head round it, said Milan, sitting down in the grass next to Ondra. If it's here we want to find it before the Ruskies do. Why did they

161

send a tank to attack the Patent Office? Why are they coming here?

Dunno, said Ondra.

You want to give it to the Ruskies, Pavel said angrily and kicked him. Not too hard, though.

We can hide you, said Milan. Look, the Ruskies will come. They'll arrest both you and Squirt. And they'll also ask you questions, don't think they won't. And they'll say: What are these boys doing here? Whose are they? And no one will say anything, get it? The people will be shit scared. Aha, the Ruskies will say to themselves. They haven't got papers? All right then, bam. And into the transport train with both of you, mate. History repeated. Ask Ploughman. And others. And then you're on the train for a week or two, the train keeps going, you don't know where. You drink your own piss. Ask anyone what it's like. Squirt will bite the dust.

No, said Ondra.

Then help him, you wuss. Remember. Does your mother know? Where is she? That was Pavel talking.

Do you want to flee from Bohemia? asked Milan. Aha, I get it, he chuckled, your mum has left you up shit creek. She's buggered off to a free country. Lots of people from Prague are doing a runner now. The roads to the free countries are jammed. People sell everything and run.

Yep, said Pavel.

I'm a Líman now. So what's your problem?

They stared at him.

Did I pass the test? I did!

You did, said Milan. You're a Líman and you're a Praguer.

I passed the test!

You're a Líman, and you're not. It's different today, said Pavel.

Well, fuck you then, you cretins.

What did you say? said Pavel angrily.

Ondra knew he couldn't say anything, otherwise he'd start blubbing, he said: I want him here. Of course I do.

Look, he's blubbing already, said Pavel and kicked Ondra with his trainer.

Who do you want to be here?

My dad, said Ondra.

Aha.

If he was here, then you two could just go fuck yourselves.

Oh yeah?

If I knew where he was, then I'd go there, wouldn't I? With Squirt.

He can't walk, you twat! Got run over by a car.

I'd carry him, get it?

They were watching him and Pavel said: Yeah. Then Pavel turned to Milan and said: Look, he probably doesn't know.

Ondra glanced at the shed. The sheet metal flowers were still glisten-ing. The church tower chimed for the last time. He hadn't been counting. He knew the funeral bier was in there. The one that had carried the coffin. No boy had had to do the test before when his granddad had just been lying in the mortuary.

You're stupid, he said. What time is it?

He knew they wouldn't beat him any more. They hadn't given it their all anyway. He heard dogs barking. The test was over. What would the hero Nemura say if he was being tortured by fiends from the Zador galaxy to reveal the parameters of his spaceship? He sneered.

You're boneheads, mate. The Patent Office, that's not like when your old man goes poaching and you know all about it.

I don't like this, said Milan. You're being a clever dick. And let me tell you something. They're taking away all the folders from all the blokes here who worked with your dad. They want to dismantle all the machines.

Some of the people have already smashed their contraptions. But not our old man.

Documents, thought Ondra. He could see the fire tossing little bits of paper towards him. The destruction of documents, he thought.

And you know what? said Milan. Come on, he grabbed Ondra by the hand, Ondra resisted, kicking him. Milan was dragging him to the mortuary. Pavel walked behind them.

They pushed him inside. Knocked him down into the corner by the bier.

You can do some thinking in there, you twat, said Milan. Seeing as you're so clever. And he closed the door.

They were laughing. He shook the door, it was reinforced with black metal. There were no flowers on the inside. The moonlight was reflecting off the metal. It came in through a little window.

He turned round and hit the metal door with his fist. He recalled the door of the bunker. He recalled the steel door of the safe. Dad had taken a folder out of it. Full of papers. It was tied with a ribbon.

That's what he'd tell them! Lads! he called out again.

The bier stood on wooden blocks. Even if he climbed up on it, he wouldn't be able to reach the little window. And it was small. He wouldn't be able to pull himself through it.

He paced around. He stamped on the ground. The floor was made of soil strewn with grit.

He could be locked up in there for decades ... he'd come out a venerable old man ... his mind would have encompassed the mystery of the world ... Squirt wouldn't recognise him, nor would anyone else ... the cleverest prisoners exercised their minds by solving mathematical equations ... he tripped over the dagger, he'd completely forgotten about it. They'd also forgotten about it. They'll return for it. They can. In Prague, boys couldn't be out at night. They'd be picked up by the police.

It started raining. The clouds obscuring the moon had sprung a leak. He sat down on the grit. Maybe he slumbered for a short while. It was still raining. Prisoners do exercises, he said to himself. So he had a go. But the dagger was on his mind. If the brave Papillon had a dagger like that he'd fight his way off Devil's Island. He'd open any lock.

He poked around in the lock with the point of the knife. He heard little stones crunching. Steps. They're coming for the dagger. Something fell on the roof. He heard roof tiles breaking. He was crouching in the corner. He wasn't looking at the bier. Fuck your stupid japes, they won't scare me, he said to himself.

Someone was climbing up the sloping roof. They were crawling, using their elbows, their knees. The window broke, shards of glass spilled out onto the grit-covered floor. Ondra saw an arm and a leg. Someone was pushing their body inside through the little window, wriggling in. Their dangling appendages looked like they'd been broken, they straightened up again, helping the body squeeze through by pulling and pushing.

Only tank drivers can crawl like that, thought Ondra, tank drivers as tiny as jockeys, tank drivers who have to crawl through narrow access hatches.

The body was hanging from the window by its arms, swinging to and fro, the person let go, landed on the grit and glass.

Ondra pressed himself up against the wall, then he heard: Jesus Christ, Our Saviour, Hail Mary, full of grace, pray for us sinners, hallowed be thy name and thy will be done on earth, Amen!

He saw a boy. He was kneeling by the bier, now he stood up. He was small. Close by. Ondra could see the ragged elbows of his tracksuit top.

Ugh, said Ondra. He was afraid of a little boy. A little gypo. The dagger fell out of his hand. He stretched his legs. He had pins and needles. Ugh! he said once again.

The boy shrieked, hopping around so much he almost knocked the bier down, he leapt up on top of the bier, tried to crawl up the wall to the little window.

Don't wreck the bier, cried Ondra. What's your name?

He didn't know what to say next. Do you guys also do tests? he asked.

The boy stood clinging to the wall. Ondra yawned. It'll be morning soon, he said.

Yeah, said the boy.

You doing a test of courage here, are you? Ondra said again.

I've come to get some varnish. Are you on guard here? Can I take some? What?

The boy raised his arm.

What is it?

Sandpaper. Can I? Please, please! I'll only take a tiny little bit.

Ondra was enjoying this. After all that fear. After the Límans.

You can!

The boy turned his back on him again.

He's sanding varnish off the bier, Ondra said to himself. He coughed. You live on the other side of the river, yeah?

Yeah. The boy glanced over at Ondra. With one hand he was sanding the bier. Ondra was waiting for the bell. Maybe it had already chimed.

They buried my granddad yesterday!

Aha, said the boy. So you'll be here till morning, eh?

Of course, said Ondra.

The boy took a few steps towards Ondra. Thanks, he said. Now you can hear dogs barking, later you'll hear the cocks crowing. Then everything will be okay. I startled you, eh?

Bollocks! said Ondra. You were afraid of me. I would have run you through.

You wouldn't if I was a ghost.

You're not.

You couldn't have known that. I thought you were a ghost. But they look different.

The boy sat down next to Ondra, his back leaning on the wall.

How? Please do tell.

Dreadful. So horrible you can't say it. Their hair is made of flames. They slither like snakes. They fly through the air. When they're really little, they crawl among the little stones on the ground. They're everywhere.

You're a nutcase!

I know, nodded the boy. Everyone says that. But who do they call when they want varnish? Me! Because I'm not afraid. You startled me something dreadful, though. I haven't got white hair, have I?

Ondra looked and chuckled.

Black as death, mate.

I got such a fright, I thought I might freeze with fear, that my bones might crack. That I'd be struck dumb. If I'd known you were here, I wouldn't have crawled in. I didn't know you lot stay on guard the night after as well.

Yeah, said Ondra. Normal procedure. Granddad was a good man.

No doubt, said the boy quickly. Your granddad was no doubt a most highly esteemed good man. He was very good indeed, yeah! He was wealthy, gave everything to everyone. Got to know the world in his lifetime. He knew everything, been everywhere. Everyone loved him. I kiss his hands, his feet.

What are you on about? The gypsy was darker than Standa. His jacket was ragged and torn. His hair was curly. He was tiny.

What do you want the varnish for? Varnish from a bier. That's weird!

Blimey, what a knife. Let me see it.

Nope, said Ondra. He tightened his grip on the dagger. He tapped a pebble with the point of the dagger. He scrawled some squiggles with it in the soil. The handle was too long for his hand. I could hold it like a two-handed sword. And knock flaming Tatar arrows off the battlements. Nothing doing! he said.

I'll buy your granddad a candle, said the boy. Not one, ten. Everyone will. And wreaths. You'll be amazed. It'll be the most beautiful grave of all. Lots of flowers, you'll see.

Hm, said Ondra.

It'll be heaped with flowers. And there'll be a thousand shining candles, day and night, all the time.

Right.

Hey, the boy leant towards him. We're not in the cemetery any more, right, this is just an outhouse. There aren't any dead here, right?

No, said Ondra. We're in an outhouse. The graveyard is behind the church. This is just a building of sorts.

Yeah, said the boy. It's just a building! He moved closer to Ondra, whispered in his ear, jabbering: Those girls! One of them went blueberry picking, the other to fetch wood. They found them in the forest. So we crossed the river. When someone dies and they bury them, then you go and get varnish from a bier. It's a good thing to do. I didn't know you'd be here.

What girls?

It wasn't any one of us who done it! said the boy. We all know each other. When someone does something like that, everyone has to get together and find them. I'm going to wait for my brothers and then I'm off. Thanks a lot. I'm grateful to you, much obliged, I hold you in high regard, most high! jabbered the boy.

What? Who are you waiting for?

My brothers.

Aha. Ondra stood up. He went through the motions of stretching. He wanted to scarper. Leave the boy there. But they were locked in. He sat down again. He heard rain. But no rain fell in. Not even a drop fell on them through the little window.

They'll come when they come. They'll find something.

What?

We've got a little boat. So they went foraging. See if there's anything useful about. You know what I mean.

A little boat, said Ondra. Where did you get it?

What do you mean where did we get it? We didn't get it anywhere. We never take anything. It was just lying there, all battered.

But it's my little boat, exclaimed Ondra.

Good, your little boat, all right. But what are you trying to say? That I'm not allowed over the river? And how am I supposed to go to school, if not over the bridge? The boy was jabbering again, thrashing about as he spoke. He struck Ondra on the nose with his elbow.

But it's possible even without the bridge. Or your stupid little boat. You'd be goggle-eyed with amazement! Mertek. He walked over the water whenever he liked. He caught thunderbolts in his hand and hurled them across the water, just like that. If he felt like it, he tossed a bolt of lightning on the road, maybe, he wasn't scared of anything. He'd slam a lightning bolt on a farm and walk off. Or he took gold and jewels from bad people and then walked on water again to somewhere and there he sold it. He went all the way to Prague. There the most holy and most venerable pope cursed him: Fall into the water, unclean power, he said. Mertek didn't fall in, he was a good person. He jumped around there and everyone laughed. Then the pope and the others forgave him. Oh yeah, Mertek. We never had it so good. He gave everything to everyone. They searched for him everywhere. They shot all the horses. But why? He didn't need horses at all.

Ondra was rubbing his nose. He thought about hitting the boy back. Nah, he hadn't done it on purpose.

Who shot the horses? he asked. And keep your voice down!

The Communists. Some horses were shot by Communists, some by Germans. There were a lot of horses.

You're talking a load of bollocks! Why would they do that?

I'm not talking bollocks! They locked the people up in a huge building and closed it off by winding wire around it. That's when they were on the manhunt for Mertek. He gave them the slip! The gendarmes and the police shot at him, but he escaped. Made his getaway over the water. He walked and walked, no one spotted him. He walked, he didn't even get a tiny bit wet.

Oh please, how do you know all that?

Common knowledge. Everyone says it. Everyone knows it.

And what's with him now?

They blamed him for everything! Said he steals, rummaging through attics and that sort of thing. That he abducts people. He was old by then, he couldn't run as fast as before. He came back home. That's where they captured him. Tied him up with ropes, but they snapped. They grabbed other ropes, real quick! Then they tied him up with sixty ropes. They snapped too! And they added six, and six more. They blamed him for everything. Said that he steals. But that wasn't true. The people caught him here and stuck him in a grave. On the other side of the wall, legs into the water! Gypo, show us what you can do! Crawl out, jump up, scarper over the water. Come on, then! Ha ha ha! He couldn't do it any more. He was old. So he stayed there. And you know what, hey!

What?

I try it sometimes. I think about him, about Mertek. Think about him awfully hard. I made a carving of him. I try it like him.

What?

Well, to walk . . .

On water, yeah? You're a fruitcake.

It must be possible. It's all about the first step.

You always go under, chortled Ondra. You go plop in the water, don't you?

Yeah. There's always a splash and . . .

Kerplunk, you twat! And you sink to the bottom, cackled Ondra.

Yeah, swallowing water! Hee-hee!

Ondra wanted to tell him about the time he'd plunged into the river. How horrible it was, how he thought he was going to choke. The leeches everywhere. He was up to his waist in mud. Up to his neck!

You saw it, said the boy. You saw where the wall's caved in, the thunderbolts did that.

I saw it.

And do you know why the lightning bolts smashed it to pieces? They wanted to join Mertek. Because they'd got used to him. He walked over the river and played with a thunderbolt like it was a kitten. The bolt of lightning flew over and Mertek caught it in his hand and said: Fly! and hurled it and the bolt flew off, and then came back again to Mertek.

Hah!

Mind boggling, eh!

Ha ha, what a load of cobblers. The lightning struck the trees and they knocked down the wall.

But that's the same thing. Thunderbolts do as they please. Come and see me sometime. I'll show you my carving. I found a piece of wood in the forest, got my knife out. And that was it. I've got Mertek at home. I'm going to paint him as well.

Sure, Ondra said to himself. I'll go to see him and the Límans will drown me. I'll go into a gypsy house and no one will ever talk to me again, yeah right. Well, maybe I'll stop by sometime, he said.

Come over, I'll show you the notebooks. I've even got everyone's notebooks.

What?

Well everyone writes their own thing, don't they? I want to know everything. So I took them from them.

Yeah?

Yeah, that's why I'm not allowed to go to school now. I've also got a fever all the time.

Aha.

Hm.

Ondra yawned.

Hey, why don't we go outside? said the boy. It's not raining any more. It was raining all the time before, now I can hear the birds.

Yeah, the birds are making a racket, said Ondra. We're locked in.

Yeah? The boy got up and tried the door handle.

Ondra stretched his legs, dug his heels into the grit, closed his eyes for a moment. The boy will pull himself through the little window. What am I going to say? That I wanted to have a look at where Granddad had been resting. That's what I'll say. I'll make a terribly sad face. The door clicked shut behind me, that's all. And weren't you afraid, laddie? Not at all. Granddaddy was a kind person, after all. What should I be afraid of? What an intelligent and brave boy, they'll all say.

Let's go, come on, said the boy, opening the door.

Ondra dawdled behind him. White mist was rising from the water. He'd never seen so much fog before. The sun was in the fog on the other side of the river. He could only see part of it. My brothers, said the boy.

They were walking away from the church. Avoiding the graves. Their eyes are fixed on the ground, was what occurred to Ondra. They're old, at least thirty, he said to himself.

One of them was wearing overalls. The one with the sack. He had it slung over his shoulder. The other one was also carrying something. His hands were full. The boy ran up to them.

They're annoyed that I'm not by the little boat, he turned round to Ondra. They're afraid here, the boy chuckled.

They were climbing over the wall. The one in the overalls climbed over first. Then his hands appeared, grabbed the sack, pulled it over. His arms in loose sleeves swished like branches. The other bloke was sitting on the wall. Under a tree.

You're supposed to go to him, said the boy.

The bloke was swinging his legs.

Mister, that's my little boat! said Ondra. He took a few steps towards the wall. He knew what the lads would say. A gypsy like that carries a switchblade in his pocket. Cuts your throat, walks off.

Come here. Got something for you, said the bloke. Lend us your boat. I'll give you five crowns. Look, he showed him the coin. He spat on it and polished it on his sleeve. He was rubbing the coin, his hair was flying about. His hair could get caught in the branches, thought Ondra. He'll jump down and hang there in the air.

I'll polish this one for you, boy. The bloke flashed the coin in the palm of his hand. He put it on the wall. I've got another one. Come and get them.

You speak Czech? Ondra was almost next to him. He stayed on the spot.

Can't you hear?

The man reached out with his hand and yanked the dagger from Ondra's hand.

This is nice, this. Where'd you find it?

Ondra's legs started shaking. He couldn't stop them.

What you juddering for? You daft bugger. You and Kája are the two likely lads, I'll tell you that!

He's sitting down directly beneath the tree, thought Ondra. No one can see us from the road. He could easily strangle me here.

The bloke yawned. We take Kája over here every now and then, you know, he won't have it otherwise. He's got all that from books, those superstitions. Varnish from a bier and that sort of thing. The bloke was chortling quietly. He tapped the stack of coins. Five crowns. We always leave this for the verger, you know. For the glazier, like. Our little one always has to go in through the little window. Got that from books. Everything he told you is a load of piffle, get it? Everything's all right on our side, get it? said the bloke. He leaned down. His eyes were fixed on Ondra. Keep the coin. We'll borrow the little boat.

Give me back the dagger, mister, please, or I'll scream.

You won't scream, said the gypsy. You'd be screaming by now. What were you up to around here? You two were made for each other. The man pushed off with one hand and jumped off the wall.

I don't make stuff up, hissed the boy. Come with us, he said, grabbing on to protruding stones with his fingers, wriggling upwards, feeling for support on the crumbling wall with the tips of his trainers, then he was at the top. Come on! he yelled, Ondra heard branches breaking, the boy slid down into the thicket.

He climbed onto the wall, almost knocking the coins off, looked down, jumped. He fell on his back. The boy was standing there. Move it, he said, lifting Ondra up by his elbow.

Ondra scrambled after him through the thicket, panting. They were walking down his path, the one used by geese and ducks.

I can see the water, whispered the boy over his shoulder. The water has risen. Move it.

The river bank had almost disappeared. After a few more strides down the path they were by the boat. There was a sack lying in the boat. It was moving. The blokes were putting other things into the boat.

Look, said the boy. He was standing in the mud. There was goose and duck shit everywhere. Shed feathers. Plucked out when a duck got a caught on a branch, maybe.

I think Mertek discovered some kind of knack, you know, said the boy. He held on to the air somehow, yeah? The boy spread his arms out. The palms of his hands were stretched taught, fingers bent upwards. Swoooosh, the boy waved his arms. He compressed the air, right? The boy slapped his thighs with his arms. It's all in the first step, you know.

The knife, said Ondra. Please!

As he took a few quick strides to the boat, the boy's boots filled with water, he climbed in, said something to the blokes, jabbering constantly. The boat moved. Ondra stared at the sack. It was moving. They'll eat the poor mutt, he said to himself. The bloke in the overalls swung his arm towards Ondra. The dagger flashed through the air, fell into the water by his feet with a splash.

He groped around in the river bottom with both hands, brushing against slimy pebbles and rotten little branches, he heard the boat creaking, it always creaked.

Cold water splashed onto his face.

I told them he was your granddad! he heard the boy say.

Thanks for the dagger, said Ondra, standing up, his hands had found it.

I'll tie it up on the other side, you'll see, said the boy. I promise. The man pushed off with the barge pole, there was a splash, they were in the fog.

The fog was also surging upwards from the water around him.

The water had risen. A strong current was now flowing over what had previously been shallows. There was lots of dirty yellow foam on the edges of the current.

He turned back to the path. He walked with his arms stretched out just to be safe. Because of the thorn bushes. Thin branches. They could whip him in the face.

He was standing on the little bridge. Fog was drifting up from the river, rising up from the surface of the water in slivers, they were rolling over each other, coalescing into an impenetrable white curtain . . . fog was also rising from the stream, standing on the little bridge, he was staring into the soft milky whiteness through which the road, the avenue lined by shattered trees, led up the hill towards the pub.

He heard chains jangling, in the cowsheds, most likely, he heard the gaggling of geese, a gate creaked on its hinges, people were getting up, going out to survey the devastation, the fog was rising all around, making the air swirl. He was breathing the fog, the gravel was crunching on the track along the stream where their house was, someone was coming towards him.

He lowered his arm, hiding the dagger behind it, pressing it to his waist, he pulled Standa's sweater over the dagger, it felt cold on his stomach.

Someone was walking through the fog towards him, to the little bridge, arduously dragging themselves along, Ondra heard whimpering: Boo hoo. Squirt's looking for me! he thought. A head in a flat cap emerged from the fog, it was Berka, he walked into the section of fog where Ondra was standing, pressing a handkerchief to his nose, he said: Boy! Have you seen my Mašík? Have you seen him?

He took his rifle off his back, pointed it above his head, pressed the trigger, the bang of the gunshot instantly drowned out all other sounds, Ondra whispered: Can I have a go, yeah?

Oh no, laddie, that's not allowed, said Berka, breaking the shotgun open over his knee, he pulled a cartridge out of his pocket, loaded, raised the gun again and fired.

They were both deafened by the gunshots. Berka recounted: They took my Mašík, my little chappie, my drooling darling . . . he slung the gun over his back, pulled a grubby red hankie out of his pocket, blew his nose, sniffle, sniffle.

Ondra was turning round to various noises, picking up the voices approaching them in the fog, he heard stamping on both sides of the bridge, then the movements of their bodies were making the fog on the bridge move, it was rolling about on their faces, their bodies, rising above them.

Zuza's dad was holding a hammer in his hand, saying: They were in our cellar too! Someone pushed Ondra up against the iron railing of the bridge, squeezing into the little throng, now the person was standing next to old Škvorová, she had a blanket over her nightshirt, she said: They ripped the laundry off the line at Horvát's place! And then Ondra almost spluttered because Škvorová said: I'll run round to the other girls' places! By that she meant the old women who went to church. Who could have done such a thing, said Berka, everybody knows my Mašík around here . . . It's obvious, isn't it, said Zuza's dad, swinging his hammer, my old lady caught a glimpse of them, the black devils, there were at least ten of them, she didn't let out a peep, though, they'd have slit her throat.

So it was the devils, said Ploughman, he'd just come running up, stuffing his shirt in his overalls, there was hardly any more room for them on the little bridge and then someone cried: Listen! The milk jug's gone too. The municipal one!

In that case, let's go! someone said, and all at once they were crossing the bridge over the stream, tearing the fog apart with their elbows and knees, they were on the road now, walking uphill, every now and then someone ran out of the throng and then they heard banging, rapping on the doors of the houses, the lights of candles and lamps were now flickering in all the windows, the men were putting on boots and blindly joining the crowd still half asleep, one arm in the sleeve of a shirt or a dungaree jacket, the other holding a stick, an axe or a hoe, anything they got their hands on in the woodshed or in the yard, Ondra heard people saying: Devils, devils . . . Berka was holding on to him tightly, they were climbing over hunks of trees, avoiding fallen branches, Berka kept stumbling and Ondra was helping him.

He was glad to be near the rifle. He was wondering whether Berka would shoot again. They went uphill along the road, a few other men were standing in front of the pub, there wasn't as much fog there up on the hillside, the men stood around smoking, Ondra saw one of them swinging a plank through the air, another had a hammer like Zuza's dad, Mr Líman had an axe.

The old women who'd been walking with them up the hill through the fog had stayed back on the road, they probably couldn't climb over all those branches, maybe they were clearing the branches and the mud away . . . only the men were standing around in front of the pub. There were at least forty of them! said someone. And the living room window at the

Fejfar house has been prised open! someone else said. Hiya! said Milan to Ondra, he was standing in front of him. Pavel stood behind Ondra. Milan said: Got it? and Ondra chuckled because if they'd ambushed Captain Fredegard the Scout like that, the dagger would already be in the interrogating officer's belly . . . Ondra lifted his sweater and said: Of course I do! and handed the dagger to Milan. Milan thumped his shoulder and said: Good. The blow made Ondra groan slightly, the men started to move, they turned behind the pub, kept walking, by now they were by the bridge, a few strides later they plunged into the fog on the bridge, Líman walked at the head of the throng, Zuza's dad was propping up Berka and someone said that Churchy should fire the first shot, that he should set that gypo rubbish dump on fire with the first blast . . . seeing as they filched his piggy . . . Milan glanced at Ondra, saying: Weren't you afraid there? Ondra said: Not one bit! And how did you get out? said Pavel. Normally . . . They were watching him, one on either side. We were on our way to open the door for you, said Pavel, but there was a hailstorm, we might have got killed . . . That's a fact, matey, hailstones the size of a fist, mate . . . Like toddlers' heads, said Pavel, smashed up the sweet corn, all the maize has been mashed to a slurry. They were walking over the bridge, the shoulders and backs of the men were in front of them, the sticks and the hammers, bobbing up and down, the men were stomping over the bridge, it was covered with branches and mud, a tree had got caught on the railing, Ondra heard water splashing, heard the river flowing under the bridge, it was close, one of the men near the front was now leaning over the railing, saying: Jesus Christ, check this out! They all saw it, the water had risen, flooded the banks, branches and whole tree trunks, massive wooden logs were snagging on the bridge, and more branches and logs were hurtling towards them in the current, and when it looked like they were just about to knock them all off the bridge, the whole lot disappeared under the arches beneath them with a roar, the foaming muddy water was dragging along bits of plank, tree trunks, a broken punt, branches, at a frantic speed . . . they saw some kind of box rolling around in the waves and all around it there were wreaths, funeral wreaths, perhaps it was kept afloat by the plastic flowers . . . The cemetery's been overrun! someone said . . . Ondra saw a dog kennel, it careered under the bridge, a cat was cowering on the crest, the cat on the kennel was a black smudge flashing by between the pillars, the current was tossing torn fences against the bridge, they were bristling with the branches tangled up in them, scraping against the pillars . . . one of the men said: We'll clear it all away with barge poles later! Yeah, later! exclaimed another . . . Let's go get the devils! shouted someone else, they moved.

Ondra would have most liked to stand there goggling at the river but those behind him were pushing him forwards and then someone right at the front hissed: Stub out your fags . . . Quietly now! said someone else, Ondra was astonished because now they were edging forward really quietly, not even a pebble scraped, not one shoe heel tapped, not a single hobnailed boot clanged against the bridge, he didn't hear the swish of wellies, not one heel-plated boot clicked against a cobblestone, those at the front were vanishing in the fog.

Ondra and Milan were walking behind Zuza's dad, they walked as quietly as possible behind Líman and Berka, Ondra's eyes were fixed on the nape of Zuza's dad's neck and suddenly they heard a sound in front of them, they heard rattling, as though someone was riding along in a cart. Líman raised his arm. Everyone stopped.

They were standing about halfway over the bridge, cocking their ears, their eyes searching in the fog, the entire river was covered with fog, the river looked like it was covered in snow.

The creaking and rattling was drawing near. Someone was riding a bicycle slowly towards them, pushing through the fog, someone in the huddle of men raised a plank, Líman said: Who could that be . . . then they saw who it was and they could hear his breathing, his arduous panting.

He was wearing a long green overcoat and a peaked cap, two more rode out of the fog behind him, those two had hats down to their ears, automatic rifles across their chests, the officer dismounted, leaning his bike on the railing, he straightened up, gave them a salute and said: Greetings, tovarishes. Where is the road to Praga?

The two behind him also stopped, but did not get off their bikes. They stood there, straddling their bikes. They were aiming their guns at the men. Fingers on the triggers.

The man next to Ondra swung his arm, tossing his axe into the river. It made a splash.

Ondra glimpsed a movement, it was Berka staggering, no one was propping him up now, Berka straightened his shoulders laboriously, gave a salute and said out loud: At your service, Herr Officer . . . the officer immediately moved towards him, pushing Zuza's dad away with his black-gloved hand and shouldering Mr Líman to one side, he reached into the huddle of men and grabbed Berka's rifle. The strap slid off Berka's shoulder, the officer yanked the rifle away and in two strides he was back by his bicycle.

Weapons forbidden, said the officer. He raised the gun above his head. Understand? And he chucked the rifle in the river.

Where is Praga? he asked.

A ripple of movement, a quiver passed through the huddle, someone said: Boys, you speak Russian . . . and arms extended from the huddle, someone grabbed Ondra by the scruff of the neck and his elbow, Ondra and Milan were now standing in front of the men, Líman shifted his weight a little, almost entirely obscuring Milan with his shoulder and massive arm, Ondra was now staring directly into the barrel of the machine gun, the man in the hat with slanting eyes that looked like they'd been carved into his face made the slightest movement with the automatic. He was gunned down by the Chinks on the bridge! the words flashed through Ondra's mind and then a warm tingle of relief spread through him, the soldier was aiming at Mr Líman's head.

Milan took two steps towards the officer, waved his arm in the direction of the main road and said: Praga, that way!

Spasiba, little one, said the officer, reaching into his pocket . . . he extended his hand towards Milan.

The officer took no notice of the axes and the hammers, he turned his back on the men, mounted his bicycle, pressed down on the pedals, rode between the two with automatic rifles. After he'd ridden a few metres, one of the soldiers lowered his gun barrel, the other waved his automatic rifle around, aiming the barrel at the head of one man for a moment, then at the belly of another . . . the soldier lowered his firearm, turned his bike around in a single movement, pushed down on the pedals, rode off after the officer . . . he stopped, whistled, they could no longer see either his face or his weapon, they only saw a dark splotch in the fog, now the other soldier also turned round on his bike in a single manoeuvre, leaning into the pedals he rode past the black splotch, and when he'd completely vanished in the fog, the splotch moved as well . . . they rode off.

Someone lit a cigarette, Zuza's dad said: So that's that, he was the first to turn around, elbowing his way back through the throng of men, he yelled out: I'm opening early today! Now! . . . Hm, said someone, they dawdled after him, all at once they started coughing and blowing their noses, giving each other sidelong glances . . . Fucking hell! someone exclaimed, stamping his feet, Líman was leading Berka by the hand, he was fumbling for his handkerchief, saying: Ahem, ahem, someone chuckled

and said: Those weren't Austrians or Germans, Granddad, that's for sure
... and Berka said: The devils took my pig, this lot my gun, might as well
bugger it all to hell, ahem, ahem... Milan and Ondra were dragging their
feet almost at the back, the man in the beanie said to Milan: What did
he give you? Milan showed them his cupped hand ... sweets wrapped
in cellophane ... bonbons! Milan stuck one in his mouth, trying to bite
into it for show, the men cackled and someone said: Give us one! and also
tried to crunch through the boiled sweet, couldn't do it, by then they were
standing in front of the pub, the fog wasn't as thick there and someone
said: Rum is the order of the day ... and someone else said: This is terrible
... they were silent, but then someone laughed and shouted: Míra Cragg's
axe jumped in the water, ha ha ... and the bloke in the beanie who'd just
come out of the fog said: I'd like to see you in my place, the Mongol was
aiming right at my face, you twat ... Hm, hm, they were all saying ... and
someone still standing on the bridge yelled out from the fog: We'll burn
you down anyway, devils ... and someone who'd already walked into the
pub hallway mumbled: Yeah! We'll burn them down ... they filed into the
pub, one by one, Pavel and Milan went in with the men, but no one said
anything to Ondra, so he was walking slowly down the hill, it was early,
it was actually still dark, and Zuza wouldn't be there yet at this hour! he
said to himself, though if she were there, he'd probably be embarrassed in
front of so many men ... he was covered in mud and yawning all the time
... buy yourself a stepladder, boy, they'd snigger ... I'm almost asleep!
Ondra was saying to himself, drowsily stepping over branches, he walked
past the old women, they probably hadn't noticed him in the fog, they
were sweeping the mud off the road with birch brooms, he was standing
on the little bridge, the damp mist from the stream wafted up towards
him like a column of smoke, he inhaled it, then he heard: Dingalingaling!
and he jumped out of the way at the last moment.

Polka almost ran him over, he was towing a cart behind his bike. He stopped, said: Lad, you gave me a fright. I almost ran you over!

Too right! cried Ondra. What's the cart for?

Well, lad, did you see them?

Yep, said Ondra. The Ruskies.

I was out scouting, you see. What about the test?

All good.

You know what then, hero? Try the cart out. It's for our little prince, seeing as his hooves are giving him trouble. I'll take you home, okey-dokey?

Oh all right then, said Ondra. He climbed into the cart. Polka pushed down hard on the pedals, they flew over the little bridge, riding downhill beside the stream, Ondra wanted to shout: It's bumpy! But he clenched his teeth, almost biting through his tongue, he held on to the netting of the cart, his legs were bent, it hurt. Yeah, I'll put some rags in here for Squirt, so he doesn't get bruised, he thought.

The fog from the river was mixing with the mist from the stream, enveloping it. Ondra watched the mudguard of the bike, it was slicing through the misty air like a cutlass. The stream had spilled over its banks, muddy pools had formed on the riverside. Little islands of brown slurry were slithering through the grass like tongues. They were carrying sods of grass and sticks. The cart bounced along, the wheels scraped over pebbles, skidded over wet branches. Dingalingaling! heard Ondra, they passed an old woman with a scythe over her shoulder, she jumped out the way. Ondra stuck his tongue out at her, he knew he wouldn't be visible in the fog anyway.

And we're here! said Polka. They were in front of the house.

Ondra dug himself out of the cart, blurted: Thanks. Polka turned the bike round, said: Burrow into the bed sheets, maybe there's a surprise for you there. He mounted, pushed down on the pedals. Ondra jumped out of the way. Polka waved at him, rang the bell. Dingalingaling! the sound faded as the cart disappeared down the road behind a bend in the stream.

He was fumbling across the yard, groping around with his arms so he wouldn't bump into the door, smash his head into the wall, he was shuffling forward so as not to hit the bench, there was light in the window, the flickering lights of candles, the fluttering of the flames was accompanied by a sound: Bzzz, bzzz, bzzz . . . the window was rippling with wings, little black wings, grey ones, midges, mosquitos, flies, large-winged moths were writhing around clumped together in a seething mass in the light, crawling over each other, wings beating against wings, the midges flitting about made it look like the pores of the wall were moving. He was staring at the bed illuminated by the candles, the girls were lying one on top of the other, heads swathed in a tangle of hair, one of them was wearing a long nightshirt, it was hitched around her waist, the one next to her was lying on her back, another girl sat up in the bed, she put her hand over her mouth, yawned, stretched, raked her hand through her hair, grabbed a pillow, slapped the girl in the nightshirt with it, she shook her head, tossed her hair up and down, she wasn't wearing anything at all, her hair tumbled over her body, the girl lying on her back raised herself up on her elbows, glanced out of the window, the girl in the nightshirt slid off the bed to the floor, the one that had wielded the pillow opened her mouth, covered her breasts with her hands, he couldn't hear her, she was giggling.

He stepped back from the window, his knee hit the bench, a hand grabbed his shoulder, it was pulling him down to the bench, it was Mr Frantla, he said: Who are you?

Ondra yelped out, muttered something.

Well isn't that a coincidence, he heard Mr Frantla say. Why, you're the elder Lipka son. Or isn't it a coincidence? Why, I was just thinking about your granddaddy. I heard you breathing. Huffing and puffing more like! Like a red-hot stove. I also thought you might be a big dog.

Yeah? said Ondra. Aren't you cold out here?

Mr Frantla was still holding him by the shoulder. What about the service, lad? Did you like it? Did you find it dignified? Now and then your granddad thought about being cremated. But he wasn't sure. You're right, the evenings are cold.

But it's morning! Let go of me.

But no one's holding you, boy. Your little brother is very brave. The way he was yelling and biting, I can't remember anything like it. Morning, you say? Well, never you mind.

Ondra moved his shoulder. Mr Frantla was still gripping him, with all his strength, it hurt. Ondra jerked to the side. He grabbed the arm, tugged on it. He was starting to make out the bench, he could also see Mr Frantla, he could see into his face now. He was squinting into the fog.

The door creaked, Zuza was standing on the threshold in a tracksuit jacket, she said: Hi! Her hands were in her hair, her arms raised, elbows jutting out towards him. She was giving off heat. He wanted to touch her, then another girl glided past them, she didn't say anything, went to the gate. It was the one who'd tossed her hair about.

Ondra said: Hello.

Make him a coffee later, yeah? said Zuza, nodding her head in Mr Frantla's direction.

And crumble some bread in it for him, called the girl by the gate.

The hand slid off Ondra's shoulder. Ondra heard him fumbling around, he found his walking stick, it knocked against the bench, Ondra walked towards the house, pressed up against Zuza, another girl came out of the hall, bumped into them. Ondra felt the girl's breath on his neck, she pushed him away, yawned. Ondra tried to grab Zuza, she'd already moved aside, she stepped out, she was standing in the yard.

Go and lie down. There's a place for you.

There's a sweet-smelling place for you, said the girl by the gate.

Yeah right, said Ondra.

They set off down the road.

In the hall he took off Standa's jumper, chucked it somewhere, kicked off his shoes, glancing at the candle holder in the window, the candles, the dark splodge on the bed was Squirt, he said: I'm still sleeping! Where have you been?

Oh, you know, said Ondra. He rolled up in a ball on the bed.

Where were you, you twat! There was a dreadful storm, a tree bashed into the roof!

Ondra yawned. Let me be, he closed his eyes. I'm going to sleep, he announced. I've not slept a wink yet.

Hey, I know a secret. Me and the girls found a secret, want me to tell you?

No.

You're stupid. Why didn't you come with us? They baptised me.

What?

Yeah, the way it's normally done, they dunked me in water, they baptised me all over.

And why? said Ondra, listening to the murmuring rolling around in his head, and Squirt was saying: They say it's better that way. When there's a war. The third world war's started, so they baptised me.

Aha, said Ondra, he was thinking about the weir, listening to the rumbling of the weir in his head, he was already asleep.

*

The light hurt his eyes as he was squinting, he closed them again firmly, he heard voices. Squirt was kneeling on the bed and yelling at the window, the gate was creaking.

He grabbed the white shirt, it was lying on the bed where the girl had taken it off, he threw the shirt over his eyes, Squirt was calling: I'm not going anywhere, I went yesterday and my brother's asleep! Berka entered, as did Mrs Škvorová, Ondra had a peek, the shirt on his head, squinted at them, old Ferdinandka was also pushing her way in, there was someone else there too: Let me be! cried Ondra. Mr Berka was saying: You should come, boy, for any day now could be the last . . . Ondra shouted: Leave me alone! Squirt on the bed shrieked: Leave my brother alone! and then he exclaimed: Blimey, thank you! Ondra looked, there was a basket by the bed, Squirt exclaimed: Yay, eggs! Berka tugged on the shirt that Ondra was pressing to his head, saying: It would certainly be good for you . . . I'm not going anywhere, I'm ill! said Ondra and Squirt shrieked: Let my brother be! Mrs Škvorová said: Well, well . . . and old Ferdinandka said: Well, perhaps if the boy has caught a chill . . . Another time, then, said Mrs Škvorová, Berka said: There might not ever be another . . . Oh, come on, don't overdo it, said Mrs Škvorová, pulling Berka out of the door by his sleeve . . . Squirt was giggling by the window. Look! They've got flags today, that's funny . . . Ondra crawled over to the window, the gate was creaking constantly, they were leading Mr Frantla by the hand, the old women were bracing him by the shoulders, there were more people there than the previous day, they were carrying flags above their heads, the man who was walking directly behind Mr Frantla was carrying a chalice, it was glimmering with a golden glow, the sun was almost directly above them.

That's a monstrance, said Squirt. They had it hidden away the whole time.

Ondra wriggled deeper under the quilt. Squirt was tugging on his leg:

Where were you yesterday? They say the church is knee-high full of water. And mud! The whole place is flooded. The coffins have been washed out.

Stop hassling me! Ondra kicked at him.

You left me here!

Oh well, I'm not going to get any more sleep, bloody hell, said Ondra to himself. What's the time?

Squirt was shuffling around on the bed, his little face tense with indignation. I'd like to see you in the bunker, thought Ondra. Squirt shuffled down the hallway, Ondra waited for him start to blubbing, and sure enough, he heard him not long after . . . that quiet whimpering.

He was sniffing the girly scent from the nightshirt. He sniffed the smell of the girl, imagining the girl by the weir, imagining a girl, Zuza did not wear the nightshirt. That's Mum's shirt! he realised. Squirt was still whimpering, so he got up.

He was kneeling by the linen cupboard in the back room, his head hidden in a pile of togs. When Ondra walked into the room he started whimpering even more.

Ondra went to the adjacent wardrobe, opened it, rummaged through Dad's T-shirts and shirts. They'll probably be too big for me, he said. He put a T-shirt on. He went over to Squirt.

Those are Mum's clothes! Ondra tried to close the drawer but Squirt was gripping it tightly. Mum's skirts, shirts were lying there. Also her necklaces. Necklaces, lipsticks, other things.

Actually, said Squirt. The girls like Mum very much. Other women here said: The Lady from Prague! Likes to doll herself up. But how does she doll up, for goodness' sake! She just washes her hair. Wears a polo neck. So she puts lipstick on, so what! The girls like that. Did you know that the nearest chemist's is in Osikov? Mum let the girls borrow things from her.

Hm, said Ondra. He sat down on a chair. Put his hands on the table.

I don't even know if I could lift this table, he proclaimed. I reckon I probably could!

Squirt kept rummaging through the clothes. His fingers were flitting about.

The girls told me that people here say that Eluzína was a little girl.

No doubting that, said Ondra.

But that she wasn't our sister. She was a little girl that wasn't anybody's. So Mum took her in as her own. Why not? the girls said. She could have taken her to Prague, the girl could have gone to a Gymnasium. She could have been a salesgirl in a department store. Or a teacher. Good! Why not?

Yeah, we were still little back then, yawned Ondra. He was thrumming his fingers on the table.

Bollocks, we weren't little! cried Squirt. We weren't alive yet. I think about it sometimes. I was waiting here for Mum. For you! If Mum hadn't lost that little girl, maybe we wouldn't even be here. She wouldn't have wanted us.

Yeah? said Ondra. But we are here. That's a load of twaddle.

And the girls said that it isn't true at all.

What?

Well, that terrible thing. That Mum got plastered and the little girl fell in the water. They say it wasn't like that, not at all!

Hm. That was a long time ago.

The girls said that the little girl just left, normal like. Seeing as she'd come from somewhere before that. Mum was sloshed so she didn't realise, that's all! Maybe only the girl's straw hat fell in the water. And people think that all of her floated off. But she just walked away, get it? She was running away all the time, apparently. What are you going to do with the girl? If she's running away into the woods all the time? What if she gets lost in the woods? Will the gypsies steal her? Will someone kidnap her?

And then what? She doesn't belong to anyone. The little girl's looking around: What am I going to do here? Tend to the geese, carry the water, do the laundry, cook the old man lunch, feed the pig and that sort of thing. Girls don't enjoy that stuff either. So Mum thought that she, a Praguer, would take her in as her own, and maybe the little girl wouldn't leave. And she left!

Is there anything to eat here?

You saw the basket, didn't you? I already had breakfast, ages ago. The girls said that it happened a long time ago. Apparently people say that the little girl belonged to people who hid out in the woods around here.

In the woods, eh? Krauts, yeah? Ondra slammed the palm of his hand on the table, trying to squash a fly. It just scurried off and stopped. He tried again and this time hit the mark.

No one knows! Or maybe they were people that were hiding from the Germans? Zuza said that people don't know. And Vendula says that maybe some people hid from the Communists for so long, they died. Except for the little girl!

We should put a roll of flypaper in here.

Not flypaper. That's really gross. And people asked the little girl: Who are you? Where are you from? They asked in all kinds of languages. Russian, Polish, even Krautish. They know how to. But when someone asks them, they say they don't. Odd that, eh?

Squirt stuck his head in the pile of Mum's togs again. He'd pulled some of them out and now they were strewn over the floor.

You're not dressing up again, you twat, Ondra hooted at him.

Squirt was holding on to the drawer of the linen cupboard. He blubbed again for a little while. Quietly. Then he wiped his eyes with the sleeve of his tracksuit jacket.

You spaz, he shouted at Ondra. I had to change my clothes otherwise they'd have taken me away. I had a necklace around my neck! I was even wearing Jolana's earrings! Clip-ons!

Taken you away? Who? enquired Ondra. You said they'd already baptised you. I'm hungry.

I don't mean them. They've already baptised me, so they don't give a shit about me any more. I mean the secret police, yesterday. It was during the storm. The girls were here. We found something. You'll be amazed. In the attic.

Secret police? They were here, yeah? Really? Ondra tucked Dad's T-shirt into his shorts.

Listen! It hadn't started raining yet. The old cop was leaning on the table here and he goes: Lassies, where are the Lipka brothers? We don't know! We don't know anything! said Vendula and Jolana. Aha! Well, try and remember, the old one banged the table. Comrade, question these lassies! That's an order! The young one stands to attention. The old one goes up to the attic, you know, and the young one says to Zuza: You'd better start remembering, missy, don't think you can refuse to talk like some princess. You come here to be at their beck and call, do you? he says. He flicks her chin with his finger. And Zuza doesn't even move. She's looking right through him, like he didn't even exist. That fucks him off, that. He's tapping his fingers on the table, says: Well! We can hear the old cop walking around in the attic, stomping. Stomp, stomp! And Vendula says: Beck and call, he says! Girls, I'm going to faint! What's he trying to say, this mister hotshot? I'm going to have a fit.

And right away the cop is standing next to Vendula, saying: What are you going on about, lassie?

And Vendula screams at him: Who're you calling a lassie, you clot. I'll have you know I'm a Miss, you clot! Miss Líman! And don't you dare touch me, keep your paws off. Vendula shrieked. And Jolana also shrieked.

You should have seen it. The cop went red. Who's touching you, girl?

Heeelp! squealed Vendula. Jolana and Zuza were in stitches, the red-faced cop jumped backwards. Vendula touched him! Ha ha! Squirt cackled. She touched him right there, no kidding, on his trousers. I was cackling too, of course I was! And Vendula yelled again: Heeelp! The cop's standing by the wall, he's blushing deep red and we hear the old one, stomp, stomp, running back down from the attic: What's going on here! he shouts. Comrade . . . jabbers the clot, Jolana and Zuza aren't giggling, me neither, and Vendula is suddenly blubbing! She's blubbing, when before she was laughing her head off, she's clever, isn't she? So I blubbed too.

And Vendula goes up to the old one and between sobs she tells him: Major, sir, comrade, please, tell this officer to leave us alone . . . boo hoo . . . and the old one screams at the young one: Out, comrade! And the young one cleared off, ran like blazes out the door.

The old one goes: Girls, what happened should not have happened . . . Vendula keeps blubbing, says: Comrade, that other comrade is horrible, we'd prefer you to examine us . . . she takes a couple of steps towards the old cop, touching his shoulder, sort of stroking him there, you know? The old one leaps back, he's standing in front of me, I was wearing Mum's shawl and that sort of thing, things that the girls had given me beforehand, and says: Don't cry, little girl. And he got the hell out of here! How about that, eh?

He was staring at Squirt with his mouth wide open. He closed his mouth, his teeth snapping shut.

Squirt was no longer blubbing. He'd already wiped his tears away. He was waving his arms while telling the story.

We'll hide in the bunker! The lads will hide us! Don't worry!

Yeah, sure, said Squirt. Look! he exclaimed, pulling a bottle out of the pile of crumpled dresses. That's probably wine, right? You reckon it's gone off?

What if they come back, said Ondra. He wanted to tell Squirt what he knew from Milan. About the transports. They'll stuff them in a railway car and take them somewhere. Like Granddad Ploughman. They'll not come back from Siberia until who knows when. Half-starved to death.

I'm not going to any bunker! said Squirt. The girls said that it's gross down there. There are fag butts lying all over the place, bottles, skulls. There are spiders there. It's dark.

The girls don't know, said Ondra. He snatched the bottle from Squirt and examined it against the light. I don't know if it's gone off. Girls aren't allowed in the bunker.

Heh, sputtered Squirt. The girls don't want to go there. And they know full well where the bunker is. The girls also walk in the woods, don't think they don't. But they don't give a damn about the bunker. They've got the hayloft.

Hah, exclaimed Ondra. The girly hayloft.

Actually! They've got a little roof there for when it rains. Zuza brings cigarettes from the pub. Easy! She puts a cigarette in a holder and looks like an actress, you'd be amazed.

Squirt closed the linen cupboard. He was holding on to the table and chairs for support. He hobbled across the hall.

The basket was sitting on the floor next to their bed.

Hey, bread rolls, exclaimed Ondra. Cheese, excellent!

Squirt was crawling over the bed and plumping up the pillows. Smoothing down the sheet.

Ondra wolfed down another roll. He was standing by the window. He was looking out.

Before, the girls used to go to the cinema, to Osikov. When the roads were empty. They've seen lots of films, you'd be surprised. But now . . . Zuza also wants to get out of here. Like Renata!

Which Renata, who are you talking about now? mumbled Ondra, his mouth full of bread roll. Look, he pointed at the window. It's raining. He was picking at the wax in the candle holder. He made a ball of wax and flicked it at Squirt. Where did you get the candle holder?

That's a secret. I'm not allowed to tell you that.

It's foul again outside, said Ondra. He could see a solid curtain of rain through the glass.

Squirt was beating the mattress with his fists. There was lot of dust in it.

Renata went wherever she liked. She wasn't at all afraid. Girls aren't allowed to walk around at night, their dads would give them a hiding. But Renata! She drew a moustache under her nose with some charcoal, put on some work boots, grabbed a jacket or some overalls and went down the pub. In Osikov. Or she went to a rock concert, a gig, why not? Now she's working in a bar in Prague, apparently. A decent girl shouldn't do that, I guess. But on the other hand she gets to go wherever she likes, buys whatever she wants. What do you think?

Hm. You want a gherkin?

Squirt was darting around on the bed, stretching the sheet. Each time he got it folded under the mattress, stretching it flat, he creased it again with his knees.

Eat all of it if you want, said Squirt. Vendula wants to go to the Gymnasium in Osikov. So does Zuza. But their old men always say: No way! Vendula says: What is there to do around here? Walk behind cows' arses for the rest of time, waiting for death to come knocking, till I'm nothing but an old cow myself? Sure! Hey, did you know that in Osikov there's a chemist's right by the station?

That I didn't know.

There are soldiers in Osikov. Renata said to Zuza: He shows off with his uniform and when he takes it off he's as much of a country bumpkin as the lads here. Renata always told the girls: You've got to get out of here. And what did Vendula say? I'd also like to go. But how? Where? And Jolana! She goes: I'm going to be a nun. I don't know about that! said Vendula.

Squirt was waving his arms. He was standing on tiptoes, shaking his head, rolling his eyes. He was talking like the girls talk.

Hey, don't talk like that, said Ondra. You can't talk like that.

I'm just having a laugh. Squirt stretched out on the bed. He folded his arms under his head.

It's almost dark outside, look! The cops won't come then. Not in the rain! When it's raining the girls crawl into the hayloft. They want to make a bonfire. But a terrible thing happened with that ointment!

They're in the hayloft, yeah? Ondra yawned. He closed his eyes. He stretched until his joints popped. He also stretched out on the bed. He also put his arms under his head. They were gawping at the ceiling.

When they make a bonfire, everyone leaves them alone. One brother goes to cut the grass, another goes off collecting brushwood, another takes the geese out, or something. The girls are out all night. Well, and then they're tired. Where would girls traipse at night when they've come all the way from Zásmuky? From Bělá? So they stay together. Like their mums did. And you know what? No men are allowed there!

No?

They smear themselves with ointment and that's the trouble. They've always smeared themselves with ointment. But now they don't have any, so Zuza thinks it's going to be bad. But I still think that Zuza's going to jump the highest. Before, Renata used to be the one who jumped the highest.

Yeah?

The girls always smear the ointment all over their bodies. They're naked, hah! Then they wash. To get the ash off, too. They have to go home clean. And if someone was ogling them, they'd tell! All the fathers and brothers of all the girls would then work them over, you know? A bloke like that wouldn't stand a chance, not at all.

No?

No. When they smear that stuff on, they become light as feathers and leap high over the fire. But that other thing is horrible. I promised the girls I wouldn't tell anyone. Do you want me to tell you?

Squirt leaned forward. He leant on his elbows.

Hey, he whispered. They always got the ointment from the gypsy women. Every time. This time Jaruna and Vendula went. So, they're supposed to meet this gypsy woman, right? The one they swap things with. Various necklaces, they've also got nice hair clips, combs, never mind where they come from. No one cares about that. Jaruna and Vendula are going to a place in the woods. And they've got crown coins with them, of course.

Aha. Don't talk through your nose!

They've already spotted her. The gypsy's lying down, the girls are calling to her: Ilonka, get up, you lazy cow! They go to her, look at her: She's dead. There's blood all over her kisser. Her eyes are open. They scarpered right away. Who could have done it? Some bloke? Wolves from Poland? Now they don't have the ointment. That's something, eh?

Hm. That's a load of bull . . .

No it's not! yelped Squirt. He was silent. He was angry.

I'll light the candles, said Ondra. It's dark.

They'll see we're here.

Aha, said Ondra.

I wouldn't go up to the attic on my own. But we had to go there. The tree bashed the roof in. What a bang that was! There was lightning, so we could see. We found the candle holder. And we found the place. Where you said Shogun lived, that one time, remember? You were trying to frighten me on purpose! Sometimes I think you're a right imbecile!

What did you find?

We crept over the planks. The lightning smashed into the roof, I told you! There's a little gate there, hanging off its hinges, you can see it now. We found the place where Granddad spent the whole war. Ten years, mate, fifteen! Hey...

You really are a total bonehead. The war didn't last that long.

Let me think. We could hide out there. From the cops. The girls will bring us food.

Ondra got up. I'm going up there. He smoothed down his T-shirt, took a step, two, then he was holding the door handle.

Don't leave me here. Wait!

Ondra took the candle holder. Squirt had the matches. Squirt pulled himself across the hallway hand over hand, but Ondra carried him up the stairs and into the attic. Squirt put his arms around his neck, latching on to his back. Ondra carried the candle holder in one hand, holding on to the banister with the other. Squirt was tittering. Ondra stopped in front of the prised-open door, catching his breath.

What's with the giggling all the time? he rebuked Squirt.

Zuza carried me like this, see. And you know what?

Hm.

I touched her knockers, blimey! chortled Squirt. For a laugh! Do that again and I'll drop you right on your coconut, she said, ha ha! And you know what Vendula said?

No!

Put him on my back, then, if it bothers you that much, you dippy cow. Put him down! You've got plenty to carry as it is! She was also giggling. Jolana was too. We were afraid. But not her! She went first. The other girls were afraid of the lightning. Jolana not one bit. And you know what? They kept pushing her ahead. She was giggling like a lunatic.

Get off, he said to Squirt. I'm going to light it.

The door slammed. They both heard it.

The cops, whispered Squirt. They found their raincoats.

The door to the attic opened. Now they were standing in a beam of light.

He was coming towards them up the stairs, slowly, pointing the light at them the whole time. He grabbed Ondra's shoulder. Is that you?

They could see into his face. Squirt squealed.

What are you wearing, boy? said Polka. I took you for a spectre, flapping around in an oversized T-shirt like that.

He stared wide-eyed at Ondra for a while longer. He lowered the torch. They started climbing down. Going down didn't give Squirt as much trouble.

The thing is, said Polka, stopping. You were wearing that ace T-shirt with the beast.

Ondra was leading Squirt by the hand. He shrugged his shoulders.

Oh well, I sure made a mistake there, then, said Polka, chuckling. Now he was walking in front of them, slowly, stiffly. Like a dummy, thought Ondra. He was wearing Dad's suit. He must have taken the suit from downstairs.

Squirt was shuffling down one stair at a time. I thought, he tugged on Ondra's arm. For a moment I thought that it's . . . that he'd come! he whispered.

I know, said Ondra.

He was waiting for them in the hall. May I? he took the candle holder from Ondra's hand.

In the living room he walked over to the window, examining the candle holder, blowing out the flames. A few had already gone out on the stairs.

So you found it, boys. Old Lipka's hideout, yeah? I brooded over it, racked my brains, rummaged through the cellar, in the end I thought he might have had some kind of hideout in a hole somewhere near the house. So it's up in the attic, eh?

A tree crashed into the roof! Squirt was explaining. There's a little gate there, cried Squirt, stretching for the candle holder. Polka kept lifting the candle holder higher and higher. Squirt couldn't reach it.

We use it for light, said Squirt, stamping his foot. We want to use it to have some light.

Oh certainly, certainly, he said. There's more up there where this came from, right?

Mostly books, said Squirt. They're weird. Also little cups, or something. Candle holders, but little ones. Necklaces. Bit and bobs.

We'll check it out together later. Why are you gawping at me like that?

He was wearing the jacket. The whole suit. He must have taken it from the wardrobe. He kept smiling. Just with his mouth, his cheeks seemed to be made of rubber.

He's different, it occurred to Ondra. He's like Polka, and not like Polka. Ondra had goose bumps everywhere.

Why are you wearing Dad's clothes? said Squirt.

I borrowed them. He stood the candle holder on the window ledge. I was afraid there were burglars in the house, see? The mess next door, the togs on the floor. Lookie here, what I found. He pulled the wine bottle out of his pocket. He started pushing the cork down the neck of the bottle with his finger.

That candle holder is made of gold, yelped Squirt. I found it.

He pushed the cork past the neck of the bottle, a few drops splashed onto his hand, he licked it.

You wouldn't believe what you can find in houses around here, boys. You know, I'm even considering the idea . . . he stuck the neck of the bottle in his mouth, took a swig . . . I'm entertaining the notion of establishing a little museum here. Right next to Blahoš. Why, boys, around here we might even find, and now I'm exaggerating a little, the boot of Forefather Czech himself! he was saying . . . That's a good thing, right! Recently, for example, I found an exquisite girl's head wreath! Imagine! And now the adventure, boys, he chuckled, thumping Ondra in the shoulder so hard it made him stagger . . . of trying to find the crown that the girl thrust on her head after she took off that wreath. Enticing, right? You'd enjoy that, wouldn't you? Shake on it? But seriously, now! If you find something, I'll give you a reward. There are still things in attics around here. Cellars. Hah! The reward is as good as yours. I've also got a showpiece right here in this sack.

The sack was lying on the floor by his feet.

Don't touch that. I've got a pair of wolf's jaw tongs in there. Could cleave your hand right off, ouch.

And was Granddad really hidden there for the entire time of the war? And why, said Ondra. Was he a resistance fighter?

Unngggghh, Polka spluttered, the wine spraying from his mouth. He tilted his head back, wiped the jacket, smearing the drops around.

No, drinking's no good for you! Ask the reverend. That's what he's here for. He helped your grandfather. Throughout the war. In the end they were always sitting around together, talking like when they were young. Kept on about cremation like old funeral directors. Argh! He tilted his head back, pouring wine down his throat till his Adam's apple was bobbing up and down . . . It's Polka all right, said Ondra to himself, he was relieved . . . Polka fumbled around in the top pocket of the jacket. Aha! He exclaimed, pulling out a folded piece of paper, he kneaded it, gobbled up the pill, swallowed, his Adam's apple jumped . . . No, drink doesn't do it for me, my dear gentlemen, but anything hypnotic makes me feel poetic, he cried . . . And you know, to be completely honest, and why shouldn't I be after all, the idea about the little museum at the foot of Blahoš isn't entirely mine. The teacher came up with it, he's an educated man. The time is right to preserve the treasures of Czechness, is it not? Down in the mine shafts under Blahoš they'd even survive a nuclear war, would they not? And then we the Czechs could all die blissfully, why not? Why, the remnants of Czechness will hold their own even in an eventual encounter with an extraterrestrial civilisation, at least as a touching and noteworthy memento of humanity, right? What do you say to that, boys? Get your kit on. The teacher is back! He was shot in the head and now he's telling stories down the pub. And Berka too, yippee! This is going to be a lesson and a half! Everybody's been down there since early morning. You washed?

Yep! they said in unison.

Let's go then. Check this out first!

He fished around in the sack, pulled out the tongs, swinging them through the air, the teeth bared, he snapped them shut, something small peeled off from the jaws of the tongs, something like a tiny leaf dropped to the floor, dripped almost. Probably a speck of rust, said Ondra to himself, there were stains all over the teeth of the tongs.

That's something, eh, boys? One of my helpers found these too. And he got some coins for his trouble, cash in hand! These are ancient wolf's jaw tongs, oh yes, hand crafted! They'll be the showpiece of the entire exhibition. Makes you wonder, eh?

They were gawking at the tongs.

Polka made the tongs snap again.

This iron has already bitten through a little wolf's neck, would you believe it?

Yeah, said Squirt.

They used to do that in the old days, apparently, so the wolf wouldn't come back. Though that doesn't make any sense, how could it have come back, when it was already dead, eh?

Yeah, said Squirt.

Polka was running his hand over the jacket, over the wine stains.

It is a nice suit, he was saying, tongs in his hand. I'll return it, don't you worry. And I'll return it, prick up your ears now! Polka lowered his voice, directly to its owner. Get it?! he roared.

Ondra nodded immediately. His whole body tensed. He almost jumped up into the air. But he was embarrassed. It took Squirt a moment to get it.

To Dad, yeah? Dad's coming!

Yep! said Polka. Not a peep to anyone, okay? Mum's the word! Be wary, at a time like this, with a war on, or whatever it is, damn it, no one knows . . . he swung the tongs through the air, almost knocking the candle holder off the window ledge. He put the tongs in the sack. He threw the sack over his shoulder. And off we go. The drink's finished. The rain has stopped.

There was enough room in the cart for both of them. They tossed in rags, blankets, a tattered tracksuit jacket, whatever they could find. Ondra stuck Standa's sweater in there. Squirt nestled himself in the pile. Polka pushed down on the pedals, hurtling off along the stream. Hah hah, exclaimed Polka, I can take on any hill!

They whizzed over the little bridge, Polka pedalled a few times up the hill, stopped. He was taking deep breaths. Ondra climbed out of the cart. Polka threw in the sack with the tongs in it. He pushed the bike holding the handlebars. Squirt was loafing around on the blankets. He kept his legs as far away from the sack as possible. The trees lining the road had been cleaved by lightning. The branches and the mud were gone. They'd been cleared away. They went up the hill in silence. Soon they saw the pub.

I knew she wouldn't be here, he was saying to himself, scanning the place for Zuza for a long time before his face finally became downcast. Hiya, Pepa Líman said to him. I've come to get you. Have you seen Jindra, said Ondra, he was supposed to bring the Monolith . . . What? What are you going on about? said Pepa, surprised. Ondra's jaw dropped, he saw Bohadlo.

Berka was sitting at the table in the middle of the pub, Bohadlo next to him, his face was a mask, a white ball, his entire head was a white sphere, there was a hole in the sphere and in it there was a straw, Bohadlo was drinking a snifter through the straw, the hands of the old men were handing him another one, full to the brim, it passed from hand to hand, some of the hands were leathery, scrawny with tremulous fingers, others were so wrinkled the shot glass almost got lost in the folds of the skin, the tough flesh, the nails of the old men were like shards of glass overgrown with flesh, they were broken, corroded. Bohadlo drank the shot in one slurp, the empty glass passed through the line of hands again, clinked against the beer tap. Yep, all those years I lied to them, the bandaged head was prattling in a hoarse voice, I lied to the children, Bohadlo was saying, the sound emanating from the head, from the orifice in the bandages, the old men were nudging each other with their elbows, winking at each other, the white head swayed forwards, backwards . . . at the blokes' table someone said lazily, as if slapping a card down on the table, as if he'd already said it many times: Well, Teachy's gone bonkers . . . Not at all, cried Bohadlo, that piece of shrapnel has enlightened me with understanding . . . Atone for your sins then, said Berka, taking out his handkerchief . . . Are there enough young people of school age in the establishment? cried Bohadlo.

Yes, comrade, called Pepa, he was pushing Ondra and Squirt forward. Yeah, comrade, squealed Squirt, they squeezed through to the table, Zuza's mum put plates in front of them. Yay, thank you, said Squirt, he whispered to Ondra: I'm not going to eat that, look, Ondra looked, there was flypaper above them, a trail of yellow slime glistened above their heads, a red streak swept through the curtain of cigarette and pipe smoke, Berka blew his nose in his red handkerchief, making a sound like a trumpet . . . Eat, Ondra told Squirt, you have to eat! Squirt tossed the food under the table. There were little dogs down there. Outside the sun was shining. The patches of light on the wooden floor looked like faces.

I have lied to schoolchildren all my life, the bandaged head was saying, I tormented them with false heroic epics about our kind . . . Give us your testimony, said Berka. I will! cried Bohadlo. This is better than the radio, Karel, said one of the men . . . Except you can't turn it off, ha ha ha! They listened, the old women, sitting in the hall, the children, jostling by the door, here and there a chair creaked, a glass clinked, a dog howled . . . got a kick under the table, they were all listening, they were quiet, so that they could hear the Head.

The truth is that two brothers came to Blahoš Hill, Lech and Czech, with a horde of their people who'd escaped from servitude in Egypt . . . originally there were three of them, but brother Rus quarrelled with the other two brothers. He was a huge bloke and a cantankerous pain in the arse. So the brothers Lech and Czech preferred to give him the slip, taking their people to another country. They were standing on Blahoš. We'll stay here, said Czech, he was knackered. But Lech sniffed the air, he said: I want to go to the sea. Piracy and trade, remember? That's why they threw them out of Egypt. But Czech didn't feel like going anywhere else. Lech left him there. The way the old and infirm used to be abandoned in the woods. Lech went away together with the wise greybeards and the august warriors with their wives and virgins, all the capable tradesmen went too, that's common knowledge. When Czech looked around, he tore out his beard and wept. The only people left were old and sick, there were all kinds of pregnant whores and drunkards riddled with depression. There were also hordes of little children, the kind no one wanted. Czech said: Only wretched folk are left. So dig a trench and we'll all die in it, that's the best thing to do. Those who could still speak tried to talk him out of it with their weak voices, but Czech refused to yield. Give me my club, I'm going to strike you all down, disgrace to the earth that you are. When they saw there was no other way, they were a cowardly and slavish rabble, they dug a trench and lay down it. At night those that could still move strangled Czech. They wept terribly and said he'd been bitten by a snake. And in your memory, dear Forefather, let us be called the Czechs. So. But because they were abysmally lazy, they lived in that trench, seeing as they'd toiled so hard on it. They made dens in there and little smoky fires and continued to multiply. The little children gathered berries and roots. Somehow they made a life for themselves. That's how it was.

Excellent! a bloke in overalls cried out, slamming his beer mug down on the table. Hah hah! someone howled. Arms with snifters were now being extended from all sides towards the table with the old men. They took them, of course they did. They stuck the straw in Bohadlo's mouth. But he spat it out.

I've been saying the truth since early morning, he said. I've changed my ways.

Well, you're a sheaf ready to be taken to the barn of Christ, said Berka.

Pepa nudged Ondra. It's a lark, eh? You know what he said? That he's going to abandon human habitations. That he's going to live like a hermit. I reckon he'll soon be running around in the woods, eating frogs and scaring people, that's something, eh?

Hm, said Ondra. That is.

Dear friends, cried Bohadlo. You know that today is a special day. He's right! cried Berka. You know what happened! You know what day it is.

So listen to the tale of an evil mother, said the bandaged head, swaying. There once was a pretty woman, you'd all like the look of her. She walked around wearing make-up, her lips were lovely, she was lovely all over, you all ogled her. There was also a little girl here, remember? Where was she from? A little child, unknown to all. Whose are you? What do you want? You don't talk like us. So that strange woman took her in as her own, why not, they were both different. So the little girl and the woman, now her mother, went for a walk, and then Blahoš Hill opened up, the Mother walked right in and Eluzína stood guard. And what did she see there! Mountains of gold and pearls and precious things. Coins, jewels galore. A tremendous treasure accumulated over centuries. Ho ho! The Treasure of the Tatars. The little girl stood guard by the stolen goods, and when she heard how that terrible Mother was straining with yet more things, fearless Eluzína went in there intending to help her, but being a vain girl she kept putting on royal togs, the dresses of some princesses, and didn't help her mother none when she was carrying out strings of pearls and trinkets, and outside the Mother shouted: Where's my little girl? And it had just turned midnight and the crag closed over. Eluzína stayed inside. The Mother lost her mind, all her hair fell out. And Eluzína's day is celebrated to this day. Bohadlo put his head in his hands.

The men at the bar were clapping. Everyone was laughing. More! someone shouted. Ondra had put his cutlery on his plate a long time before the end. Next to him Pepa was smiling inanely. Squirt was giving presents to the dogs. He was winking at Ondra. He was tugging on his sleeve.

Berka stood up. Everybody listen! You're all invited! There's a special evening service tonight. A procession in all its splendour, yes! Berka sat down again. Boys, he leant over to Ondra. Just imagine! Everyone here already knows. The church has been flooded. And boys, it's not exactly easy for me to tell you this, you especially . . . the current ripped up the new soil, yeah, flushed out the coffin into the river. The current carried it away.

Yeah? said Ondra.

Hm, said Squirt.

Squirt had been kicking Ondra under the table for a while.

At that moment Polka hurtled past them and that was funny! Squirt's eyes went wide. Polka had a shot glass on his head, and probably because he was running around the place really fast, his head was sort of . . . twisted at an odd angle . . . the glass didn't fall off! . . . Blimey! exhaled Pepa . . . Polka was standing next to Bohadlo, he took the glass off his head, grabbed Bohadlo's bandaged chin, pulled it forward, tossed the liquor in his mouth . . . Bohadlo was choking and spluttering, but he swallowed it. The men were doubling up with laughter.

Squirt kicked Ondra under the table.

And Pepa tugged on Ondra's sleeve and whispered: Let's go, come on!

And Squirt cried: Don't go anywhere!

And Polka shouted: Hey, everybody in the house! Teachy's back! Cheers! Listen everybody! continued Polka after they'd banged their beer mugs and shot glasses down on the table . . . while you were fending off the Ruskies on the bridge . . . Yeah, yeah! bellowed someone . . . I went on reconnaissance. And look here, look what I found on the railway track. Polka reached into his pocket. And, probably just because he happened to be standing by their table, he tossed a steel nut in front of Ondra. Straight away he was pulling more out of his pocket. The old men were passing them to each other. A few men came over from the bar.

Lookie here, said Polka. Seems the Ruskies shoot steel nuts from catapults, right?

Show me! the constable was reaching over to the table. He grabbed one of the steel nuts. He passed it on.

Pepa said to Ondra: Let's go.

Squirt grabbed Ondra's hand.

Polka was showing the men a catapult. The handle of the catapult had green plastic wire coiled round it. One of the men reached for the catapult and it fell on the floor.

Move it, whispered Pepa. They slipped past the bar, into the hall and out of the pub.

8.

Ondra was pulling Standa's sweater out of the cart. He won't be giving us any more tests, not him! sniggered Pepa. Líman up to the blackboard! No chance.

Ondra tied the sweater around his waist.

Pepa kept guffawing. Wait till Jindra sees Bohadlo. Beyond his expectations that, you betcha.

And where is Jindra?

Dunno, Pepa shrugged his shoulders. Haven't seen him. Secret cops are looking for you. And your brother.

Yeah?

We led them off, into the bogs, the woods. Come on, let's run!

They ran all the way to the little bridge. Then they walked briskly.

Hey, said Ondra in the forest. So what about the cops?

So I ran into the cops, said Pepa. And the cop goes: Laddie, aren't you Ondra Lipka? I'm an uncle from Prague. I've got something for you from your daddy. Chocolate too! Yeah, right! I says, scarpering. The other one screams: Stop, child! He comes after me. By then I'm on the hillside. They're scrambling after me. The old one's having trouble. The young one's dragging him up the slope. By his arm, his elbow. They're stumbling over rocks. I'm already up at the top, so I'm well happy. Laughing at them. I see Venca and Láďa Ploughman above me, taking cover in the bushes, watching. They want to take the cattle out to pasture with us in the evening. Little lads, tiddlers. So I give them an order, you know! And the tiddlers know what I mean. We've got a present for you! the cop shouts up the hillside. But by then he was bellowing at Venca, see. And Venca says to the cops: Yeah. Give us the present, then! He led them off through the bushes, nicely done. There were other boys up at the top. The cops clambered from one hillside to another. Tonda led them to the bog. They almost didn't make it out! Arms and legs flailing about. That's what we wanted, for them to not make it out. We're not playing around any more! the cops called. You're going to get a good slapping, boy, just you wait! And Tonda scarpered. They ran after him like dimwits. He led them to Blahoš. Beyond the barbed-wire fence. By then the old one was limping. The young one's jacket was torn. They've both got bruises all over. Where are they? Maybe they got stuck somewhere, what do you reckon?

Maybe they'll step on a mine!

And get blown up!

Chance would be a fine thing.

And you know what? The tiddlers have found something. Come on, let's run.

There was a bevy of boys in front of the bunker. Tiddlers. There were lots he didn't know. Some of them were brothers of the Límans or the other lads. There were some big lads there too. Milan. Pavel. Craggy was sitting on a rock. Valeš in the grass. Jindra wasn't there. Valeš waved at Ondra.

The tiddlers were shouting over each other. They kept together, at short intervals one of them would run out of the huddle. They were hopping around in the grass in front of the bunker. Jostling each other.

It's ginormous! cried the boy with the haversack over his shoulder. It's a monster. It flies. It's like an octopus.

We were in the attic, said another boy. We looked towards the church. The thing was flying!

Yeah, said the boy with the haversack. Maybe it's . . . Poskina, someone said.

Booo, Poskina! Someone laughed loudly. They went quiet.

Valeš sniggered too. He got up. That's bollocks! Poskina runs, everyone knows that, said Valeš. Or leaps!

Like a dog, said someone. Leaps like a wolf. Ten metres, easy!

One of the tiddlers started crying. Poskina, they were whispering.

Go be with the lousy scumbags! yelled Valeš, admonishing them. Go hide in a room with thick walls. Poskina can't go there. Wussies!

Poskina's not a wolf. Nor a dog, said Pavel, joining in. He slapped his palms together. You, tiddlers, listen! Poskina doesn't fly. Everyone knows that.

That's right! He doesn't fly! said various voices.

You imagined you saw something, said Milan.

Did not! exclaimed the boy with the haversack. It was flying over the river near the church.

It flew out of the horses' hollow . . .

Leeches the size of a grown man live in there . . .

They stick to a bloke, drag him down to the bottom of the river!

Yeah, the bloke bursts and the gypos have a river full of soup, ha ha ha . . .

Wait, shouted Milan. Don't laugh. Don't talk over each other. Stop screaming. So what did you actually see?

The tiddlers were jostling each other. They all wanted to tell the story. The ones at the back were elbowing their way towards Milan.

The wind grew stronger! The monster was flying in the wind. It's here. Up on the hill! It's dreadful!

And it reeks, someone exclaimed.

Let's go then! cried Pepa. What could it be?

Tonda went to check it out, said Pavel. The boys thought they saw something. Or they're talking crap. They want to be with us.

And why not? said Ploughman. Ondra hadn't noticed him till then. Ploughman came out of the bunker.

Look, said Milan. First you're a tiddler. Then you get bigger. You pass the test and then you're a Líman. And then you're one of us.

That's how it's always been.

We want to be with you lot, said the boy with the haversack. We want to take the cattle out to pasture. We want to get out of here.

Listen! said Ploughman. Before, there were no Ruskies here. Before was ages ago. Who's for the tiddlers going with us?

We're not voting, said Milan. I've got the dagger.

Fuck that, said Ploughman. Today's different. I want to be with my brothers.

The boy with the haversack and another even smaller one were standing next to Ploughman.

And what about me, you twat? said Valeš. I've only got sisters.

They all burst out laughing.

Sure! Might as well take girls down the bunker now! said Pavel.

Tiddlers see monsters everywhere, said Milan. They don't listen. They talk over each other. They don't know how to walk in the woods.

Monsters don't exist, said Pavel. Maybe Poskina. Poskina doesn't fly. And as long as you're not on your own, he won't do anything. And who's seen him?

Well, said Craggy. My brother, maybe, mate. He might have seen him, no shit, matey.

One of the tiddliest boys started whimpering. They all started chattering again.

It was dreadful! We were scoping the terrain, it had stopped raining. There was a black cloud flying towards us. What's that? We went closer. It flew out of the water.

It was flying right at us, it was dreadful!

Well, how about it then, said Ploughman, his eyes fixed on Milan.

He said how about it then, fuck it, didn't he? cried Craggy.

No, said Milan.

You twat! Ploughman shook his arm at Milan. You! You know what they call you?

What? said Milan.

Sovpet, that's what you are, you twat! A Soviet pet. You took sweets from the Ruskies. You sent the tanks on Prague. Everyone saw it!

Milan said: What? What? Ondra saw that he was gripping the dagger tightly. He was adjusting his fingers on the handle.

Fucking hell! whispered Pepa into his ear. He's going to stab him.

You'll take that back, said Milan.

Fuck off! Ploughman didn't budge an inch. He too was eyeballing the dagger in Milan's hand. Everyone was watching.

He's going to knife him! whispered Pepa. He has to, now.

You were standing on the bridge! cried Ploughman. You sent the Russians to Prague. Sovpet!

Milan took a step forward. Ploughman didn't budge. Nor did his brothers. The older one had his hand in his haversack.

Craggy stood up.

Leave it out, cried Valeš.

No fucking Sovpet's going to give orders around here, said Ploughman. He put his hand in his pocket. One of the tiddlers sniggered. Stupid Sovpet! someone shouted.

They heard stamping. They heard branches breaking.

The bushes shook, Tonda fell into the grass, gasping for breath. I've seen it, he said. It's there.

One of the tiddlers yelped: The monster. Let's get out of here, cried the boy with the haversack.

No, said Milan. I'm going after it. I'll run it through with the dagger. Who's with me? I'm not afraid.

Don't go! said Tonda. It's huge. Wrapped around a tree. Breathing. Never seen anything like it.

It'll see you and leap at you, shouted one of the tiddlers. It'll eat you! The tiddlers were whimpering. A few of them ran towards the hillside. They came back again.

Let's go, said Pavel. Who's coming? He was looking at Ondra.

Me, said Ondra.

Get up, said Milan, poking Tonda. He turned round to the others. Spat in the grass. Go and be with the girls. Put some lipstick on. Go and hide in the hayloft!

Milan went first. They followed him up the slope.

It was windy on the hilltop. The wind was swishing among the trees. They saw it at the edge of the wood. In the thicket around a tree.

Ondra stopped. He was sweating. Pavel walked behind Milan. He was walking slowly. He was sharpening the end of a stick.

He could smell the stench. His stomach was heaving. He kept sweating. They could hear it breathing.

Milan didn't stop.

Pavel was walking right behind him.

His eyes were fixed on the bush. Something was gleaming inside. The light was gloomy in there. He could see the eyes of the monster flashing.

Milan jumped into the bush. He was jabbing the knife in all directions. Screaming. It was falling on top of him.

Tonda yelled out. Ondra was standing next to him. They saw Milan stabbing and slashing with the dagger. The monster had wound itself around him.

I'm going in, shouted Pavel, and set off, pointing the sharpened end of the stick forward. He stopped.

Milan was crawling out of the bush. He was holding his nose with two fingers. His whole face was twitching, he was grimacing.

You stabbed it, yelped Pavel.

Milan was laughing. He was in stitches. He was holding on to a branch. He threw the knife into the ground.

I went up to it! I wasn't afraid!

Yeah! shouted Pavel. You weren't afraid, said Ondra.

It's not a monster, said Milan. It's a parachutist.

They were looking into the bushes. The parachute was inflating and deflating again with each blast of the wind. He'd got caught on the branches. They stared into the dead man's face. It had been disfigured by an explosion, or the face was decomposing. His round glasses were twinkling. The straps of the parachute had gotten tangled up with the branches. The bush was lifting the dead man up and down a little. He was wearing a green uniform. His legs in boots were trailing in the grass.

Monster! Fuck me! Pavel chuckled, thumping Tonda's shoulder.

Milan was unbuttoning the breast pockets, Pavel was rifling through the trousers. Nothing, said Pavel. Everything must have fallen out.

He hasn't even got any insignia, said Milan. Too bad.

Ondra approached more closely. He blocked his nose with two fingers. You couldn't see the eyes behind the glasses.

Ha ha! laughed Milan. Monster, they said. He hasn't got binoculars, nothing. Not even a handgun. Someone picked him clean.

The tiddlers said he was blown over the river, said Pavel. From the gypos.

Aha, said Milan.

They came back out of the thickets. Tonda was running away. With a few strides he vanished in the woods.

He's ashamed, said Pavel.

Let's get out of here, said Milan. So they ran. Ran down the hillside. They didn't stop until they'd reached the footpath. They were walking side by side.

There was no one at the bunker. Trampled grass was all that the boys had left behind. They walked down the slope, through the forest, they crossed the wire fences. They jumped over the tree trunks left behind by the storm.

You're coming with us in the evening, said Milan.

We've got to grab the best places. Before the lads from Bělá turn up. The Zásmuky boys, mate, said Pavel.

Sure, said Ondra.

They were walking along the tree-lined avenue. Between the first houses on the outskirts of the village. There were still puddles everywhere.

They were plodding towards them over the little bridge. They were propping each other up. The young one's jacket was missing a sleeve, his face was covered in scratches, the old one was limping, holding on to the railing for support.

Hello there, boys.

Ondra wanted to say: Hello, but Milan said: What do you want?

Boys, we need some information, said the older one.

What? Who're you looking for? Where you from? said Milan.

What are your names, boys?

I'm Milan. I'm a Líman. Who are you?

Boy, we're the ones asking the questions. What's your name? The older one pointed to Pavel with his chin.

I'm Pavel Líman. Why you asking? We haven't done anything.

This is my brother, said Milan. He put his hand on Ondra's shoulder.

Líman, I expect, said the older one.

Yep, said Ondra.

You wouldn't happen to know where we could find Ondra or Kamil Lipka, I suppose?

We wouldn't, said Milan.

Don't you play with them?

They're Praguers, chief. Fucking wankers. We don't give a shit about them, said Milan.

Clear off, boys. Clear off right now.

They walked round them.

Scum, said the older cop. They're scum, he said. He leant over the railing. Spat into the stream.

They were trotting up the road, they didn't stop until they were in front of the pub.

We'll go when it gets dark.

Where from?

From the river, said Milan, waving his arm.

All right then, said Ondra and started running again. He passed the pub, ran up the hill. Then he slowed down. He didn't want to be completely out of breath when he got to Standa's place.

That's it exactly, she said to herself. She moved away from the window immediately. She didn't want him to catch a glimpse of her. No doubt he'd come inside, all red in the face, he wouldn't take his eyes off her. He'd put a coin on the counter, saying: One Kofola! Your suitor's here, the men would say, choking with laughter. Get the stepladder out, Zuza! Ha ha ha.

That's exactly it. Men don't run around like that all the time. They don't gawp at everything. I do like him, a lot. But. I raise my elbows, arch my back like this, then he's on top of me like a sack of potatoes, pushing me up against the wall. The girls were laughing their heads off at the way he gawked at us through the window. He's running off somewhere again, in his shorts. I've got work to do, she gave the table a cursory wipe with the rag.

The pub was closed. They never shut this early. They closed because of the Old Hag.

I got such a fright when I saw her. Everyone got up, picked up their things and got the hell out. Dad said: Just sweep up in the evening, get the middle table ready. Then be on your way, shove off.

Oh Daddy, how I'd love to shove off from these shores, to float away, you've got no idea. She rinsed the beer mugs. I'll just give the spit-covered floor a few slaps of the mop and I'll be off to the bonfire. That Vendula: You're not going to leap over the bonfire, she'd said it quietly so the girls wouldn't hear. You might hurt it . . . is that what you want?

Of course I don't want that!

You haven't been to see the Old Hag, every girl would like someone to get rid of it for them, every girl would.

You too? Zuza blurted out.

Me, what about me, said Vendula, wavering.

There you go then.

The first time he came to her was that night he'd made all the punters dance again, she heard him, the stairs creaked, she could tell when it was Mum, she always stopped to catch her breath, he walked up quickly, two steps at a time, everyone had been in stitches that evening, she'd laughed too, they laughed at what he said, at the way he said it. He came to her, he talked, encircled her with his arms, ensnaring her with sweet talk. He's mesmerising me, she'd said to herself.

My little doe, prick up your ears and listen to me! I'll take you away from here, you'll get to see the whole wide world. We'll have kids, we have to, otherwise you'd run away. I'll love them, I'll love you too, I'll take care of you all. Would you like that?

How many times she'd laughed in his face. Just then she was crying.

My little doe, I know. Life is hard, but death isn't much of a lark either, trust me.

She was afraid Dad might hear. But she couldn't stop it, she was laughing into the pillow.

Polka. Everyone wanted his advice. They went to see him. He wasn't afraid of anyone. Not even the secret police. He even took the Mickey out of Bohadlo. That slimebag, who kept crawling after her, always snooping on her. Polka saw through him. Oh well, Bohadlo, Teachy, poor wretch. What happened to him? What was he prattling on about here? Everyone laughed at him. Poor wretch . . . but! . . . he kept her in detention after school, whenever he liked, Bohadlo, then she had to go with him from Bělá through the woods that time, with that slobberer, people talked about that . . . Hey! Polka had whacked Teachy in the back, he'd slumped down on the table, snoring, he was plastered again, Dad never threw him out, everyone was afraid to say anything to him. Hey, you! The little museum's a good idea, but will you even have time? . . . Wake up, Polka kept slapping his back, you're tired, you keep traipsing after girls through the woods . . . you've got a fever, Teachy, girl-fever, you keep thinking about her . . . she doesn't want you, right? . . . you lie down somewhere among the trees, sweating in the heat, sweating on the inside, eh? yelled Polka, thumping Teachy again, waving his forefinger, making a sign: Do not disturb! . . . the old men were sniggering, the women sitting on sacks who'd been nattering incessantly were now cocking their ears, peeking in from the hallway . . . You can't stand those drops of sweat, it's a viscous kind of sweat that's dribbling from your bones into your insides, cried Polka, Zuza was cringing in the corner behind the beer tap, they didn't know Polka was doing this to impress her . . . You look at your hands and what do you see? They're all hairy, suddenly your fingers are longer than before, your crooked nails are glistening, you're rolling around in the forest, touching your belly with those weird fingers, touching your chest, you've got a thick coat of hair all over your body . . . not like a bloke normally does! cried Polka, winking . . . and they all roared with laughter, only Teachy was holding his head in his hands, Polka was taking long stork-like strides, running around Bohadlo, and when the laughter died down and the old men had stretched their legs again, scraping their chairs towards their beers, he says . . . There's a thick coat of fur on your back, a chill runs down your spine, it's like a spasm and that's your ecstasy, your back is near the earth, your head too, you're sniffing around in the earth, then you start running, you're running on all fours, you're running quickly, you can smell the forest, you can smell the rotting leaves, you can smell the moss, you can smell the scent of everyone who's been through there, you can smell everyone who's walking through the woods, and you're running . . . Polka stopped, froze, one stork-like leg

221

placed in front of him, they froze with him, no one was laughing, they almost weren't moving, not even the boys peeping in through the open windows, their faces hanging on the window ledges on the inside of the pub . . . here and there one of the old women fiddled with her fingers, quickly putting her middle finger over her forefinger, a little cross won't do any harm, he's talking about the little wolf, isn't he? . . . only Polka was laughing, but quietly . . . And then you wake up in the morning in your bed . . . and there's blood all over your mouth and you don't know why! Ha ha, laughed Polka, snatching a snifter from the old men's table with a sweep of the hand, he moved towards the bar, standing in front of her he whispered: To your good health, my little doe . . . he slammed the empty shot glass on the counter and the chairs started creaking again, the men were lifting their arms with fingers raised, ordering beer and spirits, as though their throats had gone dry in that short time, now they were all burbling at full tilt again, the boys were sticking their heads through the windows, scrounging for chewing gum, beer mugs and shot glasses were clinking again, the constable called out: Hey, quit clowning around all the time . . . and stop talking shit . . . he waved his arm.

That's how it was.

She'd already put the chairs up on the tables. I shouldn't be lifting them, but who else is going to lift them? She only left the middle table. The pub's closed. Everyone's gone. At least I've got some time. She ran the cloth over the middle table. She pulled the wick up in the lamp. They made a quick exit because the Old Hag had come in. The wick looked like a worm. It made her cry once when she was little. She thought they were burning the little worm's head off.

She'd seen her through the window. She got a fright. She thought she'd come to tell on her. Come to tell her dad about it. She'd already hidden the bottle, as well as the bag with the herbs. The Old Hag shuffled along with her walking stick, outside she always walked like she was a doddery old bag. She makes herself different to make an impression.

She was hobbling along, limping, her dirty hair braided into a knot. Zuza heard the walking stick tapping down the hall, the old women recoiled from the Old Hag . . . she fell over on the doorstep.

The first to get up was the constable, he ran his hands over his uniform and said: On your feet, citizen! He leaned down to her, she was whispering something to him, he was leaning over so much he almost fell over, he kept sweeping his hands over his uniform. He called out: Karel, close the door . . . someone brought the Old Hag a glass of water, she drank, she'd also have liked to help her, but it was better not to even look at her.

Closed! We're closed! Dad was shouting and clapping his hands, the men were getting up, scraping their chairs back, even the old men left, straggling past the Old Hag sitting there on the doorstep, glass in her hand. They left immediately, no one had anything to say in parting and that was odd.

What happened? she'd asked Dad. Give it a once-over, get the middle table ready, then off with you. They were leaving, Mum too, her head in a shawl, she followed the women who were now leading the Old Hag by the hand. She closed the door.

The quiet of the empty pub. She was familiar with that. From night-time. In the mornings she mostly had to hurry, getting everything ready.

She walked around the tables, emptied the ashtrays. She left the beer mugs and other glasses out to dry, letting the water drip off them. Onto the counter, onto the rag.

Weird. My legs never used to hurt. How could I jump this time? I won't. But what will I say? I can't tell them anything. I don't even know if I can do it, be with the girls.

She put the bottle in a bag. The pouch with the herbs too. I'll drink it on my own. In the woods. I'll get drunk. No one will see me. I'll be on my own. It will die.

She sat down at the middle table.

What was it he said to me, what was it he said to me today? I never know when he's taking the Mickey and when he's not. He says he doesn't drink, and he drinks. He swears at people. They wouldn't let a stranger do that. He's an outsider. And he's not.

She stuck her finger in a damp patch on the table, drew a head. She drew two heads. She stuck her finger in her mouth and daubed a heart around the two little heads with her saliva. After all, he'd said: We'll get out of here.

He knows how to get out of here. No one would go after us. Not even Dad. The roads were jammed.

They could return later. When everything had changed.

She picked up the rag. Wiped the heart off the table. Rubbed off her girl's saliva.

She was looking at her tummy. From up here it's funny. Looks like my legs are growing straight out of my belly. My two legs, like sticks.

Polka. No one dares say anything bad to him. In the morning the men stagger out of the pub, off to get some sleep. Women find them all hateful at that moment, except for Polka! He gives them the eye, mumbles something, and there they are, simpering. He's friends with the reverend, even the constable takes advice from him. Berka goes to see him, even Bohadlo swears by him. There's no one like Polka. He makes fun of Líman. Do the bear! When Polka gives the order, even Líman dances. How many times has it happened that Dad was drunk, Mum was asleep, and Polka was on his own downstairs, pouring himself another beer from the tap? And when he comes to her, he's never drunk.

And why are you like that? Why do you carry on like that?

Because I can. I do bad things too.

Then don't do bad things, she kicked his leg. He took hold of her head, her head was nestled between his elbows, he lay on top of her.

I have to do bad things, because I can. But I draw the line when it comes to you, girl.

She hadn't seen him do that before. Really whimper like that.

They were lying on their backs.

Sometimes I even weep, would you believe it? You wouldn't, eh? A big man like me. Wouldn't think I had it in me!

Look. You've got a grey hair here. Completely grey! She coiled the hair around her finger and tore it out.

I cry because life is huge. I don't have any other explanation. I like it when you kiss me there, keep doing it. And hey! Don't close your eyes! That means you're thinking about someone else. If you are, say so. I'll be glad to get the stepladder for him! Don't get upset right off. What about this? You like this? Yeah? Me too.

Shut up, then.

When he fell asleep, she watched him. Listening in case she heard the stairs creak. Her mum might come up the stairs. Mum did that when Zuza was a little girl. Sometimes she'd come up to check on her at night. Whenever she fell asleep, his snoring woke her up. He must have cast a spell on her parents, she said to herself. Otherwise there's no way they wouldn't hear it. He was snoring, grinding his teeth. She thumped his side, he rolled over. She watched him, the pillow was too small for him. Then she'd hear the cocks crowing. First one, then the others joined in.

She stood up. She surveyed the pub. Most of the light was coming from the oil lamp. The wick behind the smoke-stained glass was quivering. It was drawing in light from outside. Shattering the light. What was it he said? Get yourself ready, girl. We'll be off. We'll disappear. Soon the only sun shining here will be black.

Oh well, she said to herself. We'll leave together. Every girl would like to hear that.

She went behind the counter, pulled out the bag. She took out the bottle and the pouch. I'll just wrap the bottle in a dishcloth. Night will fall. No one will see me.

The door handle moved, someone was pulling the door open, she wanted to call out: We're closed! She had a quick peep and then lowered her head again. She squatted down, crouching. But she couldn't help herself. She craned her neck, leant her chin on the counter, put her head between the beer mugs.

They shuffled over to the middle table. The old one was grabbing on to chairs for support. Their shadows flitted over the wall. Their faces and arms were covered in scratches. They sat down immediately.

Someone else walked in, she recognised Dad by his footsteps, she pressed her chin into the wet rag.

Evening all, he said, scraping back his chair. Evening, comrade, said the older cop, and before the door slammed shut, Líman walked in. How am I going get out of here? said Zuza to herself, the light of the petrol lamp flashed off the buttons of a uniform, dazzling her. Salutations, comrades! said Constable Frída, Líman didn't say anything, he pushed his chair towards the light. Praised be the Lord, whispered old man Berka, also sitting down, and there was someone else there too.

They talked over one another, she was watching them through the gap between the beer mugs, then Dad stood up, scraped his chair back, almost shouting: I've got all my papers in order, damn it, but who am I supposed to hand them over to and why? I don't want to, he said, sitting down again . . . people trudged all over the hills, he added quietly.

They were paid fair and square, however, said the older cop.

The point is that you can't force us, said Zuza's dad. If there's a Tatar treasure around here somewhere, then it rightfully belongs to us who've lived here all these years. We won't have it swallowed up by somebody from Prague, for example.

Too right! exclaimed Líman, banging his fist on the table.

This really isn't about archaeological research, said the old cop.

Look here, our forefathers lived here a long time ago, and if you want to dig in the ground . . . said the man who'd come in with Berka. Craggy.

Nonsense, comrade! the young cop shouted at him. This is about the country's defence capabilities.

Tell him not to interrupt me, yeah? said Craggy. We've come together for a discussion, right? I've got my rights, haven't I?

Of course, said the older cop.

Comrades, said Líman. Pardon the question, right? How come you're both so much worse for wear? You look like you've been playing tag with our boys all day.

Ha ha, Craggy was doubling up with laughter. He had to hold on to the chair. Ha ha!

Hmph, hmph, snorted old man Berka.

Well! exclaimed the young cop. The local boys . . .

What? bellowed Líman. He banged his fist on the table again. In front of the young cop. He got a fright. He winced. Zuza drew her head back. She hid behind the counter. She couldn't stop herself from laughing. She stuffed her fist in her mouth.

Oh dear, comrade. Did I startle you? Why, just now you jumped up like that little flame. Do forgive me, alrightey? I'll give my boys a good hiding. You can count on that.

Fathers, do not belittle your children, so that they don't become weak-minded, said Berka. Commentaries on Proverbs, numbers three and twelve. I'm going to the service, he said, standing up and pushing back his chair.

We haven't finished talking, said the older cop. Líman's whole body tensed in his chair.

Sit down for a bit longer, then, old man, said Zuza's dad.

Sit down, neighbour, said Frída.

In view of the international situation, said the older cop, we have the authority to hold a military tribunal.

Oh shit, said Líman. With him in charge, eh? The Cougher? So you're going to execute us in the end, are you? Well, fuck me sideways. He poked the constable with his elbow. They were sitting next to each other.

We should drink to that, comrades. Just imagine that the last thing I'll see before all eternal death is this here snout belonging to the Coughy Boy! It's like not having lived at all, fuck it.

He got up, went up to the bar. She was completely still. Líman reached for the shelf, grabbed a bottle. He went to the table, sat down on his chair, he'd already opened the bottle. He took a swig. He put the bottle in front of Craggy. He also took a swig.

I want to inform you all, said Berka, standing up, about a special religious service.

Hah, said Craggy. Ha ha!

Let us pray, said Berka. We'll march in a procession! We'll form a procession in all its glory. He was fumbling for something in his pockets, pulled out a handkerchief, hid his face in it. Plopped down in his chair again.

All right, said the younger cop. You have a service to attend? Very well. You belong to a particular denomination? All right. But first let's conclude the matter of the documentation. And the devices. He banged his fist on the table. But it was risible. No one was listening to him.

Do you want to give it to the Ruskies or don't you? said Líman. What's it for? What was being measured here?

Is it really just about the weather? chimed in Craggy.

We heard stories about a motorway, said Zuza's father. And a tank training area. We know bugger all. What's it about?

We're the ones asking the questions around here, said the older cop.

And what if I tell you to fuck off with your questions? said Líman. What then?

Not giving you anything, said Zuza's dad.

Come on now, men, said the constable, don't be daft!

You keep your trap shut, said Líman. No one's asking you.

Comrades, is that your last word? said the older cop.

The Russians are in Osikov, said Líman. Nachty's done a runner. There's you two here. And who are you? What do you want? You want a drink? Please, Líman pushed the bottle towards the older cop. It wobbled, almost falling over. The cop caught it and pushed it away.

Pardon me, said Líman. Maybe the gentlemen from Prague would like glasses. In Russia they only drink from glasses, isn't that so? Why don't you tell us about it.

Ha ha ha, Craggy laughed.

So, said the older cop. I'm going to call on the comrade here, he nodded towards the constable, Comrade Frída.

All right then, the constable nodded.

Comrade Frída, I would like you to preside over the discussion from now on.

Someone spluttered with laughter. Berka was getting up again. Líman took a swig from the bottle and passed it to Craggy.

Very well, then, said the constable. He reached out, grabbed the bottle.

Put it on the table beside him. Craggy fixed his eyes on him. But he let him.

I didn't want this, said Frída. But if you won't have it any other way . . . Men! You think that this little light here, he waved his arm at the petrol lamp, isn't enough for me to be able to see inside a human being? Sit down again, Granddad.

What are you going on about? said Zuza's dad.

Clown, added Líman.

Craggy rocked back and forth in his chair. He folded his arms across his chest. He didn't even glance at the bottle.

So, said Frída. No need for any military tribunals, eh? We're all neighbours here. The comrades were just saying that. Lead is no good for the health, after all. Damages the body even after death. Lead is harmful and will soon be declared inhumane.

Get to the point, comrade, said the older one.

Yeah. I'm going about it in a roundabout sort of way, I know. In neighbourly fashion. There's no other way. Men. You know! The Soviets are putting the squeeze on us a little right now, despite all our fraternity. They have left the steppes. They're here. In our ancient basin. They crossed over the garland of our mountains, easy peasy. Even with heavy military hardware. That's how things stand. We're Czechs, that's clear. And men! Aren't you a lost cause for the future of humanity? That's the question that me and the comrades here are asking ourselves. Try to understand, after all. Whoever tries to resist the new law will get fucked.

Hmph, said Berka. My dear lad, my dear lad.

Has it sunk in yet? said Frída. The new life wants happiness for humankind here on earth. And you can't defy that. That kind of happiness just gets into a man of its own accord. Like a tiny little egg. Even if a person crawled under ground, that happiness will hatch in them. And the tanks? You say, tanks! Yeah, there are tanks here. There's a great kinship between machines and humans in the new world order. You've heard about satellites? Even the sky will be completely new.

You've completely fucking lost it, you fuckwit, said Líman.

Old Smoky is stirring up shit, chuckled Craggy.

Míra, that laugh wasn't really meant from the heart, said Frída. As a parent you surely know that violence is sometimes necessary to achieve happiness, right? Why have you gone as pale as ash all of a sudden, Míra?

No one said anything.

You're angry at me, aren't you, Craggy? Your misfortune is my grief too, don't doubt that. Why, it's the same with potatoes. One tiny little patch of mildew in one potato and the whole lot's ruined. You know that. And sweet corn? Nature's anger can even sweep away thick stalks like that. That's been visited upon us here too. Men, let's not beat about the bush any longer. The comrades would like the Patent Office documentation. You're the last ones refusing to hand over your contraptions. Is that so? Are you sure I'm not mistaken? Really?

Hmph, hmph, said Berka. I managed to lose it all, somehow!

Zuza's dad applauded. Now they were laughing.

Oh come on, Granddad, the constable patted Berka lightly on the shoulder. Maybe you'll remember. What about you, Jarda my lad?

Nothing, said Líman.

Aha, said the constable. Comrade, should I?

Frída didn't wait for the cop to nod. He wasn't looking at him. His eyes were fixed on the table in front of him. The buttons on his uniform were still glistening. They hurt her eyes. Must be their reflection in the beer mugs.

Jarda, my boy, said Frída, what would you say if I and one of the other comrades here sort of put you under our protection, eh? After all, as an officer of the law I own a pistol and the comrade here is no doubt also equipped for action, am I right? And the other comrade here, with your permission, would go and take a peek in your woodshed, yeah? He'd find a useful little pickaxe there. Because you didn't throw it out, you miserly git. I know that, I keep a record of all those sorts of things. It's been quite a few years, eh! We were still young back then. But what's a few years to a skeleton? Now the experts from Prague can see if they match. The marks on the bones and your little pickaxe. They'll take out the remains from the churchyard. They'll exhume him. That's no trouble at all for the comrades.

Her nose was full of the pong of beer. The wetness of the rag. She kept pressing her chin on it. Her neck was getting stiff.

Eh? You piece of shit, said Frída. He reached out with his arm, tugged on Líman's sleeve. You've been taking the piss out of me all these years. Smoky. The Cougher. Coughy Boy. A different age is upon us. It has arrived just in time, like I'd rung for it. And now you're going to see.

What's the matter with you? said Líman. You held him down. You were there.

Not likely, said Frída. Craggy got up. The younger cop moved into the corner behind Craggy. He looked like a shadow to her. The older one was also holding a pistol. He tapped it on the table.

Keep your gob shut, said Zuza's dad. Belt up. Both of you.

You were there too, said Líman. By the deep pool next to the church. You fell in and got soaked.

Frída waved his hand dismissively. Religious people are right about some things, he said. The mills of God grind slowly, but they grind. And now, men, you're going to get pulverised.

You were there, said Líman. My old woman dried all your togs in our house. You fell in the water. You slipped down the bank.

Oh, come on, said Frída. You don't believe that nonsense, do you, comrades?

No, said the older one. Not in the least.

And what about you two numbskulls? You, innkeeper! You were there too. Churchy! You arranged everything so niftily, we actually put him in a grave. By the wall. And what about you, Míra? And the others? You held the stinker under the water. He thrashed about. The pickaxe in the head didn't do the trick. You finished him off in the water. A rope around your neck and in you go, you thieving bastard. Well, every decent village has beaten at least one gypo to death at some point, I'm not saying they haven't. People don't get shot for it. Screw that. But get this: if they dig him out, you're going to do time. Eh?

You can't do that, not that, said Zuza's dad.

Oh but I can, said Frída. Ten, fifteen years. To the court it'll be murder, it's all just paperwork to them, one person is like another to them, am I right, comrades? Stop behaving like imbeciles. Hand over your contraptions. Or do you want to give them to the Americans? All right then. So that would be espionage and grand treason. Well that's suicide. Stop behaving like lunatics.

He looked them over, one by one.

Nod your heads in agreement, men, he said. And we'll drink to it. Give us a nod. I'm imploring you now! What about your boys, Jarda? They'll go feral without you. And you? That Zuza of yours, what a lovely girl. What would she do on her own? What would become of her? We both know what, Karel. We went to school together, for crying out loud. Don't let me be the only one to speak. Why are you keeping quiet? Churchy? You crying?

She wanted to have a look at Dad. She wanted to see what he was doing. This rag has made me drunk. And I've got pins and needles in my feet. Berka spotted her first. He almost dropped his handkerchief. By then the younger cop was moving towards her.

At that moment they heard the sound of motors. They rose immediately, pushing their chairs back. The sound erupted, deafening them. The explosion blasted the door open, smashed the windows, knocked the petrol lamp over. The place was now full of light. The air was white hot, hissing. The door kept flying open and slamming shut again.

9

What was it that happened to you? I have no tears, seeing as I'm the Mother of the Dead, they were all here again, for the second time since back then, but now they came for you, to carry you away, oh what is it that has befallen you? A boy like you, so brave, you went everywhere on your own, it's dreadful, this thing that has happened to you, but maybe it's better this way, forgive me for saying so, you were neither one of us nor one of them, you couldn't go to the other side of the river, and here? Here they laughed at you, there was no one like you here, I know you found me repulsive. Nan! You called me nice names, when your hand was reaching out for coins, you found me repulsive, and where were you supposed to go?

The Mother of the Dead, that's what that cheeky girl called me, so that's who I am, the Mother of the Dead. They're here everywhere, tiny newborn babies, blind little sucklings, little lambs, the girls stick them in the muddy banks, raking up the sand between the roots of the trees, they make a hollow where the dike slopes, that's where they ditch them, rejected little balls, slimy with blood, those little lights in the marshes, those are the ones expelled from their bodies, later the girl goes to fetch wood, walking through the forest she hears something go peep, she remembers, she hears crying, wailing in the trees, all the little ones start screaming at her, their voices sliding down the leaves, the girl walks by the river and coming from the reeds she hears: Mummy? Is that you? They come to see me after they hear their little ones, years afterwards they start trembling, the moment they get here they say to me: Old Hag, but I was so young and stupid, a stupid girl, why didn't you say anything to me?

But I did! You'll end up with him anyway, the little one will be somewhere, you didn't hear me then.

They come, they say: Granny, help! I'm supposed to help you now, girl? You weren't careful! But I did it out of love, they whisper, then that love turns to nothing but wailing, the sound of bubbles bursting in a muddy hollow, that's where she shoved it, the rustle of grass on the slope of the river bank, that's where she interred it, its tiny mouth smeared closed with mud, to begin with they are jumping from the attic with sacks of grain on their backs, later they vomit when they see Mum's knitting needle, after that they come to me, they don't say anything to their mums, they wouldn't, even if they knew their mums also used to come to see me.

Mother of the Dead, said the girl, and where is she now? Vanished, she took off, cheeky girl, they change right before my eyes like that, the one who washes dishes in the pub, she's still like a doe, with that startled look, her hair in her eyes so you can't see her face, she blushes when she speaks, she says: Granny, and if this doesn't help, will you do it yourself? Sure, and then for years whenever I look into your eyes all I'll see is hate, you'll change, so I'm the Mother of the Dead, well then that's who I am.

Some Nan you have. Something's rotting in the back of my mind, I can't catch sight of it, it's this crazy notion that the Evil One chose you because of me, and straight away I'm hurrying to tell you, I know I shouldn't say it: What would you have done with yourself here?

There was no one like you here, you were always hanging around the locomotive, you kept pleading for attention, from him, he let you call him: Dad. But he had dodgy dealings with us here, you used to go to meet him on his way home, all sad, as if he'd pinched your heart.

So they were here again, all of the them, the innkeeper, the policeman, the verger, a few of the others, back then they brought her, saying: Old Hag, take care of her, the way only you know how, we'll honour our debt to you. They brought a little girl, a little child.

Take care of her, they said, and we'll turn a blind eye to everything, Old Hag, you'll be able to live here. Neither you nor your people need ever go to the other side of the river, I promise you that for all days, said the constable.

They left her here, little blondie, straw hat on her head, just like the other one who came on her own, but where had she come from? Was she the one from the train? But where would she have got that dress from, she was like a little princess, all perfumed, she reminded them of all of that, that's why they didn't want her, a piece of wood would do the job, easier than doing a rabbit in, a little girl like that, shove her down a well, push her off a slippery river bank, lure her off the path somewhere in the woods, they didn't have the guts for that, so they brought her to me.

I took care of her all right, but in a different way than you all think.

And now they were here again, to take a look at the horror, oh the horror, how could you have done this to me, you miscreant, he was such a brave boy, went everywhere on his own, a fiend mauled you, my boy, you managed to crawl back to me here, I screamed at you in front of everyone and beat you with my fists, tearing my hair out, they stared at me.

But then again. You kept waiting for him all the time, going to the locomotive, you believed that the blighter would return, he left you in the lurch, he never did give a shit about you, if he'd been here it wouldn't have happened, maybe.

They carried you off on the shed door, I rolled around in the dirt, they weren't expecting anything else from me.

Looks like he's been mauled by dogs, someone said. Russian saboteurs, said another. But they were staring at the ground. They know. These people!

They know, they have to know who's doing it. They're from here, after all. They know everything. But they didn't send this boy. He's been hiding from them.

This one in particular. He's got his granddad's eyes, protruding ears, and why is he hiding here? Does he want something from me? Does he want to hear it? I'll tell him then. I'll take him inside.

He jumped into the ditch, she passed him by, striding down the road to the village, her body held upright, striking the stones hard with her walking stick, her eye flashing briefly towards the place where he'd made the nettles stir, she didn't stop.

He was walking around the ramshackle house. He didn't dare go inside. Standa! he called.

He was staring into the gloom through the dirty window. He spotted the tip of a trainer, the other one next to it.

Oi, mate! He chucked gravel at the window pane. Doss all day for all I care, just hand over my Numa T-shirt! He pushed his way right up to the window through the nettles, the high grass, tapped on the window pane. Standa didn't stir. Didn't move his head.

Then he heard them. Even though they were still far away. The lamentations rose towards him up the road, hovering above it. He saw them. She was lumbering along with her walking stick, stumbling. The women were dragging her.

The constable opened the door, they went in immediately.

He stayed in the grass, crouching down, catching sounds. She was wailing, the women were speaking to her. Come, come, they were saying.

They're talking to her as though she was their sister or something, he thought, hiding his head.

Zuza's dad came out with a bloke wearing a beanie and a scarf wrapped loosely around his neck, they went behind the ramshackle house, came back with a door. People were coming out. Berka, Prošek. The old men he knew from the pub. Horror, such horror, people were saying.

Zuza's dad was walking backwards, carrying the door, holding it with both hands. Someone threw a blanket over Standa.

The Old Hag broke free from the huddle of women, they came out last, she was clutching at the door, hitting Standa with her fists, weeping, almost all the women were crying, they were holding her arms, pulling her inside, the constable slammed the door shut behind them.

It's dreadful, said Berka. That it is, Granddad, said the constable. Oh dear, said one of the men. Let's go, said the bloke with the beanie on his head, he was also carrying the door, he prodded Zuza's dad with it, they set off down the road. Gravel, tiny little stones went flying from under their feet. They walked down the hill, soon they were out of sight.

Then the women started trailing out. What a tragedy! one of them cried. She stumbled over a pothole, grabbed her ankle. They braced her up, they walked together. A little old granny was the last to walk past Ondra, wiping her eyes with her apron. Twilight had already set in.

He stayed crouching in the grass. Something twinkled in the gravel, he crawled towards the sun. It was descending into the village. He untied Standa's sweater, let it drop from his waist, crawled towards the fence.

A crown coin was lying among the little stones. So he reached for it. I'll polish it on my sleeve, he thought. But there was blood on it. He wiped his fingers on the grass.

The Old Hag was standing on the threshold, the door had just flown open. Come here, boy, she said. Move it. He didn't want to. He had no choice.

It was almost pitch black inside. He saw bones and yelled out.

Don't make a racket. They're bird bones. What are you nosing around here for? She gave him a shove, he stumbled right into the room. The bones were embedded in every part of the wall. They jutted out from the plaster like ribs. The weak light of the petrol lamp flickered over them.

He saw a stove. There was a tablecloth on the table. It was warm. It smelled nice.

Her unfastened hair tumbled down her back. She was taller than Ondra. She passed him a tin cup. It felt cold in his fingers.

Nosing around here. Why?

I came to see Standa, madam.

Don't lie. You came because of your grandfather.

You knew him? He drank. Yum, Kofola! he said. He wiped his mouth.

If you finish it, you'll get another. Standa put this stove here. Nice, eh? His dad was supposed to bring us an electric log. Sit down. She tapped a chair.

He sat down. He was staring at the tiny flowers on the plastic table-cloth. The flowers were crawling over the gleaming plastic like little black bugs, as if they'd been drawn out of it by the light of the petrol lamp. He tried to squash one of the flower bugs with his thumb. He thought about what Standa had told him. That his nan talks to the dead. He glanced at the couch. That's where he was lying. He'd seen his trainers. He looked up at the wall. The flame of the petrol lamp was flashing over the bones. The bones were passing the light to each other.

Maybe they're not all bird bones, the Old Hag said. No one checked on that, believe me. This house used to belong to a strange old woman. People had got used to her. Where was I supposed to go? Standa's dad wanted to put the place in order, make some repairs, leave it, I said. Looks better as it is. Your dad also used to come to see me. For advice.

He did? said Ondra. Can I have some more?

She refilled his cup.

Where is your dad?

I don't know! Everyone keeps asking me. I don't know anything.

If you don't know, you don't know. I know why you're here. They do that sometimes. Come for an answer.

Who?

The dead.

What?! He almost knocked the cup over.

Yep. That's why you've come. You've got his eyes, and flappy ears, too. I reckon he's climbed inside you and he's looking at me now. They do that sort of thing.

Look, madam, I . . .

That's how it is, said the Old Hag. So you want me to forgive you? Eh? After all that happened?

She leant into him, her shoulder was almost touching him. He gave out a yelp. His breath got stuck in his throat, refusing to budge and pass through his lips. The flowers on the tablecloth scarpered in all directions.

Back then you said: Ilonka, please don't be angry with me, but you have to leave. You'll slip through the woods somehow, your own people will hide you. But my people had all gone by then. And now you turn up. They buried you yesterday. So this time you've hidden yourself good and proper! You were a master at that, hiding away, that you were. Under a cross in a cemetery. You've hidden yourself permanently this time.

Madam, I'll be on my way, said Ondra, standing up. I've got to go now!

The Old Hag grabbed his shoulder and pushed him back down into the chair. She held him there for a moment. Until he stopped resisting.

Why, I had a dream about your granddaddy. I was at the funeral, standing behind a wall. And I had a dream about him.

That's not my fault, yelped Ondra. She kept hold of his shoulder.

They drove them all into the freight cars, they shot the horses, I was out gathering wood when the soldiers came, I was a little girl and I stayed in the woods. During the day I stayed hidden, during the night I traipsed around, looking for people. You can eat anything that grows, and my tummy swelled up. I used to see him in the same place. He went there to breathe. I could tell he was also hiding, so I wasn't afraid. He couldn't see me until I wanted him to. When he saw me he liked me straight away. He took me to his place, I was happy. Could I have made it otherwise? In the forest in the winter? Alone? You've lost your mind!

I guess so, said Ondra. He was no longer trying to get away.

We breathed on each other all winter. In the summer the roof was scorching hot. We lived intertwined. We knew each other's every smell. No one knows another person like that. I wasn't a little girl any more. I gave off the scent of a young woman. That's how the reverend found me. Only Frantla came to that house, whose former occupants had all been led away. Bring food in, take shit out. That's an adage the local folk have about people in hiding.

Please, lady! exclaimed Ondra. That was a long time ago. I don't know anything. He tried to wrench his shoulder free. She kept hold of him.

You think it was a long time ago? But I'm not that old, she said, tightening her grip. She jerked her head, her hair skimmed over Ondra's face.

Ouch! he said. When he spoke, she dug her fingers into his shoulder. So he kept his mouth shut.

I had to stay hidden, when he came I listened to their disputations. Your granddad taught me to speak the way normal people speak, before I only spoke like our lot. They deliberated and argued over books, all the time. What else was there for them to do, after all? Ones like them don't play cards.

If the war carries on, I'll convert you, the reverend used to say. I'll be the one to convert you, more like, you'll see, you smirked.

They loved that. To talk about God. They only laughed quietly. Into their cupped hands, like this: keh, keh. Why, we couldn't even speak aloud. They would have shot us. Maybe they'd have shot everyone in the village, who knows. Trust me, it was hard in that hideout. I was growing up, after all.

You can't live like this, like an animal, the reverend used to say to you. She can't leave now, you can see that for yourself.

Oh yes, you stood up for me, the Old Hag laughed. She slapped Ondra's head.

It wasn't me! he yelled. He tried pulling away from the Old Hag. She didn't let him. She was sitting opposite him. Her elbow was leaning on the table. She held his shoulder with her other arm. She was breathing on him.

She's a wild child. She's a little animal from the woods. You've lost your wits because of her. You've got a task. To guard all this. The reverend waved his arm over the books, over all those things you had there, that you squatted on. Maybe you're the last one, who knows, the reverend used to say to you. He kept wrinkling his nose, he could smell me, my scent was that strong, and what was I supposed to do?

It'll scream when it's born, they all scream, and I was supposed to smear soil over its little mouth, bury it under a sod of grass?

Then Frantla stopped coming. As long as she's here, you won't see a cracker from me, not a piece of sinewy meat. We collected water through a slit in the roof.

I was showing. That's why I smelled so good. You sat there with your book like you were intoxicated, it was stronger than any other scent. All the dogs went berserk, dragging their chains around their kennels, getting tangled up in them, barking at shadows, at the slightest flurry of wind. The cocks crowed all night, it was impossible to sleep, the trumpeter pigeons inflated their crops, they descended on the attic in flocks. We ate them. All you had to do was reach out, grab the pigeon by the neck, we heard them all day, all night, beating each other with their wings, climbing over each other, the attic was filled with a horde of pigeons, yet more came flying in. My scent wafted through slits in the roof, at night the cracks were blocked by moths and midges, forcing their way in, we had to tear down layers of moths, with our nails at first, then with a stick. During the day butterflies clogged the slits and cracks, they pursued my scent, we pushed their bodies out, stuck together with wings, we had to, otherwise we'd have suffocated.

The rafters in the attic were coated with forest ants, they even crawled over you, sitting there intoxicated by the scent exuding from me, they crawled over your arms, your head, you swept them off with your fingers, they crawled around in your beard, fell on the book, and as you turned the pages, the leaves of the book teemed with their tiny bodies. The people in the village could smell the scent, it reached the little bridge, wafted over the water, soldiers sweating in their uniforms could smell it, the barrels of their rifles shimmering above their heads in the scorching heat, their rifles slung over their shoulders on straps, how many times we saw them through a chink in the roof, my scent was so strong that it drove the animals in the village into a frenzy, the horses broke troughs with their hooves, the bulls in the cowsheds tugged on their chains, making them jangle, birds swooped on the roof, thud! thud! I can still hear the sound their bodies made on impact . . . and just now that scent came back to me and I want to vomit.

We knew they'd find us as soon as it started screaming. I wanted to drown myself in the river. Slippery slowworms slithered under my feet in the grass on the river bank, making my progress difficult, grass snakes, yellow and black adders coiled round my feet, ensnaring me, the fish that swallow air bubbles covered the surface of the water. The scent attracted water rats, they jumped from holes under my feet to make me slip and go no further. Dace swished through the water beside the river bank. Flies, dragonflies, wasps, bees swarmed, interweaving to form a solid barrier, they covered me and my tummy, holding me in place. I didn't go into the river.

I said to you: Come, let's go outside, we'll follow the road like normal folks, we'll report to the soldiers.

You pointed to the books, you pointed to the scrolls from which you read, at the candle holders that we couldn't light. I can't leave this. I might be the last. The very last one of us all.

Come, I said, we'll go through the woods to another country, since I'd been a little girl I'd been able to drive dogs wild, could make them turn on those that had set them upon us.

You said: Forgive me, Ilonka, but you have to go, so I went.

And now you want to know whether I've forgiven you? All that? But of course I have.

Ouch, said Ondra. The Old Hag let go of him.

Madam, I don't understand what you're talking about.

He was rubbing his shoulder, glancing at the Kofola. He drank.

Well, no one's talking to you anyway, said the Old Hag. She stretched. She put her hands behind her neck and stretched again. Her hair swished around.

Madam? What happened to Standa? He was my mate. We were down the pub together. He was my second.

What happened to him. The Evil One, he met someone evil.

Aha.

You shouldn't be running around here like this on your own either. You could read to me. I never learnt to do that. There wasn't time.

Read?

That's right, read to me about the latest advancements. Standa's dad used to get me all kinds of magazines. When he finds out about it. Well, he did push the boy away, sometimes. He was a whitey, after your grand-dad.

Aha, said Ondra. Where is he?

He went to get a tomcat. In the locomotive, naturally. They were in a tunnel. The men in the locomotive drove on. Standa's dad, he's different. He drove inside the mountain in his own shadow, in the shadow of the locomotive, that's where he wanted to make a deal on the tomcat. I guess it didn't work out.

A deal? Who with?

Don't even ask!

I won't, said Ondra to himself.

Standa's dad. He wouldn't even say hello to your grandmother.

I never knew her! said Ondra quickly. We didn't come here then!

She came back. But crippled, didn't even have a face, she was a veritable corpse, I tell you. So they got married. After all, could your granddad have taken a gypo for a wife? This lot marry their own kind, too. I didn't like her, that's a fact. She also came to me for herbs, don't think she didn't! I always helped her, I'll have you know. She had easy deliveries and an easy death. What more does a woman want from life?

Lady! I have to go now, said Ondra. We're going into the woods. The Russians are here, lady! We'll catch the one who did it to Standa.

Catch him, will you, eh? Who? She laughed.

We'll catch it. The animal.

Animal, eh? Well . . . boy, it's very nice of you to be mourning with me like this. No doubt Standa would be glad to have a friend that's sitting with his forsaken nan.

The Old Hag bent down, ran her fingers through her hair and started sort of rocking in the chair. To and fro. Ondra flicked the metal cup. Then he banged the table with the metal cup. She didn't lift her head. She just kept swaying.

I'll make a run for it now, thought Ondra. He turned his shoulder towards the door. He already knew the Old Hag was strong. She's got strength. She mustn't catch me. He went for it. She grabbed him with both hands.

The odd thing is, the Evil One changed Standa's clothes. Dressed him in a T-shirt with a beast painted on it. Standa never had one like that.

The Old Hag's hands were sweeping erratically over the tablecloth, she was tapping the flowers with her fingers. When she held him, her hands didn't shake.

And he took Standa's sweater.

Ondra snapped his teeth together. Kept his trap shut, clenching his teeth. Pretended to drink. There was nothing left in the cup.

Before I actually glimpsed you, I'd only noticed that someone was snooping around. And I thought maybe the Evil One had come. As though nothing had happened. Bringing Standa's sweater, tossing it on the fence. What do you think?

I don't know.

They do that sort of thing sometimes. They enjoy it.

I don't know! said Ondra. He stood up. She made a grab for him. He sat down again.

At the funeral I stood behind a wall. No one saw me. I heard mud squelching. And in my dream I saw a coffin. It was floating down the river, there were a thousand candles and a thousand wreaths on it, you could see all those flowers in the candlelight, he was sitting on the coffin, I was standing on the bridge, he was waving and calling: Ilonka, so I finally ran away! And he didn't look like an old man. He looked handsome. Like back then.

Yeah? And what did you say?

Nothing. I just waved. As if to say everything's all right.

And you ... but you said that you would have wanted ... to marry him.

But that was before. Who'd want to marry an old geezer? Who's floating off somewhere on a coffin? What's wrong with you, boy?

Oh, said Ondra. I don't know this minute.

What?

What's real, he said.

Go, then. It's evening.

All right then, said Ondra, getting up, he had to grab the chair to steady himself. His legs were buckling under him. He'd been sitting down for so long. He made a move to the door. He stood there, hand on the handle. He wanted to say something. Thank you very much, he said.

Don't mention it, she said. She pushed him out.

*

She moved, springing towards the light, they were getting up from the table, the overturned petrol lamp had smashed on the floor, it was rolling around by their feet, trailing a little flame behind it, the flame was licking the shards of broken glass. They were reeling in the light, it was pounding into the room through the smashed windows, they were staggering around the room, deafened by the explosion, Zuza was gripping the neck of the bottle tightly, pressing the package from the Old Hag to her body. Out of my way! she shrieked, knocking into Dad with her shoulder, he was standing there with his arms outstretched, he wanted to catch her, squeeze her tight, when she pushed him out of the way his trap snapped shut. The door of the pub flew open, the draft was forcing them all outside, out into the quivering, red-hot air, the barrel of a tank was belching shells, white light, it was a dazzling spectacle.

She was standing in front of the pub. The barrel of the tank was aiming at her forehead. She ran. My hair is crackling, she thought, crackling like wires made of fire.

She ran off the road. She was scrambling down the hillside, she couldn't use her arms for support. The village was plunged into darkness, she heard explosions. She heard rumbling. More tanks were arriving.

She was running down, the air was moist there. Light was falling onto the grass through the treetops. The moon was hanging above the reeds, the light of the moon was grinding the sand in the hollows, making a grating sound. There were shallows by the river bank. Trees jutted out of the fog.

Now I'll sit down, said Zuza, and that's when he ran into her, he'd tripped over a root, got startled, collided with her, the bottle fell out of her hand and broke on a rock.

You cretin, she said. You stupid cretin, she got down on her knees, groping around in the darkness with her fingers, carefully touching the jagged pieces of glass, the moss was soaking up the wine, his face was right next to hers. I love you, he was saying, pressing his face to her face, he too was fumbling around in the grass with his hands. The shards of glass were everywhere. She pushed him, she grabbed his hand. I love you too, very much, she said, she slid down to the ground, curled up into a ball. He lay down next to her, put his arms around her. We'll run away together, he whispered. Her shoulders were shaking, her mouth was in the grass, he was stroking her neck, her shoulders, her head. He kept stroking her. She was no longer crying, she was laughing. He kept repeating that they would run away. Together. Tomorrow!

He kept saying it over and over, she said: No! He didn't hear her, she raised her head and said it to him again.

I'll do anything you want, he whispered. Anything. Always! He kept pressing himself against her. His saliva pasted her hair to her neck. She pushed him away.

But I, she exclaimed, I need someone who'll tell me what to do! Not a little boy. Scared shitless. She pushed him again. He shrank back. Lay down on his stomach. He groped around in the grass with his hands. She could hear him swallowing. He'll start blubbering in the end, she said to herself. Then she threw herself on top of him, lay down on him, held him tight. They pressed each other to the ground.

It came out of the river. Snorting, kicking up water. Drops of water streamed down its mane. The rider was lying on the horse's neck, the barrel of a rifle flashed above the rider's head. They came out onto the river bank, water was drizzling off them. The horse moved its muzzle, snapped at some grass, took a step forward, then another. The saddle creaked, the rider jerked back, now he was sitting upright.

The smell covered them like a horse blanket. He felt her breath on his neck. Her hair, he thought. Her pale hair must stay out of sight. The rider and the horse moved. Then they heard it. Coming from the forest. The wind swerved, tossing sounds over the water. Cattle chains jangled against each other, hooves got caught on roots, they heard mooing, the clamour produced by heavy herds of cattle walking through undergrowth, crushing the thicket, every fallen branch. They heard voices: And if the Zásmuky boys are there, mate! He sent the steel nut flying at his head so hard the bloke puked his brains out, I'm telling you! Branches were breaking. The horse and the rider were among the trees now. They vanished in the forest.

Don't smother me! said Zuza, so he let her go.

He's after the lads, he said.

Hm.

We'll run away, we'll take Squirt with us.

She stood up.

I'll come for you, he told her, tomorrow. I swear!

Yeah? She opened the pouch she'd been gripping in her hand the entire time, she scattered the contents all around, she even sprinkled some herbs on Ondra's head, he was still lying there. Then she inflated the paper bag and slapped it with the palm of her hand, there was a bang, the paper burst. She laughed.

Don't muck about. There might be more of them around here!

See you, she said.

Wait, he sprang up. But she had already receded into the darkness. It had only taken a few strides. He went after her immediately. He brushed the herbs off, his eyes were full of them, he swept them off his shoulders, he stumbled around in the forest, in the dark. She'd vanished. He looked for her.

It was just a deep groove that he was staring into. Not the void, he wasn't falling. When he came round, he was dragging himself over the ground. There were grooves everywhere in the asphalt. The door of the pub was hanging off its hinges. The stench of fumes hung in the air. No lights were on in any of the windows.

He turned onto his side laboriously. Where is everyone? He wiped blood off his brow. My fingers ... are completely ... sticky ... he remembered this word, it seemed childish to him, so he laughed. Sticky fingers. His uniform was in tatters. He crawled towards the woodshed, then he probably lost consciousness. Is it night or what?

Aha. The tanks. They were only driving through. The comrades didn't really mean it. Just took a crack at a light, that's all. Force of habit, nothing personal I'm sure.

There's someone over there. Someone's standing there. I'll call to them. Before I end up in limbo. I'm all singed. I'm burnt.

He was lying in front of the shed. The person grabbed him by the shoulders and pulled him inside.

Good, whispered Frída. People shouldn't see me like this. Is that you, Karel? Or you, Líman, my lad? Listen, Craggy, matey. I didn't mean it like that with the gypo, you know me. After all, you lot are the only people I know. Listen good, then! Karel! It was the comrades fucked me up like this. Burnt down your pub. Can you smell it too? That fiery stench. Will you help me?

The rod struck his arm, smashing it against the earthy ground. Juza raised the rod again. He brought it down hard on the constable's back. The Constable bent backwards. Juza grabbed his arms, turned him round.

You? said Frída. So I guess you know about Květa, then. Don't hit my arms any more. Smash my head. Finish it. You hear?

Juza was beating him with regular strikes. He was just raising his arms. But I can't feel anything, the constable chuckled. His eyes were open. He could see broken machines in the gloom of the shed. The cabinets had been smashed to smithereens. The contraptions had been eviscerated, spilling toothed wheels, springs.

Juza, I thought you were a complete dunce, and you're clever, the constable groaned. He was no longer trying to avoid the blows. He was no longer able to. Is this because of your girl? he asked. It'll be over soon, he said. Thock. This time there was an audible squelch. Blood splattered. He was pounding his soft belly. He kept on beating him.

The candle holder was standing on the window sill. All the candles in it were burning brightly. You couldn't see in. There were boots strewn over the floor by the door. Muddy old hobnailed boots, well-worn wellies. He stepped over them, pulled on the door handle. He heard people. Women's voices. He felt the damp, steam condensing from dresses, rough sweaters, flower shawls, the woollen blankets over their shoulders. It was making his nose sting. They had made a fire in the stove.

They'd brought chairs into the room, stools, little footstools from around the house. They were sitting on them, their heads covered with headscarves. Someone was even sitting on the coal scuttle.

No one noticed him, not a single back turned even slightly towards him. Mrs Fejfarová, wrapped in a blanket, was sitting on the bed. Next to Berka. Squirt was there somewhere. Ondra craned his neck.

Mrs Prošková sat squeezed between the bodies by the window. She was enormous. That was one of the reasons why he couldn't see in. The room stank of mud. He wanted to be with Squirt. He wanted the people to go away. He was pushing past their backs.

So the last days are upon us, said Mrs Fejfarová.

The time has come for us to join the multitudes on high, said some old woman, almost singing. Soon enough, very soon.

In the pallid light the staaars doooo twiiinkle . . . came from the window.

The wretched human being is mooortal to the last, sang Mrs Škvorová.

Come now, ladies, you should be rejoicing! cried Berka. Why, it was clearly a miracle. And it happened through the medium of the teacher, who converted. So let us rejoice!

Yes, let's rejoice, someone said.

Ondra managed to elbow his way to the bed. He must be here, he said to himself. Squirt must be on the bed. I have to find him. The old women will crush him to death.

We've said a prayer together, made ourselves warm, said Mrs Škvorová. It's time to go and get ready. So that everything is in readiness, as it should be.

That's right, that's right, said Berka.

Ondra was now standing in front of him. He heard coughing coming from the bed. Squirt. Hey! he said, grabbing Berka's sleeve.

So kiiind and quieeet and gracious, he heard some woman. She too was extending the words, as though she were singing.

Suuuch a teeeerrible weight came down on hiiim, cried some other woman.

Now, now, said Berka, moving his arm.

Ondra let go of his sleeve, which slipped from his fingers. Suddenly he felt sick. His legs buckled. He could still feel her embrace. Her scent, the smell of her hair. But he couldn't have found her in the woods? Not when she didn't want him to?

And now her scent was dissolving. Among the people. In the steam rising from their backs, their shoulders.

Suuuch a weeeight, cried the woman again.

They were talking about Standa. He thought about him. He could see his trainers. Standa lying there. He felt tears welling up inside him. Rising within him from below. His eyes were going to fill with tears. He mustn't allow that. Squirt mustn't see him crying. Youngsters shouldn't see their elders crying.

I'm his friend! he blurted.

Look, the boy's here, said Berka. The woman wearing a headscarf, who was sitting next to Mrs Fejfarová, chuckled. Squirt peeked out from behind their backs.

Ondra squeezed through the people sitting on the bed, crawling in to join Squirt at the back by the wall. It was almost dark there.

Blimey! blurted Squirt. Where were you? He was wearing a scarf around his neck. His cheeks were on fire.

I was outside.

The Russians ran the reverend over, said Squirt. The monstrance fell in the water. We were walking through the mud in front of the tanks, the whole procession. We had to jump into the river. I caught a cold!

Yeah? Are you ill?

I sank all the way to the bottom of the river. They pulled me out. We were going home from the service and suddenly a tank appeared! Coming right at us. Everyone jumped in the water. Bohadlo carried the reverend on his back. Someone carried me too. Squirt wrinkled his nose. I dunno who carried me.

Don't blub. Is your throat sore?

You left me in the pub. You're a pillock!

Frantla's dead, yeah?

No, said Squirt. The reverend got run over by a tank, but then he got up and walked, man!

They heard the door creak. A wave of movement rippled along the wall of backs separating them from the people, from the light. Ferdinandka stood by the bed. She held a cup in her hand. There was steam coming off it.

Drink this! she told Squirt. Thank goodness he didn't fall on the rocks, said Škvorová. True, true, said Fejfarová. You were very fortunate, boy.

Ondra took his trainers off, kicked one off with the other. He crawled in with Squirt.

Teachy stood there in front of that infernal monster, the reverend on his shoulders, said Škvorová.

Prošková shuffled over from the window. We were walking along. Suddenly the tanks were there. No one knew which way to turn. I slid down into the water on my backside, don't even know how.

And consider the fact that Teachy, said Berka, had just been converted by the sisters of the Black House! It's a miracle, there's no other explanation.

Ferdinandka sat down on the coal scuttle. She was also drinking from a mug. In front of that monster they were like God's Warriors in the old paintings, they didn't even flinch from the metal-plated dragon, she said.

I was standing up to my waist in the river, shivering. But suddenly I felt warmth coming from my heart. And the tank drove by and they got up and walked on, alive . . .

Yeah, a miracle has been worked.

Doesn't matter how bad things get, if miracles can happen . . .

That's right . . .

They knocked them down into the mud, they rose up . . .

They did not stand aside for the Russian beast . . .

We were walking along, the procession in its full glory, and Teachy trotted before us, the reverend on his strong youthful shoulders . . .

That bandaged head of his shone through the twilight like a candle . . .

Ondra scrunched up his nose. The steam coming off their shoulders and backs was no longer so piercingly damp, he could smell the aroma of tea, he reached out, someone passed him a cup, he took a sip. Squirt was burning up next to him. He was yawning. But he wasn't asleep. They were staring at each other.

Chairs were rattling in the hallway. They were leaving. Berka stayed behind. Prošková and Škvorová too. Ferdinandka. And a few others. They continued talking.

He finished the tea. He lay his head down on the pillow. He was warm. He closed his eyes. Zuza. She's the one I want to be with, he said to himself. Suddenly he was furious. So much so it made him sweat.

Hey! He turned round to Squirt. I don't want to live like this, he said. I don't!

You promised you'd be here, said Squirt. And you weren't!

We'll go away, said Ondra.

Where? said Squirt.

Doesn't matter.

Aha, said Squirt.

We'll make a run for it!

They're leaving too, said Squirt into his ear. In the morning, apparently. With Frantla and everything. All these people.

Where are they going?

That I don't know, said Squirt.

We'll go with Zuza.

With Zuza, yeah? Hah, said Squirt.

What?

You're talking bollocks again. You'll do a runner again. Sometimes I think you're pretty stupid.

Go to sleep, then, said Ondra. Seeing as you've got a cold.

The hand of time has turned, has jammed, it's that day again, Berka was saying. A miraculous day. You know the girls are having the bonfire today? Do you know what day it is?

Our girls! Someone cried from behind the stove.

Don't worry about them, said Berka. The sons of Belial won't sniff out our girls. No tank can drive into the forest. The boys are in the woods with the cattle. We're all safe, the entire village.

Except for that boy today, whispered one of the old women.

You know, said Mr Berka, that we're a blessed village under heavenly protection. What happened to that boy is a tragedy. But it confused the Evil One, and our boys and girls can now slip through his claws more easily.

Horse trading even with the heavens above. Tit for tat . . .

Yeah, yeah, strange goings-on . . .

Yes, the mighty light of a miracle is shining from our village! Even the last lousy and snotty lad from God's House, that filthy orphanage in Osikov, will in the end be irradiated by this light as though it were a floodlight . . .

Shush, old man! That place is clean. I did the cleaning there myself for two years . . .

Women, today reminds me of another miracle we witnessed. Today is the day of fire, the day of Eluzína, as you well know. And we made it from the river unharmed, today. The entire procession. Remember the stream?

Don't drag that into this, said Ferdinandka. She shuffled over to the bed with a mug. Here. Squirt raised his head. He drank. She held the mug to his mouth.

Today has reminded me of a day like this one long ago, a day long gone has slipped into the present. The days of miracles are intertwining. Like the beads on a rosary. Remember the little girl?

It's been heaps of time, said one of the women.

Do you remember?

Let it rest, said Mrs Fejfarová. The Day of Eluzína. Yeah.

I remember, of course I do, I don't mind saying so, we're among our own kind here, said a woman by the window. A pretty little girl, blonde, wearing a dress from the city and a hat, a little doll, a pleasure to behold.

What are you prattling on about, for goodness' sake? said Mrs Škvorová. You're talking rubbish. You've got it wrong. She came from the woods, like a little animal, like a wild child, all covered in ash from a gypsy camp fire, unwashed, her belly bloated. Towards the end of the war it was.

No! It was later, said Fejfarová.

Ladies! What do you mean end of the war, said Berka. And blonde? A little Jew she was, people were throwing them off the trains, by then they knew they were being transported to Poland to their deaths. They tore the floorboards out and pushed the kids through. They threw the kids out and the guards shot at them with their rifles, and they didn't always hit their mark. I know, I saw it. And what happened with those kids after that? Well?

What are you blathering on about? You always muddle everything up, you daft old scatterbrain! The woman lowered her voice. The little girl was the child of lunatic Kunhart. Not Jewish at all. Not likely! A little German. Kunhart kept her in a remote house. She didn't speak our tongue. It wasn't till he croaked, the scoundrel, that she came out. She was hungry, wretched little runt. She came to the girls' bonfire! The woman pulled out a handkerchief. Tears were running down her cheeks.

None of the ones from the trains survived. Or did they? We're among our own kind here, said Berka. Women. They were slippery, those young ones, eh? Did they wriggle in your hands by the stream back then?

What are you jabbering on about? Wash your mouth out, you old fart! You were there too. On guard. So just let it rest.

Why are you bringing it up now, dredging it up from the past? It's been ages, we had to do it, you know that.

And one of them, Berka was saying, wrestled free, her body was greasy because of the soot from the train, your hands slid over that little body and the little lass broke free and ran over the water. You drowned the others, I know that, I was on watch.

Who knows what you saw! You'd been on the bottle!

I saw how she ran away over the water, I saw it. She walked, her heels didn't even make a splash. It was a miracle. We're a village blessed with God's mercy.

Mrs Fejfarová was also weeping. Her hands were shaking. Her cup was wobbling, she splashed her skirt.

I wasn't by the stream, said Prošková. You all know that. I was tending to the flowers at the vicarage and at the very moment when the little girl broke free and ran over the water, the Most Sacred Heart of Jesus on the wall started throbbing like thiiiis and a thimbleful of the sweetest blood spurted from it. I'll testify to that!

We know you weren't by the stream, some of us were, we had to do it, they would've shot those kids anyway . . .

That's right, that's right. And who knows, maybe they would've shot everyone in the village.

Yep, we had to do it. We did it. My heart died by that stream.

Yep. Oh dear. Dear, oh dear . . .

Mrs Fejfarová was wiping her eyes. She blew her nose. Ferdinandka's tears were streaming freely down her face.

And now the Ruskies are here. What's it going to be like? What's going to happen?

Ruskies? Dear neighbours, you don't need to tell me anything about them. When they occupied us after the war, they went to see the reverend in the vicarage straight away, saw a picture of our most holy Lord, Jesus Christ, then they heard the toilet flushing, and blasted the loo to smithereens. We know the Ruskies!

True, we're familiar with the Riders of Belial, we know them well . . .

He was no longer listening. He'd go to see Zuza. As soon as it was light. When morning came. They'll run away together. They'll be together. Then it won't matter what happens next.

Then he thought about Standa. He didn't want to. He tossed his head from side to side, opened and closed his eyes. Next to him, Squirt was whistling through his nose.

He might have fallen asleep for a while. He opened his eyes. Only Ferdinandka remained in the room. She was sitting on the coal scuttle. Light from the candles was reflecting off the scuttle and the stove. They were burning out. He tossed his head from side to side again, rolled over the pillow, the old woman and the scuttle she was sitting on seemed to be levitating. Hovering back and forth. Tee hee, chuckled Ondra.

Ferdinandka was standing in front of him, her gaze fixed on his face. She shuffled over to the bed. You're crying, boy. In your sleep. I can hear you. Now you're laughing for a change. Why?

I went to see Standa, he said.

Are you thinking about that boy? About the Old Hag? I know her well. She's not that old, don't think she is. People just say that.

He nodded. He closed his eyes. Ferdinandka sat down on the bed.

Listen, boys, there are still fairy tales to be told. Even though there's the radio, uranium, and that sort of thing. They still survive. When you grow up, lonely old crones like me won't be allowed to live any more. Nothing to be done about it, you can't stop progress. So you listen for just a little while. And you'll be sure to fall asleep, that I know.

Hm, said Ondra. Oh dear, he thought.

They say there's a creature, you know . . . he flies around . . . he's flying through the clouds, laughing maybe, bolts of lightning are flying all around him and he's catching them, the bolts are slithering around him, he sends them wherever takes his fancy, then he stretches in the air like this . . . and falls back to the ground, he sinks his paws into the soil, runs over the leaves, over the moist earth, sniffing around, he catches a scent and runs . . . his mouth is so big he can drink an entire river dry, he can quaff the whole lot, but he can make himself so tiny that he can take a sip from a thimble . . .

Squirt rolled over and gave out a snore. Ondra grabbed his hand. The palm of Squirt's hand was dry and hot. Ondra listened to his breathing. It was like his own. He'd stopped tossing about.

You know, boys . . . he's not a dog, but he can howl, he's not a wolf, but he can run so fast that you can't see him, between the trees or in a grey field, sometimes you can hear him when his claws slide over a rock or when he's flying through the branches above you . . . and he lives off what people do, lives off what people do to each other . . . but he's a human being too, imagine that! He's walking towards you, maybe in a white shirt over the village common, and you'd never guess what he's really like, he looks like a man . . . at other times he's tiny, like the tiniest ferret, he ferrets around in houses, around the cooking pots when the women are sitting down nattering, gossiping about what, who and when . . . and he puffs up with every lie, he's happy when people deceive each other, he's at their sides straight away, jumping with joy, and he loves it when children blubber, he makes sure never to miss that, and when someone pushes away a child like that, all grimy and smeared with tears, they're giving him a big present, he knows all the tricks and ploys, he's old and young at the same time, and he's familiar with everything, knows it all . . . are you asleep yet, boys?

Hm, Ondra wanted to say. So he moved his lips.

Almost. Well I'll tell you a little more. He even knows all the hollows that have swallowed up drowned people, and he rolls around down there in the dead ooze at the bottom of those hollows like a wicked black cockerel who only takes his dust bath in a burial ground, he likes that, he likes it when people worry themselves to death everlasting. This Evil One makes a hanging man dance on the gallows with his reeking breath, huffing, puffing, tossing the dead person around the tree on the rope to scare the children out picking strawberries, they drop their baskets, start screaming with fear and he likes that very much, makes him a little stronger again, they all know him, they're all afraid of him, that's why he's so strong. You see? So, you're not so afraid any more. Eh? Well, you're asleep. You've fallen asleep, boy. That's good. That's what I wanted.

Then he felt her making a cross on his brow. With a finger so thin it felt like a little dry stick. It scratched a little. She leant over Squirt and blessed him as well.

He dreamt he was a little animal. He was running over the little bridge. Running between the legs of the villagers, they were walking, he was zig-zagging between shoes, wellies, boots with horseshoe heel plates, battered old clogs, legs wrapped in rags up to the knee, he was jumping between them. He woke up with the dream still playing out on the back of his eyelids. It was morning. Cold. He opened his eyes. A man was standing in the middle of the room. Snow was melting on the epaulettes of his uniform. The man's arms were outstretched, he was lowering them to his sides. And Squirt! He was sitting on the bed, fidgeting, twittering: Dad. It's Dad! Dad?

Ondra also sat up. Everywhere outside, snow was falling through the light. Snowflakes were sliding down the windowpanes. Suddenly the snowstorm was also inside. Dad was standing by the bed, he was hugging them, both of them. He'd never hugged them like that before. Squirt was squealing: Yippee, they were rolling around on the bed, holding each other tight, the pillow tore open, the down feathers went flying in the air, falling into their hair. Then Dad stood up, clapped his hands, said: All right then, lads, up you get! Come on. We're heading out! He went next door, turned on his heels, and was gone. The door slammed.

Blimey, he was actually blubbing, said Squirt.

Bollocks, said Ondra.

No, his tears wet my face.

He was wet from the snow! said Ondra, setting him straight. He stood up. It occurred to him that Dad had gone again. Vanished. He didn't tell Squirt that. Hop it! he exclaimed.

They were wriggling into their clothes quickly, pulling on trousers, T-shirts, sweaters, whatever was there. Squirt was limping, fumbling around for his socks. Ondra pushed them towards him with his foot. It was cold, they wrapped up warm.

I think we're going home, said Ondra.

Bollocks, said Squirt. We're going to the free countries. Everyone's going there right now.

Yeah?

They were walking down the hall, pushing the chairs left behind by the people out of the way, groping around, reaching out with their arms, there wasn't much light there, they walked towards the back room. They spotted Dad immediately. He was now wearing a suit. He was standing with his back to them. They could see him through the gap in the door. They saw clothes scattered over the floor, saw the dresser with its drawers thrown out. There was someone else standing there. Squirt wanted to go in, rushed forward, Ondra put his hand on his shoulder, grabbed him with his fingers.

There you are in all your glory, they heard. An officer of the Czechoslovak People's Army. I'm simply astonished. I'm trembling all over!

That was Polka talking. He was standing with his back to them in their father's jacket, flinging his arms about.

You have to believe me. You'll make it across with the boys if you look like a villager, a simple bloke. I've already propitiously scuffed this festive jacket of yours, hah. They'll detain me, not you. You'll make it with the boys and the documents. You've got to trust me.

But it's not that easy.

Yeah. I had to do some bad things. But that's over now. I'm done with all that already. You're looking at a different person!

Something fell on the floor. Ondra was holding his hand over Squirt's mouth, he peeked in, moving his head out of the gloom. They saw Dad over Polka's back. Polka bent down. Dad let the army coat drop off his shoulders. The thud they'd heard was his belt falling on the floor. Dad took off the uniform jacket. Polka was already holding his jacket in his hand. They were taking their trousers off.

I'll make it somehow. I'll risk it for the homeland. For you. You'll make it across and hand over the documentation to the free world! The free world will fall to its knees. You'll take care of me, if anything happens. Get it? They'll detain me, an officer. You'll make it. Easy.

We'll see, Ondra heard Dad say. Hopefully it'll work out.

I always envied you, Polka was saying, trousers in hand. I envy what you've achieved. You could say I was left with the task of performing minor deeds among the people. All over the world, you'd be surprised. Hopefully I make people feel at least a little happy when they're with me. What do you think?

Dad chucked his trousers at Polka. Chucked them on his head.

Look, one whistle and they've got you. What do you think? They've been snooping around the village looking for you, the secret cops. That old man of ours, our dad. It kept messing with my head. What was it all for? Why did he survive? What was he guarding? Why did he not give a shit about anybody all his life? Mother, me. He never talked to anyone. Your boys found it immediately, at the snap of a finger. And I'd been slogging away at it. I brought the reverend over, so Dad wouldn't be alone. They just sat in silence, the pair of them. Well, your boys found it. Treasure, indeed! A pile of old rubbish. A flea market treasure. Stupid menorahs. Yeah, you were the brains. I was supposed to stay here looking after the well-being of the Great Guardian. And what was it he'd been guarding all those years from the Nazis, the Commies, from us? A pile of rubbish, fuck it! When you left he stopped talking altogether. Not only with me. And what became of me? I had to stay here in these pestilential hills. I got infected by that deadly mildew. I couldn't leave for keeps like you. Until now.

Polka did his trousers up.

Undershirts too? said Dad.

Sure, brother. The checks can be thorough. But what's that compared to the final check of Our Looord? Now Polka squawked like the old women in church. Squirt spluttered. Ondra felt his saliva on his hand.

Shirt, said Dad. He tossed the army one to Polka.

You know what I can't figure out? asked Dad. How come no one's stabbed you by now. That's how they do it, isn't it? A pitchfork in the back? In the woods, somewhere. Shoot you from a bush with a poacher's rifle. They're clever, aren't they? They know everything. I really don't get that, Dad said, putting on his trousers. The suit trousers. He fastened the belt.

What do you know? said Polka, fastening the army belt on his trousers. Maybe they have stabbed me. Maybe they've done it many times!

Ha ha, said Dad.

But maybe the Lord singled me out to make someone happy. He made me exeeempt from deeeathhh, made me into one of his seeervants, said Polka in a high-pitched voice.

Hah, said Dad. Still bullshitting, I see.

Maybe.

Dad bent down, reached into his overcoat and pulled out a thick envelope. It was bound with a pink ribbon. He stuffed the envelope under his shirt.

Polka put a fur hat on Dad's head. Suits you. You look just like a local. Even the storks that nest in the village will think you're a bumpkin, a clodhopper, a simple peasant.

Thanks.

Polka did up the last buttons on his uniform. He moved towards the door. Ondra let go of Squirt, turned round, ran down the hallway. He was standing outside. There was a motorbike in the yard. A Jawa. With a sidecar. He could smell petrol. We'll go to the free country in this, he said to himself. No they will. Dad and my brother. I'll never see them again.

He went to the gate through the snow. He wasn't sinking in, though. It was just a light sprinkling of powder. The snow stuck to his trainers, he was walking on soil. He could see his breath. There was a continuous layer of mist between the snow on the ground and him. The snow was still falling. He broke into a trot. He ran up the tree-lined avenue, through the snowflakes. Past all those trees.

The door of the pub was hanging off its hinges. The common was covered with ruts made by tank treads. He ran through the pub. The chairs were overturned. Shards of glass from the petrol lamp and beer mugs were scattered over the floor. He could smell fumes, the reek of burning. He ran up the stairs, pulled on the handles. He stood by the door to Zuza's room. He was gripping the handle.

There was no one in the shed either. Nor the yard. Not anywhere. In the hall of the pub he collided with Polka's cart. The pain darkened his vision. He was holding his knee, saying to himself: Now I've hit my knee. That's normal. That doesn't matter! There was a stack of sacks in the cart, old blankets. I hit myself pretty hard, he said to himself. She's not here. Not here. That's awful. There were bits of paper in the cart, the comic book cover with Nemura on it. The comic book was in tatters, someone had ripped it to shreds. In the past he'd have been compelled to start reading, wouldn't have been able to tear himself away, eager as a beaver. Now he didn't even touch the book. He was holding on to the cart, vomiting a little. Outside I'd scoop some snow over it. At least there are no flies in here. He spat, went outside. Then he ran. He ran back.

They had to wait. A throng was rolling over the little bridge. The whole village, it seemed. They were walking on foot, riding on carts. Dogs with tongues sticking out were darting around under everyone's feet. Snapping at horses. The dogs that were normally chained up, the ones that never moved from their kennels. Now they'd released them. They were wreaking havoc together with the strays. No one had ever been as surprised by life as them.

He was staring at them. Gawping. Squirt, on the other hand, was fidgeting. He kept looking round at Dad over his shoulder. Look, Dad, look! Prošek's taking his billy goat. Look at those quilts, Dad. They're stripey, aren't they? Dad, why is it so cold? Do you know?

They were sitting in the sidecar. Squirt was wriggling in Ondra's lap. They were wrapped up in thick sweaters. They were wearing as much as they were able to get their hands on. Now and then Squirt coughed, sharply, it sounded like a crack coming from his little throat. But he wasn't feverish.

Ondra reaped some sharp reprimands for his late arrival. You're over-sensitive, almost like a woman. Did you want to say farewell to the entire village, or what? Don't you understand how important our assignment is? We're a combat unit.

Dad, Dad, he kept doing a runner on me!

Dad reached under his coat, fished around in the pocket of his jacket, pulled out a little glass bottle, tapped it on the palm of his hand. He took the pill between his thumb and index finger, stuck it in his mouth, tilted his head back, swallowed, his Adam's apple jerked.

My heart, boys, he said. That's from worrying all the time. But it'll hold out, have no fear.

Sure, Dad, said Squirt.

Well, boys. How were the holidays? Have fun, did you? A new life will begin for you now.

Yeah, Dad! said Squirt. Brilliant!

You've got no idea how worried I was about you. How I suffered.

Look, blurted Squirt. They're even hauling their washtub. The Horváts have got a tub on their cart, what a mess, Dad, look, look!

They had to let them pass. Dad didn't want to weave his way through them. We'll overtake them when there's more room on the road, you'll see, boys! He was wearing the fur hat, a scarf around his neck. He was wearing an old coat over his jacket. He didn't look like a soldier.

They were all going along the tree-lined avenue to the bridge. They went past the church, vanishing where the road turned. They went on foot, pedalled on bikes, towed carts. Carts packed with all kinds of stuff were pulled by tractors, horses. The old women sat on quilts, holding tightly on to children and chickens. The men walked next to the carts, or drove them. At short intervals someone spat from the bridge. They trailed around the church and up the hill. There weren't that many of them. A few latecomers hurrying along with bundles and rucksacks on their backs were wading through a thick slurry of trampled snow on the little bridge.

The motorbike jerked and set off. Yippee, squealed Squirt, here we go, Dad's driving . . . they set off towards the bridge, Dad was making a turn and that's when they caught sight of them. They were standing in front of the church. Two or three were on the road. Dad put the brakes on. He had to. They were looking at each other.

Líman had a rifle over his shoulder. It was like the one Berka had, a poacher's gun. The one that everyone called Craggy, Míra Cragg, was holding an axe. A long scarf was wrapped around his neck. Zuza's dad was also standing there. And a few other men were there too. They were watching.

Are you off as well? said Líman.

We are now. Father nodded his head. And you?

We've still got some work to do. Líman sniggered.

Aha, the welcoming committee, Dad said, nodding his head. May courage be with you, then. And see you in better times.

You bet, Lipka, said Craggy. And goodbye to you. And your sons.

Byeee, squeaked Squirt. Ondra didn't say anything. He no longer wanted to see them. Then they were on their way.

10

And the air they were swallowing was so cold. It coated the trees in the forest, hardening to ice. It rushed towards the crags. Shimmered above the water. Froze to the ice floes above the river hollows, they were full of twigs, pebbles, sand, they broke up in the current.

There was slush in the ditch beside the road. Coated with snow, the branches lashing across the road in the wind grew heavy, hanging above their heads. The motorbike with the sidecar whizzed over puddles, slashing the tracks left in the snow by the carts. The wind blasted against them, Ondra's nose was full of the new, cold air, his mouth too, he heard Squirt shrieking and babbling with excitement, the wind snatched the words from his mouth. Then they passed them. They waved at them, the people on the carts, their acquaintances, Dad just raised his leather-gloved hand and honked the horn a few times. Ondra spotted Frantla, he was wrapped in a blanket, the man next to him looked like a giant, he was swaying, his white bandaged head was rocking to and fro. They flashed by in the blink of an eye. They passed them so quickly, all those people, carts, tractors, horses, dogs, that all they really saw was a smudge. Those they passed were vanishing in the fog. Ondra pressed his back into the leather seat, Squirt on his lap, the sidecar was tossing them about.

Every part of the motorbike rattled at the same time. They held on to each other. Grit went flying wherever they went. They weaved between carts, the asphalt-covered side roads and the field tracks were full of people, they were joining the main stream of people trailing along the road. They drove uphill, further into the hills, they came to a railway crossing. They waited for the train to pass. They stood by the barrier, the carts were slowly catching up with them. The railway cars zoomed by before their eyes. Old wooden freight cars, cattle wagons. Some of them had sloppily painted red crosses on them. There were splashes of paint all over the wood around them. A white flag fluttered on the locomotive. White flags also hung from the barred windows of the last cars.

Bedsheets on a broomstick, said Squirt, cackling.

The barriers lifted, they headed off. Sometimes they had to slow down to walking pace, weaving between people. Sometimes they were the only ones on the road, then they drove quickly.

He tilted his head back. They were going uphill. They'd been the only ones on the road for a long time. He glimpsed the pointy red spire of a church. Everywhere, mist was rising from the forest. He could even see Blahoš, dark in the fog, the highest of the hills. It was behind them. He'd never been so far beyond the village.

They stopped at the top of a hill, there was forest on both sides of the road. There was silence.

He reached into his jacket pocket, pulled out the little bottle, tipped a pill out into the palm of his hand, tilted his head back, swallowed. Ondra saw his Adam's apple bob up and down. Aha, he said to himself. He felt a chill run down his back. That's not him. That's not Dad.

Over there, boys, the leather-gloved hand waved down the road. That's where the checkpoint is. We'll wait a moment. And then we'll go through it. That's where free territory is. That's where the future is.

Will Mum come there? said Squirt.

Then they heard it. Dingalingaling. Dingalingaling, they heard it from the fog behind them.

He put the little bottle back, shook his head, chuckling. My dear boy, my dear boy, he said.

So where is Mum then? asked Squirt inquisitively.

They could feel the cold coming from the forest around them. He felt warmth coming from Squirt on his lap. He was no longer fidgeting. They'll ride down. To the checkpoint. That's where we'll make a run for it, he said to himself. From Polka. Or whoever that is. It's not Dad. That's certain.

Everything he'd experienced up to that point was helping him now. His experience meant he saw the man with absolute clarity. He saw the dark colour of his silhouette. For a moment he had the feeling that he could also see the landscape through him. He saw sharply. Even a few centimetres in front of his eyes . . .

He grabbed Squirt's shoulder and squeezed it.

Ouch, you pillock, yelped Squirt.

They heard the sound of the bell behind their backs, a creaking noise was labouring up the hill. The yellowy light of a lamp pierced the fog. And then he was next to them. He was pedalling, covered in sweat. He didn't stop. Then he was riding downhill, he no longer had to pedal. The overcoat of an officer of the People's Army was done up to the last button. Squirt thumped Ondra's knee.

Look, said Squirt.

She was sitting in the little cart, holding on to the netting with her fingers. She was crouching down on the sacks, wrapped in blankets, a scarf. Her hair was all over her shoulders. He could see the way she was breathing. The bike kept squeaking. She raised her head, smiled at him.

He saw her nose, eyes, lips. She was passing by him. Something inside him burst. Black blood flooded his stomach, chest, all his organs. She was no longer looking at him. She was watching the road, looking down. He saw the back of the man on the bike. The forest surrounding them was enormous. He needed all the air that was in it to breathe. The black blood murmured in his ears. It was rolling around. Nothing will ever be the same again. The bike with the cart rode into the fog.

Ondra heard: Get ready, boys.

Yeah, Dad, bleated Squirt.

A few moments later they were riding down the hill. Slowly. They rode out of the forest, they saw the checkpoint. The fog wasn't as thick here on the other side of the hill. The checkpoint was on a bridge over a brook. They were sliding towards it through a wood. A barbed-wire barricade stood in front of a row of sandbags. Soldiers in long coats with machine guns across their chests were pushing it aside. The cart passed close by the barrier. The wheels of the cart scraped against the wire.

She must be cold, said Ondra to himself. His teeth were chattering.

The bloke on the bicycle was speaking to the soldiers, pointing behind him with his finger. He didn't even dismount, standing up straight leaning into the pedals, pointing backwards. At them. He saluted. He flicked his hat with his finger. Rode on.

Dad, Dad, Squirt was yelling, they made it!

And then they were on the bridge. The barrier bristled with barbed wire. It stood in their way. As though some invisible mechanism had instantly turned it against them.

The man on the bike, receding into the distance with the cart, was pedalling, pedalling hard, he turned round, waved.

They stopped. The sidecar always rocked from side to side when they did that. He was gripping the seat with tensed fingers, his fingers were slipping on the leather. Squirt's hands were fumbling for him. Squirt grabbed on to him.

They were on the bridge, the brook was flowing beneath them, they heard it, through the railing they could see a snow-covered plain. Ondra's knee was touching the railing. He grabbed Squirt's shoulder. The soldiers were all around them. An officer wearing a peaked cap was holding a pistol in his hand. A soldier who'd ambled over to them from behind raised his arm, striking downwards with the butt of his rifle. The body shook from the blow, falling down on to the handlebars. Daddy, shrieked Squirt. The fur hat fell down to the officer's feet. He stepped over it, sliding the man's coat open with the barrel of the pistol, feeling for the pockets with his hand.

Ondra put his weight into the footboard of the sidecar, he leant over the railing pulling Squirt with him, they dropped down, rolling down the slope. They were falling through the snow, there were thickets all around them down there, it felt like being in a den, they were pressing against each other. They heard motors. They remained lying down.

The Evil One was now flying through the air. He did what he had to do, for his own pleasure. He'd always been like that. And now he could take a rest. He flew.

While his body was pedalling tirelessly, like a machine, the face of the man had become transfixed into a mask. The girl in the cart was slumbering, curled up into a ball. The child inside her moved, stretched slowly, tapped from the inside, softly, gently, sharply. She chuckled. She wasn't one bit afraid. She was looking at the road.

The man pedalled all day. He didn't need to rest. They rode through a valley and then uphill again, past houses, through villages. They didn't need to talk. Later. Once they stop, at some point the bike will stop.

The Evil One up above stretched in ecstasy, doing somersaults in the air. He was laughing. And yesterday? He was also laughing! Laughing a lot. Then he'd seen a woman by the river. That's where it happened. He saw her and her death. She carried her death in her belly. That's why the Evil One didn't want her any more.

Standing behind her ready to pounce, he'd shrunk back, turned around with a yelp, his massive body weaved through the coppice, a branch plucked a tuft of black fur from his back. His paws were cold. Snowflakes were falling.

She'd arrived. This is where she'd been heading. She walked out of the milky white fog and into the diaphanous mist by the water. The landscape in front of her was white.

Those snowflakes are falling wherever I breathe. I'm blowing the snow in front of me. The soil under my heels is turning to ice. So I might be dead, she thought. Well, at least I won't get old, look at it that way, Shaved Head, she said to herself.

I can never ask for anything again, she'd said to herself that morning when she'd moved her body after waking up and the straps had slid off. And the door was open. Thank you, she said. Thank you, very much.

The roads had been jammed. Clogged up with waves of humans. Then some men in a car took pity on her. They gave her a ride even though she was barefoot, but so what, it was summer.

Snow started falling, but I didn't care. I'm bounding along. Like a she-wolf. Bounding, frost under my heels, my belly pushed out, now I could play a march on this drum of mine, calling: Mum's here! Come out, my sons! Which hole are you hiding in? Watch out for yourselves! I have noticed that at night the stars in the sky stick out like holes . . .

She reached the water.

It was here. Here I held her by the hand, that little girl of mine, the one that had come to me. I stopped here. I had to! All right, I'm on my way. I'll be with them in a moment.

She was stumbling through the forest. She fell. She tripped over a rock or slipped. For a while she crawled along on all fours. Just like a she-wolf, she chuckled . . . if hunters come across me, she said to herself, they'll shoot me like game. There're hunters everywhere now. But they're hunting people. She was stumbling through the darkness again. She was clutching her tummy with both hands. She saw sparks, a bonfire between the trees.

A body was flying over the fire. Charred branches flickered among the trees. They were flying like bolts of lightning. She walked towards them. She fell over on the clearing. They saw her and started screaming. Straight away they started screaming. Then they were all around her, shoving her, scratching. She wanted to stand up, one of them struck her on the head with a burning stick. She almost fell into the fire, they were beating her, kicking her. Screaming all the time. She fell again, this time she fell into darkness.

They were breathing like one body, wrapped in blankets, they'd thrown all the rags that were there over themselves . . . the girls had arrived from everywhere, bringing gifts, girls I didn't even know, from the surrounding villages, from isolated settlements, they'd walked through the forest, over footpaths, roads were out of the question, some of them had been walking all day long, two days, they slept in the woods, they showed them their scratches, told them about how they could still hear the forest in their ears. There's howling all night! Stamping in the thickets! All around you branches go snap! They bragged, straight away they were kneeling down by the water with their combs, dolling themselves up, putting on make-up, gazing into mirrors, we were done up already, us local girls.

Only a few of us hadn't made our first leap yet, I didn't know the others, we were the first to go into the water, moving through the water glistening like dace, we were laughing, drinking also, a little vodka, oh well, those were the presents, a little vodka and some sweets, the bonfire was already burning when I entered the water, it was cold outside, but immediately I felt the water seething around me, there was hot water all around my body, oh yeah, it'll be my first leap . . . and so I jumped . . . Jolana nestled up to the body next to her now, before she had recoiled, the woman lying next to her had frightened her a little, breathing loudly through open lips, Jolana pressed herself against her warm body, they were lying under one blanket, Vendula too . . . I wonder if she at least is asleep, because I can't, well, this other one's sleeping like a log, snoring! Lucky her . . . we jumped, flying over the flames, not one got burnt by the fire, from above the bonfire looked like it was made of metal and from the ground I could see how the blaze was lifting up the girls, it lifted me too, holding me up, the girls flew up high, pushing off one leg was enough, our hair got tangled above the flames, not one girl fell over, got hurt, when the fire died down at the edges we picked up hot powdery clumps of ash, smearing it on our bodies, and we leapt even higher, we were even lighter, that's what those that had given us the ointment had told us: Leap and you'll be young, beautiful, pure as a jewel, always . . . we were smearing ourselves with ash, later we'd go and wash in the river again, we had to make sure no one saw us . . . she staggered out of the forest, she sank down by the fire on all fours like an animal, she gave us such a fright! They pounced on her immediately. They beat her like an evil animal from the forest, like a frenzied animal that had come to maul them, they all swooped down on her, knocked her down, beat her with branches. Then we recognised her. The Lady. The Praguer. But how were we supposed to recognise her? Her belly was big, her head was shaven. She came out of the forest on all fours. No one would have recognised her.

They came after her. The wind was whistling through the trees, tearing off leaves, bending and breaking branches, driving snowflakes before it. The shadows of the trees came alive, lengthening, breaking off from the forest, riders came darting out of the snowstorm, in twos, threes, suddenly they were everywhere, riding over the clearing, logs seething with sparks hissed in the grass, we scarpered, girls jumped into the water, I slipped and collided with a horse's belly, one of the riders grabbed a girl by the neck, by the arm, threw her over his horse like a sack, Vendula yanked me to the side, we ran. Now we're here. Where are the girls? I can't sleep. I'm cold.

She whistles through her nose when she sleeps, this Jolana, like a bird tweeting, where are they all, where are the others? They'd have come, wouldn't they, they'd come here. And what are we going to do with this one . . . we were running with Jolana, she was scrabbling after us, like she was sniffing around for a scent, her head close to the ground, we helped her, what should we do with her now? Should I fetch Mum? I can't go and get Mum. What's she doing here? Why did she come crawling after us? What are we going to do, oh dear, I'm a cow, a wicked cow. She came in useful once, we liked her then, the Praguer. Liked her things. That was a long time ago. The girls scarpered, sparks on their naked backs. Hopefully they got away like we did, it'll be morning soon. And Zuza, the brothers? One day passes and suddenly everyone's gone. What will become of us? She's screaming again. Vendula's body jerked, she put her hands over her ears, sat up.

She didn't know she was screaming. She was thinking: This is probably it, life is leaving my body. Both our bodies. She wanted to laugh. She thought

279

she was laughing, but she was screaming. She saw branches through the roof of the hayloft. They were swaying slowly and quietly, to and fro. They kept moving. Blown by the wind. At the very top there were stars. She saw it all.

The girls were no longer pressing up against her, they'd drawn back, they were looking at her. One on each side. Jolana had her hand over her mouth.

Don't be afraid, little girls. Watch. So this is how it is. She laughed again. Quick, quick, so what does one think about ... give me a drink, at least a little snow.

Vendula yanked the blanket off her, felt her tummy, slid her hand between her legs. She wiped her hand on some rags. She was staring at her belly. Now it looked enormous. White. It quivered. And then again. And once more.

Blimey! whispered Jolana. You think?

Yeah, it's time, said Vendula. Get up.

We can't leave!

The stars are out. You'll be able to see.

What?

Go. Go and get the Old Hag.

The Old Hag? Not her.

Go. Hop it!

He was walking slowly, dragging his feet. He'd loaded Squirt onto his back. Now and then he looked over his left shoulder at Blahoš. Sometimes it was completely obscured by the fog. Most of the time you could see the dark summit.

They'll cross the railway tracks, they'll approach the river from the other side. Squirt was holding on to his shoulders. He was no longer bombarding him with questions. Beneath the bridge his tiny face had been warped with anger. Ondra had gagged him by sticking his hand in his mouth. He'd kept it there even after Squirt bit him. It was only a nip. He'd held him until the soldiers left. Held him under himself. Squirt had thrashed about, writhing, his arms flailing. Then he'd wanted to stay in the snow. Ondra hadn't let him. He put him on his back. Squirt was grumbling all the time. At least he wasn't kicking any more.

It occurred to him that he could come off the road. Off the road around Blahoš. He could go somewhere else. No one would care, after all. He'd reach some valley or other. Some remote valley where it's always quiet. He stopped.

Squirt kicked him. But only softly. He was scared. He didn't want Ondra to leave him there, somewhere.

You say it wasn't Dad. That soldiers have heaters in their cars. You're an imbecile! Where're you going?

We'll hide.

Quite frankly I'd really quite like to die right now, that's a fact, Squirt declared.

You'd die with the soldiers. They'd haul us off to Siberia. That's happened here before, you twat. Ask Grandfather Ploughman, said Ondra in a deep voice. Ask anyone! he shouted. He strode on.

Don't shout at me, said Squirt. His head was dropping down onto Ondra's shoulder. He was probably snoozing. He was quiet now. Ondra was indignant. He was pounding the snow with his feet. He was indignant all the time these days. Someone was always telling him what to do. That's going to change now.

He was walking down the hillside. Towards the railways tracks. Squirt hooked his arms around his neck. He wasn't fidgeting any more. He wasn't coughing. Ondra didn't mind carrying him. He was sweating.

Somewhere down there must be the cool valley. There was snow on the trees, everywhere. No track leads there. They could find a place to hide there. They'll cross the river. Hide. Something will happen.

He sank into a snowdrift. He'd spotted the black dots a while back. They were moving. They could be dogs or crows. Crows in summer, he chuckled. He worked his legs free. He rested standing up. He looked at his feet. I'm wearing trainers. And I'm not cold. Strange.

At first the railway cars looked like black smudges. In the snowstorm they repeatedly appeared and vanished again. Then it stopped snowing. He was walking beside the railway line, his gaze following the tracks as far as the eye could see. Some boys emerged from the fog. They were carrying a plank. Squirt tensed up. He wasn't asleep any more, he was watching.

The slope of the embankment was strewn with broken planks, bits of iron, lumps of coal fused into larger lumps. There were holes all over the embankment, the blast had blown the snow out of them. There was grit in the holes. Warped sections of track rolled about between torn-up, crushed sleepers. Only two cars stood on the tracks. Dark, map-like patterns extended over the wooden sides of the cars, that's where they'd been licked by the blaze. They were bristling with sharp splinters, as though they'd been slashed by lightning. Broom handles jutted out of the windows, limp white sheets hung down from them.

The children were trudging over the embankment, up and down it, their feet slipping in the snow, they hobbled along a well-trodden path, pulling bits of wood from the tracks. They were carrying this jumbled mess, this wreckage, heaping it up. A little camp fire was burning next to one of the cars. A girl wearing tracksuit bottoms was dipping a mess tin into a pot above the fire, she was pouring out black tea. They were reaching out to her with empty tin mugs. Boys and girls. Smaller than

Ondra. They were sitting in the open doorways of the cars, bunched up together. Hay was falling onto the tracks. They were wearing tracksuit jackets, raincoats. Even though it was no longer snowing.

He walked up to the car. From here he could see the locomotive. It was lying at the bottom of the hill, in the ravine. It had smashed all the trees to pieces. There was nothing in the ravine except for shattered trees stripped of bark. He couldn't see the treetops, their crushed remains were probably beneath the locomotive. It was lying in the ravine, deep down below, enormous. Its wheels jutted skywards like the discs of angle grinders. There were bodies lying next to the locomotive. Women in black robes were standing there. He was watching them from above. He leaned over so that Squirt could also see. The kids in the car were silent. He heard a mess tin scrape against a tin cup. He heard the girl pouring out tea. Two women in black robes were walking up the slope beneath them. They were walking slowly, each carrying a bucket packed with snow. More children were walking behind them.

They're the lousy kids, the scumbags, said Squirt.

Hm, said Ondra.

Well, this is no Pioneer Camp, that's for sure, said Squirt, chuckling. Put me down.

There was now a boy sitting in the doorway of the car. The kids were thronging around him. They'd made room for him. His head was shaven, he was wearing a black cape over his tracksuit jacket, dangling his black-booted legs in the air. Behind him kids were huddling in the gloom. They were eyeing Ondra and Squirt. Slurping from tin cups. The girl had stopped serving. She was also eyeballing them. Puckering her lips, waving her arm in the air, going: tut, tut. She'd probably burnt herself. What do you want? Where are you from? she said.

The boy said: We're waiting for a handcar. He stuck his hands in his pocket, spat. Or a locomotive, he said. Where are you going? He was smaller than Ondra. Ondra envied him those boots of his. But maybe they wouldn't even fit me, he said to himself.

I want a drink, said Squirt. You'll give me some tea, yeah? He said it loudly, extending the words in supplication. Ondra was embarrassed. He didn't want anything. He was never going to want anything from anyone again. He was done with that. He felt like throwing Squirt off his back.

You're not on the list, said the girl. We're full up!

We've got nowhere to go! squealed Squirt. Ondra arched his back, stamped his foot. Squirt's head wobbled. The children laughed.

You can come with us, Ondra heard behind him. He turned round. This was her moment, the time for her to appear. Her hair fell down over her face from beneath the black hood. She was looking at him, neither her eyes nor her lips were moving, yet she was laughing. Her eyes were blue. He averted his gaze, he could still see her. His eyes skimmed over the tracks, the grit, but still her face remained inside him. They were tugging on her sleeves, twittering: Sister Eli, Sister Eli!

The girl was pushing the little children away, pointing at Ondra and Squirt.

Sister Eluza, these two boys . . . she almost poked Ondra in the face with her finger.

Where have you come from? asked the nun.

From the village. We've come from the river, said Squirt. But there's nobody there now! Squirt waved his arm to the side, Ondra also looked over in that direction. He squinted, because of the sun. It was sliding out of the fog. It was above them. He caught a glimpse of the river, far away, glistening, incised into the landscape.

That's where you've come from? said the nun. I know that place well.

I also came from there. Give them some tea, she said to the girl. Put them on the list.

They were all staring at her. She walked off down the slope.

Squirt slapped Ondra on the shoulder.

What are your names? said the girl. The name of your mother, your father, out with it. But you're not sleeping on the straw. Don't get any ideas. She handed Squirt a tin cup. He drank from it immediately.

We've been evacuated, said the boy in the cape.

Oh yeah, really? said Ondra.

We hit a mine! said the boy.

Oh rubbish, said the girl. It was a collision.

No, it was a mine!

Blimey! A mine! chimed in Squirt from above. This is no Pioneer Camp, then!

Yeah, said the boy, nodding. It was terrible. He smoothed down his cape. Dreadful, it was. He was kicking his feet. The girl pulled a notebook and pencil out of her pocket.

Where are you going, Ondra muttered. He'd heard talk about trains like this. He became furious again. Before he'd talked all the time. But now he was angry. He wasn't going to talk any more. That's how he's going to be. Always. He took a step towards the boy.

A mine, and so what? Piss off! His fists were clenched. He was breathing rapidly. He felt the rage in his stomach. The skin on his knuckles went white. He liked it.

You piss off! yelped the boy. The children in the car were silent. Ondra bent down, Squirt slid down his back onto his feet. He came down in a heap, spilling everything from the tin cup. He started coughing immediately.

You're on your way to Russia, aren't you, you lousy scumbag? Ondra erupted at the boy. Scumbags! he cried. Where are you going? Squirt was tugging on his sleeve.

He turned round. He walked downhill quickly, through the children. If he had a scarf, he'd also wrap it round his face. He almost knocked over a girl swathed like that. He was walking past the lousy kids, between them, taking no notice of them. He stepped over a plank blackened with smoke, it was bristling with nails. He went all the way down to the bottom of the slope, there were no footprints down there. He'd walk through the untouched snow all the way to the river. He knows where his little boat is, after all. He's known all along. He'd never taken Zuza out on the little boat. That's never going to happen now. But he'll find the place. He was thinking about the valley, far away, cold. The snow there is sparkling because the sun is shining. There's snow everywhere, even on the branches. He could also see people there. Standing under trees. They were all his people, people he wanted to be with. He'd find faces and names for them. He won't be alone there, that's for sure. It'll be quiet there.

Squirt shot past him, sank into the snow, churned it up. He was digging his way out right away, trying to stand up. He reached out with his hand, grabbed him.

She went about it the right way, that girl, turning up here all of a sudden in the middle of the night . . . goggle-eyed with the news she was bearing, jabbering, stuttering . . . and the moment she caught sight of them in their black boots she jumped behind a stack of logs, crouching down, hardly breathing, hardly existing . . . they've got it in them from birth, these girls, consider those blokes, from a distance they reek of the meat they eat, they stink with every breath they exhale, even the air must recoil from them, they don't know how to walk at night or in the dark, they've got bellies like pots, those murderous comrades of ours, cleverly she made her escape, the little girl, I know those ugly mugs, their kind always came on the roofs of trucks, nice and warm up there, reeking of booze and dirt, knocking a little girl like that down to the ground, defenceless, fucking her brains out, for them it's like blowing your nose, burning down a village like skimming a stone over a pond or snapping a dry branch, it's nothing to them, nowadays they wear jackets and ties, unfortunately . . . Welcome, comrades, at your service, I welcomed them nicely and they said: Let's go, now . . . Alrightey, then, whatever you say . . . You'll get yours, traipsing around till dawn, I'll keep you busy, climbing over rocks, struggling with thistles and prickly branches, you won't believe your eyes, an old woman, sliding over rocks like an adder, a black adder, you'll say . . . if you could only catch your breath, you pot-bellied swine, sweating all over, men are supposed to be dry and hard like fence posts, like rocks, not like you.

She was leaping over rocks ahead of them, they couldn't keep up. She led them through the forest, along paths they couldn't see, up a muddy slope, uphill all the time. They suspected she was taking them round in circles. That she was stealing as much of their time as she could. Stealing their time to give to others. They didn't know the area. What could they say? She laughed at them. She couldn't do more than that.

Once, twice they got stuck in the snow. Despite their boots they were soaked through. For hours they trudged through the undergrowth, initially the darkness was so black you could feel it with your hand. Up here there was more light. Dawn's coming, the younger cop realised. Low shoes are more suited to work at the police station, or for questioning a suspect already in custody. But he's going to wear different footwear on his next assignment. For sure.

The older one stopped often, he had to catch his breath. She was careering ahead of them. Slow down, citizen! howled the younger cop, astonished. Where does that person get the energy from?

An unreliable person of gypsy gender. She exploits the superstitious nature of the inhabitants. That's what the local constable wrote about her in his reports. She's an excellent informer. She even communicates with the deceased. That's what the teacher wrote, the one who lost his mind. Well, even the news has been deranged at times recently, the younger cop said to himself. That's evident. But still. Those comrades on horseback. Where did they come from? Where? The advance units of the allied armies? Odd. We must investigate that. Once we've closed this case.

They had the woman under surveillance the entire time. That was the easiest part. Comrade-informers are everywhere, like psychic feelers. Acting in concert, they collaborate like a perfect machine, as verbalised in regular reports. They opened the door of the guarded facility. They let the woman out, gave her a ride in the car. They knew she'd lead them there. The family would reunite, such is the instinctive behaviour of families, the young cop creased his nose. The female will lead us to the male and the young. And then? The trap will snap shut. Mr Inventor. Ha, ha, ha! Well, we'll see, Mr High Traitor. It's a first-class operation, the cop almost whooped. My first operation. He lifted his head.

She was above them all the time. Her hair was flying around as she climbed up the slope, holding on to trees. They were gasping for breath far below her. The older one could hardly keep going. He'd twisted his ankle or something. The younger one climbed down the slope and braced him up. They clambered, the older one's face had turned almost purple. He was clutching at his heart. But he kept walking, crawling like a beetle. He keeled over once again, face first in a puddle. He was rasping. The younger one lifted him. Wiped his mud-blackened face with a handkerchief. They had almost made it to the top.

The Old Hag went first, then the younger cop, the muddied old cop kept slogging along at the back. He was limping. If anything happens

I'll take command, thought the younger one, blushing. It made him feel ashamed. He waited, took the older one by the arm. They clambered over a tree trunk. The Old Hag was waiting for them. They could hear the river. They were at the hayloft.

Oh dear, exhaled the younger one.

She looked like she had frozen stiff. The woman's face was hideous, the cold had turned it blue, through and through. Her nose stuck out like a hook. Her face had stiffened in a smile, her teeth were bared. She had a blanket over her. That's where the sound was coming from, the crying. A kind of howling, moaning, but soft. It didn't grate on the ears.

All right then, said the Old Hag, stooping down, she slid her arms under the blanket. She was ready. She had a clean nappy with her. She lifted the baby so quickly! They didn't even see it. She wrapped the nappy around it, rocking it in her arms. It kept screaming.

She'd been breast feeding it, she said. There was enough spirit left in her for that.

Is she . . . is she dead? said the young one.

See for yourself.

The old one bent down to the woman. He drew the blanket aside. He covered the woman again quickly, straightened up. Drew back. Even so . . . it was as though the blanket had moved.

But he hadn't seen that. He staggered. He was as pale as ash.

You too, then, said the Old Hag to herself. And you must have seen a few things in your time. Even the biggest ones turn into little runts when confronted with the affairs of women.

She was holding the baby firmly. It wasn't screaming any more, just sort of purring. There you go! she said to the child. She was rocking it.

The young cop overcame his nausea. He was smiling. He was watching the baby, smiling. Light was falling on them through holes in the roof of the hayloft. The countryside was thrusting itself upon them with all its scents. Reaching even to the stars that were still everywhere. But soon enough . . . dawn was breaking. The young cop raised his arms: Comrade, he said, half-choking, and you, comrade . . . the baby started screaming, he took a tiny step back . . . could I, comrade citizen, he glanced back at the old cop with a look of alarm . . . maybe, could I? The old cop nodded.

Could I . . . hold the baby? said the young one. His cheeks were ablaze.

See, the Old Hag was saying to the little one . . . your first day and you've got me here . . . and two uncles like scarecrows, bogeymen, some life you're going to have, I'm not even sure I want to see that . . . she was rocking the tiny munchkin that she held in her arms, carefully she passed it to the cop.

He took hold of the baby, holding it like the Old Hag. It's quiet! he blurted. It's happy! His face lit up brightly. His emotions surged. The old cop was now standing next to him . . . I think, the young one lowered his eyes, maybe for once even we could . . .

Yes. That would be beautiful, said the old cop.

The new law is human, said the young cop. It's so human. His chin started quivering.

The old one nodded again. Now he was frowning. He was wiping mud off the little face with one of his mitts. She stepped towards the young one. He handed back the baby. That tiny little head . . . and those teeny paws . . . he whispered.

Take care of it, said the old cop emphatically, turning round. He went outside.

The young one stood there. He was rifling through his pockets. I . . . hopefully, a little present, something . . . he pulled out a little knife, a penknife, thrust it in the Old Hag's hand, she clenched it tight. He left immediately.

Well, there, you see, she said to the child again. You little rascal. And you've been saved. I'll look after you, have no fear, she was rocking it, it was crying quietly. I don't even know if you're a girl or a boy. Back then they shoved a girl into my arms and said take care of it. Oh yeah, I took care of her all right, but not how they wanted, I did it my own way. It'll be the same with you. I'll take you to the Black House too, you little nestling. There's plenty of room there. They'll give you a home. Not crying any more? Sleeping...

Easy! We'll build a hut in the valley. We'll make ourselves snowshoes. We'll go hunting. It'll be good, don't you worry.

If you reckon...

They must have left a lighter in the village, some matches. Sweaters, blankets. We'll need a small axe. They couldn't have taken it all with them, didn't have enough room, get it?

Oh all right.

And after that! We won't be able to find the lads in the woods, if no army can find them, that's obvious. But they'll find us. See? They'll be amazed when they see our hut, you'll see!

Hm.

Don't sleep. You can't sleep now. We'll be there soon. We're basically there.

They were walking through a blizzard again. His trainers were soaked right through now. Even so he was sweating. He'd never felt so strong before. He didn't know where the strength had come from. Something external was pulling him along, something in the landscape. As if the thin, tenacious fingers of an invisible hand endowed with dreadful strength had hooked into his ribs, dragging him towards the invisible body connected to the arm, somewhere. He hardly felt Squirt on his back. He could see clearly even in the fog and through the snowflakes. He saw the outlines of the trees on the river bank so clearly, it was as though they were radiating light. He saw houses. The boat must be somewhere around here.

But that's a gypsy house, you twat, said Squirt. Those are gypsy houses, you gone daft?

He was already fumbling for the door handle. He stopped.

If you want, wait here.

Squirt clasped his back: No way.

He opened the door, the hinges creaked. He smelled smoke immediately. Inside, the house looked huge. There was no furniture in there. There was just a table in the corner and a few chairs. They were piled up in a heap. They looked like they'd been hacked with an axe. A straw hat was lying on the floor, someone had ripped it apart. The straw stank. Everything in there reeked. Soot stains slithered over the walls. Light was falling in through broken windows with torn-off shutters.

I don't even know if it's getting dark. Or maybe it's morning, Ondra said to himself.

There's nobody anywhere, said Squirt. Not even dogs.

There were piles of rags between the houses. There was also a campfire ring. It was still smouldering a little. In spite of the snow. A charred kettle lay on the ashes. The roof of the other house had caved in, the rafters were charred.

Don't go in there, said Squirt. Then he shrieked. Ondra took a step, two, they were inside the gloomy house.

What is it? Who is it? Let's get out of here! yelled Squirt, kicking him in the back.

The body was lying on the floor, the legs stuck out towards them, they couldn't see the face, the head, it petered out in the gloom, reaching all the way to the other side of the room, there the darkness was as thick as a cloud, the arms thrown to the sides stretched all the way to the walls somewhere. Dust hovered in the light above its chest.

Squirt was shaking him, yelling. Hold on, you twat, shouted Ondra. It's a piece of wood!

And to make Squirt believe him, he kicked one of the legs.

Look, it's painted. There's a rag on it.

There was a piece of cloth wrapped around the waist of the wooden person. His body stretched as far as they could see in the feeble light. In places the paint was flaking off the body. It looked like it had little blisters.

Squirt quietened down.

Yeah. It's carved from wood. I can smell the paint. I got startled, that's all.

Don't kick me any more.

I won't.

I guess the wood swelled up. Because of the sudden cold. It puffed up because of the damp here, you know?

Guess so, said Squirt. Ondra backed out and closed the door.

He walked towards the river bank. He could still feel that strange strength. He was taking care Squirt didn't snag on the branches and get knocked off. He was no longer coughing at all. He was holding on tight.

The water had risen right up to the tree branches. The bark was covered with hoar frost. He grabbed a branch, swung up above the water. His eyes were scouring the river bank. The bark felt cold on his hand. He promised, he was saying to himself. He promised, the lying gypo . . . then he spotted it. The barge pole was in it.

Squirt fell into the little boat like a sack of potatoes. But he was cackling. Ondra had to laugh too. He broke the thin icy crust around the little boat with the pole.

Blimey, he chuckled, I cut myself on an iceberg, look. He was showing Squirt his finger.

Ha ha, Captain, bellowed Squirt. Setting course for the North Pole!

In the fog the trees looked like crooked people. Soon they were no longer visible. They vanished just like the silhouettes of the houses. They could only hear the water, the barge pole creaked in Ondra's hands. He was pushing off the bottom. They had almost reached the deep part of the river. They heard a roaring sound.

What's that? said Squirt.

Something's making a roaring sound, that's all. Ondra shrugged his shoulders. Now that Squirt was off his back he felt his strength even more. He felt a tingling in his shoulders. He could break the barge pole in half like a toothpick.

And hey, at the North Pole, right. We'll wolf down a polar bear!

Squirt nodded. He put his hand in the water and watched the little ripples.

The roaring sound was coming from the ice floes. The current in the middle of the river was undercutting them. And more and more of them were floating towards them. They were stacking up. Sometimes an ice floe broke in half with a mighty snap, sliding under the water.

Head over to that, called Squirt.

One of the ice floes was rushing towards them. It struck the little boat, soaking them. It pressed the little boat up against the wall of ice floes. The impact knocked the barge pole out of his hand.

The ice was rough, full of fissures. Only in places where the ice floes had stacked up was it smooth, polished by the wind. It was slippery there. They scrambled up. Holding on to Squirt, he kicked the boat. It vanished immediately. He lost one of his trainers in a fissure. He didn't care. I'm not cold, he said aloud. They walked over the ice in pitch black darkness.

They slipped, fell, rolled over each other. Then he loaded Squirt on his back again, kept walking. Squirt felt warm on his back.

I messed up, said Ondra. I've been walking downstream the whole time. Not towards the river bank.

Squirt laughed. You really are a pillock!

We'll wait, said Ondra. He let Squirt down.

All right then. Squirt sat there curled up in a ball.

But we're not going to sleep, said Ondra. That could be dangerous.

That's clear, said Squirt. He stretched out his arm. Ondra grabbed it. There were ice floes all around them. They were creaking on the edges where the current was eroding them. They were on dark, hard ice. They couldn't hear the water beneath them.

Good job I took my hat with me, said Squirt.

Ondra sat down next to him.

Look, there's a light over there, said Squirt.

A light was bobbing around above the river bank where the village was supposed to be, high up in the black darkness. It was shimmering on the edges of the clouds, you could see them wherever the light went. It was looking for them, growing bigger all the time. Reflecting off the ice. It was close.

Some people with lanterns, probably, said Squirt.

Maybe.

Or those spaceships of yours, hah.

Might be.

Maybe it's falling from a star.

That's possible, too.

Waldberta, Mont Noir
2000/2001